WOLVES OF WISTERIA

Wisteria Witches Mysteries

BOOK #6

ANGELA PEPPER

CHAPTER 1

Zinnia Riddle woke up Tuesday morning with one ghost in her heart and another waiting in her kitchen.

Her bed was too warm to leave. She'd kept the window open overnight, and the chill of January had taken over the room. She could use some extra help getting up, so she did what any witch would do. She cast a spell to yank the bed covers away.

Magic sparkles whizzed from her fingertips as the spell took hold. The blankets fluffed up, hovered, then settled down again squarely, tucking in their edges all around her. That wasn't right. Tucking in was the exact opposite of yanking away. The tucking was vigorous, too. Zinnia groaned from the force. *Floopy doop.* She realized her mistake. She'd accidentally inverted the spell. Served her right for not keeping up her spellwork practice! Her magic had gotten rusty.

She tried to wrestle her way out of the tightly made bed. The spell did not want to give up. Her floral-patterned comforter wrapped around her legs like a boa constrictor. When she finally broke free, Zinnia's down-stuffed pillow made a half-hearted attempt at smothering her.

She punched the pillow away, got her feet on the floor, and backed away from the bed, making a tsk-tsk sound. "You, too, pillow?" The pillow gave her a lackadaisical shrug before settling neatly on the bed.

It was going to be one of those days.

* * *

In the kitchen, the first rays of sunlight were filtering in through the floral curtains that covered the window above the sink. Zinnia flicked on the overhead light, but it didn't do much to dispel the room's gloominess. She opened the curtains, freeing a cloud of dust. She immediately sneezed. The dust motes swirled around her like misguided insects.

Dusty, she noted. *My magic is rusty and my house is dusty.* The two things were connected. She could have used spellwork to tame the dust before she left for work, but she didn't trust herself. The way things were going today, she'd probably end up with a black eye, wearing a mop bucket as a hat.

She turned on the tea kettle manually and opened the door of her vintage refrigerator. She yawned and closed her eyes as she reached for the orange juice. A moment later, she let out a startled cry as she found herself pouring a glass of... not juice, but eyeballs. Eyeballs of various sizes, from newt to cow. The orbs were useful for many things, but not as a breakfast beverage.

"I really need to declutter," she muttered to herself. And why not? Decluttering was a normal thing to do. The other women at her office often talked about the "life-changing magic of decluttering." Zinnia had to bite her tongue whenever the topic arose. She knew there wasn't anything magic about throwing useless things away, not unless you were chucking them into a swirling vortex that led to another dimension.

She tossed a few eyeballs into a Ziploc bag in her purse. A good witch doesn't believe in coincidence. If a magic item finds its way to your hand, take the hint! Magic knows more about the future than any witch.

Zinnia returned the jar of eyeballs to the hidden compartment at the back of the fridge, retrieved the orange juice, and got breakfast started. She drummed her fingers on the counter as she waited for her toast to pop. She leaned forward to make sure the internal elements were hot. As she leaned back, she caught sight of her reflection on the side of the appliance.

She was struck by how dark and deep her hazel eyes looked. How long had it been since her eyes had shone brightly? Too long. She actually looked her age this morning. Or did she? How old was she, anyway? Forty-seven. She forced a smile at the reflection. The image of a lightly freckled, classically beautiful redhead with long, wavy red locks smiled back at her. She was no supermodel, but she looked pleasant enough when she mustered a smile.

Something itched at the back of her consciousness. Something about the date. Had she missed garbage pick-up day? She whipped her head to check the calendar on the refrigerator. Today was Tuesday, which meant... her birthday was today. *Double darn and triple trouble!* She wasn't forty-seven anymore. She was forty-eight. She'd forgotten her own birthday. Again.

The realization made her feel weak, emotionally and then physically. Her legs shook and her knees threatened to buckle. It had been over a year now, and nothing had improved. She still hadn't recovered.

She gripped the edge of the counter and forced herself to stand up straight. Now was not the time to dig up the most painful memories of her life. The right time for that was... never. But even as she commanded herself to stay focused, her brain offered up all the usual shoulda-coulda-wouldas. If only she had tried something different, been quicker to solve the puzzle, known more than she could have. Why hadn't she been brave enough to—

The toaster popped, breaking the unproductive thought cycle, bringing her back to the present.

As she buttered the toast, she heard the words of her wise mentor in her head. *Worrying about the past is about as useful as playing the accordion on a deer hunt.*

Wise words. Her mentor had also pointed out that her birthday was a lucky date. It came around when people were giving up on their New Year's resolutions. That meant there was a lot of unused "change magic" floating around, looking for a person to help. If Zinnia opened herself to this magic, every birthday could be the catalyst for transformation. Maybe it would happen this year. Or maybe it already had. Career-wise, her job was simple, but she enjoyed it. She even had a new man in her life. Thinking about him caused her cheeks to heat up—in a good way.

Blushing, she grabbed an avocado and continued preparing her breakfast.

As she leaned forward, a cool breeze brushed her from behind. It felt as though someone had walked past her in a hurry, or blown cool air at the back of her neck. She cocked her head and rotated her body as she looked around the kitchen. It was empty. She was alone, as usual. And yet, the motes of dust hanging in the sunlight swirled frantically, as though caught in a localized whirlwind. Someone was there. Someone who could not be seen. She still held the knife she'd been using to slice the avocado. She gripped the handle instinctively—not that a knife would do much to scare off an invisible foe.

She slowly turned back to the counter and continued her work quietly while her senses—both human and witch—buzzed. As she smeared the avocado on her toast, the scratching sound was like a roar. She hadn't made avocado toast in a long time. It had been his favorite. A lump rose up in her throat.

Could it be him? Had he chosen her birthday to visit?

The ghostly presence hadn't made a move, but it hadn't left, either. The hopeful lump in her throat made it hard to breathe.

She opened her mouth. "Ai—?" The lump in her throat cut off his name. She coughed and tried again. "Aiden? Aiden, is that you?"

The energy in the room shifted with a crackling sound. The light grew brighter, then darker, then brighter again. The magic afoot was in conflict. Zinnia set down the knife and turned around slowly, hands up and ready to blast.

The darkness from the corners of the room gathered together, focusing into a swirling vortex before her. The light bulbs in the ceiling fixture buzzed and grew brighter, increasing the contrast in the room. The tasteful flowers on the room's wallpaper became bright and joyful, and then brighter still, until they were lurid, shades of fluorescent orange and yellow.

"Aiden?" As she uttered his name for the third time, she heard the hope in her voice die. It wasn't Aiden. He wouldn't come to her like this. His heart was too pure, unblemished by time and experience. He could never have worn such dark shadows.

But the dark presence was a ghost. Of that fact, Zinnia Riddle was absolutely certain.

"Who are you?" She squinted at the shadowy form. The specter was no more solid than static on a television, or pouring rain. It could be seen yet not seen, flickering between the world of the living and the world of the dead. Two dark spots coalesced, forming eyes. But the eyes disappeared as quickly as they had formed, and there was only static again.

Zinnia tensed her core muscles deliberately, silently rehearsed a reveal spell, and then cast it in whispered Witch Tongue.

The darkness obeyed her command and took form. The ghost glanced down at its body, seemingly as surprised as Zinnia that the spell was working.

Zinnia gasped. "No!"

But denial changed nothing. Zinnia recognized the ghost even before the spell had finished. She reached a hand forward, her voice croaking as she gushed apologies.

And then, with a pop of light, the spirit was gone, pulled through to the other side as easily as a plucked thread.

So, *that happened.*

Zinnia clenched her teeth. If she relaxed any part of her body now, her lips would quiver, and then she would be lost.

She checked the time. She was in danger of being late for work. More time had passed than seemed possible. It was always like that when ghosts were around. They had a way of warping light and time around them, along with their other, deadlier powers. But she had no time to ponder the physics now. Not if she was to stick to her regular schedule and avoid suspicion. The world didn't know about witches, and they weren't going to find out through a slip-up by Zinnia Riddle.

Zinnia dumped the contents of her teapot into a thermos, and then hurriedly tossed some magical supplies into her purse until it bulged. Then she headed for the door. She paused to put on her boots, gazing up at her painted ceiling while she tied her laces. The ceiling had a fresco-style painting of an English garden. The image usually relaxed her, but this morning it did nothing for her nerves.

She checked her appearance in the hall mirror. Her flowered blouse matched the wallpaper behind her so closely that she appeared to be a semi-visible woman. A ghost. She put her hands on her hips and struck a sassy pose to bolster her confidence.

"Zinnia Riddle, you can handle this," she told her reflection.

Her hazel eyes brightened.

"Simply remember your training, and keep your wits about you."

Now her eyes twinkled.

"And for goodness' sake, don't do anything foolish."

The gleam went out of her eyes. The lump returned to her throat. The woman before her faded into the background, becoming a literal wallflower.

So much for confidence. There was no sassy pose or pep talk that could change the grim facts revealed that morning.

The dead woman was Annette Scholem. She was a coworker whose face Zinnia knew well, since they had seen each other every weekday for the past year. Annette was older than Zinnia, but still healthy and vital, kind and fun-loving. Annette was the one who'd wrangled the whole office into forming a bowling team. She was organizing their float for the summer parade. Annette was a dynamic powerhouse of a woman with big plans for the future.

But the dead don't organize parade floats, and they don't go bowling. Annette's big plans had died with her.

Zinnia leaned against the wall to steady herself. *Pull it together*, she told herself. *For Annette's sake. She came to you for a reason.*

She pulled on a warm jacket and then shivered in spite of it as she stepped outside. The chill in her bones wasn't just from the January air.

Zinnia furtively glanced left and right as she walked to where her car was parked next to the sidewalk, and climbed in. She locked the doors.

Danger was never far away in the town of Wisteria. Zinnia's house was relatively safe, thanks to the protective wards, but tragedy could be waiting around any corner. Zinnia couldn't shake a terrible image from her mind's eye.

Back in the kitchen, the ghost had revealed her identity, and something else. Something even more troubling. Her death wounds.

Whoever or whatever had killed Annette Scholem, it had left deep, bloody marks on her chest. She'd practically been torn open. The poor woman had not died peacefully.

Zinnia blew a warming breath onto her trembling hands, gripped the steering wheel, and drove toward City Hall.

"Happy birthday to me," she muttered grimly.

CHAPTER 2

WISTERIA CITY HALL

8:20 AM

Zinnia parked her car in an unmarked space in the staff parking lot. She glanced around to see if anyone was watching as she exited her car. A maintenance worker was sprinkling salt on the icy patches of walkway. He gave her a friendly nod and continued his work.

The magic ingredients she had shoved into her purse clanked together as she walked toward the staff entrance. Some of the items could only be safely stored in glass. She used recycled baby food jars that were magically charmed to be shatter resistant, but the noise was still disconcerting.

Zinnia's pace slowed as she neared Annette Scholem's parked car. The red Mustang convertible was empty inside, and parked on an angle, with one tire crossing the white line. It wasn't unusual for Annette to be sloppy at parking. She was often distracted when she arrived, listening to a self-help audiobook or a comedy podcast during her morning drive. The woman loved to either improve herself or have a laugh. Her coworkers teased her about her bad parking, but she'd tell them it was a small sacrifice for putting herself in a happy mood for the day. Nobody could argue with that. Annette Scholem was a cheerful soul who would be missed.

Zinnia pulled her gaze off the Mustang and continued walking at a measured pace. Were her footsteps extra loud this morning? She stepped more lightly. Her palms were sweating despite the chill in the air. Seeing the car had made Zinnia uneasy. Since Annette rarely went anywhere without her Mustang, that meant Annette's body wasn't far away. The death might have happened inside City Hall.

Zinnia reached the staff entrance at the side of the building and pressed her ID card against the card reader. The speaker let out a sad BLOOP sound. The flashing red light remained red. The building's security system had broken a week ago. Apparently, it was still busted. Zinnia tried the door and found it unlocked. So much for security at City Hall.

A hot blast of heated air pushed Zinnia's hair back as she stepped inside. She unfurled her clenched fists to dry the sweat on her palms.

She walked down the hallway and turned the corner. Up ahead, three of her Permits Department coworkers stood in a group. They were talking to each other with loose hand gestures. They clearly didn't know about Annette's death.

Zinnia's stomach felt heavier than ever as she approached the trio. She hoped that she was wrong about the ghost, that they would open the door and find their charismatic coworker typing away at her computer. She hoped today could be just another regular, boring Tuesday.

Zinnia forced a smile and said to her three coworkers, "Don't tell me this door's busted, too." The dryness in the back of her throat made her voice crack. She couldn't bear to look anyone in the eyes, so she leaned over to peer through the interior window at the side of the door. The window was frosted for privacy, so the only thing she could determine about the other side was that the lights were off.

Gavin Gorman was the first to speak up. "Actually, we're on strike," Gavin said in a joking tone. "Didn't you get the memo about our department-wide walkout?"

Zinnia turned to meet the man's gaze. Gavin Gorman was an athletic man in his forties. He was tall, over six feet two, and had the good looks of someone who worked very hard to have good looks. Occasionally, he went too far with his efforts, such as the time he bleached his teeth so bright they scared an elderly customer. That Tuesday morning, Gavin was wearing a stylish wool jacket over a fitted dress shirt and gray slacks. He would have easily been the best-dressed person at City Hall if only he'd pick clothes that were his size instead of half a size too small.

Gavin grinned, showing his blue-white teeth. "Nah, we're not really on strike, Zinnia. What would be the point? As much as I'd love to see them put a juice bar in the cafeteria, I know nothing ever changes around here." He kicked the bottom of the door with the toe of his shoe. "The door is jammed."

The other two coworkers held back, yawning and muttering about coffee.

Zinnia asked, "Did you call maintenance yet?" She thought of the man she'd seen putting salt on the icy walkway. She could pop outside to ask him for help with the door. Then again, he'd probably scowl and tell her to go through official channels. Some of the people at City Hall could be rigid about the rules.

Gavin crossed his arms and narrowed his eyes. "Why would we need to call maintenance? We figured you'd be along soon, and you always have your special way with things, Zinnia."

"Right." Zinnia pursed her lips and reached for the doorknob. The knob turned freely, but when she attempted to push the door open, it only cracked an inch before bumping against something on the other side.

"The door's hitting something," Gavin said.

Zinnia bit back a sarcastic remark. Gavin had a habit of explaining the obvious to people.

"If we had a screwdriver, we could take the door off its hinges," he said.

"The hinges are on the other side."

Gavin snorted. "Fine, Zinnia. What do you suggest we do? Throw a book through the glass? At least then we could see what's blocking the door."

Zinnia ignored him and asked the others, "Do you think Annette is around here somewhere? I saw her car in the parking lot."

The others, Karl and Dawna, both shrugged.

Gavin said, "I saw her Mustang, too. Annette has lousy parking skills, but I suppose that's to be expected, considering her age." He grinned. "Plus, she is a woman." He laughed at his own joke.

Zinnia shot him an icy look.

Gavin's expression turned serious. "Annette's probably in there, sitting in the dark and laughing at us."

"Annette? She doesn't laugh at people. She laughs *with* people." *Or at least she used to*, Zinnia thought sadly.

Gavin put one hand on his slim hip and eyed the door. "Then maybe she pushed something in front of the door for privacy. I bet she's sleeping on the reception couch again."

"Sleeping on the couch? That explains what she was doing last week," Zinnia said. "I got here early last Wednesday, and Annette was walking around shoeless, brushing her teeth." Zinnia shook her head. "She must have been here late last night, working on that mysterious project of hers." Lately, Annette had been staying after hours to work on something personal. She didn't have a computer at home, and nobody minded if she used the one at her desk after hours.

Gavin pushed the door until it stopped against the object with a thud. And then again. *Thud.* To Zinnia, who believed the object was the body of their coworker, the thud was sickening.

Zinnia cocked her head and pointed a finger at Gavin. "You were the last one to leave yesterday. Was Annette still at her desk when you walked out?"

He scratched his chin. "Come to think of it, she was. And she did say she might pull an all-nighter to work on that mysterious secret project of hers."

"Any idea what the secret project is?"

He shrugged with apathy. "I figured she'd tell us when she was good and ready. I was scared to show too much interest, actually. You know how Annette is. Always trying to get people to have fun and play those lame party games."

Zinnia gave the door another push. She could have used magic to boost her strength, but if it was Annette on the other side, she didn't want to disturb the body. Zinnia took a step back and placed a hand on each hip. There were countless ways she could get through the door, but she couldn't do magic with her coworkers standing around.

Gavin pounded his fist against the window, hard enough to make a loud noise but not hard enough to shatter the frosted pane. "Annette, you've had your beauty rest. Time to wake up, sleepyhead!"

They waited quietly for a response, but there was none.

"I have an idea," Zinnia said to Gavin. "You should go look for Annette in the lobby. If she's not there, try the cafeteria. Take Karl and Dawna with you."

Gavin snorted. "If the old broad's anywhere in this building, she's obviously inside this office where the coffee is free, not getting that swill from the cafeteria."

"Check anyway."

"And leave you here?"

"Gavin, you know I have my ways." Zinnia raised her eyebrows and widened her eyes to make her point. "Please go look around elsewhere."

"Fine," he huffed. He turned to the other two yawning coworkers. "Dawna, do you want to come with me?"

Dawna, who seemed to be sleeping on her feet, woke up at the sound of her name. "Sure. Whatever."

"I'm going, too," Karl said in his usual grumpy morning voice. "I need a coffee anyway, even if it's from the stinkin' cafeteria. Something tells me it's going to be a long day."

The three of them walked away. Once they were out of sight, Zinnia dropped her purse on the floor and started rummaging. She had a dozen baby food jars, each filled with things you'd never feed a baby—not unless you wanted the baby to grow tentacles. Everything clanked together noisily until she reached the Ziploc bag with the eyeballs. Bingo. Her fridge had once again given her exactly what she needed. And that was why she kept the old thing, even though it was decades past its prime and cost a fortune in electricity to run.

She stood up, checking over her shoulders to make sure the coast was clear. Then she poked a small, blue-tinged eyeball—an eyeball that had been sustainably harvested from a magical species of fish—onto the tip of her pinkie finger.

She pushed the door so that there was a crack wide enough for her to stick her fingers through. Then she closed her own eyes and let the magic do the work. With the fish eye's view, she could see the reception area clearly, including the object that was blocking the door.

Zinnia breathed a sigh of relief. It was just a chair blocking the door, not a body. But the relief didn't last for long. Beyond the chair, there were signs of a struggle. Another chair lay upside down, and the carpet was littered with papers and folders.

Zinnia was lifting her hand higher to get a better view beyond the reception counter when she felt a hand fall upon her shoulder. The scent of Gavin Gorman's cologne tickled her nose.

"Careful you don't lose a finger," Gavin said. "You need all ten for typing up permit applications."

She withdrew her hand, palmed the fish eye, and dropped it into the pocket of her jacket as she turned to face Gavin. He had already returned with Dawna in tow. She was focused on her phone, ignoring them.

"Any luck?" Zinnia asked.

"The lobby was practically empty," Gavin reported. "But at least I got a head start on my exercise steps for the day." He leaned over Zinnia to give the door a test push. "No luck here, I see."

Zinnia turned back to the door and stuck her fingers through the crack again. She gave the air a little twirl of magic—just enough to change the angle of the chair.

Gavin gave her a wary look. "What's blocking the door?"

"Beats me." She shrugged. "The cleaning staff is always moving stuff around at night. Every now and then, they get creative."

Gavin furrowed his brow. "But if they blocked the door, how could they get out? That's the only exit, unless you count the window in Karl's office."

Just then, Karl rounded the corner with his steaming cup of coffee. "Are you talking about me?" His eyes bugged out. "Is this whole door thing some sort of joke, Zinnia? Did Margaret put you up to this? That woman has gotten too big for her britches."

Dawna glanced up from her phone. "It's not a very good joke, Zinnia."

Zinnia sighed. "If it's a joke, I'm not in on it. I swear."

Gavin crossed his arms. "Isn't it your birthday today, Zinnia?"

She nodded.

Karl muttered a lackluster, "Happy birthday."

Dawna frowned. "If I'd known, I would have gotten you a scratch-off ticket."

Gavin continued to stare at Zinnia with suspicion. "Is there a birthday cake on the other side of this door? It had better be gluten free. You can't use the general expense fund if the cake isn't suitable for everyone."

Zinnia sighed. Her coworkers were lucky that the existence of witches was a secret. If she didn't have to worry about blowing her cover, she might have turned them all into frogs ages ago.

"Let's give the door one more try," she said. "We can push together."

Nobody made a move to help her.

Dawna said, "I just had my nails done." She flashed orange talons.

"We wouldn't want to mess up your nails," Zinnia said. "Dawna, you stay right there and continue to look fabulous while I do my impression of a battering ram." Nobody laughed at her joke. People didn't find Zinnia nearly as funny as she thought she was. Annette was the funny one. Everyone would have laughed if she'd made the crack about Dawna's nails, or about being a battering ram.

Zinnia braced her body against the door and put on a show of grunting as she pushed. The door moved easily now that the chair wasn't acting as a wedge, but she put on a good performance, letting it open slowly, breathing heavily the whole time.

"There," she said at last, brushing make-believe dust from her hands.

The other three continued to stand in the hallway, unconcerned. Karl was grumpily adjusting the lid on his coffee container, Dawna was glued to her phone, and Gavin was trying to look over Dawna's shoulder to see what was so captivating on her screen.

Zinnia barked, "Get to work, already!"

The trio jolted and entered the dark office. Dawna flipped on the lights and gasped at the messy sight.

"We've been robbed," Karl said.

"Either that, or a tornado passed through here," Gavin said.

The magazines in the reception area were spread all over the floor. The fresh flower bouquet that had been on the reception counter the day before was now on the floor in a pile of petals and broken glass. Zinnia walked in with trepidation.

She called out, "Annette?" No response. She prepared herself for the worst.

"I don't think the cleaning crew did this," Gavin said, kicking a magazine. "This isn't cleaning. This is demolition."

Zinnia took in the chaos with a slow sweep of her eyes. In front of her were six desks arranged into four work stations. To the left, there were four doors that led into four different rooms—a storage room, a break room with kitchen facilities, and two offices. The other rooms were dark. There was a chill in the air. It wasn't a magical chill, though. Either the heating system wasn't working, or someone had left the window in Karl's office open.

Dawna screamed.

Zinnia turned to look at the one spot she'd been avoiding. Annette's desk.

Annette's limp body lay in a pool of blood. The darkness stained her emerald green dress. Her eyes were wide open. In life, she had been tall and pleasantly curvy, with curly brown hair. She had a wide face, a pointed nose, and a round chin. Annette had always smelled like the sweetest of spices. Now she would only smell of death.

Dawna screamed a second time, and then the office was eerily silent.

Gavin pushed past Zinnia, jostling her on his way to Annette's body. He dropped to his knees next to the older woman's body and began touching her arms and shoulders.

Dawna shrieked, "Gavin! Don't touch her!"

Gavin ignored Dawna and continued to move his hands around the body, as though he was searching for something. Zinnia quickly realized Gavin was up to something. What could he be looking for on their dead coworker's body?

Zinnia swallowed down her revulsion and kneeled next to him to get a better look.

CHAPTER 3

As Zinnia got closer to the body of Annette Scholem, she couldn't help but see the woman's face, and as Zinnia did, the hard coating around her heart threatened to crack. Annette's eyes were completely, utterly blank. At least she didn't look terrified; death had relaxed her expression. Yesterday, those big brown eyes had been so lively. All the vitality was gone now. And there were those deep wounds in her chest, exactly like the wounds the ghost had worn. She'd been ripped into. Seeing Annette this way was enough to break a regular person's heart in half.

Gavin, meanwhile, was patting down the bloodied body as though it were nothing more than an inanimate object.

Zinnia, who was kneeling next to Gavin, nudged her shoulder against his. She asked evenly, "What do you think you're doing?"

He didn't seem to notice her presence, let alone hear her words.

She sharpened her voice. "If you're checking for a pulse, your hands should be on her neck, not all over her."

Her well-dressed coworker kept pawing at Annette's body. He was careful not to stain his wool jacket, but blood was on his fingers and spreading all over Annette's dress. The dark liquid appeared almost black against the emerald-green fabric.

"Gavin," Zinnia said with maximum sharpness. "Check her pulse or get out of the way so I can do it."

"That's what I'm doing," he said. "I'm, uh, trying to find a pulse." More clumsy patting, and then a ripping sound. "Oh, no," he exclaimed. "No, no, no!"

Dawna shrieked behind them, then asked, "Is she moving around? Bodies can move after they're dead. It's the gas and stuff."

"No, that's not it," Gavin said sheepishly, his bright white teeth covered by drooping lips. "I just split the seam of my pants." He sighed. "What a disaster."

Zinnia's mouth dropped open in disbelief. Splitting his pants was the disaster? She couldn't hold back any longer. She reached out and slapped Gavin across the face. He reacted with a bug-eyed, startled look.

"You hit me," Gavin said.

Zinnia felt her nostrils flare. Perhaps she shouldn't have slapped him, but it was done now.

She replied calmly, "I only did that to get your attention because you were acting hysterical, talking about your split pants when our dear Annette is—" She couldn't finish the sentence. *Deader than roadkill.*

"But you slapped me."

Zinnia blinked. "Stay calm or I'll have to slap you again. Now check her pulse."

Gavin's bugged-out eyes returned to normal. He pressed two of his bloodied fingers against the side of Annette's throat.

"No pulse," Gavin reported. "She's as dead as she looks."

The other two said nothing. Zinnia looked up to see their reactions. Karl was slack jawed. The hand holding his coffee cup was tilting sideways, and the coffee was dribbling onto the carpet. Dawna had her long orange fingernails pressed to her mouth as though they were the only things stopping her from shrieking again.

Out of the corner of her eye, Zinnia caught Gavin dropping one bloodied hand into the hip pocket of Annette's green dress. He was definitely looking for something.

From where Zinnia was kneeling, she could see the edge of something purple and plastic poking out from underneath the body. It was Annette's beloved writing pen. Was that what Gavin was after? She couldn't imagine why he'd be searching for the dead woman's cheap plastic pen, but she had a hunch it could be valuable. Zinnia used her body to shield her actions from Gavin's view while she grabbed the pen with one hand and sent it rolling underneath a nearby bookshelf.

Karl abruptly cleared his throat with his signature HARUMPH sound. Everyone turned to look at him.

"Stop what you're doing," Karl said gruffly. "Get away from Annette. Hasn't she suffered enough? Give the poor woman some space." They didn't move right away, so he barked again. "I said, give the woman some space!"

Gavin immediately did as he was told, backing away. Gavin's listening skills were much better when it was Karl that was issuing commands, even though Gavin didn't respect the older man.

"Stay where you are and don't touch anything," Karl ordered, his face turning red as he blustered. "I'm in charge of this department, which means I'm in charge of whatever —" he waved both hands, spilling more coffee "—*this* is. You have to listen to me."

Zinnia raised her hands like a captured criminal. "Easy now, Karl. We're all in this together."

Karl set his now-empty coffee cup on a desk and loosened his tie. The redness in his face faded as he unbuttoned his top shirt button.

Karl Kormac was a portly guy who turned red at any insult to his ego, and insults to his poor fragile ego were frequent. He was the department supervisor, technically, but he didn't have much real power. People did as he said mainly because they didn't want to be responsible for him getting upset and dropping dead. Annette had jokingly referred to Karl as the Coworker Most Likely To Have a Heart Attack While Screaming at the Photocopier. Karl was sixty-three years old, and less than two years from retirement—a fact he mentioned often, along with the current countdown number of days. Despite his age, he still had a full head of hair, mostly brown. Karl must have known the rest of the office didn't take him as seriously as he took himself. He kept trying to command respect anyway. He always wore suits, even on Casual Fridays.

With everyone's attention on him, Karl grabbed an overturned chair, flipped it over, and sat down with a loud groan. Ever since the incident with Annette in the boardroom last fall, he'd been groaning loudly whenever he stood up or sat down. Karl picked up the phone on the desk, punched an outside line, and jabbed at the digits for emergency services. The chair squeaked as he rotated from side to side impatiently.

"There's been an accident here at City Hall," he barked into the phone. "Yes, *Wisteria* City Hall. Can't you tell where I'm calling from?" He barely paused for a response. "This is Karl Kormac, the supervisor of the WPD. No, not the police department. I wouldn't be calling you from the WPD that's the police department, now, would I? No. I would not." His face turned as red as a ripe strawberry. "I'll speak more slowly so you can follow along. This is Karl Kormac, the supervisor of the Wisteria Permits Department at Wisteria City Hall. You need to send the police over here immediately. There's been an accident. Or maybe it's not an accident." He glanced over at the body. "Nope. Not an accident. Someone has been... murdered."

Dawna shrieked into her orange fingernails.

"Murdered," Gavin muttered as he lunged for a box of tissues on the desk. He frantically rubbed off the blood on his fingers.

While Karl continued giving details over the phone, Zinnia quietly stepped away from the others. She followed the chilly breeze she'd noticed earlier into Karl's corner office, which had the only window that opened. Sure enough, the window was wide open, and the bug screen had been ripped apart. It wasn't a huge window, but even a bigger person like Karl could have squeezed through. Annette's attacker must have gained entry through the window. Zinnia peered through the torn screen at the frost-covered grass and the trees beyond the lawn. City Hall backed onto a woodsy area known as Pacific Spirit Park. The local kids claimed the park was full of ghosts and unspeakable creatures. *Kids and their wild imaginations.*

Zinnia stepped back from the window, careful not to touch anything. If Annette's attacker had been the regular human kind, the police might be able to get fingerprints or other physical evidence from the window frame. Then again, the attacker might not have been the regular human kind. They were in Wisteria, after all. And the vicious slashes in Annette's chest didn't seem very human.

Pulling her winter jacket tighter, Zinnia left Karl's office. She popped her head into Jesse Berman's office briefly without entering. He hadn't arrived yet, but that wasn't unusual for Jesse. Nor was it unusual for the other two employees who hadn't shown up yet, either. She continued on to the next room. The staff break room was small but efficient, with a microwave and coffee pot on the counter, and an apartment-sized refrigerator in the corner. Sitting on the counter was a teapot full of Annette's favorite tea. Zinnia touched her hand to the side of the pot. It was full, but cool. There were two mugs sitting next to the teapot. Had Annette been entertaining someone? Zinnia stepped back. The counter was actually full of glasses and mugs, like a typical office kitchen. It was impossible to be sure how many mugs Annette had been planning to use for tea last night.

Zinnia turned to leave the break room. She whirled quickly and bumped into someone who'd snuck up behind her. A tall, solid man. Jesse Berman.

She exclaimed breathlessly, "Jesse!"

"Looks like I picked the wrong day to sleep in," he said.

His masculine voice was almost magical. It changed the shape of the emotions roiling within Zinnia, softening all her feelings, smoothing down all her edges. She had never been more glad to see him, and she was *always* glad to see him.

Jesse Berman stood six feet tall and bore the commanding presence of someone even taller. Unlike Gavin Gorman, with his fake tans and bleached teeth, Jesse didn't have to work at his good looks. He had the facial bone structure of an action movie actor—rugged and strong, but not like a caveman. Jesse's looks were refined, almost beautiful. His eyes were a transfixing shade of light blue, and their brightness gave him a boyish look. He was thirty-six, and his dark hair showed no signs of turning gray. He wore his dark brown hair cropped short, but not too short. There was a natural curl that made the longer hair on top swirl in an interesting new direction every day. Zinnia had spent a lot of blissful moments during her first months at the office daydreaming about running her fingers through Jesse's thick, wavy hair. He was a dozen years younger than her, and being in the same room with him made her feel young. She might have quit her job ages ago if not for the added benefit of working so close to Jesse.

He looked into her eyes and asked, "Are you okay?"

"Me?" She found the question absurd. "Annette is the one who's dead."

"I saw." He pointed his transfixing blue eyes at the floor and put his hands in his pockets. "You poor thing. I know you were fond of her. We all were."

Zinnia studied his face. His usually clean-shaven jaw had a smattering of stubble today. She pointed at his chin, resisting a girlish urge to touch it and feel the sharp hairs under her fingers.

"You didn't shave this morning," she said. "That's not like you."

He shrugged. "Like I said, I slept in. I stayed up too late watching the end of a TV series, and then this morning, my arm must have turned off the alarm clock without waking me up." He rubbed his dark stubble and grinned. "I haven't stayed up that late since college days. If my dad were still alive, he'd whoop my butt for being such a slob."

"Oh, Jesse." She rolled her eyes. "You're the opposite of a slob."

He waggled his eyebrows. "Compliments will get you everywhere."

Zinnia sighed inwardly. She could flirt with Jesse all day. It was the best part of her job.

They smiled at each other until the grating sound of Karl being irate over the phone drifted into the break room. Jesse's handsome face took on a grim expression, his smile lines turning to frown lines. "Do you have any idea what happened to Annette? Was it a burglary gone wrong?"

She almost laughed at the absurdity of his question. "It couldn't have been a burglary. We don't have anything to steal. The computers in here are so old, you'd have to pay someone to take them away."

"True." Jesse crossed over to the sink and poured two glasses of water from the filtered tap. He handed her one. "But how are you doing? You don't seem very shaken up. You must be in shock."

"I think we're all in shock." She took a small sip of water and nearly choked. With all the upheaval, she'd forgotten how to swallow. Stress did funny things to the body.

Jesse opened his mouth to speak but stopped, turning his head to listen as the main office door opened and closed with a slam. Two seconds later, Margaret Mills stomped her way into the break room, breathing heavily. She'd come in so quickly, she must not have noticed the dead coworker on her way through the office. Margaret was what some people would call a Force of Nature. She could have tunnel vision at times, the way a cyclone has tunnel vision.

Margaret dropped her purse on the room's table and sighed wearily. "I am so exhausted. You're all going to have to excuse my mistakes today. I feel like the walking dead."

Jesse said, "Margaret, there's—"

She cut him off with a wave of her hand. "I know, I know. We all have our problems. We shouldn't drag issues from our personal lives into work. Goodness knows that's the main reason I come here every day, to get away from..." She waved one arm as shorthand for all the things they heard about regularly.

Jesse glanced over at Zinnia, quirked an eyebrow, and handed the other glass of water to Margaret. The woman would find out about Annette soon enough, and it was good to stay hydrated.

The tardy coworker drank the water with loud, unselfconscious gulps, blissfully unaware of the grave situation in the next room.

Margaret Mills was short and solid, with rounded shoulders and a forward-leaning posture that made her appear to be charging ahead, rhinoceros-like, at all times. She had once had lustrous light brown hair, but now it was gray—entirely gray, even though she was only forty-two. The hair made her look much older than she was, but she liked the degree of anonymity it gave her. Every woman of a certain age knows about becoming invisible as the years progress. Margaret used her gray hair to her advantage. For example, she could browse in any store without being bothered by salespeople. Margaret was defiantly proud of her ability to blend in anywhere. Her gray hair was naturally curly, and she styled it one of two ways: frizzy or extra-frizzy. Today, it was relatively smooth. However, as she gulped her glass of water, her gray curls seemed to frizz up from the extra hydration.

Margaret set the empty glass on the counter and picked up right where she'd left off. "Who knew having four kids would be like working in a circus? I tell you, it's non-stop, with the monkey business and the jibber-jabber. They had a goldfish go missing this morning—allegedly—so they missed the school bus, and I had to load them all in with me for an extra-fun drive. That's when I found out what *really* happened to the goldfish, and trust me, you do *not* want to know the sordid details."

"Probably not," Zinnia agreed.

Jesse gave Zinnia's shoulder a friendly squeeze. "Mind if I leave you two lovely ladies while I go check on the rest of the gang?"

"Go ahead," Zinnia said. "I'll handle the news. Good luck out there."

Jesse eyed the door with trepidation. "The least I can do is give Karl someone else to order around so he can enjoy his last moments on earth before he gets that overdue aneurysm." He grinned.

Zinnia gave him a head shake.

He stifled his grin. "Too soon? Too dark?"

"Both," she said.

He took a deep breath, puffing up his handsome chest, and left the break room.

Margaret gave Zinnia a raised eyebrow. "Flirty, flirty," she said. "You're like a giddy schoolgirl."

"I'm a grown woman," Zinnia said. "I'm forty-eight now. Today's my birthday."

Margaret stepped back and looked Zinnia up and down. "Is that what's different today? There's something in the air. I noticed it as soon as I walked in, because I don't miss a beat."

Zinnia bit her tongue.

Margaret said, "Look at you. Zinnia Riddle, another year closer to fifty. Fifty! Don't you dare drag me with you, woman!"

Unpleasant though it was to have her proximity to fifty be highlighted, Zinnia had something much worse to discuss with Margaret. She put one hand on each of Margaret's shoulders and looked down into the other woman's eyes, which were as gray as her hair. "Margaret, Annette is dead. She's lying in a pool of blood next to her desk, with deep-looking wounds in her chest."

Margaret blinked and drew her head back, increasing her number of chins. Then she blinked again, thrust her chin out, and straightened up until she was only a few inches shorter than Zinnia.

In a serious tone, she said, "That does explain why I saw her ghost this morning when I was in the shower."

Zinnia repeated back, "You saw her ghost when you were in the shower,"

Margaret nodded, making the single frizzy curl that adorned the center of her forehead like a horn bounce up and down. "She was wearing the same emerald-green dress she was wearing yesterday. I remember because she paired it with that cute pink cardigan I've always admired. The one with the pearl buttons."

"The pink cardigan is on the back of her chair," Zinnia said. "She didn't go home last night. She never left the office."

Margaret took in the news and frowned. "Someone came here, into our office, and killed Annette. How could that happen?" She lowered her voice to a whisper. "Don't we have protective wards set up on the building, or at least around our little office?"

"You know those wards don't do much on public spaces."

Margaret shook her head. "We're a couple of lousy, good-for-nothing witches. And now one of our coworkers has paid the price."

"We can't protect every non-magical person in the whole town."

Margaret inhaled sharply and reached for her purse. "I have to check on my kids. If anything were to happen to my little angels, I would die, Zinnia. I would just die."

"I know," Zinnia said softly.

Margaret pulled her phone out and paused. "Who would want to hurt Annette? It doesn't make any sense. She was just a regular person. Do you think there's a crazed killer on the loose?" Her gray eyes widened. "A serial killer?" Her hair seemed to frizz up at the suggestion.

"We must not get ahead of ourselves."

"But Annette's not the kind of woman who has enemies." Margaret's voice had gotten loud, so she lowered it again. "She didn't have any powers, did she? Not a full-blown witch, of course, but maybe some minor mage thing?"

"Not that I know of, but you know how paranoid some —" Zinnia cut herself off because someone was entering the break room.

Dawna walked in, looking shaky. She plopped into a chair across from Margaret. "Are you two talking about who might have killed Annette? Do you have any ideas?"

Zinnia and Margaret exchanged a look.

"No ideas," the two said in unison.

Dawna arched her back, sticking out her chest. She was apparently getting over the shock, and her usual sass was returning. "Well, I know who did it."

"Oh?" Zinnia and Margaret grabbed chairs and joined Dawna at the break-room table.

CHAPTER 4

Zinnia and Margaret sat quietly across from their coworker, Dawna. What had she meant about knowing who killed Annette?

Dawna Jones was a watchful woman who kept quiet until it suited her to speak up. She had dark skin, and dark natural hair that she wore pushed back from her face, often with a headband, accenting her orange eyes. She was lithe and moved quietly, like a cat. Dawna had cats, between two and five of them—nobody was quite sure how many. She could be strangely private about her private life. A person looking for clues into Dawna's internal life might notice her desk was decorated with a healthy jade plant, a framed four-leaf clover, and a white elephant—all symbols of good luck from various cultures. She was one of the younger employees in the office. At thirty, she was a decade younger than her on and off again lover, Gavin.

Dawna had always gotten along well with Annette, but they did disagree about one thing. Gavin Gorman. Dawna felt that Gavin was suitable dating material about fifty percent of the time, which explained their frequent breakups. Conversely, Annette found him suitable for Dawna exactly zero percent of the time. Whenever the couple reconciled after a breakup, Annette would roll her eyes and say to Dawna, "I don't know what you see in that man." Dawna always pointed out that at least she had a man, unlike Annette. The only man at City Hall that Annette did approve of was Jesse Berman, but he wasn't Dawna's type at all.

Dawna tapped her long orange nails on the table and savored the attention of the two women present.

"You were saying something," Zinnia prodded.

Margaret chimed in. "About some enemy that Annette had?"

Dawna nodded sagely, relishing her knowledge. "I have a pretty good idea who killed her," she said.

"Are you going to tell us?" Zinnia asked.

"Maybe you should wait until the police get here," Margaret said.

Dawna's forehead wrinkled. "The police? No way. They'll think I'm crazy. Unless... can you two nice, respectable ladies back me up?"

Zinnia and Margaret muttered "sure" and exchanged a look. What were they agreeing to?

Dawna drew herself up with a big breath. "My theory is that the person who went all scary-movie-hack-job on Annette must have been someone who didn't appreciate having all of their secrets gettin' spelled out in that new book she was writing."

In unison, Zinnia and Margaret took in a breath and asked, "What book?"

"Don't you know?" Dawna's voice pitched higher and higher. "That book she was writing!" When the other two didn't respond, she said, "Oh, don't tell me you didn't know all about Annette and her side hustle. Aren't you two usually up in everyone's business?"

Margaret made a scoffing sound.

Just then, their three male coworkers came into the break room. Karl's face was red and splotchy, even though he'd unbuttoned more shirt buttons and abandoned his tie somewhere. Gavin went to the sink and started washing his hands vigorously. Jesse held back, leaning against the wall next to the door.

"Oh, good," Dawna said, twirling her long orange fingernails in the air. "Staff meeting. This saves me from having to repeat myself to everyone one at a time."

Margaret explained to the others, "Annette was writing a book." She turned to Dawna and asked, "Is that what her secret project was? The one she was staying after hours to work on."

Dawna nodded. "You got it, girl."

Margaret turned to the men and explained, as though they hadn't been standing right there, "Annette's secret project was a book. That's why she was staying late all those nights."

"Shush," Dawna said waving a hand between Margaret and the men. "Let me tell it." She rotated her chair so she was facing the male coworkers. "You fellows won't know nothin' about this, but Annette asked me to help her with some computer stuff one night. I wanted to get home to feed my cats, but the old lady needed help with the computer, and you know me, I gotta be helpful because I'm lucky at computers, right? So, we got to talking. Did you ever hear of an author called AJ Scholem?" Everyone exchanged puzzled looks. "Me, neither," Dawna said. "But that's the name that Annette's been using for her fantasy books."

Gavin scoffed. "Fantasy? You mean romance?"

Karl's eyes bulged out as he stammered, "Wha-wha-what? Romance? What? Annette? What?"

Jesse patted Karl on the shoulder. "Take it easy, Karl. Deep breaths. In through the nose, out through the mouth. Let the lady speak."

Dawna rolled her eyes. "Not that kind of fantasy. You men have a one-track mind. I meant *fantasy*. You know. Like The Lords of the Rings and stuff."

"*Lord of the Rings*," Gavin corrected.

"Whatever." Dawna squared her shoulders with pride. "Annette is a real, genuine author, and she told me all about it. She trusted me."

Jesse pulled out his phone, tapped the screen, then read aloud, "AJ Scholem is the pen name for a mid-list author who lives in the rainy part of the West Coast, in harmony with nature." He looked up, eyebrows tented. "That's all it says. No picture. It doesn't even say if AJ is male or female. I guess it could be Annette."

"It's her, dummy," Dawna said with a sassy head bob.

Jesse stifled a grin. He was no dummy, but he didn't have Karl's fragile ego, so he let it go.

"I was sworn to secrecy by Annette," Dawna said. None of them spoke or moved. Dawna continued. "But now that she's dead, everything's going to come out. That woman had secrets, just like the rest of us, except she wrote hers in a book. And somebody didn't like that, so they killed her."

Margaret scowled. "You said you knew who killed her."

Dawna shrugged. "I don't know their name," she said in a high voice. "Do I look like the FBI?"

Karl grunted. "But why would someone kill Annette for writing a book? This is ridiculous."

Jesse said, "When the police get here, let's not waste their time with this book stuff."

Gavin, who was still washing his hands, said, "I've got your back, Dawna, but are you sure about any of this?"

"Ridiculous," Karl said again, snorting.

Dawna raised her hand and turned her palm toward Karl. "Haters gonna hate," she said. Addressing the others, she continued. "You see, Annette already had this one series that was doing okay. Last fall, she started writing this new spin-off book. That's like a book that's part of a series but not really, depending on how you look at it. She told me it was gonna be her breakout hit, the big one that takes her from being a nobody to being a household name. You know, like the Harry Potter lady." She paused to catch her breath before letting out a light, nervous chuckle. "Here's the weird part. All of the people in her book, well, they're us." She looked around the room with her orange, catlike eyes wide, pausing on each person. "We're all in the book!"

A moment of silence passed.

"Oh," Jesse said in his usual irreverent tone. "Well, that explains everything." He balled his hands into fists and held them to his chin in mock fear. "Someone must have killed Annette because her book was going to reveal all their secrets."

Karl snapped his fingers. "It's like a poison pen mystery."

Gavin asked, "What? A poisoned pen?" He paused his vigorous hand washing.

Karl made a HARUMPH before explaining, "That's when a group of people, usually in a small town, like a quaint English village, get anonymous letters full of all sorts of nasty lies and accusations. This all leads to somebody getting murdered, and then some plucky or brilliant detective has to figure out who the killer is." He tried to straighten his tie, even though he wasn't wearing one. "And usually there are cakes. Not my sort of thing, but I've spent some time in bookstores over the years."

"So, this poison pen thing happens in books," Jesse said flatly. "In novels."

Gavin chimed in. "Yeah, Karl. That sort of thing only happens in books."

Karl's face flushed to a plum shade. He let out another HARUMPH.

Margaret banged on the break-room table with her fist. "I need to see this scandalous book of Annette's immediately. Where is it?"

Dawna bobbed her head from side to side. "Beats me! Probably on the computer network. She might have had a printout somewhere, too. Like, for proofreading or whatever."

Jesse said, "Wacky as it sounds, I'd like to see that book, too."

"We need to find it now," Gavin said. "Before the police get here and lock everything down."

Zinnia spoke up. "Speaking of which, why aren't they here yet?"

Everyone started speaking at once about their experiences with the town's law enforcement agency.

Karl waved both hands to get everyone's attention. "I'm in charge here, and I'm ordering everyone to look for Annette's book. And when you find it, give it to me."

Jesse grinned at Karl. "You're not in charge of me, man. I'm technically my own department. Special Buildings Permits."

"Fine," Karl blustered. "Don't help us look for the book. Make yourself useful anyway. Put on a fresh pot of coffee."

Jesse gave Karl an army salute. "Your wish is my command."

The three women got up from the table and followed Gavin and Karl out to the main area of the office. Zinnia tried not to look anywhere near the body of Annette Scholem, but her eyes kept pointing there anyway. Poor Annette. They hadn't even taken the time to close the poor woman's eyes.

Gavin stepped over Annette's body as though it was nothing but a pile of clothes. He yanked open the drawers of her desk and started ransacking them.

"Gavin, not like that," Karl barked. "Look with your eyes, not your hands. Don't get your bloody fingerprints all over everything."

Gavin waved both his hands at Karl. "Look. It's okay," he said. "I washed all the blood off."

"You're standing in blood," Karl said.

Dawna made an un-Dawna-like burp. "I'm gonna be sick," she said. "You people are all crazy. You act like Annette's not lying right there on the floor, staring up at heaven."

Gavin continued rummaging through Annette's desk drawers, muttering, "If I was an author, where would I hide my book?"

Yeah, right. Zinnia was fairly certain Gavin was still looking for the pen. She used her magic to roll it deeper under the bookcase for safekeeping.

Karl went to the filing cabinets on the far wall and started opening file folders and binders frantically.

Margaret stood off to the side, talking on her phone to someone at her kids' school. She wouldn't be of much help until she checked on her family and eased her fears.

Jesse called out from the break room, "Coffee will be ready in five minutes."

Zinnia pressed her hand to her forehead. The morning couldn't get any more surreal, not unless she and Margaret started busting out spells, using magic to search for Annette's book. But they couldn't do that. If their coworkers learned about magic, there'd be a big mess to clean up, and it would be dealt with by the scary people who worked in the shadows. Those people would start by wiping the memories of the non-magical folks, and they might not stop there. They might even wipe the two witches, returning both Zinnia and Margaret to "factory default settings," whatever that meant.

Zinnia turned in a slow circle, scanning the office for clues. The authorities would be arriving eventually. Once they did, she would no longer have access to the scene of the crime. She slowed her breathing and calmed her mind. What did she know so far? She looked at Gavin, who was digging through Annette's desk drawers. Gavin had been the last to leave the day before, the last one of them to see Annette alive. And now he was frantically searching for something in her desk. That was certainly suspicious.

Zinnia turned to Dawna and gave her an encouraging smile. Dawna scarcely noticed, since she was throwing up into a garbage bin. That wasn't suspicious. It was perfectly normal behavior for a person who was standing in the same room as her deceased coworker.

Zinnia looked over at the other office witch. Margaret finished talking on the phone, and, without even making eye contact with Zinnia, marched into Karl's office. Karl followed, hot on her heels. "Stay out of my office, Margaret. The book isn't in here."

Margaret replied, "How would you know if you haven't looked?"

The two of them argued with each other while Margaret searched his drawers and shelves.

Zinnia pulled out her phone and started taking pictures of the scene. She had an excellent memory, but her coworkers were making a mess of everything faster than she could capture all the details. And she still needed to retrieve Annette's pen from under the bookcase before Gavin found it.

Suddenly, someone reached over her shoulder and yanked the phone from her hand.

An authoritative male voice boomed behind her, "Freeze, everyone! Don't move a muscle. I've got guns and Tasers. Which ones I use is up to you."

CHAPTER 5

WISTERIA POLICE DEPARTMENT

OFFICE OF DETECTIVE ETHAN FUNG

5:35 PM

Zinnia watched in awe as Detective Ethan Fung typed quickly on his computer keyboard. The man could type!

"What's your speed?" Zinnia asked playfully. "Is that ninety words a minute I'm hearing? Over a hundred?"

He smiled and kept typing.

She leaned forward, looking down her nose at his hands. "You're fast, all right, but how's the accuracy?"

He snorted but continued to smile and type. "Never you mind about my speed, Ms. Riddle, let alone my accuracy. I don't get any complaints."

"Mm-hmm." Zinnia leaned back and let him type, the tappity-tap-tap sounds filling the small office. Unlike the other plain, white rooms inside the Wisteria Police Department, Detective Fung's office was painted a cheery ocher color that reminded Zinnia of a chain coffee shop. The walls were decorated with peaceful pictures of nature. A large painting of the sea filled the space behind Fung's head. His desk was dark brown, oil-finished natural walnut, and very tidy. Against the side wall was a bar-sized mini-fridge and a tall bookshelf filled with books on a wide range of subjects: weather almanacs, forensic science, medical manuals, geography, history, and a whole shelf of new age and self-help books. Detective Fung was a well-read man who could make small talk with anyone. It was part of what made him an excellent detective.

Sometimes he played the role of the tough meathead cop, such as when he'd shown up at the Permits Department that morning. Sure, he had threatened to shock people with his Tasers, but that was just to get their attention. In reality, he was calm and thoughtful, and almost never shot people without provocation.

Zinnia glanced around the office for current clues into his personal life. There was no "World's Greatest" coffee mug. No personal snapshots. No clues at all, not even any indication he existed outside of the WPD. And he still didn't have a wedding band on his ring finger. Was that driving his poor mother crazy? Was Mrs. Fung still trying to set him up by ambush? Zinnia wondered why his mother's ploys hadn't worked, why he hadn't been snapped up by a woman. He was a catch, and not hard to look at.

Detective Ethan Fung had a pleasantly oval face and perfectly trimmed black hair. His eyes were dark brown, small and active, topped by thick, straight eyebrows—*two* eyebrows, with plenty of hair-free light brown skin between them. Having two separate eyebrows was one of many signs he wasn't like the other police officers in town. Fung's male coworkers took pride in having as much facial hair as regulations allowed. Most had a unibrow as well as a bushy mustache. Fung's face was always clean-shaven, revealing the laugh lines at the corners of his mouth. His wrinkles weren't very deep for his age. He had been born the same year as Zinnia, so he would also be forty-eight soon enough, but he didn't look ready. Then again, who was ready for forty-eight?

Fung punched the final keystrokes with a flourish. "And that's the story thus far," he said in a deep yet playful storyteller voice. "Unless you have something to add, *Ms. Riddle*?" He placed an especially formal emphasis on her name.

"I've told you everything I know, which I'm afraid isn't much," Zinnia said.

He pushed the keyboard away and turned to face her. "And now you just want to go home."

She arched her back, catlike, and stretched her arms above her head. "It's been a long day." It had been eight hours since the detective had arrived at the office and taken charge of the crime scene. The time in between had passed in a blur, a series of phone calls and interviews, most of it at the police station, solemn and businesslike, punctuated with outbursts of grieving.

Zinnia and Margaret had both been kept busy, tracking down Annette's distant next of kin and trying to keep their coworkers from imploding. Gavin had a meltdown when Karl ordered fast food for everyone to eat for lunch. Jesse had to go track down vegetable juice—freshly squeezed— to prevent a second homicide. Poor Dawna couldn't keep down any food, healthy or otherwise, and she'd also chipped three nails. The two witches hadn't found a single minute to privately discuss the situation from a magical perspective.

"You think *your* day has been long," Fung said. "Mine is just beginning. And today was supposed to be my day off."

"You love it," she said.

He wrinkled his nose. "I do."

She looked down at her hands. Her pale skin looked fragile, nearly blue, in the artificial light of the office. Annette's skin had looked pale, too. Zinnia swallowed down the lump that kept returning to her throat.

Softly, Fung said, "Zinnia, I'm sorry for the loss of your friend." He exhaled audibly. "I truly am."

She flicked her gaze up to meet his. Her voice, when it finally came out, was as hard as a rock. "Then be a good detective and catch the bad guy... or girl... or whoever it was." *Or whatever it was.*

He propped his elbows on his tidy desk and folded his hands together. "The WPD will be putting all available resources to work in solving this horrific crime."

"Will that include the type of resources that aren't so traditional?" Zinnia met his gaze confidently. "The *special* resources?"

He smirked. "Of course. Jerry Lund is conducting the autopsy even as we speak, and he's the best. Until we close this case, it will remain our number one priority."

"Good," Zinnia said. "It's the least we can do for Annette. Out of all the people working at City Hall, Annette Scholem deserved this the least." She cleared her throat. "Not that anyone deserves to be shredded like that."

Fung leaned back in his chair and allowed his arms to rest on the sides. "I didn't know Annette. She'd only been living in Wisteria for about a year and a half, and our paths haven't crossed until now. From what I've learned today, Annette Scholem was the kind of woman who wouldn't hurt a fly."

Zinnia nodded. "She was the kind of woman who would convince the fly to join her bowling team."

"It takes a real monster to hurt someone so nice."

"Maybe it *was* a monster." Her mouth went dry. "As much as I'd like to stick my head in the sand and pretend monsters don't exist, I know better."

Fung blinked once before turning toward his bookshelf. "You know, maybe I should have become a doctor."

Zinnia didn't respond. Maybe he should have become a doctor, somewhere far away from Wisteria. He would probably have a ring on his finger by now, and photos of chubby-cheeked babies on his doctor's office desk.

The little office was silent, yet a frenzy of noise continued just beyond the closed door, with police officers and support staff rushing around, speaking in clipped tones. Homicides did happen in Wisteria, but they didn't happen often, and today was going to be a long one for many people. For Zinnia, sitting in Fung's pleasant, ocher-colored office felt like being in the eye of a hurricane. Her gaze kept going to the painting of the seascape behind his head. She remembered him telling her about the painting once, when she'd been helping him with something years ago. He'd put the painting there on the advice of a feng shui consultant his mother had sent in.

Fung was still looking at his bookshelf, imagining life on a path he hadn't taken.

Zinnia broke the silence. "You would have been an excellent doctor."

He broke out of the dream. "Yes, but fate had other plans," he said wearily. "*Fate. Magic.* Same difference, as they say."

Zinnia nodded. She knew Fung's history. He'd been about to graduate from medical school when a close friend—possibly his girlfriend, but he'd never said—had been murdered. Her death changed the whole trajectory of his life. He dropped out of medical school and became a police officer six months later. Then he solved his friend's murder while he was supposed to be handing out traffic violations. Rather than getting punished or thrown off the force, young Ethan Fung found himself promoted to detective. Someone clever—someone far up the command chain—had seen his value. And now here he was, all these years later, with a tasteful ocher office and no ring on his finger.

Zinnia asked, "Is today one of those days you regret making the switch?"

"Yes." He drew himself up tall in his chair. "But by the end of the week, the regrets will be gone." He paused. "By Friday."

She let out a low whistle. "Today's Tuesday, Detective. Are you telling me you're going to close this case by Friday?"

His small, quick-moving eyes took on a boyish gleam. "Guaranteed by Friday, or you get your money back."

"Guaranteed, hmm?"

A loud knock on the door surprised both of them. The air in the room sucked out as someone yanked open the door without waiting for an invitation. Zinnia turned to see her boss, Karl Kormac, standing at the doorway.

Karl said to the detective in a low, gruff voice, "Do you have a minute?" Karl looked ashen and sweaty.

"I've got a minute," Fung said evenly. "Is there something you wanted to ask me about the case?"

Karl chewed his lower lip and eyed Zinnia. "I need to..." He looked down at his feet. "I need to change my statement."

"Sure thing." Fung turned to his computer and typed rapid-fire on his keyboard. "Okay, shoot. I've got the file open."

"Now?" Karl frowned at Zinnia.

Zinnia patted the empty chair next to her. "Take a load off, boss."

Karl remained in the doorway. He liked being called boss, and he liked sitting down, but apparently he didn't like either enough to sit beside her right now.

"Go ahead," Fung said. "What's the change to the statement?"

"It's, uh, more of an addition." Karl gripped the door frame and swayed, looking like a little kid reluctant to face the principal. "Last night, I couldn't sleep, so I went for a drive. And right around the time I was driving by City Hall, my stomach growled, so I decided to get a snack from the only place that was open in the middle of the night."

Fung paused his typing. "What time was this?"

"About three in the morning. I parked in the staff parking lot—out of habit, of course. And then I walked up to the street to Lindell's."

"The Korean grocer?"

Karl wrung his hands. "Yeah. It's the only place in town that sells azuki bean rice balls. Plus, they're open all night." He stopped wringing his hands long enough to rub both hands against his wrinkled suit trousers.

Fung asked, "Did you enter the City Hall building?"

"No." Karl shook his head vigorously.

Fung muttered, "Not that the broken security system would have logged your keycard if you had."

Karl didn't say anything.

Fung asked, "Did you see anyone else in the staff parking lot?"

Karl kept shaking his head. "I saw Annette's Mustang, but that was it."

Fung stopped typing and turned to look at Karl with a cool expression. "So you knew Annette was alone in the office at three in the morning."

Karl shoved both hands into his pockets. "I know, I know. It sounds pretty bad, but you have to believe me. Would I come to you voluntarily and change my statement if I... had done something wrong?"

Fung's expression remained impassive. "I don't know. You tell me. Would you?"

Karl huffed and puffed, his face turning a deep, dangerous-looking red. He withdrew one hand from his pocket and thrust it toward Fung.

His sudden movement put Zinnia on red alert—or, to be specific, *blue lightning alert*. Her fingers crackled with power. She was prepared to let some blue plasma fly when she saw Karl didn't have a weapon in his hand. A crumpled piece of paper left Karl's hand like a tiny bowling ball and landed on Fung's desk.

Fung raised his eyebrows. "What's this?"

"Proof," Karl said. "My receipt from Lindell's."

Fung slowly smoothed out the receipt on his desk. "Thank you, Mr. Kormac. I will add this to the file."

Karl took one step backward, into the hall. "It was the receipt that reminded me. I totally forgot that I went out last night until I saw that in my pocket."

"Perfectly understandable," Fung said. "I'm satisfied with your explanation. Is there anything else?"

"Nope." Karl turned and left.

Zinnia waited until Karl was out of hearing range before she said dryly, "That wasn't suspicious or anything."

Fung tapped his fingers on his desk and clicked his tongue. "How well do you know your coworkers?"

"That depends. When you spend forty-plus hours a week with people, you get to know them, but only their office side."

"How long have you been slaving away there, anyway?"

She didn't need to look at a calendar to remind herself. "Exactly one year to the day," she said.

"Really?" His eyes widened. "That long at one job?"

She shifted her position in the chair. She didn't like what Fung was implying, even though she felt the same way.

Fung said, conversationally, "Why not start at the beginning and tell me all about it? It's about time for me to eat something, anyway." He got to his feet, opened the mini-fridge, and started pulling out vegetables, charcuterie, and crackers. He spread everything on his desk between them. "I've got more than enough to share. How do you feel about having a picnic dinner with me?"

"Someone ought to help you eat all this food." Zinnia furrowed her brow as she looked over the food. It was all appetizing and healthy. Something had changed dramatically since the last time she'd been inside Fung's office. She gave him a questioning look. "Celery sticks? What happened to your drawer full of Pringles and Mars bars?"

He gave her a sly wink, closed the mini-fridge door, and returned to his seat across from her. "That's a long story, and not the one you want to hear right now." He ripped open a box of whole-grain crackers. "Tell me about your first impressions of everyone at the parking department."

"Permits Department."

He almost smiled. "Duly noted. What made you take a job there, anyway?"

"It's not a what but a who." She leaned back in her chair. "Margaret Mills."

He chuckled. "Go on."

This wasn't how Zinnia had planned to spend her Tuesday evening, but if the detective thought her perspective might help him with the investigation, she would oblige. Like most witches, Zinnia was attuned to the needs of others. She was happiest when helping.

Zinnia grabbed her purse, pushed aside the jars of magic supplies, and pulled out a couple of square, thin packages. She tossed one over the desk to Ethan.

"Sure," she said. "Let's do this."

Ethan's eyebrows shot up as he caught the foil square. "Zinnia! I'm flattered, but..." He blinked rapidly at the square packet. "Oh. This is one of those moist hand wipes."

Zinnia felt her cheeks flush but kept an even tone. "What did you think it was, Detective?"

"Nothing. Never mind." He ripped open the square foil packet and started cleaning his fingers with the moist towelette. "Tell me about the day you met Karl Kormac."

She wiped her fingers with her own towelette, even though she didn't need to. Witches have an extremely high tolerance to bacteria. If anything, a good dose of bugs makes them stronger.

She began the tale. "The first time I met my boss, he showed me how to use the coffee maker. Try not to get too excited, because there's more. We were alone in the break room together, and it took me about two minutes flat to figure out Karl's big secret."

"Which was?" Ethan leaned forward in anticipation.

CHAPTER 6

ONE YEAR AGO

After only two hours at her new job, Zinnia was sent for a coffee break by the woman training her. Zinnia was ready and willing to keep going, but the woman, Annette Scholem, was getting hoarse from talking non-stop. She'd been bubbling about the staff picnic they'd have on the first day of spring, and the summer parade float, and the bowling league she wanted them all to join. "What do you think of this for a name? The Incredibowls!" Annette hadn't waited for a response before crinkling up her big, brown eyes and giggling. "It's perfect, right?" Zinnia had to agree that it was a great name for a bowling team. Annette's enthusiasm was just that contagious.

They hadn't covered much about issuing permits. Zinnia had barely learned how to log on to the internal network before getting sent off for a breather. It was a good thing she was a quick study on computer systems. Annette Scholem was instantly lovable, but she was no trainer.

Zinnia walked into the break room, took one look at the calendar on the staff refrigerator, and stopped in her tracks. Pump the brakes! Today was *that* day. All thoughts about the morning's training session screeched to a halt.

She double checked with her phone. It was true. Today was that very special day in January. Statistically speaking, it was the date the average person gave up their New Year's resolutions. It was also Zinnia's birthday. She'd completely forgotten.

An older male coworker joined her in the break room. What was his name again? He had a funny name, with Ks that might have been Cs, and so he'd spelled it out for her when they'd met two hours earlier. Karl Kormac. That was it.

Karl was the only person in the office who wore a traditional suit and tie—albeit a cheap, off-the-rack version. The other two men were more casual. Gavin Gorman, the sporty guy with the eerily white teeth, had come in wearing a turtleneck sweater one size too small. All the better to show off his chiseled physique. The other one, Jesse Berman, had barely introduced himself to Zinnia before disappearing into his private office. It was probably for the best that their interaction had been brief. Zinnia's usually nimble tongue had gotten mischievous, trying to tie itself into a knot. Jesse was younger than Zinnia, by a full decade if not more, so her crush was highly inappropriate. But he was effortlessly attractive in his business casual clothes. He smelled like the woods and fresh winter air. He made a woman have feelings. Even now, standing in the break room with boring old Karl, Zinnia was blushing as she thought about Jesse. Worries about job training and even her birthday grew distant. What was wrong with forgetting a birthday, anyway? It could be the secret to preventing aging.

Karl's gruff voice broke through her daydreams. "That coffee pot beat you, too, huh?"

She started to say no, it hadn't, and she preferred to drink tea from the thermos she'd brought from home, but Karl didn't wait for a response.

"Stupid contraption," he said. "We used to have the kind that takes the pods, for individual cups, but then Gavin had a different idea." He rolled his eyes. "Mr. Gourmet Fancypants insisted we go back to brewing full pots so we could use the coffee pod fund for buying organic beans, hand sorted and air roasted or some nonsense. We get it delivered from Dreamland Coffee every week." He picked up a foil bag of beans and poured a third of the bag into the top of the coffee machine. "It's probably just Nabob from the warehouse store, and they put it into new packages to sell it for twice as much. Who can tell?"

Zinnia could tell. She could tell by the smell of the beans alone that it was the highest quality coffee a person could buy. And she had seen the air roasting process herself a time or two.

"Dreamland does make the best coffee," Zinnia said. "I know—" She was about to say she knew the owner, Maisy Nix, but stopped herself. A wise witch doesn't name drop.

Karl descended on the coffee maker's control buttons, muttering under his breath at the "stupid contraption." Little did he know, he was using the exact tone a magical person would use to curse a machine into not working. Zinnia watched with interest. Non-magical people could accidentally perform spells. It wasn't common, but it had been known to happen, especially in a town as magical as Wisteria.

Sure enough, the machine started flashing all its lights at once.

With a discreet wave of one hand, Zinnia sent a positive counterspell at the coffee pot. It made an obedient BEEP sound and began grinding the beans.

Karl beamed, evidently proud of himself. "See, I told you I could beat this thing. And I'm not even a rocket scientist." He struck one finger in the air. "Although, I could have been a rocket scientist if I'd had more interest in engineering."

Zinnia suppressed a smirk. "You could have been a rocket scientist, but instead you decided to work at City Hall, giving out permits for parades and special events?"

"That's right." By the way he stared blankly at the brown stream of coffee filling the pot, Zinnia could tell he hadn't picked up on her subtle sarcasm. "It's very important work," he said. "We have to make sure the appropriate permits are in place. It's what separates us from the animals."

"Permits are what separate us from the animals?" Zinnia chuckled. "I hadn't thought of it that way."

"Yep." He rolled his shoulders back and adjusted his belt, thrusting out his belly to the limits of his jacket. "It's a tough job, but someone's gotta do it. I'm happy to report that nobody's ever died on my watch."

"That's comforting to hear." She glanced at the door. Had she given Annette's vocal chords enough of a break?

Karl yanked out the glass coffee pot before the machine had finished brewing. He poured himself a mug of nearly-black brew. Then he raised the steaming cup to his lips and took a big sip. He didn't flinch. He took another, bigger sip, seemingly unbothered by the heat of the steaming drink.

He lowered the volume of his voice and asked, "How are things going with Annette?"

"Good," Zinnia said carefully. She hadn't yet gotten a handle on the local office politics, and didn't want to give away too much.

"Annette sure likes to talk."

"Yes."

"She's a fine woman," he said.

"She sure is."

"It's too bad she doesn't have a man in her life." Karl slowly tilted his head to the side. "Or does she? Has she said anything to you about a boyfriend?"

"No. She's mostly been telling me about office, uh, procedures."

He made a tsk noise. "She should get out more. Annette's a lively woman. She should find herself a man." He stared into Zinnia's eyes and added, "A real man."

Zinnia was starting to get a handle on the local office politics. She had figured out Karl's big secret in no time at all.

"She's not getting any younger," Karl said. "None of us are."

Zinnia smiled knowingly. "Karl, it sounds to me like there's a man right here at the office that Annette could find if she wanted to."

His eyes widened. "Who? What have you heard?"

She tapped her chin thoughtfully. "I think someone in this break room has a crush on her."

His eyes grew even wider. "You do? But you just got here."

She laughed and swatted him on the shoulder playfully. "Silly. I mean you."

The pink in his cheeks deepened. With a low, gravelly voice, he asked, "Is it that obvious?"

"Only to people who are as perceptive as the two of us." She stepped back and made a point of looking down at his hand. "There's no ring on your finger, Karl. Divorced?"

"Widower," he said neutrally. "My wife passed a few years back. She was a talker, just like our Annette."

Zinnia pulled a mug from the cupboard and poured a cup of coffee. She was feeling funny that morning. Not funny-ha-ha, but something else. Like she'd caught Spring Fever, even though it was only January. She felt herself shifting into this new persona. Zinnia Riddle, Permits Department clerk. Zinnia Riddle, regular woman, going to work at an office every day to perform rote tasks without the use of magic. Zinnia Riddle, matchmaker?

"Karl," she said with a honey-sweet voice. "Do you like riddles?"

He frowned. "Is that a joke? Because your last name is Riddle?"

She laughed it off and pressed on with the riddle. "What is useless to one person but indispensable for two?"

"Beats me."

"Love." She paused for impact. "Love is the one thing that's useless to one and indispensable for two."

He took a step back and eyed her warily. "I don't know what you're getting at, but you're not my type. Sorry. Redheads give me the heebie-jeebies."

Zinnia let the insult bounce off her like water off the back of a butter gargoyle. Karl Kormac was not the sharpest pencil in the office. She smiled sweetly and offered him the coffee cup. "I'm not your type, but it sounds like Annette is. Why don't you take her a coffee?"

"Ah! Gotcha." He took the cup and set it on the counter. "She likes it with two cream and one sugar. Not that I've been spying on her when she fixes her coffee. Not on purpose. It's just that a guy like me picks up on certain things. I do have excellent powers of perception."

"Your perceptive powers won't do you any good if you don't use them." It was true. Powers of all kinds got rusty with disuse.

He laughed nervously. "Are you some kind of love guru?"

"Not at all." Despite her denial, something fluttered in her chest. Helping someone else had relaxed her, and now her true feelings were coming out, unguarded. "I can never love again." She paused and continued in a dramatic, theatrical voice, "For, you see, my heart has been turned to stone."

Karl looked away from her. He cleared his throat. The spoon went ting-ting-ting as he stirred Annette's coffee.

Zinnia fidgeted with the sugar packets. So much for keeping her cool at her new job.

"Thanks for the dating advice," he said, finally. "But I wouldn't want to do anything risky. I'm kind of old, in case you didn't notice. I'm sixty-two. I've got six hundred and fifty-two days of work left before retirement. I'll get a gold watch from this place, then I'll start collecting those retirement checks. That's when I'll pursue my dreams."

"Don't wait, Karl. My heart is stone, but yours still beats. You can take a chance on love."

"You think? My doctor says the ol' ticker is in good shape. Maybe you're right." His shoulders rose within his cheap suit with new-found confidence. "You know what? You're right. I should take a chance and tell Annette how I feel. I'm going to tell her right now. Everything."

Zinnia held up one hand. "Not so fast. Maybe you should start by asking her to spend some time with you outside of the office."

"But we're already here together all day. And I'm her supervisor, so I can tell her whatever I want, whenever I want. I could move her desk into my office."

Zinnia's stomach lurched. "Wait, Karl. I didn't realize that. You're her supervisor?"

"And yours."

"Oh, dear." Zinnia rubbed her hands on her clothes. Two hours into her new job and she'd already made a huge mess. If she'd known a spell that could wind back time five minutes, she'd cast it right now, never mind the cost.

Karl, meanwhile, seemed unperturbed. "I may be the supervisor, but it's just a title. I don't have much real authority."

"Sure, but it's still there. If you're her boss, then you can't put the wrong kind of pressure on her."

His cheeks reddened. "I'm not a monster."

"Of course not. I didn't mean to—"

"I'm just taking a cup of coffee to my *friend*," he said, and he left the break room with both cups, stomping and dribbling coffee on the floor as he went.

Zinnia grabbed a paper towel to mop up the coffee drips on the floor. She was alone with her regrets.

Karl hadn't even tried to ask about her story, about why she'd said her heart was stone, but that was okay. Nobody ever wanted to know.

The First Day of Spring

The whole office was enjoying their lunch-time picnic on the lawn between City Hall and the forest of Pacific Spirit Park. Annette was beyond pleased at how much fun everyone seemed to be having. While the others played croquet, Annette and Zinnia took a break from the competition and settled on a picnic blanket in the sun.

Annette handed Zinnia a cluster of grapes. "Thanks," Zinnia said, popping one into her mouth.

The older woman rolled onto her back and opened her mouth wide. "Now peel them and feed them to me," she said with a giggle. "One at a time."

"Ah! So this is why you've spent months talking up today's spring picnic. You wanted to enslave us."

The two women laughed together. It was March now, and they'd grown closer since meeting in January. Zinnia felt comfortable and unselfconscious as she attempted to peel a grape and then lob it into Annette's mouth.

After a few minutes and several wet grapes on the face, Annette rolled to face Zinnia again. Annette propped her head up with one arm, letting her curly brown hair hang free. Her big, brown eyes were hidden behind sunglasses, but Zinnia could tell Annette was smiling with her whole face. The whole office was playing together outside, goofing around and teasing each other like an unconventional family. Annette kicked off her shoes so she could wiggle her toes in the sun.

"Psst," Annette said. "If you see Karl coming this way, give me a heads-up so I can put my shoes on again. I wouldn't want to drive him wild with the sight of my bare feet."

Zinnia wrinkled her nose. "Is he still bugging you to go on a date with him?"

"Worse," Annette replied. "I went for a walk with him last week to Lindell's because I wanted a diet iced tea, and now he thinks we are actively dating. He's been trying to line up our," she made air quotes with her fingers, "second date."

"My condolences," Zinnia said. "When I first met him, I thought he was nice enough. I didn't realize he could also be..."

"A creepy little troll?"

Zinnia cast a guilty glance at the others to make sure they were still absorbed in their croquet match. Jesse had taken off his shirt for some reason, and now Gavin had to do the same so he could show off his spray tan. Karl was waving his arms, quibbling over the rules with Dawna. He saw Zinnia looking his way and stopped arguing to stare back at the two women on the picnic blanket.

Annette said, "If I ever find out who encouraged Karl to declare his love for me, I will strangle that person to death."

Zinnia groaned. "Okay, but can you make it quick?"

Annette whipped off her sunglasses and blinked at Zinnia in disbelief. "You?" She held one hand to her bosom in mock horror. "I thought we were friends. That you were the little sister I never had!"

"I'm sorry, Annette. I'm so sorry. It was my first day at the office, and I wanted to fit in and be normal. I thought it would be sweet if I could help some romance blossom."

Annette rolled onto her back again. "I'll forgive you, but only if you peel five grapes and get them into my mouth."

"Deal," Zinnia said. "And I am so sorry about the Karl thing. Maybe I can do something about it."

"If you're so sorry, you can feed Karl an anti-love potion."

"What?" Zinnia's whole body tensed. Why was Annette talking about potions? Did she know something about Zinnia, or about Margaret? Was this her way of starting a conversation about witchcraft?

Annette laughed. "Just kidding. I know there's no such thing."

Ah, but there *was* such a thing, and Zinnia knew all about it. She also knew a certain gnome who might be able to procure the ingredients for an anti-love potion. But dealing with such magic was almost always a terrible idea.

"I'll take care of Karl myself," Annette said. "He's not the only one who can share his feelings."

"Oh, Annette. Promise you'll let him down easy. He's only got six hundred and nine working days left until retirement."

They collapsed into each other, giggling.

The First Day of Fall

The staff meeting to discuss reports about other reports was the most boring event Zinnia had ever attended. She was seriously considering shocking herself with magic just to stay awake when the mood in the boardroom suddenly shifted.

Karl got to his feet and yelled at Annette across the table. "Your reports were late again, which made my reports late! You have to stop letting down the members of your team! There are other people in the world besides you, Annette!"

Annette blinked rapidly and rolled her chair back. "Karl, I sent you the reports as an email attachment." Her voice was trembling. "I was only a few minutes late, if that. It's not my fault it took you three hours to figure out how to open the file in the right application."

He jabbed his finger at her. "You did something to my computer!"

Annette looked around at the others, who were just as flabbergasted as she was. "Karl, calm down. I did not—"

He banged both fists on the table. "You're fired! Clear out your desk and go!"

Nobody moved.

Zinnia wanted to do something, but what? Wave her hands in the air and take full blame for pushing Karl into pursuing Annette back in January? Zinnia held herself steady. Speaking up now would only make things worse. She should have prepared some kind of potion for just such an event. Karl's boardroom blowup wasn't exactly coming out of the ether. It had been building for months, ever since Annette's attempt to let him down easy. There'd been an increasing number of snide comments and passive-aggressive overtures. And it certainly hadn't helped morale in the office that the heating and cooling system was on the fritz. The air was freezing one moment, boiling the next. Maintenance couldn't figure out why. The only good thing about being up in the boardroom today talking about reports was the room's steady temperature. Not that it was cooling down Karl's foul mood.

"You're fired," Karl said to Annette again. "Just go. I'll have someone else clean out your desk."

Dawna waved a hand to draw everyone's attention. "Nuh-uh. No you don't, Karl. You can't fire her for some imaginary thing she didn't do. If you're computer's wrecked, you did it yourself. You probably downloaded a virus. Let me look at it for you when we get back. Stop all this nonsense about firing people."

"Dawna's right," Gavin said. "There's a process here. You need to file an official report, and then—"

Karl banged his fists on the table again. "I'm the boss here, and I'll fire whoever I want to fire!"

Softly, Gavin corrected him. "Whomever."

"Gavin, you're fired," Karl said. He pointed at Dawna. "You're fired, too. Don't think I'm not onto you, Dawna, with your expensive purses and jewelry. I'm not a complete idiot. You've got money. I've seen the car you drive and the house you live in. There's no way you paid for that with your Permits Department salary."

Everyone looked left and right in astonishment at their coworkers. Now that Zinnia thought about it, Dawna *did* have a lot of nice purses and jewelry. And her car was a newer model.

Gavin said, "You can't fire Dawna for having good taste, Karl. Now sit down. You haven't had your post-lunch snack, and you always get like this in the afternoon. I've explained to you how metabolic disease happens. You've got to push aside the processed carbs and have a vegetable now and then."

Karl lifted one fist and waved it at Gavin. "Don't you tell me about vegetables, Mr. Fashion Pants. I'll turn *you* into a vegetable."

A stunned silence followed, and then a chortle. It was Jesse laughing. Zinnia kicked his shin under the table and shot him a look. *Not here.* Laughing at Karl would only make the situation a thousand percent worse.

Karl turned in slow motion until he was facing Annette again. "This mess is all your fault, woman. You're... a witch."

Margaret, who was seated next to him, gasped audibly. The word *witch* has a special sting to someone who secretly is one. Zinnia could feel her pulse in her throat.

"Witch," he repeated, getting louder. "Witch, witch, witch!"

Margaret jumped up from her chair, pulled back her arm, and slapped Karl across the face.

Detective Fung's Office
Now
"And that was more or less what went down in the boardroom," Zinnia explained to Fung.

He nodded thoughtfully, one finger at the corner of his mouth. "Interesting."

She agreed. "It does shed some light on the Karl-Annette dynamic."

"No, I meant the part about Margaret slapping Karl. Didn't you slap Gavin Gorman earlier today?"

"That was different," Zinnia replied.

"There's a lot of slapping going on in your office."

"Just two slaps. And to be precise, Margaret didn't slap Karl in the office. We were upstairs on the third floor, in the big boardroom."

"Ah, well that clears everything up." Fung dropped his hand from his mouth and smiled broadly. "What happened next? Did you all pile on each other for a big slap fight?"

"Karl fired every single one of us. Then someone from another department heard the kerfuffle in the boardroom, and came running in with donuts. After two rainbow sprinkle donuts, Karl offered to hire us all back, but for half our pay. There might have been more yelling and slapping, but the mayor walked in right about then and shut everything down." Zinnia reached for the second-to-last celery stick on Fung's desk and gave it a good crunch. "Human Resources sent Karl out for counseling, or maybe rabies testing, or who knows what. He wouldn't say. But he's been fine ever since."

"No hard feelings?"

"It's Karl, so there are always hard feelings, but it's down to a manageable level."

"Until last night, when he snapped and killed your coworker."

Zinnia's celery-chewing slowed to a stop. "I think Karl's just one of those guys whose bark is worse than his bite. Maybe you're half right. Maybe there's another guy out there who she also rejected. Annette treasured her friendships, but she didn't seem interested in romance."

Fung's dark eyes twinkled. "There's nothing wrong with friendship and dedication to one's work."

"True."

"We have officers canvassing her neighbors right now. Annette was on her own here, no family in town. She didn't have many friends outside work, so it won't take long to track down her other rejected suitors, assuming there are any."

"Don't forget, there's also the book she was writing."

Fung laughed. "Good one."

"I'm serious. Dawna has very strong feelings about Annette's book. We were all trying to find it when you busted into the office this morning with your SWAT Team impression."

Fung could barely restrain his amusement. "Yes, the secret book must be the key to everything. I bet it's full of more clues than *The Da Vinci Code*. I'll have our technician pull it off Annette's computer and I'll send you a copy."

Zinnia was not nearly as amused as the detective. "Send it to everyone in the office," she said evenly.

"So I can have all your coworkers sniffing for clues in a work of fiction?" He dropped his head to the side, feigning weariness. "I'll need to hire an assistant to deal with all their screwball theories."

Zinnia said nothing. Smart witches know that the true power of having a voice is knowing when not to use it. If she waited, Fung would hear his words echo back in the silence and change his mind.

"Then again," he mused, rubbing his chin. And there it was. "Screwball theories might not cut it in other towns, but we live in Wisteria, where the truth really is stranger than fiction."

She nodded.

"I'll even read the book myself," he said. "Right after I rule out Karl Kormac as a suspect."

"That sounds logical to me. One must never jump to strange theories when an ordinary explanation will do."

He agreed, "There's nothing more ordinary than a jilted lover." Fung looked pointedly at Karl's crumpled receipt from the convenience store. "Zinnia, you do realize this alibi of Karl's is practically a confession, don't you?"

"If that's what you believe, I trust your judgment."

He looked up at her, his small, quick eyes flicking around her face, searching for clues. "What about Annette, anyway? Was she the type of person Karl accused her of being that day in the boardroom? Was she... a *witch*?"

"No," Zinnia answered without hesitation. "She was one of the nicest people I've ever met."

He looked at her through his eyelashes. "Ms. Riddle, you know what I mean."

She turned her head to check that nobody was standing near the open doorway. She turned back to Fung. "Annette Scholem had no supernatural powers that either Margaret or I were aware of. That is the truth. I give you my word." The air between them filled with a shimmering mist that only a witch such as herself could see. She completed the pledge with the final phrase. "My word is my bond."

CHAPTER 7

WEDNESDAY

EARLY MORNING

Zinnia woke up before dawn and couldn't get back to sleep. How could the exact same bed feel so luxurious some mornings but inhospitable on others? Was her bed angry at her for the previous day's misunderstanding? It was possible. Sometimes the objects around witches took on magical properties, and magic *did* have a mind of its own. She tossed the covers aside—using her hands, not magic—and got up. It was 5:35 am.

After getting dressed in a tasteful everyday outfit of green pants and a ruffled floral print shirt, Zinnia sat in her quiet, dark kitchen, sipping her first cup of tea of the day. She would consume a dozen cups by nightfall. The tea was a special herbal blend of her own design. The chamomile calmed her nerves, the licorice made it sweet, and the two drops of black scarabyce blood kept the spell around her heart working. The blood of the deadly black scarabyce was versatile, and GRAS—Generally Recognized As Safe —in small doses. In large quantities, it could be used for all sorts of things, including preventing tissue rejection. In theory, a witch could play Dr. Frankenstein and attach assorted body parts together in ways nature had not intended. A four-armed woman? Why not! Who couldn't use an extra set of hands? Rumor in the witch community had it that some enterprising—and almost certainly criminally insane—witch had used black scarabyce blood to create actual flying monkeys. Like the ones in *The Wizard of Oz*. Ah, the twisted creations of a witch gone mad with power.

The blood itself was not black, but a pale lavender hue. It even smelled similar to the purple flowers. Over the last year, all of Zinnia's coworkers had shown an interest in her special drink at one time or another, so she'd been keeping packets of store-bought herbal tea handy for them to try. But the decoy tea didn't always work as planned.

One time, just before Halloween, Annette had been showing Zinnia how to fill out a particularly tricky permit application, and she had absent-mindedly taken a sip of Zinnia's tea. As the tea took effect in her mouth, Annette's big brown eyes had widened as the normal redness at the corners turned bright white. Before Zinnia could stop her, Annette had swallowed down the whole mug.

"That was so refreshing," Annette said, blinking her redness-free eyes. "I've tried brewing your tea, but it never comes out the same for me. Is it something about your thermos, or the fact you make it at home?" She snapped her fingers and shook her head, her brown curls sweeping her round shoulders. "I know! You must have magic water coming out of your kitchen tap."

"That must be it," Zinnia replied with an enigmatic smile. "Magic tap water."

Across the workstation Zinnia shared with the other office witch, Margaret cleared her throat and shot Zinnia a behave-yourself look. Thanks to having four rambunctious children, Margaret's behave-yourself look had been honed to maximum effectiveness. It cut through Zinnia's playful mood like a sharp razor. A little bit must have caught Annette, too, because she began to shiver. Then again, it could have been the cooling qualities of the tea.

Annette rubbed her arms. "Does it feel chilly in here to you two ladies?" She reached for Zinnia's thermos. "I could use more of this tea. You don't mind, do you, Zinnia?"

Zinnia felt a sharp pain on her shin. Margaret didn't have the leg length to kick Zinnia from where she sat, so she must have used a spell that mimicked a kick. Times like these, Zinnia regretted taking the desk across from a witch.

Zinnia jumped up from her chair and grabbed her thermos before Annette could pour a single drop. "We could all use more tea," Zinnia announced. "I'll go boil up a fresh pot for everyone, so it's nice and hot."

Margaret also got to her feet. She was wearing the hard-soled boots that made her sound like a hoofed mammal, even on the room's threadbare commercial carpet. She clip-clopped her way to Annette's chair and grabbed the woman's new cardigan, which was pink with pearl buttons.

"Here you go," Margaret said, draping the cardigan over Annette's shoulders. "That should warm you right up. And I do love this pretty sweater of yours."

Annette patted Margaret's hand atop her shoulder. "You're a good one," she said. Annette looked over at Zinnia, her eyes twinkling in that endearing way she had. "You, too, Zinnia. I'm so lucky to have you both as friends. We make quite the trio, us women of wisdom!"

* * *

As the memory faded, Zinnia wiped her eyes with a square of paper towel, and then poured another cup of tea.

She could feel sorry for Annette all day, or she could do something useful. She started to make breakfast but stopped herself. She'd been using her hands for everything these days, which was probably why her magic was so rusty. If she ever wanted to send a shin kick back to Margaret under their desk, she'd need to work on her speed and accuracy. Making breakfast in the privacy of her own home was the perfect opportunity to practice. What would it be today?

Egg drills! She heard the suggestion in her mentor's voice.

No, she thought. *Not egg drills. Not today.*

Soft-boiled eggs and toast sounded warm, salty, and comforting. She cast a spell to open the refrigerator door then got everything in motion. The eggs wiggled out of the carton obediently. So far, so good.

While the breakfast made itself, she ran upstairs. Inside her bedroom, she opened a magically hidden cabinet and pulled out a stack of dusty books. She also grabbed Annette's purple writing pen from the place she had stashed it the night before. She'd mentioned the pen to Fung, but he'd been even less interested in it than in Annette's fiction, so Zinnia had promised to assess it for spells and report back to the detective. She loaded her arms and lugged everything downstairs, where she could spread the books out on the table. She turned the corner and entered the kitchen just in time to run smack-dab into her toast and soft-boiled eggs, which had been circling the room waiting for her. The food bounced off her arm and clattered to the floor. Hot yellow yolk erupted from the two eggs like twin exploding volcanoes. Eggs that were soft-boiled by magic were much more volatile than standard eggs!

Zinnia scrunched her face and uttered her favorite curse. "Floopy doop!"

* * *

Two and a half hours later, Zinnia sighed and pushed aside her dusty magic books. She had checked her resources for magical enchantments that could be placed on pens, and so far her search had been fruitless. She had tested the pen for the usual spells, everything from never-ending ink to heat-seeking mini-missile, but it sat lifeless on the table. It seemed to be just a regular pen.

The fact that Gavin Gorman seemed interested in the pen was the only thing that made her suspect it was enchanted. She didn't know if Gavin had any magical abilities, or even if he knew about magic—people were understandably secretive about such things—but she did know Gavin's uncle Griebel Gorman. Griebel had his small gnome hands in several pies, from potion ingredients to magically enhanced mechanical devices. He ran an appliance repair shop in town as a cover, but due to the changing of the times, appliance repair was becoming less of a disguise. New stuff was so inexpensive these days that most folks tossed broken toasters aside and bought new ones rather than deal with the cost and bother of repairs.

Griebel kept talking about changing his storefront, but he was a busy little man, buying and selling things to the highest bidder, with no qualms about where objects of power ended up.

If Gavin Gorman had been after Annette's pen, he might have been tipped off about its value by his uncle. Or perhaps by someone more dangerous than the Gormans. Someone who also knew about the enchanted object, and killed Annette for it.

Unfortunately, as tidy as Zinnia's theory was, it couldn't be true if the pen was worthless. Sure, the attacker could have taken the magical pen and replaced it with an ordinary duplicate, but that didn't match up with the murder method. An attack that violent spoke of anger, a fit of rage—the opposite of planning.

Zinnia had only one test left.

She went to her fridge and grabbed the grocery list. She paused to look at the photographs that were also stuck there with magnets. The pictures were from the office's first night bowling as The Incredibowls. There were several group shots, and one of Jesse and Zinnia together in the retro arcade, posing by the Donkey Kong machine. They had their cheeks pressed together, and Jesse had taken the picture himself, with his phone.

Zinnia looked away. Thinking of happier times right now only made her feel sad, yet she was grateful to have the evidence in front of her. Better times existed, and they would come around again. That was the whole point of putting such things on one's fridge door.

She returned to the table and wrote *cucumbers* on the grocery list. She didn't feel anything magical in her fingers. A common yet low-value pen enchantment was a spell for tidy handwriting. Unfortunately, the word *cucumbers* came out no more tidy than usual. The cursive letters were very round and tidy, but that was normal for Zinnia. She wondered, could one even improve on perfection? She had a little snort to herself. Zinnia had excellent penmanship, unlike so many young people these days, and she allowed herself to feel pride in that.

She switched the pen to her non-dominant hand and wrote *peas and carrots, peas and carrots, peas and carrots*. The writing was about as scratchy and awkward as she'd expected. There was no tidy handwriting spell in place.

She unscrewed the cap and cast a magnifying glass spell so she could get a close look at the components. There were no secret spy devices inside. No computer data drive or valuable metals. So why had Gavin been trying to grab this pen off Annette's corpse? Had he actually been after something else? She screwed the pen back together and wrote another line of *peas and carrots*. Still nothing magical.

Her internal timer dinged. It was the time she would normally be leaving for work. Should she go to City Hall? It hadn't been discussed yesterday. The department wouldn't be operating as though it was an ordinary day, would it?

Bright words flashed in her head.

It was a magical preview of the flood of text messages that would be coming to her phone over the next few minutes. Zinnia was blessed with a psychic ability that had very specific limitations. She knew when someone was about to text or phone her, but her prescience was limited to a range of thirty seconds to two minutes. Less time than a television station's commercial break. It could be handy at times, but it took a clever witch to turn such a limited gift into something useful.

She mentally read the full message while sending her second breakfast plate toward the sink. The dish smashed into the wall behind her. Zinnia winced. Multi-tasking wasn't the most efficient way to work, and her telekinesis was still rusty, apparently.

She brought the books and pen upstairs to their hiding places. She was heading for the front door when the first text message came in the regular way. She didn't have to look at her phone. She already knew it was from Karl, and it was a group message that he had sent to the whole office, including Annette Scholem. Either he didn't know how or couldn't be bothered to remove the dead woman from the group email.

The text of his email said that word had come down from the Powers That Be, and the Permits Department would be open for business today as usual, no matter what.

CHAPTER 8

WISTERIA CITY HALL

8:25 AM

When Zinnia arrived at work, two members of the local forensics team were in the hallway, removing black and yellow crime scene tape from the door.

One of them, a chipper young woman with big lips and a low ponytail, held the door open for Zinnia and cheerfully said, "After you!"

Zinnia stood still in the hallway. "Are you sure your team has gotten everything?"

"The body has been cleared out."

The body. She meant Annette's body. It wasn't just "any ol' body." Annette was a real person.

And yet, now that twenty-four hours had passed, the shock was not quite as sharp. The loss was not quite as dark and bottomless. Zinnia wondered, was it the tea, or just time? Was it so easy to get over the loss of an unmarried, childless woman of a certain age? How long until Miss Ponytail was cheerfully removing "the body" from Zinnia's house?

Miss Ponytail looked into Zinnia's eyes. "I said you can go ahead, ma'am."

"What about the other evidence? Isn't it unusual for a crime scene to be opened so quickly?"

Miss Ponytail glanced at her partner before answering. "Ma'am, we were sent here by the mayor herself, Paula Paladini, to make sure everything was open and ready for business today. I don't know what you people do in here—"

"We issue permits," Zinnia said flatly. "Permits for everything from sport fishing to throwing parades."

Miss Ponytail took the information in stride and continued in a professional tone. "Well, whatever it is you do, it must be very important to the town."

Her partner, an older man who was crumpling black and yellow tape in his hands, shifted the ball to one hand and reached for a business card. "Ma'am, here's the case file number in case you have any questions for Detective Fung."

Zinnia had Fung's number, but she took the card anyway. She thanked the forensics crew for their service and walked into the office to find her coworkers standing in the reception area.

Twenty-four hours after the discovery of Annette's death, the office was still in disarray. Only now instead of a corpse, a pool of blood, and a ripped window screen, the chaos centered on a maintenance crew of six people. Three of them were cutting carpet into strips and rolling up the strips, and the other three were scrubbing the concrete under the carpet pad with what smelled like undiluted bleach.

Dawna waved her long orange fingernails under her nose. "Peee-ew! Those chemicals are making my eyes water."

Jesse put his arm around Dawna's shoulders in a protective gesture. "The smell is awfully strong," he said. "Let's get you into the break room and see if you can keep down some coffee today. Were you still throwing up last night at home?"

Gavin sidled over to Dawna and squeezed his arm under Jesse's so that he was the one hugging her shoulders. Gavin lifted his chin and sniped at Jesse, "Never mind about what Dawna does at home."

Jesse pulled his arm away and held up both hands. "Easy now. It's going to be a long day for all of us. Let's not start off on the wrong foot."

Gavin puffed up his chest. "Then keep your arms to yourself, Lover Boy."

In response to being called Lover Boy, Jesse only grinned. That was just like Jesse Berman. Whenever someone insulted him, he found it more amusing than upsetting. It was one of his most endearing qualities. He was as good-natured as he was effortlessly good-looking.

The two men stared at each other. Gavin kept raising his chin and leaning forward, as though he meant to hit Jesse with his chin.

Dawna rolled her eyes. "Gavin, this is why I keep breaking up with you. You always pick the wrong moments to man up. And your interpretation of manning up is not normal."

That only made Gavin thrust his chin around more, which made Jesse chortle.

Gavin said to Jesse, "What are you laughing at? I'll give you something to laugh about."

Jesse replied, "No, Gavin. You've already given us all so much."

Then Karl decided to weigh in with his opinion about both of them. "You two young bucks dress too casual. You should dress for the job you want, not the one you have!"

Dawna continued berating Gavin about his flaws, Karl continued giving wardrobe advice, and everyone got louder and louder.

Margaret, who was the only person other than Zinnia who wasn't making noise, put two fingers in her mouth and let out a loud whistle. Zinnia detected a little magic oomph in the whistle.

Everyone immediately stopped what they were doing. Even the cleanup crew stopped rolling and scrubbing to give their full attention to the stout, gray-haired woman with the commanding whistle.

"Thank you for your attention," Margaret said, clapping her hands once. "Now, children, here's how things are going to go down today. Obviously nobody can work in the main area until the new carpet's been installed, so we'll have to split up and share desks. Jesse and Karl, you're each going to take a person into your office."

Karl gulped and looked dismayed, but didn't disagree.

Margaret clapped her hands again, and ordered the maintenance crew to get back to work. All six did as they were told.

Dawna muttered, "Coffee."

They all murmured in agreement and walked as a group into the break room, still discussing who was going to sit in which office. Nobody wanted to double up with Karl, even though his office had the only window. Surprise, surprise.

9:45 am

Nobody had to share an office with Karl after all.

The maintenance crew had been incredibly speedy. The new carpet was laid down and the desks had been returned to their usual spots by the time the group had wandered out of the break room. With nothing left to argue about, they'd all gotten down to work.

After working quietly for what felt like five hours, Zinnia looked at the clock. It was only 9:45 am. But it wasn't coffee time yet, which meant the break room would be empty.

Zinnia tossed a wadded-up ball of paper at Margaret. When Margaret looked up from her work, Zinnia said softly, "We should probably take a moment to talk in private.

Margaret said, "You read my mind." She jumped to her feet. "I'll go first. Give me a few minutes to go ahead and get everything set up."

Zinnia agreed, then she killed time by twirling in her swivel chair and looking around the office. The maintenance crew had been as tidy as they'd been fast. The air smelled of bleach, mingled with the chemical tang of new commercial carpet. Everything had been returned to normal on the surface. A stranger walking in for a permit wouldn't have any clue something terrible had happened there the night before. They would never guess that the desk in the back corner was empty because the person who normally sat there had been brutally slain only two feet away.

As Zinnia was looking at Annette's empty desk, Annette's phone began to ring.

There was a collective gasp in the office. Everyone turned to look at the ringing phone.

From inside his office, Karl called out, "Grab that incoming line, Zinnia. You're the closest."

Zinnia answered the phone, her voice trembling. "Good morning. Wisteria Permits Department. Zinnia Riddle speaking. How may I help you?"

A man replied, his voice cracked from age, "Good. You're open today. Bye." His end of the line clattered and went dead.

Zinnia hung up the phone and turned to Dawna and Gavin, who were both watching her with saucer eyes. "Just a random citizen," she said. "An older gentleman checking to see that we're open."

"We sure are." Dawna rubbed her arms. Yesterday's broken nails had been repaired and painted an even brighter orange than the day before. Dawna continued, "It's so creepy being here without Annette."

"Not as creepy as being here *with her yesterday*," Gavin said. "On account of how she was dead."

Dawna turned away from her on-again off-again boyfriend, shaking her head in disgust.

Dawna asked Zinnia, "Do you think Annette would have wanted us to be working here today?"

Zinnia had gotten up to meet Margaret in the break room. She slowed by Dawna and Gavin's shared work station.

"Yes," Zinnia said. "Annette would have wanted us all to be together, to support each other."

Dawna jumped up and threw her arms around a surprised Zinnia. "You're so nice, Aunt Zinnia," she said.

Zinnia pulled back to look into Dawna's face. "What did you call me?"

Dawna used a knuckle to wipe a tear from her eye. "Aunt Zinnia. That's funny, isn't it? Maybe I called you that because you remind me of my aunties. Not on account of your looks, of course, but because you're so nice."

Gavin snorted. "You wouldn't feel that way if Zinnia had slapped *you*."

Zinnia jokingly waved her hand at Gavin, as if to imply she'd happily slap him again.

Gavin quickly got back to work, as did Dawna.

Zinnia continued on her way to the break room. She encountered a putrid smell just outside the doorway. What was that? Had the carpet installation crew inadvertently released something toxic into the air? It smelled like a cross between burned popcorn and a sewage treatment plant. Had someone microwaved popcorn and durian fruit for twenty minutes too long? She pinched her nose and pushed through. The break room was thankfully stench free.

Margaret was beaming proudly. "Great stink bubble, don't you think?"

Zinnia whispered, "I thought you needed a few minutes to set up a sound bubble." The witches used the simple sound barrier spell whenever they needed privacy in a public space.

"I did." Margaret kept beaming. "It's a sound bubble that I custom blended with a stink bomb."

"You mixed two spells?"

"Sure. I do it all the time. I whipped this particular one up a couple years back so I could enjoy a few minutes of privacy in my bathroom without the kids barging in. I don't get to use it much these days, now that the little ones have grown past that phase. And not a minute too soon. Have you ever seen eight little hands trying to wiggle through the crack under the bathroom door? Do you know how many wiggly fingers that adds up to? It's a terrifying sight. Possibly more terrifying than disrupting a nest of bone-crawlers."

Zinnia shuddered at the thought of either.

Margaret started making a fresh pot of coffee. "What's on your mind?"

Zinnia cut to the chase. "Do you think Karl is capable of murder?"

"Karl Kormac? Our Karl? No way. That bulldog is all bark, no bite."

"Hah," Zinnia said. "That's exactly what I said to Fung last night."

Margaret shot her a look of concern. "Karl is a suspect?"

Zinnia explained what she'd witnessed the previous day, when Karl had changed his alibi to what Fung felt was a confession.

When she was done, Margaret said, "That is suspicious." She checked that the sound barrier was still in place and continued. "So, Karl was in the staff parking lot at three in the morning. He saw Annette's car there, but he says he didn't go in?"

"They'll have to take his word for it, since the security system was down."

Margaret twirled the single gray curl that hung in the center of her forehead like a rhino horn. "Poor Karl never got over Annette rejecting him."

"He had a motive, and the opportunity," Zinnia said. "As for the means, I don't know."

"Did Fung say what kind of murder weapon was used?"

"No." Zinnia gulped down the tightness in her throat. She thought of Annette's emerald-green dress, and how it turned black from her blood.

"Shame," Margaret said.

In a hoarse tone, Zinnia said, "I wish they'd kept the office closed at least a day or two."

"Same here." Margaret twirled her gray forehead curl into a tight ball.

They stared at each other in solemn silence. After a moment, the corners of Margaret's eyes began tilting up.

"Uh-oh," Zinnia said. "You're getting that look, Margaret."

"What look?"

"The one you get right before you decide that breaking the rules is completely acceptable when you're the one doing it."

Margaret snorted. "No, I'm not. And I don't do that." The corners of her eyes tilted up even more.

"Whatever you're thinking about doing, don't."

Margaret turned away to pour herself a cup of coffee. She said over her shoulder, "I suppose you have a better idea than whatever it is I may or may not be planning?"

"As a matter of fact, I do." Zinnia withdrew from her pocket a slip of paper containing a spell she'd copied out of one of her books earlier that morning. She handed the paper to the other witch.

Margaret's eyes widened as she looked over the spell. "This is for contacting the other side."

"Yes, it is."

"But we can't do that."

"Yes, we can. We ought not to do so, but we can."

"Oh, Zinnia." Margaret shook her head. "I don't know about that."

"If we want to know whether or not it was Karl who murdered Annette last night, the most direct way to find out is to ask Annette ourselves. She already visited both of us. You, in your shower, and me, in my kitchen. Honestly, I think she'd be open to it."

Margaret frowned.

Zinnia said, "We ought to do something. Annette was our friend. She called us the Three Wise Women, remember? She's counting on us."

"Nope, nope, nope." Margaret set down her coffee, leaned back against the counter, and crossed her arms. "A big fat mountain of *nope*!"

"We could do it tonight. This spell is very mild. All it does is summon the ghost to appear at a window or a mirror. That sounds safe enough, right? The ghost can come up to the glass, but not all the way through."

Margaret remained unconvinced.

Zinnia said, "The book says that even a solo witch could cast this spell, if she's experienced, but it is recommended for two or more witches." Zinnia put on a positive, winning smile. "Which is why you and I should cast it together, tonight."

"Nope, nope, nope." Margaret shook her head. "A big marching band spelling out the word NOPE on a football field."

"I could whip up a batch of those brownies you love."

"Nope, nope, nope with a big, mean grizzly bear on top."

"So... are you saying you're not sure? You want some time to think about it?"

Margaret gave Zinnia the look she gave her kids when she was down to her last nerve and there would be no more warnings.

"Very well, then," Zinnia said. "I'll cast the spell myself." She turned to leave.

Margaret lunged out and grabbed Zinnia's arm. "Don't do it," she said. "Everybody thinks ghosts are so cute and harmless when they're haunting a spooky old hotel, but spirits are dangerous. Extremely dangerous. Especially when they encounter a person who harmed them in life." Her eyes glistened and her lower lip quivered. "Zinnia, I forbid you to cast the summoning spell by yourself."

Zinnia sniffed. "You're not my elder."

"Please. Promise you won't cast that spell. If you promise, I'll go along with the next thing you ask of me. Anything you want."

Zinnia sighed. "Fine. I promise I won't cast that mirror spell for Annette." She sighed again. "My word is my bond."

The air twinkled. Zinnia's promise was sealed.

Margaret relaxed visibly, melting against the counter behind her. "Good," she said. "We have to be more careful than ever with what we cast. We have to be sure that whatever actions we take, no matter how extreme, are *absolutely* necessary."

Zinnia gave Margaret a sidelong look. Margaret liked to get extra preachy about the rules right before she broke them all herself.

CHAPTER 9

2:30 PM

Zinnia was keeping an eye on Margaret Mills, who still had that devious rule-breaking look on her face. What was she up to? Every few minutes, Margaret would crane her neck to peer into Karl's office through his open door, as though she expected something to happen at any minute. It was perfectly understandable for her to be keeping an eye on Karl if she believed he was the person who killed Annette two nights before, but Margaret didn't appear to be fearful at all. If anything, she seemed excited.

"You did something," Zinnia said in a low tone. "Something you know you shouldn't have."

Margaret gave her a wide-eyed, innocent look and twirled her forehead curl. "Huh?"

"You did something to Karl." Zinnia couldn't say *spell* or *magic*, because they were in the middle of a busy office.

The other witch kept twirling her rhino-horn curl. "What makes you say that?"

"Margaret Mills, I can read you like a book."

"Me? Are you implying that I have a *tell*?"

"You have *so many* tells," Zinnia said. "Where do I even start? How about the fact that you keep getting cups of coffee but not drinking them? Look at yourself, Margaret. You've got six full mugs on your desk. Not only have you done something you ought not to have done, but you're hoarding the office china."

Margaret released her curl and swirled one hand over the mugs. "I'm going to drink all these. I'm, uh, cooling them to the perfect temperature." She glanced into Karl's office once again, then stared into Zinnia's eyes with an indignant expression. "Unlike Karl, I don't drink my coffee scorching hot."

"Sure. A likely story."

"Since when are you the coffee police?"

"Somebody's got to keep an eye on you."

Margaret narrowed her eyes. "Is that why you took the job here? To keep an eye on me?"

"No, Margaret. I took this job because you said it would be *fun*."

"Fun? I said no such thing. I may be a lot of things, but I'm not a liar."

Zinnia sniffed.

Margaret inhaled, and puffed up straight in her chair. She spoke quickly. "Zinnia Riddle, I told you to take this job because I knew I couldn't leave you haunting around that house of yours all day and all night, going mad."

"Going mad?" Zinnia was so offended that she could only repeat the absurd words.

"You heard me," Margaret said. "You were already half mad last January. It's a good thing that we needed another warm body here in the department."

"A warm body? Is that all I am to you?"

"Of course not. Don't change the subject. You always take things so literally, and you're always so quick to be offended."

Zinnia snorted and returned her gaze to her computer screen. She had a lot of work to do, and if Margaret was going to be so combative, there was no point in talking to her.

"Honestly," Margaret muttered. "You try to do something good for someone and it comes back to bite you in the rear end."

Zinnia ignored the comment. She did have a spell that made the recipient feel the sensation of something biting their rear end. Margaret shouldn't give her so many ideas!

"I know you can hear me," Margaret said. "The truth is, you've got things backwards. I brought you into this department so that I," she pointed at her chest, "could keep an eye on you." She pointed at Zinnia.

Zinnia pursed her lips and continued ignoring Margaret. She didn't need anyone to keep an eye on her, let alone bossy Margaret.

Margaret sighed. "You weren't doing anyone any good holed up in that house of yours, decorating and redecorating those rooms. How much money did you spend at the Chintz Boutique?"

Zinnia frowned. Neither her redecorating nor her finances were any of Margaret's business.

"I hope Mrs. Puddikin gave you a discount," Margaret said. "Between the wallpaper and the—"

She was interrupted by the sound of movement coming from Karl's office. Margaret craned her neck and watched his doorway with her lips parted. Karl emerged from his office looking the way he did every day by midafternoon: tired and rumpled. His posture got worse throughout the day, too. His hunched slouch made him look shorter and rounder. By five o'clock, Karl Kormac resembled a walking basket of laundry.

Karl noticed both women looking at him and stopped in his tracks. "What are you two looking at?"

In unison, Margaret and Zinnia said, "Nothing." They both looked down and shuffled papers.

"If you two busybodies must know," Karl said with an air of indignation, "I'm going for a walk in the fresh air to clear my head."

This caught the attention of Dawna, who'd just finished helping a walk-in customer. Dawna waved her bright orange nails in the air. "Ooh, Karl. If you're going to Lindell's, get me a Diet Coke."

Gavin interrupted. "Not Diet Coke," he said to Dawna. "That stuff is poison. I keep telling you."

"Whatever," Dawna said to Gavin. "You're the one who ate a whole ice cream cake by himself last night."

Gavin, who'd been taking a sip of triple-filtered water from his stainless steel bottle, choked and started coughing.

Karl meanwhile, continued to look like an irritated pile of laundry. He shook his head, and as he did, there was the tell-tale sound of gas being expelled. That was another thing Karl did midafternoon. He quickly made a HARUMPH sound to cover it, and started walking again, crop-dusting Margaret's work space as he did.

Zinnia watched carefully for a reaction from Margaret. Whatever spell she'd cast on Karl, it had not prevented his midafternoon fart-bombing. Margaret didn't even fan her hand beneath her nose as she typically did. She just kept on staring at Karl, as though any minute now fireworks were going to shoot from his ears.

With another HARUMPH, Karl passed gas again on his way to Dawna. He snapped up her money for the Diet Coke.

"Dawna, I'll get you whatever you want," he said sweetly, tucking the money into his wrinkled trousers. "I'm the kind of boss who takes care of his people." He turned to look back at the two witches. "Can I get you anything for you two eager beavers? A little squeeze bottle of honey for the busy worker bees?"

Margaret's eyes widened. "Do you need any company for the walk? Someone to talk to?"

That wasn't normal midafternoon behavior for Margaret, and Zinnia knew it. *Oh, no, you don't*, Zinnia thought. Before Karl could answer, Zinnia got to her feet. She wasn't about to let Margaret be alone with Karl and cast whatever spell she'd been cooking up. Why torture the guy? Zinnia didn't believe for a minute that Karl had done anything to Annette. Both Fung and Margaret were barking up the wrong tree.

"A walk sounds great," Zinnia said, smiling. "Margaret's too busy to go, because she's working on a *very* important report, but I'll go with you, boss." Zinnia looked at Margaret and asked, "Is there anything at the store I can pick up for you, since you're so busy?"

Margaret swallowed audibly. "Just keep your eyes open," she said weakly.

Zinnia raised an eyebrow. "You think I'll see something interesting?" Had Margaret already done something to their boss?

Margaret shrugged one of her round shoulders. "You never know. Keep your eyes and ears open."

"Always," Zinnia said through a thin smile.

While Zinnia was gathering her purse and jacket, Karl made two more HARUMPH noises, but they weren't the same ones he used to cover fart-bombing. They were the HARUMPHS of Karl changing his mind about something. When Zinnia met him at the door, he handed her the Diet Coke money Dawna had given him.

"On second thought, I don't need a walk," Karl said. "We had a late start this morning, so I should get back to my desk, push through, and deal with all my emails."

Over at her desk, Margaret made a strangled sound. She gestured that Zinnia should get Karl to go outside. Zinnia sighed inwardly. Whatever it was Margaret had in mind, Zinnia would try to help, regardless of how she felt. It was best for a witch to go along with whatever a fellow witch requested. Trust was tantamount in coven relationships.

What could Zinnia do about Karl? She had to think fast and act faster. Normally, Zinnia wouldn't cast spells at work, but she sensed that charm alone wouldn't get Karl to change his mind again.

She had a few options, but it was best to stick to the basics, the so-called "bread and butter" magic. A bluffing spell would increase her charisma while simultaneously making Karl more gullible. She'd never understood the exact mechanism, but it was a handy bit of magic for getting people to be more cooperative. If she didn't have her no-spells-at-work rule, she would probably use the bluffing spell all the time. Or perhaps not. She did have her ethics, and manipulating people wasn't something a good witch did. This afternoon's situation with Karl was different because she was helping a fellow witch. Plus why was she so worried about Karl's feelings, anyway? He was both a murder suspect and a fart-bomber.

She looked Karl in the eyes, and then, while weaving a web of Witch Tongue around her words, she said, "Come on, boss. I *know* you want to go for a *walk* to the *store*. Put on your jacket and we'll *go* together."

The sparks that only Zinnia could see fluttered around the sixty-three-year-old man. The air around them tightened up, becoming more viscous, the way it did when the spell was working.

Karl's eyes bulged. His cheeks turned red and then back to a healthy color. He made a noise that sounded like HARUMPH, except backward: PHMURAH! He yanked his winter jacket from the coat rack. He pulled it on so quickly, Zinnia heard a seam in the lining rip. Karl didn't show any sign of noticing the tear. Moving jerkily, he gripped the door handle with both hands and yanked it open forcefully, making a breeze that blew some fliers off the front counter. With another PHMURAH, he was out the door. The man was already halfway down the hallway before Zinnia caught up.

* * *

Outside in the thin January sunlight, Karl walked down the sidewalk with surprising speed. Zinnia was nearly jogging to keep up. Karl's gait was not normal. He had stiff arms and legs, and rhythmically tilted from side to side, as though being pushed by invisible hands. He reminded Zinnia of a toy wind-up robot.

The longer they walked, the worse it got. Karl's arms fought the air as though he was underwater. He puffed loudly from the effort. His feet pointed at odd angles with every step. His butt would sag and then his hips would thrust forward. He was looking less like a wind-up robot and more like a wooden marionette. It was such a spectacle that people walking their dogs were stopping to stare. Even the dogs were staring.

Zinnia had to investigate what was controlling Karl. She reached into her purse and pulled out a pair of polarized sunglasses, along with a tube of what any onlooker might guess was sunscreen. She squirted the goop onto the lenses, smeared it with her fingers, and put on the sunglasses. Karl didn't seem to notice or even turn his head her way. Zinnia peered through the sight-enhancement gel at her boss. She didn't see any of the tell-tale streaks of light that would indicate manual control over Karl by another entity. She sighed with relief as she put away the glasses. The creatures who controlled others were the worst kinds.

Next, she pulled out what would look to onlookers like an ordinary breath mint. She cracked the capsule between her front teeth and blew the light dust in Karl's direction. The magical compound would give her insight without interacting. The powder swirled around Karl's head three times before turning a color that no witch likes to see on magic. It was a color called *bruise*, a shifting blend of sickly green and grayish purple. The revealing powder confirmed what Zinnia suspected: Margaret must have cast a powerful spell on Karl, perhaps when they'd been alone together in the break room at lunch time.

That Margaret! Why didn't she and Zinnia have better communication with each other? Zinnia wouldn't have cast her bluffing spell if she'd known Karl was already under the influence. Now the two witches had made a terrible mess, the color of *bruise*.

The thing about spells was they were like prescription medicines. One would do its intended job, but if you added in a second or third, there could be interactions. Unpredictable, undesirable, unappealing interactions. And judging by the unpredictable, undesirable, and unappealing way that Karl was robot-marionette-walking, he'd been the victim of conflicting spells.

Now what? A lesser witch with no impulse control might have cast a third spell, but Zinnia knew better. She would have to be patient and wait for the spells to fade. All she had to do was keep Karl out of trouble for a few hours. How hard could that be?

"What a lovely day," she said conversationally. "It's such a treat to see blue sky in the middle of January."

"Yes-it-is," Karl said robotically. "It-is-a-lovely-day. It-is-a-treat. The-sky-is-blue. It-is-January."

"You seem tense, boss. Would you like to stop for a moment to relax?" They were passing a small park with a children's playground. "We could sit on the swings for a bit, like kids."

"I-am-tense. I-would-like-to-relax." His robotic voice became even more choppy. "Swings. Sit. Kids. Yes. Swing."

Zinnia led the way up a grassy incline toward the playground. The grass was mostly yellow due to the season, and the play equipment was empty. Karl barreled past Zinnia at top speed—top speed for portly Karl—and launched himself at a swing. He whooped excitedly as he swung higher and higher, pumping his legs and giggling.

Zinnia settled onto a swing next to him. The chains were very cold, so she pulled the sleeves of her jacket down to act as mittens. She could have cast a hand-warming spell, but if some of the spell had sprinkled over to Karl, he very well might have spontaneously combusted.

Karl whooped again, and jumped out of his swing at the apex. He landed heavily, his joints complaining audibly.

Zinnia called after him, "What are you up to, Karl? Do you want to take turns swinging? You can push me for a bit, then I'll push you."

But Karl was already racing down the grassy hill toward someone. "Detective!" He waved his arms. "Detective, wait up! I have to tell you something!"

Zinnia jumped off her swing and chased after him.

By the time she reached Karl and Detective Fung, Karl was already well into what sounded like a confession.

Karl was saying, "I confess. Ah. That's better. I confess. I did it. I'm a bad man." He got down on his knees and held his fists up, touching his arms together at the wrists. "Arrest me," he pleaded. "I confess. Whip me, beat me, take me to jail."

Fung took a half step back and ran his fingers through his impeccably trimmed black hair. "Whip you and beat you? Mr. Kormac, that's not how arrests work. At least not on my watch."

Karl bowed his head, keeping his fists raised, and whimpered as he stared at the ground.

Fung looked over the kneeling man at Zinnia. His small, quick eyes flicked left and right, up and down, taking in the whole picture.

Zinnia said, "This isn't what it looks like."

"It's not?" Fung's eyes kept flitting between Zinnia and her boss, who was still kneeling. "I was driving by when I noticed a couple of extra-large kids on the playground. I thought I'd stop to see how much they'd been drinking, which is when this happened." He nodded at Karl.

"Arrest me," Karl pleaded. "I feel so guilty. Put some handcuffs on me. Please."

"I'm telling you, Detective, this isn't what it looks like."

"It's not?" Fung scratched his head.

Zinnia made a wand-swirling gesture, and then a second one with her other hand, trying to communicate the double spell interaction to the detective.

"Gotcha," Fung said with a wink. Then he reached for his handcuffs and snapped them onto Karl's wrists.

Zinnia shook her head. What was it with her and communicating with other people today?

"Okay, Mr. Kormac," Fung said in a soothing tone. "I've got you in handcuffs, as per your request. But technically I can't arrest you, because I don't know what you've done."

"I did something bad," Karl said in a low, growling tone that took both Zinnia and Fung by surprise. They exchanged a wide-eyed look.

Fung tentatively asked, "Did you... do something to Annette Scholem?"

Karl nodded, his head floppy and puppet like. "I wanted to hurt her like she hurt me."

Fung mouthed something at Zinnia. *Told you so.*

She did the double wand gesture again. "I really need to speak with you, Detective. In private. It's important."

He waved her off. "Go back to work. I'll call you if I need anything, Ms. Riddle."

"But—"

"I said I'll call you if I need anything. I'm the detective here, not you."

Zinnia backed away. They could sort it out over the phone. They'd probably throw Karl in the drunk tank and let him sleep it off. He was probably safer with them than with Zinnia, who was liable to give poor Karl a heart attack on the playground equipment.

Zinnia said to Fung, "Promise you won't hurt him."

Fung shot her an offended look. Not a pretend, mock-offended look, but a real one.

Then he helped Karl to his feet and walked him toward the unmarked police car.

"I only did it because I loved her," Karl said.

"That's what they all say," Fung replied. "Let's zip those lips until we get to the station, all right?"

* * *

Zinnia practically ran back to the office.

She'd barely stepped in the door when unseen forces grabbed her and yanked her into the supply closet.

To defend herself, Zinnia instinctively cast the first spell that came to mind.

CHAPTER 10

Zinnia Riddle's hastily cast spell, despite being an unconventional choice for defensive magic, worked exceedingly well.

Margaret Mills' legs flew up. Over she went, landing on her butt on the carpeted floor of the office supply closet. She wheezed as the wind got knocked out of her lungs. Her shoes floated in the air above her.

Zinnia was impressed with her own creative spellwork. Margaret was not.

Margaret's curly gray hair seemed to turn extra frizzy as she spat out, "Shoe removal? You cast a spell for shoe removal on me?" Her arms flailed as she reached for the levitating shoes.

Zinnia calmly replied, "It appears as though I have." She leaned forward to inspect Margaret's socks. One sock had a kitten pattern and the other was striped.

Margaret sputtered and flailed.

Zinnia said, "I can teach you the shoe removal spell, and also one for sock matching."

"How could you?!" Margaret continued to wave her arms and legs ineffectively, not unlike an overturned tortoise.

"Me? You're the one who grabbed me without warning and yanked me into the supply closet. How did I know you weren't the killer, trying to take your next victim?"

Margaret stammered, "But-but-but shoe removal?"

"It worked, didn't it? Any spell that throws your opponent off balance can be useful in a fight. The best defense is, well, *any* defense you can cast under pressure."

Margaret got her torso upright but remained seated. She grabbed for her shoes, her short arms flailing again. The footwear evaded her, floating higher and higher. Zinnia's shoe removal spell was supposed to act as a magical shoehorn, simply decoupling shoe from foot with minimal effort. It wasn't supposed to levitate the shoes as well. She must have been so unnerved that the spell had come out with a little extra—to use the slang of modern witches —"stank" on it.

Margaret gave up on catching her floating shoes and crossed her arms. "You've got some real bad juju in your magic right now, Zinnia."

"Me? You're the source of the bad juju around here. What sort of spell did you cast on Karl, anyway?"

Margaret's voice got high and thin, defensive. "Nothing too crazy."

"I blew a puff of revealing powder on him. Do you know what color it turned?"

Margaret batted her eyelashes. "Pink?"

"Bruise, Margaret. *Bruise.*"

"Oh."

"All I did was cast a basic bluffing spell on Karl so he'd go on his walk, like you wanted, but it mixed with your spell and then it all went sideways and turned *bruise*!" She heard her volume rising and got control of herself. The last thing they needed was their coworkers barging in to join the party. She could have cast a sound bubble within the cramped closet, but with the way things were going, it was liable to invert and become a sonic boom. When the juju around a witch got really bad, spells had a tendency to do the exact opposite of what you wanted.

Margaret asked, "What exactly happened on your walk with Karl?"

"Karl got himself arrested. He literally got down on his knees and begged to be taken away."

Margaret gasped in shock and clapped both hands to her cheeks. "Really?"

"Really," Zinnia said flatly. Margaret's "shock" seemed a little too theatrical for Zinnia to believe it was genuine.

Margaret gasped again. "Tell me exactly what happened."

Zinnia didn't want to play along with Margaret's performance, but she did anyway, quickly summarizing all of the details, from the robotic walking to the enthusiastic swing-set swinging, and then the confessing.

When Zinnia was done, Margaret said, "Good."

"No." Zinnia put her hands on her hips and glowered down at Margaret. "It's the opposite of good. It's very, very bad. And all because of that spell you cast."

Margaret stuck her nose in the air. "I'll have you know, my spell was working just fine until you polluted it with your sloppy syntax."

Sloppy syntax? Was Margaret critiquing another witch's spellwork? Yes, she was. The nerve! And after everything Zinnia had done for the other witch.

Without warning, one of Margaret's airborne shoes dropped, clunking her on the top of the head.

"Ouch," she said.

The other one dropped, and she yelped again.

"Oops," Zinnia said.

"You did that on purpose." Margaret rubbed her head.

Zinnia held her hands up. "Magic has a mind of its own."

"Oh, yeah?" Margaret made finger guns, pointed them below Zinnia's knees, and delivered a double shin kick. Hard.

Zinnia didn't flinch, even though her shins stung from the double kick. Margaret would pay for that. Zinnia flicked her wrist to whip Margaret's shoes back into the air, and then dropped them on Margaret's head again. She yelped twice, once for each shoe.

Margaret growled and batted the shoes aside. She rolled her shoulders back, changed her hand gestures, and blasted Zinnia with the butt-biting spell. Full power. Now it was Zinnia's turn to yelp.

While Zinnia was rubbing her backside, Margaret put her shoes back on her feet and stood up. She cast a steadfast spell so the shoes wouldn't come off again so easily. And then she used her telekinesis to smack Zinnia on the side of the head with a flying pad of Post-It notes, original yellow.

Zinnia returned fire using a volley of dry-erase markers.

Margaret repelled most of the markers. She was breathing heavily as she levitated a box of index cards and made them rain around Zinnia. The rain stung. Several of the cards gave Zinnia paper cuts on her hands and cheeks. The cuts would heal almost instantly thanks to her regenerative powers, but they still hurt like the dickens.

Zinnia charmed a roll of stamps so that it swirled around Margaret, twisting and tightening like a thin white boa constrictor.

Margaret fought her way free of the stamp snake and made paperclips rain down on her foe. The concentrated storm of metal was shiny, silver, and painful.

Next came the padded envelopes. Not very scary.

The pencil-top erasers weren't too bad, either.

The boxes containing printer toner, however, were just big enough to pack a punch.

Zinnia, breathing heavily by now, looked around the storage closet for new ammunition. Light bulbs? No. Too breakable. Not the scissors, either. She didn't want to kill Margaret. Not yet. Her gaze landed on the packing tape. Perfect! She worked the same snake spell she'd used on the roll of stamps. This time, the secret witch language rolled off her tongue like hot oil from the mouth of a butter gargoyle. Who had rusty magic with bad juju? Not Zinnia Riddle! Not once she got warmed up.

Ten seconds later, Margaret Mills was quiet and well behaved. She was also wrapped from head to toe in packing tape, looking not unlike a mummy.

From a crack in the tape around her mouth, Margaret croaked, "Truce?"

"What's that?" Zinnia crossed her arms and tapped her toe next to Mummy-Margaret. "I believe the word you're looking for is Uncle." Just like young children, witches used the word Uncle to tap out of fights when they'd been outmatched.

Begrudgingly, Margaret said, "Uncle." She wriggled helplessly on the floor, the triple-thick layer of packing tape crinkling. "You win, Zinnia. You beat me, fair and square. I couldn't cast so much as one of Karl's farts from in here."

"That's right. I won. Now tell me what spell you cast on Karl."

Margaret-Mummy sighed. "You already know."

Zinnia did have a strong suspicion about which spell the other witch had used, but she'd been afraid to have it confirmed. "Was it Trinada's Confession Hex?"

Margaret-Mummy made a noise partway between humming and groaning. In other words, yes.

"You've gone mad," Zinnia said. "Mad!" It was a powerful, dangerous spell.

The mummy squeaked out, "The end justifies the means."

"With any of Trinada's hexes, you need at least a triad of witches to get any control at all. And you cast it by yourself? Sloppy spellwork, Margaret. Sloppy and dangerous. But I suppose the rules don't apply to Ms. Margaret Mills, who does as she pleases."

"The spell will wear off eventually," replied the mummy on the floor. "And it worked out, so what's the harm? You should be thanking me for getting a killer out of the office and into jail where he belongs."

"Don't you see what you've done? It was a false confession. Before Detective Fung came along, Karl was swinging on a swing set without a care in the world. Karl Kormac. On a swing set. Picture that. Then he saw the detective, and literally begged to be arrested. But he didn't even know what he was saying. He was just desperate to be agreeable, to confess to whatever needed confessing."

"Oh," said the mummy. "Now that I think about it, Karl's not a murder kind of guy. He's all bark, no bite."

"Exactly. But now, thanks to you, the police are going to be fixated on the wrong person. Fung is a good cop, but he's still just a cop. If you hand him a confession, he's going to be all too happy to close the case. Don't you want him to catch the real killer?"

The mummy didn't move. Zinnia kneeled down to make sure the tape was loose enough for Margaret to breathe. Her mouth was clear, but Zinnia couldn't read her facial expression. Her eyes were covered in too much tape. Zinnia didn't dare rip it off—Margaret was probably attached to her eyebrows—so she searched her mental database for a solution.

Strangely enough, Zinnia did know a way to remove the sticky side from tape. She'd never seen the point in such a specific spell, but she'd learned it anyway, because her mentor had insisted she master all of the fundamentals, even the obscure ones. Zinnia rehearsed the spell in her mind and then cast it. The packing tape slackened around the mummy as it lost its sticky side. Margaret was free from her bonds, by magic. Zinnia noted to herself that it had been a perfectly executed spell with perfect syntax. Not that Margaret would notice and give her a compliment.

Margaret wriggled free of the non-sticky tape but stayed on the ground. She looked up at Zinnia, and then around the small room. She twisted her lips from side to side. "We've really made a mess this time."

Zinnia swiveled her head, taking in the chaos of the ruined office supplies.

"We sure have," Zinnia said. "How about you clean up this mess, and I'll go clean up the other one?"

"Deal," Margaret said. She started sweeping up paperclips with both hands. "What are you going to do?"

"I'll tell you what I *won't* do. I'm *not* going to cast any of Trinada's hexes by myself." She took in a deep breath and let go of the remainder of her outrage. Holding onto anger would only give her bad juju. Her coworker had simply been trying to help. What witch doesn't get herself in over her head from time to time?

"Of course you won't cast any of Trinada's hexes," Margaret said. "You've always been the practical one."

"Thanks." Zinnia leaned forward and picked a paperclip out of Margaret's ear. In a more gentle tone, Zinnia said, "I won't hex anyone, but I *will* go straight to the WPD to confess."

Margaret pulled a handful of stamps out of her bra. "The Wisteria Permits Department? Right here? I don't get it."

"The *other* WPD, Margaret. The other one."

CHAPTER 11

ZINNIA RIDDLE'S HOUSE

11:00 PM

Zinnia sat on her couch with her feet up on her favorite ottoman, the one with the thistle pattern that matched her vest. She read the first page of Annette Scholem's manuscript and then paused for contemplation. The content of the book was easy enough to understand, but she couldn't shake the feeling she was violating Annette's privacy.

She had received the file at ten o'clock by email, courtesy of the Wisteria Police Department. They had gotten permission from Annette's cousin, her nearest next of kin, to release the unpublished manuscript to Annette's coworkers. The computer forensics team sent the novel to everyone in the office, as per Zinnia's request. Dawna had immediately replied to the group email with a dozen animated images conveying excitement. Ten minutes later, Gavin had sent an email to the group apologizing on Dawna's behalf for her being "inappropriately joyous," considering the circumstances. Then Jesse replied passive-aggressively to say that everyone responded to grief in their own way, and Dawna had done no wrong. Then Margaret replied in all capital letters to say that everyone should STOP EMAILING AND START READING ALREADY!!! That had been the final message. Margaret had a special talent for shutting down jibber-jabber.

It had taken most of the last hour for Zinnia to get a hard copy made. The printer needed a new toner cartridge, and then she'd had to run next door to borrow more paper from a neighbor. She wondered why she didn't have one of those handy e-readers other people raved about. She could have been several chapters into the book by now. She also wondered why her neighbor had needed her to introduce herself twice. The man had lived next door to Zinnia's house for at least a decade. She wasn't that forgettable, was she? Granted, half the time her house had been boarded up vacant while she'd tried and failed to make a life for herself elsewhere, but she'd been around. Her mind took a turn down a dark hallway. Would anyone miss Zinnia if she died right now?

Zinnia blinked the blur in her eyes away and tried to focus on Annette's book. A psychic preview distracted her. She sensed that Detective Fung wanted to talk to her. She looked at her phone's blank screen and waited for a full two minutes.

No messages came in. She put the phone down. Sometimes her psychic previews were false positives, and it had been a long day, after all. She still had some tender spots from her supply closet throw down with Margaret. Zinnia smiled. The paper cuts and bruises had been worth it. Oh, the sight of Margaret trussed up in packing tape like a mummy! Zinnia would treasure the image forever.

Zinnia returned to the manuscript and read the opening for the third time. It read:

Once upon a time, there was a sweet child of fifteen who didn't know about the wolves who wore sheep's clothing. The child went about obliviously playing with friends and ignoring parental warnings about all the dangers in the world. The child ignored the adults. They were old and fearful. That child was me. Deep down, I worried that the adults who cared for me knew more about my genetic parents than they admitted. Did the kind people I called Mom and Dad have some template for my destiny? Was that why they tried to control who I spent time with?

Zinnia yawned. She wanted to be generous toward Annette's deceased spirit, but it was not the greatest opening paragraph. Where was the vitality, the warmth, the humor Annette was known for?

There did seem to be an inciting incident a few paragraphs down, but Zinnia's mind kept wandering. Her attention was bouncing all over. She rested her hands on top of the manuscript and looked up at her ceiling. How long had it been since she'd tried to read fiction? Too long. Her reading skills were as rusty from disuse as her magic.

She checked her phone again. Nothing from Fung. How rude. How dare he tickle her mind with intention and not follow through? Plus, he had promised to be in touch tonight with an update on the whole Karl situation.

Zinnia had left the office at four o'clock and gone straight to the other WPD to clean up Margaret's mess. He'd been skeptical. He didn't believe her about Trinada's Confession Hex and insisted she give him a demonstration of the spell. She told him she couldn't possibly do that, not unless he rounded up two more witches. Fung finally caved and admitted that he'd already concluded that Karl's confession was false, induced by either magic or garden-variety anxiety. Fung promised to set things right and keep her updated.

She checked the phone again. Still nothing. She pulled inward, searching her mind for the thread of the psychic preview.

A loud knock at the door startled her from a quiet, meditative state.

She opened the door to find Detective Ethan Fung standing on her porch.

"That explains it," she said, more to herself than to Fung.

"Sorry I woke you." Fung was dressed in the same light gray suit he'd been wearing that afternoon. His dark eyes were twitching left and right, and he was practically vibrating with energy, shifting his weight from one foot to the other.

"I wasn't sleeping, but you could have simply phoned," she said.

"I come bearing good news and bad news."

Zinnia nodded. "Sounds about right." Her psychic preview had come with a mix of hope and dread.

"And I could use a cup of tea." He licked his lips. "If you would be so kind as to make me a tea with something *special* to keep me going all night, I'd be your biggest fan. Your *number one* fan."

"How could I refuse an offer of such loyal devotion?" She discreetly cast a moving sound bubble around the two of them while she invited him inside.

Once they were in the kitchen, Fung took off his suit jacket and slung it over the back of a chair. "New wallpaper," he said, looking around.

"Not that new."

"I dig it." He looked up at the ceiling's exposed wood beams. "Where's all your funky plant stuff? The herbs and magical things? You usually have half a greenhouse worth of plants drying along the beams."

"Lately I've been trying to, uh, go straight."

"That explains your odd choice of employment."

"Yes. Well, I've been keeping busy."

Fung wiped some dust off an unused pepper grinder that Zinnia kept on the table. "You haven't been busy dusting."

"Detective, are you here to tell me things I already know, or do you have actual news?"

"Depends. Do you have that tea we talked about?"

She pursed her lips and tapped a cupboard so it opened backward to reveal a secret cabinet. She pulled out a slim metal canister. While she boiled the water and sprinkled a mug with small yellow flower buds, Fung caught her up on the case. Karl had been cooperative back at the station. Too cooperative. They had to keep him isolated from the other people in the holding cells because he kept offering to join people's gangs, and every time someone commented on an article of his clothing, he gave it to them.

Zinnia found herself torn between laughing and feeling really sorry for poor Karl.

"Mr. Kormac has been cooperative enough," Fung summarized at the end. "But the guy's more stunned than a bunny that's just been yanked out of a magician's hat."

"Margaret Mills is the one who's responsible for that," Zinnia said. "A confession hex always causes a confession, whether it's true or not."

"A confession can be false for many reasons," Fung said. "People confuse crushing anxiety with guilt. Most folks aren't in touch with their feelings enough to tell the difference."

"Not in touch with their feelings? That sounds like our Karl."

"It happens more often than the public would think. A person being questioned might want so badly for the horrible stress to lift that they'll say anything to shift the situation."

"Detective Fung, I *have* watched my share of true crime shows."

He gave her a tired look.

She pushed a big mug of tea toward him and took a seat at the table.

She asked, "How's Karl now? I hope you released him."

"Not yet. He fell asleep in his private cell, and he looked so peaceful that I couldn't wake him. I'll drive him home in the morning." He grinned. "He'll be better for it. Most people don't value their freedom until they get a taste of living without it."

Zinnia smiled and gestured for him to taste his tea. He took a noisy slurp.

"Good tea," he said. "Karl will be a free man in the morning. He's not even a suspect anymore. What really saved his bacon is—"

Fung was distracted by the sound of the floor creaking upstairs, then water running in the bathroom on the upper floor. He stared up at the ceiling as one hand went to his gun holster. "Someone's in the house," he said softly.

"Yes," she said at regular volume. "I know. I assure you, all parties present are accounted for." She grabbed the pepper grinder and discreetly wiped the dust from the top. "Plus I've cast a sound bubble around us, so you can keep talking. Nobody's going to hear us."

"And who is this *nobody*?"

She blinked twice. "How's the tea?"

He blinked right back. "What's in the tea?"

"Would you believe me if I told you?"

He relaxed and settled back in his chair, taking another sip. "Whatever you put in here, thank you. I'm feeling more energized already."

Little did the detective know, the *special* tea he was slurping was nothing but plain old chamomile. The herb did have psychoactive qualities, but they were very mild and well known. Chamomile was commonly used by non-magical society. The tea would either do nothing at all, or make him slightly more relaxed and sleepy. It was for his own good.

Ethan Fung was a regular person with no magic abilities of his own. If he'd been battling Margaret in the supply closet that afternoon, he would still bear the paper cut wounds. If he insisted on staying up all night working, he'd only be tired tomorrow, and not as effective at his job. He didn't need special tea. He needed rest. Like a regular human.

The floor above them creaked again, and then the house was silent.

Fung slurped his hot tea and picked up where he left off. "What saved Karl's bacon is his new alibi came through after all. We got the security camera footage from the City Hall parking lot and also from inside the convenience store. All of Karl's time near City Hall on Monday night is accounted for. He never went into the building."

"So, his story checked out," Zinnia said.

"It sure did. So that's the good news."

Zinnia sighed. "I wish I could be relieved, but now you're no closer to finding the real killer."

"And that's the bad news part of my good-news-bad-news offer."

Zinnia shifted in her seat. "Didn't you promise to have this case closed by Friday?"

"Or your money back." He nodded. "But it's only Wednesday."

She checked the time on the stove clock. It was twenty-five minutes past eleven. "Only for another thirty-five minutes, Detective."

He snorted. "We aren't exactly sitting around eating donuts back at the department." There was a defensive edge to his voice. That was another reason Fung needed sleep. He got cranky when he didn't take a break.

Zinnia said gently, "I never meant to imply you weren't working hard."

"We're chasing down some other leads right now."

"Such as...?"

"You know I can't tell you."

She gave him a contemplative look, her mouth pressed into a rosebud. "You know, I could *make you* tell me, if I wanted to."

He squinted at her. "Did you do something to me today?"

She sniffed. She wasn't even going to dignify that with a response.

"You should head home and get some sleep now," she said. "You can start again in the morning."

He gave her a mischievous smile and pushed his tea toward her. Zinnia was surprised to see the mug was still full. He'd only been pretending to drink it.

"Zinnia, I know chamomile tea when I smell it."

"And I know a man who's going to stay up all night and wear himself out when I see it."

"Plenty of time to sleep when I'm dead."

"When you get tired, you slip up."

"I promise to take a power nap when I get back to the office."

Zinnia tried to believe him. "Well, if you need something to make you drowsy, try reading Annette's book."

"Is it that bad? One of our junior agents is reading it right now. She says it's very gripping."

Zinnia waved a hand. "Maybe I'm not the target audience. Or maybe I don't feel right reading my dead friend's secret project, looking for clues into who might have wanted her dead. It's not exactly my cup of tea."

"Fair enough." He got up from the chair and pulled on his jacket. "I'll leave you to," he glanced up at the ceiling, "whatever it was you were doing when I got here."

She nodded and walked him to the front door without speaking.

He reached for the doorknob and paused, looking back at her. "Do you have protection on the house?"

She kept her voice low out of instinct, even though the sound bubble had rolled with them. "Protective wards? Yes. Why?"

"I didn't just see Karl on the parking lot footage. There was something else. An animal. Possibly a wolf. The footage was grainy, but something was there."

Zinnia's voice got loud and high. "You might have thought to mention this particular detail sooner!"

He shrugged. "Now you know. Keep it to yourself, will you? It's not been made public. We wouldn't want citizens to panic."

"You'd rather the wolves picked them off one by one?"

"I said it was *possibly* a wolf. Just one wolf. And we don't know yet."

"I shall be on the lookout for a *possible* wolf."

Fung tipped an invisible hat at her before leaving.

Zinnia locked the door, refreshed the protective ward on the entryway, and then leaned her forehead on the cool wood of the front door. A wolf? That could explain the wounds on Annette's chest. And the broken bug screen on the window in Karl's office. But who had opened the window? It was the middle of winter, and no sane person would open a window for a wolf. Not unless she knew the wolf.

Zinnia grabbed the unread sheaf of papers from the coffee table and went upstairs to get ready for bed. She brought the papers into her bedroom, where she quietly set them on her nightstand. Her bed covers shifted, but not by magic. The man who'd fallen asleep hours earlier, when she'd been sorting out the whole printer fiasco, was still there. She crawled in beside him, pleasantly surprised by the heat coming from his body. She knew spells that warmed a cold bed at night, but there was nothing quite like a man to fill it with his warmth and musky scent.

He lay on his side, facing the wall. She snuggled up behind him, her hands rolled into fists that she nestled against the small of his back.

Jesse Berman shifted in his sleep, waking up. He mumbled, "Cold hands," and wriggled away.

"If you think those are cold, you should feel my feet."

He whimpered. "Nooo! Not the feet!"

She chuckled. "Who's the big, strong man who's afraid of some chilly fingers?"

He took a deep breath and rolled onto his back, stretching his arms up and then over to embrace her. "Who are you calling afraid, little lady?"

She kissed Jesse's warm lips and stared into his captivating blue eyes. On a night like this, she was very glad she'd done something about her office crush.

CHAPTER 12

WISTERIA CITY HALL, PERMITS DEPARTMENT

8:30 AM, THURSDAY

When Zinnia arrived at work for the day, Karl Kormac wasn't there yet. She wondered if he'd been let out of his jail cell, as per Fung's promise. She didn't mention anything about Karl's incarceration to the others. Everyone but Margaret believed Karl had left early the day before due to sudden onset of a stomach bug. Zinnia hadn't even told Jesse about Karl's arrest. They shared a bed from time to time, but that was all they shared.

Zinnia set her purse and tea thermos on her desk. She glanced over at Annette's desk out of habit. The chair was empty. Zinnia looked away again quickly, before the bad feelings could take hold.

She went to the break room to get a clean cup for her tea. Gavin was in there, along with Margaret, Jesse, and Dawna. Gavin was preparing the first pot of coffee for the day while the others hung back, milling around the small room.

Jesse said, "Good morning, Zinnia."

"Good morning," she said right back.

"Your cheeks look flushed," Jesse said. "Did you go to the gym this morning or something? You look like you've been... exerting yourself."

He would know. Zinnia gave him a tight smile. "It's a new blush," she said lightly. "Thanks for noticing."

Margaret cleared her throat and raised her eyebrows.

Zinnia changed the subject. "Has anyone heard from Karl?"

Dawna, who was filing her long orange nails with an emery board, said, "Not since he left here yesterday with my Diet Coke money and then didn't come back with my Diet Coke."

Margaret patted Dawna on the shoulder. "There is a vending machine on the third floor. I can loan you a few bucks."

Dawna shrugged away the older woman's hand. "I don't need money. It's the principle."

Zinnia covered for Karl, since she was partly responsible for his sudden disappearance. "Dawna, he got sick really fast. I offered to drive him home, because he was so pale and clammy, but he jumped in his car and sped away."

Dawna's expression softened. "That's all right. Nobody should have to stay in the office if they're having *disasterpants*."

Gavin said over his shoulder, "It's no wonder Karl had stomach flu yesterday. Have you seen the way he eats?"

"Be nice," Margaret said. "He's our boss."

Gavin turned and gave Dawna a huge smile. "He's not my *real* boss, Margaret. You know I only answer to the lovely Dawna Jones."

The others groaned. Apparently, Dawna and Gavin were back together again. But of course they were. Tragedy has a way of moving relationships along their natural trajectory at a higher velocity.

Zinnia looked over at Jesse, who winked at her. Jesse had arrived at the office ten minutes before her, even though they'd shared a ride to work. Their clever tactic was for Zinnia to drop him off, then circle Pacific Spirit Park before returning. She winked back at him and quickly turned away, lest the others catch a whiff of their chemistry. Their casual arrangement was just fine how it was, thank you very much. Zinnia didn't need any external pressure to put a label on what they had.

Margaret stood on her tiptoes to peer over Gavin's shoulder as he shook out the coffee beans. She made one of her impatient rhino sounds. "What are you doing, Gavin?

Counting the beans?" She elbowed him out of the way and took over the brew. Gavin was so busy making goo-goo eyes at Dawna that he barely complained.

Zinnia noticed Gavin was wearing the same trousers he'd torn on Tuesday. He must have gotten the rear seam repaired already. She knew it was the same pair because there were spots of blood—Annette's blood—near the cuff. Zinnia looked away, mildly nauseated by the sight. It wasn't like Gavin to miss a stain on his clothes. He must have seen Annette's blood and worn the trousers anyway. Zinnia didn't have the highest opinion of Gavin in the first place, but seeing his stained trousers made her opinion sink a little lower.

Margaret announced that the coffee would be ready in five minutes, thanks to her. Everyone murmured appreciation.

"And Carrot is coming in today," Margaret said. Carrot was their other missing coworker. She had called in sick Tuesday morning and had not been in since. The others had been so busy with their extra workloads, plus all the murder intrigue, that the young woman's absence had barely been noticed

Gavin said, "Carrot must be Patient Zero. She got one of those forty-eight-hour bugs, and passed it on to Karl. I hope the rest of us don't get sick."

Jesse asked the group, "Hey, has anyone talked to Carrot about... you know?"

Margaret waved a hand. "Don't worry," she said. "Carrot knows about everything."

"Good," Jesse said, nodding. "It will be nice have her back. She's such a sweet girl. Plus it will be great to have the whole gang back together again."

Gavin cleared his throat. "The whole gang? We're missing Karl and Annette. So even with Carrot, it's only part of the gang. Six out of eight. Seventy-five percent."

Margaret frowned at Gavin. "Six out of seven. Annette's not coming back."

Gavin stuck his nose in the air. "Excuuuuuse me for getting the math wrong."

Margaret rolled her eyes. Heaven help anyone who tried to correct the corrector.

Zinnia bit her tongue. Margaret, like Gavin, also liked to correct people on technicalities, especially when it wasn't necessary.

Dawna said, "When Carrot and Karl return to the pack, we shall be made whole." She furrowed her brow. "That sounded weird coming outta my mouth, didn't it? *We shall be made whole*." She shook her head, the tight black coils of her hair swinging out. "It must be the book that's making me talk funny. I was up late reading it last night, and now I sound like one of Annette's characters."

Margaret waved to get everyone's attention. "Karl's not coming in," she said, waving her phone. "He just sent me a text message. I think he meant to send it to everyone, but he didn't hit reply-all on the chain. Typical Karl. Anyway, he's taking the rest of the week off and using up some of his vacation days."

Gavin groaned. "That's not fair. Nobody else can use their vacation days while he's away."

Dawna said to Gavin icily, "Is there somewhere else you need to be?"

"No." He flicked his finger against the glass coffee pot, ringing it like a bell. "It's the principle of the thing."

"Plus, complaining about things being unfair is your favorite sport," Dawna said.

He flicked the coffee pot again. His girlfriend was not wrong.

The main door to the office creaked, and everyone went silent, listening.

A timid female voice called out weakly, "Hello?"

Four out of six people answered in unison, like a chorus. "We're in here!"

Carrot Greyson entered the break room hesitantly, looking pale and startled—which was how she always looked, with her light skin and her big eyes.

"Hello," she said, pulling down the sleeves of her V-neck shirt to cover her hands like mittens. "Nice to see you all again."

The rest of the gang greeted her with equal politeness.

Carrot Greyson was the only person in the office who was universally adored by everyone. She was twenty-five, average height, and a bit too skinny. She had large blue eyes that bulged out of her head—but in a cute way, like the bugged-out eyeballs of a purebred purse dog. Carrot didn't just bear the name of a vegetable, she also had hair the color of pureed carrots. Her natural shade was somewhere between blonde and brunette, but she had been dying her medium-length, fine hair a bright orange since before Zinnia had met the young woman. In addition to the eye-catching hair, Carrot had a number of tattoos all over her body. Her appearance seemed designed to gather attention, and yet she shied away from such notice. She often looked surprised whenever people spoke to her, as though she'd come to believe she was invisible.

"Sorry I've been away," Carrot said softly. "I guess there are a lot of permits waiting to be processed. How are we splitting Annette's docket?"

The others exchanged guilty looks. Nobody had thought about the files that had been specifically tasked to Annette Scholem. They had barely been able to get any of their own work done over the last two days.

The coffee pot hissed to announce that its brew was ready. As they poured their mugs, the group had an uncomfortable yet necessary conversation about the logistics of splitting Annette's work and posting a job opening for the dead woman's position.

Nobody could ever fill Annette's shoes, they agreed, but they could at least get a warm body into her chair.

* * *

11:35 AM

Margaret and Zinnia were still discussing shared workload when Jesse emerged from his office and sauntered toward them. Memories from the previous night flitted to Zinnia's mind. Jesse had complained of her cold hands, but they hadn't stayed cold for long. She felt herself blushing. Jesse was a completely different person inside the office. For one, he was never naked at work. What a shame.

Jesse sat casually on the corner of the desk nearest Zinnia. He leaned across her computer screen and helped himself to the candy jar.

Margaret and Zinnia had dropped their conversation at the sight of him, which caused him to ask, "What are you two brewing up?"

Margaret snapped back, "What do you mean, *brewing up?*" Margaret was often triggered by words associated with witchcraft: brewing, casting, eye of newt, and so forth.

Jesse raised an eyebrow. "It's just an expression, Margaret. What were you talking about?"

"Work stuff," Margaret said.

"Tell me more." He rested his chin on his hand. "Work fascinates me. I could talk about it all day."

Margaret grabbed a candy from the open jar and narrowed her eyes at him as she crunched away.

After she'd swallowed the candy, she asked in a light, concerned tone, "Jesse, is there something wrong with your vehicle? I noticed you got a lift in this morning with Zinnia."

"Uh, no problems. We carpool sometimes."

"I've noticed that." She fixed him with her gaze.

He squirmed. "Well, you know how City Hall gives out those commendations to people who make an effort to reduce their environmental footprint?"

Margaret sniffed. "You never ask me to carpool with you."

"That's because your van smells like sour milk and beef jerky."

"You get used to it after a few hours." She batted her eyelashes. "Listen, I can swing by your place any time. It's on the way. You're still in your dad's old house, aren't you?"

Jesse paused, seemingly at a loss for words, before answering, "Zinnia has a great stereo in her car."

Margaret shrugged one shoulder coquettishly. "Does she? You haven't heard my singing voice. It's better than any stereo. What time should I pick you up on Monday? I wouldn't mind getting some of those environmental points."

Jesse's handsome brow furrowed. He glanced back and forth between the two women. "Will there be snacks? Zinnia keeps snacks in her glove box."

"I bet she does." Margaret licked her lips. "Okay, Jesse. You've forced my hand. I really want you to carpool with me, so I'm going to pack my glove box full of candy. Will that get you into my van?"

"Oh, Margaret." He shook his head as he got up from the desk. "You just offered me candy to get into your van. If that doesn't sound suspicious, I don't know what is."

She giggled. "You might like my candy if you tried it, Jesse."

He pointed a finger at her. "Margaret Mills, if you keep flirting with me like this, I'll have to make a report to Human Resources."

She snorted. "It'll be your word against mine."

"Zinnia will vouch for me." He turned to Zinnia, grinning. "Won't you?"

Zinnia held up a finger and pulled a white headphone out of one ear. "Won't I what? I didn't hear any of that." She blinked innocently. "You're not bothering Margaret again, are you, Jesse? Leave the poor woman alone. We're trying to get some work done here." She made a brushing-off gesture with her hand. "Shoo. Back to your cave."

Jesse leaned across her screen again, slowly helping himself to another handful of candy. He made eye contact the whole time, with those captivating blue eyes of his. And his perfect mouth was only inches from hers. What a tease! He finally finished getting his candy and left.

Both women watched his butt as he walked away. Unlike Gavin, Jesse Berman bought his trousers the exact right size.

Margaret said in a hushed tone, "He *must* know that I know about you two."

"We both promised to keep it a secret at work, so I have to keep pretending I haven't talked to you about it."

"Do you think *he* told anyone about your arrangement?"

"Men aren't like that."

"He's from a different generation than us. The men talk about their feelings now. Didn't you get the memo?"

"Very funny."

"I'm serious. And it's contagious. Last night, my husband asked me how I was feeling, then he went on for an hour about how sad he was about poor Annette. I missed the second half of my singing show. And he cried, Zinnia. The man had water coming out of both eyeballs. The last time I saw him cry was when that doctor who did his vasectomy handed him a bag of marbles and said he could keep what got removed."

Zinnia bit her lower lip to keep a straight face. The town's only vasectomy surgeon was a bit of a nut, pardon the pun. "Are we allowed to laugh about that, or is it still too soon?"

Margaret looked past Zinnia, at Annette's empty desk. "I don't know. But it does feel good to laugh. And goodness knows there's always plenty to feel sad about." She frowned. "Poor Annette." She shook her head. "Any chance we can get a look at that security footage the police have?"

Zinnia had phoned Margaret earlier that morning, while Jesse was in the shower, to tell the other witch about her late night visit from Detective Fung.

Zinnia said, "I can ask, but you know how Fung is. He prefers for the information flow to go toward him only."

"Those cops would probably be more appreciative of us and our special skills if they didn't have... *you know*. The others." She waved a hand. "Whatever the shifter bunch is calling themselves these days." She hunched forward, leaning in on the shared desk. "Sounds to me like it might have been one of them who got to Annette."

"A shifter? Yes. All signs certainly point in that direction. That's got to be the new theory Fung is working on right now."

Margaret whispered, "Or covering up."

Zinnia sighed. "You and your crazy conspiracy theories."

"It's not a crazy conspiracy theory if there really is a secret organization behind the workings of your town."

"Maybe I'm part of the conspiracy." Zinnia waggled her eyebrows. "Maybe I'm working for them."

Margaret laughed loudly enough to attract the attention of Gavin, Dawna, and Carrot.

"Good one," Margaret said to Zinnia. "They'd never let someone like you be a member."

Gavin, Dawna, and Carrot were still looking their way.

Zinnia put her headphone back in her ear and resumed her work.

* * *

12:15 PM

The whole gang crowded around the break room table at lunch time. It was a rare occasion for them to eat together in the small room. Most of them usually ate at their desks. Even Jesse, who usually went out for lunch to avoid the smell of microwaved leftovers, had ordered in delivery so he could join them.

They discovered they were one chair short. They discussed bringing in Annette's unused desk chair but settled on one from the reception area, even though it was a couple inches too low.

Everyone was munching away—Carrot in the too-low reception chair—while Margaret regaled them with her latest tale from the trenches. That morning, her four children had gotten up early to make pancakes. Margaret and her husband slept through it all, right up until the fire trucks arrived.

The anecdote was interrupted by the beeps and buzzes of everyone getting a phone message simultaneously. It was an emergency notice from the mayor's office:

The coroner has announced that the City Hall employee who was found deceased on the premises on Tuesday of this week was killed by a wild animal who gained access to the ground level office through an open window. Therefore, all employees are advised to take measures to ensure all windows are closed and locked, and to avoid being alone on the premises during non-office hours. Thank you for your utmost attention to this serious matter. We care about your safety.

Jesse made a tsk-tsk sound. "And yet, they still haven't fixed the security system at the staff entrance."

Dawna said, "It's been so long, I forgot that door was supposed to be locked."

Gavin made air quotes. "We care about your safety." He rolled his eyes.

Margaret and Zinnia exchanged a look. Fung had said they were keeping the wild animal detail from the public. What could this announcement mean? Either Fung's word was no good, or someone over his head had released the information.

Carrot looked around the room, her blue eyes even more bugged out than usual. "Is that what really happened? Annette got attacked by a wild animal?"

"According to the coroner," Jesse said.

Gavin added in, "And also according to the way her body looked. She had these deep gashes from her throat to her guts. I think some of her organs might have been missing. Don't wolves eat the liver first? Or am I thinking of some other predator?"

Carrot's lips wavered. She looked like she might burst into tears.

"Wolves go for the liver, heart, and kidneys," Jesse said. "And also the lungs and stomach lining."

Dawna started to burp-hiccup. "I'm gonna be sick again." She got to her feet and ran out, making horrible sounds as she did.

Zinnia started to follow Dawna, but Margaret was closer to the door and beat her to it.

Carrot, Gavin, Jesse, and Zinnia remained in the break room.

For some reason, everyone had lost interest in their food. They picked at their meals without eating. Talk of animals gnawing on a dear friend's organs did have that effect on appetite.

Had a wolf, or a shifter in wolf form, attacked Annette and then stood slobbering over her, eating the poor woman? The thought was too much to bear. Zinnia couldn't sit still any longer.

"Let's check the window," Zinnia said, pushing away her food and getting to her feet. "Like the memo said."

The other three jumped up and murmured agreement. They looked almost happy about checking the window. When faced with upsetting news, moving was always better than sitting still, even if it was just going into Karl's office to check a window.

In the small, private office, the four of them checked and rechecked the window latch.

"It only opens from inside," Gavin said. He opened the window and leaned out, looking down. "Not much of a drop to the ground. I could climb through here. I think any one of us could. Even Karl." He pulled his head back into the office and closed the window with a loud bang that made Carrot jump.

"This is so creepy, you guys," Carrot said. "I can't believe you were all here right after, with Annette's blood all over the carpet. Just working. Like it was a regular day."

Jesse frowned and said, "It wasn't a regular day, Carrot."

She pulled her sleeves further down over her hands. "We shouldn't even be here now."

Jesse kept frowning. "What would you suggest? Shutting down all of City Hall?"

Carrot blinked up at him. "Just for a few days."

Gavin said, "Carrot, that's not going to bring her back. Annette is gone."

Carrot stamped her foot and glared at the two men. "How can you be so cold? You men! You're the worst."

Jesse waved a hand and then brought it to his chest. "Carrot, I don't know what you're getting at, but you're wrong. We all loved Annette. My mother died when I was a baby, so I never got to know her, but Annette was like a guardian angel or something. I like to think my mother sent Annette here to look out for me." He cleared his throat. "By which I mean all of us. Not just me, of course."

Carrot took this in and agreed, "She was very motherly, for a woman with no kids."

Gavin chuckled. "Annette was nothing like my mother. She was much, much better."

Carrot's expression brightened. "We should write all this stuff down for her memorial," she said. "So Annette's family knows how much she was loved here at work."

"Good idea," Jesse said. He looked directly at Gavin and said, "Let's leave out the part about wolves eating her liver."

Zinnia gave Jesse a head shake. He was known for his breezy, irreverent attitude, but sometimes he went too far.

Carrot's mood suddenly changed again. She balled up her hands into little fists. "Stop saying bad stuff about wolves."

Jesse raised his chin and squinted down at the orange-haired young woman. "Hey, don't you have a pet wolf?"

"No," she said, a little too vehemently.

"That's right," Gavin said. "Carrot, you adopted that wild wolf a while back. What was his name again? Adolf?"

She shook her small fists at him. "Shut up, Gavin. Shut up!"

Gavin looked over at Zinnia. "Carrot has a pet wolf," he said, in the singsong manner of a child tattling.

"I do not," Carrot said.

"Do too," Gavin said.

"Do not!" She suddenly struck him in the chest with both of her little fists. Gavin, whose muscles were all for show, went sprawling over a low filing cabinet.

He landed on the floor just as Dawna and Margaret returned from the washroom and entered Karl's office to see what was happening.

Margaret's eyes widened. She took one look at Gavin, who was doing his own impression of an overturned tortoise, and she turned to Zinnia and demanded, "What's going on in here?"

Zinnia held up both hands. "This isn't what it looks like."

Gavin was still flat on his back, being pelted with file folders from the overturned filing cabinet.

Carrot was bouncing on the spot, fists raised.

Jesse could scarcely contain his amusement. He said to Margaret, "Carrot has a pet wolf named Adolf."

"Do not!" Carrot turned and tried to run out of the office, but she tripped over her own feet and went sprawling.

As she landed, her V-neck shirt skewed off one shoulder to reveal one of her many tattoos. It was a dark-furred animal with glowing orange eyes. A wolf? Zinnia came over to help Carrot to her feet, but really she was trying to get a better look at the tattoo.

CHAPTER 13

12:50 PM

Carrot looked more skinny and pale than ever, sitting at the break- room table in the too-short reception chair with an ice pack on her elbow. She reminded Zinnia of a child who insisted on playing with the big kids and then cried when the inevitable horseplay injury occurred.

Carrot peeked under the ice pack on her elbow. "That's a big boo-boo," she said of the bruise.

Zinnia snorted. Carrot was such a baby, even though she was twenty-five. Was Zinnia that old now, that she saw twenty-somethings as children? Carrot was an adult by anyone's definition. She lived on her own, held down a full-time job, and drove a big old Cadillac. Perhaps it was the dyed-orange hair that made her look like a silly puppet. Or perhaps it was the fact Jesse had slept with Carrot that made Zinnia see her in a critical way. That was probably it. Simple old-fashioned jealousy. What a cliché. The older woman, jealous of the younger threat. Zinnia wasn't happy to see herself in that light, but she certainly fit the parameters.

Carrot checked the bruise again and pouted.

Dawna rolled her eyes. "Girl, you did that to yourself. Nobody pushed you."

"I know," Carrot snapped defensively. She gave a pouty look to Jesse, probably looking for sympathy.

Jesse said, "We were just teasing you about your pet wolf. We didn't mean anything by it." He pulled out the chair next to Carrot and took a seat.

Zinnia checked the time. It was ten minutes to one, so their lunch hour wasn't over yet.

Zinnia pulled out a chair and sat by her unfinished lunch. Margaret and Dawna did the same. One chair with an unfinished lunch in front of it remained empty. Gavin had split his recently repaired trousers when he fell and lost the battle with Karl's filing cabinet. He had excused himself to drive to his apartment at the Candy Factory for a change of clothes. Now it was just the five of them in the break room.

Margaret twirled her gray forehead curl and gave Zinnia a meaningful look. Zinnia had no idea what the other witch was trying to convey. Speak up? Do something? Margaret flashed her eyes twice, whatever that meant.

Zinnia spoke gently to Carrot, the way she would speak to a fool or a child. "We've got about nine minutes left for lunch. Why don't you tell us a little about your pet wolf?"

Carrot jolted upright in her chair and dropped the ice pack on the floor. "I don't have a pet wolf," she said.

Zinnia pressed on. "What about Adolf? Gavin seemed pretty sure of himself that you know a wolf by that name."

Carrot looked over at Jesse, her blue eyes bugging out. He gave her a nod to say *go ahead*. Carrot blinked rapidly, which settled her eyes back into her head.

She drew in a labored breath and said, "The only wolf I know personally is the one I call Alfie. Not Adolf." She grimaced. "Alfie, like Alpha."

Dawna said, "Now we're getting somewhere." She poked at her tightly curled black hair with two long orange fingernails. "Gavin must have mixed up some of the letters, just like Annette used to do with everyone's names."

Jesse nodded. "Annette was not great with names."

That was an understatement. Zinnia spoke up. "When I started working here, she called me Nina for months."

Carrot looked into Zinnia's eyes across the table. "Nina is a pretty name. You'd be a beautiful Nina."

"Thanks," Zinnia said, feeling guilty for accepting a compliment from Carrot.

Margaret picked up a celery stick from her unfinished lunch. Before she took a bite, she waved it at Carrot, wand-like, and said, "Now tell us about this wolf friend of yours,

Alfie. I'm sure he has nothing to do with that memo about wolves attacking people." She crunched into the celery with gusto.

Zinnia gave Margaret an appreciative look. Margaret had just cast a minor compulsion spell—one that could only be cast with a wand, and she'd nearly done so without detection by Zinnia.

Carrot held her head higher. "Alfie would never hurt anyone," she said.

"You can't trust a wild animal," Jesse said. "They're not like—"

Margaret silenced Jesse with one of her stern motherly looks, plus a subtle shaking of a fresh celery stick.

Jesse clamped his mouth shut.

Margaret said to the group, swirling her celery stick, "Let's give Carrot and Alfie a chance, okay? No need to grab the torches and pitchforks yet." She gave Carrot one of her gentle motherly looks along with a celery stick prodding. "Go on, sweetie."

"There's not much to tell," Carrot said, frowning.

Margaret set down the celery, picked up the ice pack from the floor, and gave it back to Carrot for her elbow. "How'd you meet Alfie?"

Carrot's frown turned to a soft, wistful smile. "I was walking at Towhee Marsh last summer, and I heard something whimpering in the bushes. I thought it was somebody's dog, so I figured I would take it to the vet, Dr. Katz." She kept talking, delving into the details of the animal's injury and the effort of getting it loaded into her old Cadillac.

Zinnia and Margaret exchanged a look. They both knew of Dr. Katz and his clinic through their other coven member, Fatima Nix. Fatima worked for the veterinarian. Fatima and her aunt, Maisy Nix, rounded out the coven at a whopping four witches. Not much of a coven, but it was better than nothing. They used to also have Winona Vander Zalm as a member, even though she wasn't technically a witch, but Winnie had lost interest and stopped coming to coven meetings years ago. Zinnia wondered what Winona was up to lately. The woman was so very old, she might have passed away by now. Zinnia made a mental note to drop by Winnie's lovely red house soon to check on her, even though something in her witch's intuition told her it was already too late.

Zinnia pulled her attention back to the break room. Carrot was still sharing details about her animal rescue, specifically about having to rent a carpet steamer to clean the animal blood out of her back seat.

Margaret interrupted to say, "Lunch time's nearly over. Can you tell us more about the animal? When did you figure out it wasn't a dog?"

Carrot's pale cheeks flushed. "I asked Dr. Katz to check for a microchip or an ear tattoo, and call the owners. That was when he told me it was a wolf, not a dog." Carrot put her face in her hands. "I can be so clueless sometimes. I don't even see what's right in front of me."

Margaret patted her on the shoulder. "You did the right thing, Carrot. Whether it was a wolf or a dog, it was the right thing to do."

Jesse agreed. "Animals are innocent creatures. It was kind of you to help. You're a good person."

Carrot dropped her hands from her face and looked at Jesse with what looked to Zinnia like goo-goo eyes.

The tattooed, orange-haired young woman gushed, "Thanks, Jesse. You always know how to make a girl feel better."

Margaret asked her, "Where's Alfie now?"

"Back in the wild," Carrot said. "After Dr. Katz stitched him up, Alfie stayed in my back yard for a while. He got better and better, and then one day he jumped the fence and left forever."

Margaret asked, "How long was his recovery period?"

Carrot shrugged. "I dunno. Does it matter?"

Margaret and Zinnia exchanged a look. The recovery period did matter. It mattered a *lot* if Alfie was a shifter. Their kind didn't heal instantly, but they did heal quickly, which was critical to the supernatural creatures, because they couldn't shift from animal to human if an injury was serious.

Dawna asked, "Was it a few weeks? A few months?"

Carrot shrugged again. "A couple of weeks. Maybe a month. Not too long. He did cost me a lot of money to feed."

Margaret and Zinnia both leaned back in their chairs at the same time. A month to heal didn't sound like any supernatural creature they knew. Alfie must have been a regular wolf.

"And that was the end," Carrot said. "He went away. Probably far away."

Dawna crossed her arms and snorted. "I'm not so sure about that."

Zinnia raised an eyebrow at Dawna. Was she about to spout some new theory? Yesterday, she'd breathlessly told them all she knew who killed Annette, and then it turned out she didn't know anything. All she'd had was her wild theory about the book.

Carrot pushed back her chair with a jarring scrape. "Lunch time's over."

"Not so fast," Dawna said. "You haven't told us everything about Alfie."

Carrot's lower lip quivered.

Margaret got another celery stick ready for a compulsion spell.

Dawna stared at her pale coworker. "If you never saw that wolf again, then how come last week I saw you walking across the back lawn toward the woods with a box of Milk Bones?"

Margaret jabbed the celery stick. "Milk Bones? Spill it."

Carrot stammered, "I-I-I w-would never give a wild animal processed food. They were organic snacks I made myself. Mainly oats and coconut oil."

"I knew it," Dawna said, looking pleased with herself.

All at once, everyone asked if it was true. Had Carrot been feeding a wild wolf right outside the office?

She nodded and put her face in her hands. "Just a small wolf," she said meekly. "He might even be part dog, because he's not very big. I swear, you guys, Alfie wouldn't hurt anyone." She dropped her hands and gave them a bug-eyed look.

The group muttered to each other about the coincidence of a wolf being fed near the office and a person being attacked.

Carrot tugged at the neck of her low-cut shirt, giving Zinnia another glimpse of her tattoos. The tattoo Zinnia had glimpsed back in Karl's office was definitely an animal. Zinnia could see an outstretched animal paw, and four red lines extending from its claws. The tattoo had been drawn to look like it was scratching the young woman's skin.

Margaret berated Carrot for not saying something earlier about Alfie.

Jesse got up from his chair, circled the table, and put his hands on Carrot's shoulder's protectively. "Margaret, go easy on Carrot. She's not a tough old broad with rhino skin like you."

Margaret's shock at being spoken to like that registered as a loud gasp that was strong enough to make the napkins on the table flutter. Zinnia felt the uncontrolled energy crackling off the other witch. Someone was going to get a blue lightning blast to the chest. Possibly two someones. Jesse for saying Margaret was a tough old broad with rhino skin, and Carrot for feeding organic dog treats to a wolf right next to the office.

CHAPTER 14

Zinnia couldn't allow Margaret to zap people with blue lightning in the break room, no matter how badly some of them deserved it. Zinnia clapped her hands in a very specific, controlled way that would help dissipate the other witch's energy.

By the look of the pout on Margaret's face, the clapping was working.

Zinnia clapped once more for good measure. "That's enough, everyone," she said.

Dawna, Carrot, Jesse, and Margaret stared at Zinnia. The clapping had also served to rivet their attention on the redheaded witch.

Zinnia spoke slowly and calmly. "Even if it was Alfie who attacked Annette, he didn't do it under Carrot's orders. I think we all can agree on that."

Jesse, who was still standing behind Carrot with his hands on her shoulders, gave the young woman a reassuring shoulder rub.

"Zinnia's right," Jesse said. "Our Carrot is a sweet girl. She's got the tattoos of a bad girl, sure, but she's a good girl, deep down." He leaned forward to look down into her eyes. "Isn't that right?"

Carrot nodded, her wispy bright-orange hair flipping with the movement.

Zinnia felt a bit of her half-eaten lunch rise in the back of her throat. She wanted Jesse to play it cool at the office, but did he have to be so affectionate toward Carrot?

Margaret got to her feet. "Lunch break's over."

Dawna remained seated. "Hang on, everyone. We have two minutes left to talk about Annette's book."

The others turned their heads, looking at anything but each other.

Dawna said, "Come on, people. You didn't read it? You had all night!"

"I didn't even get started," Zinnia admitted. "I had issues with my printer."

"Same here," Jesse said, which was technically true, since he'd also gotten his copy from Zinnia's printer.

Margaret looked sheepish. "I only got one chapter in before I fell asleep with my face mashed onto it."

Carrot looked confused. "What book are you guys talking about?"

"Annette's unpublished manuscript," Dawna said. She went on, giving Carrot more details about Annette's secret career and the book she had been writing before her death. As Dawna explained, it became clear this was the first Carrot had heard of any book.

"But you got a copy last night," Dawna said. "Sent by email. Didn't you open it?

"I didn't open the attachment," Carrot said. "I don't trust attachments."

Dawna and Margaret both groaned.

Carrot said, "That's how viruses get on your computer. I was waiting to open it here at work, because we have IT people around who can fix our computers if they get viruses. But then I got here, and I had two days' worth of emails, and you know how Karl sends me a copy of everything, mostly by accident."

Dawna gave Carrot an incredulous look. "Open up that attachment, girl! All the characters in the book are based on us."

Carrot scratched the top of her head. "Really? Us?"

"You'll get a kick out of it," Dawna said. "Your character especially." She looked around at the group. "We should *all* get caught up tonight, so we can talk about it tomorrow at lunch time. Like a book club. A *real* book club."

Margaret and Zinnia exchanged a look. Sometimes they referred to their coven meetings as a book club. It wasn't the most imaginative code.

Jesse, who still had his hands on Carrot's shoulders—much to Zinnia's annoyance—said, "Imagine that. A lunchtime book club with all of us. Annette would have loved that."

Everyone was silent. Jesse was right. Annette would have loved it. She would have loved it even more if she'd been alive to take part.

* * *

Everyone got back to work after their lunch break, including Gavin, in a new pair of unripped, unstained, half-a-size-too-small trousers. Dawna caught him up on what he'd missed: Carrot's wolf's name was Alfie, not Adolf, and Carrot had recently been feeding Alfie homemade dog treats in the forested park behind City Hall. People were divided over whether or not Alfie the wolf was a suspect, but generally agreed Carrot had nothing to do with the attack. Also, Carrot hadn't opened the email attachment with Annette's book, but Dawna showed her how right after lunch, so now she had a copy.

Zinnia kept glancing over at Carrot. The young woman seemed more nervous than usual, dropping pens and bumping her computer mouse on the floor twice. Was Carrot feeling guilty about feeding a wolf near the office? She had to be. Anyone in her position would be feeling terrible after getting that City Hall memo about preventing animal attacks.

The police needed to hear about Carrot's tame wolf, Alfie. And they needed to know about Carrot's tattoo with the scratching animal paw.

Zinnia passed Margaret a handwritten note about the matter. Margaret wrote back that Zinnia should be the one to call Fung, exactly as Zinnia expected Margaret would. The words disappeared from the page as they were read by Zinnia, thanks to a handy spell. The witches tried not to pass magical notes too often, because even with disappearing words, it was risky, but it was still more secure than email.

Shortly after two o'clock, Zinnia grabbed her phone and quietly slipped out of the office. Instead of visiting the regular washroom on the ground floor, she continued on to the seldom-used special needs washroom around the corner.

Her phone call to Fung went through to voicemail, so she left a detailed message, careful not to implicate herself as a witch in case he had someone else answering his messages.

As she left the washroom, she bumped into Jesse Berman.

Jesse's captivating blue eyes widened with delight as he gave Zinnia a knowing smile. "Who's using the special washroom that we're not supposed to use unless we actually need it?" His tone was flirtatious and teasing. "I may have to report your activities, Ms. Riddle."

"Is that so?" Zinnia put her hands on her hips. "You'd report me to the department that oversees the use and misuse of the special needs facilities?"

"That's right." He used his chin to gesture at the door, with its multiple signs warning away people who didn't require its ample space. "They need to make those signs big enough so that even people like you can read them."

Zinnia snorted. "What do you mean, *people like me*?"

"Willful women." The light in his blue eyes danced. In a low, gravelly voice, he said, "Coincidentally, willful women are my favorite kind."

"I've noticed that." She narrowed her eyes, remembering his hands on Carrot's shoulders. "And you're drawn to redheads."

He waggled his eyebrows. "Guilty as charged."

"But not in a discriminating way." Her voice was brittle, sharp. "It seems *any* sort of redhead will do." She blinked twice.

The flirty look fell off his face. "What?"

"You seemed awfully eager to offer comfort to a certain fake redhead coworker of ours."

"Carrot?" He snorted. "She's just a kid, Zinnia. I only like women."

"But you used to like her."

He took a step back and slowly nodded. "Ah. I was wondering when this was going to come up." He closed his eyes briefly. "Did Margaret tell you something? She's such a gossip."

"Everyone at the office knows you used to date Carrot."

Jesse shrugged one shoulder. "Dating is such a strong word. I would say—"

Zinnia held up one hand. "Don't," she said. "I don't want to hear about it."

"You're the one who brought it up."

"Only because I also don't want to *see it*, Jesse. I don't want to see you rubbing her shoulders or putting your arm around her. I don't think it's too much to ask."

He looked left and right, then took a step back, eyes wide. "I don't know what's going on here, but what you saw at the office was nothing. The poor girl hurt her elbow, and then you other women attacked her like a pack of wol—" he stopped himself from saying *wolves* and cleared his throat. "Hyenas," he finished.

"We were nothing like hyenas. Carrot's the one who was feeding a wild animal, Jesse. Right next to the office. I don't know if it was Alfie who attacked Annette, but something did. She's dead, Jesse. Dead. Annette's not coming back."

Jesse studied her with a detached, clinical expression. "You're really worked up today," he said. "I've never seen you like this."

A wave of shame passed through Zinnia. Jesse had seen her lose control. She was acting like a jealous, crazy woman. She swallowed, fixed the collar on her blouse, and smoothed down her hair.

"I'm fine," she said, and she was. Some emotion had gotten away from her and broken through, but now everything was back to where it was supposed to be.

"You're right about Annette being gone," Jesse said softly. "We're all going to miss her, but it's her own fault."

"Her fault?" Zinnia couldn't imagine where Jesse was going with this.

"Yeah." He shoved his hands in his pockets and lifted his shoulders tight to his ears. "She was always using manipulation, trying to make us be more to each other than we are. She must have been lonely because she didn't have a family, so she tried to make the whole office into a family, with herself as the grand matriarch."

Zinnia said nothing. It was true, but the way Jesse described Annette's enthusiasm as *manipulation* made it sound unsavory. Pathetic, even.

"She knew about us," Jesse said. "About me and you."

"Oh." Zinnia was surprised, but not *that* surprised. When she and Jesse had taken their flirtation to the next level, they'd been careful, but not careful enough. Margaret had figured it out instantly. Carrot either hadn't or wouldn't let on. Dawna and Gavin were so consumed with each other and their drama that they wouldn't have clued in if Jesse and Zinnia had started making out in the break room. Annette, however, would have noticed. She'd always been good at observing people and figuring them out. It must have been her writer side.

Jesse said, "Annette liked that we were seeing each other." He paused, looking puzzled. "She even said she *approved* of you."

Zinnia frowned. She didn't like the idea of someone judging her worthiness for dating, not even someone like Annette.

"I'm going to miss her, too," Jesse said. "This whole thing, it's just so surreal." He looked down at his shoes and scuffed one on the floor. When he spoke again, his voice was low and gruff. "And to think, this all happened because Carrot couldn't tell the difference between a dog and a wolf."

Zinnia felt a chill run up her back. Jesse was on the same page as her: Alfie the wolf *did* have something to do with the attack.

Jesse said, "Actually, I came down here so I could use this private washroom to put in a call to the police about Carrot's wolf."

"No need," Zinnia said. "I already called."

He looked up at her, his blue eyes bright and gleaming. "You did?"

She nodded. "Funny how you and I think the same thing sometimes."

He grinned. "Funny."

She tilted her head to the side. "Got any plans for tonight, Mr. Berman?"

His posture slumped and he sighed. "I do, actually. My father had a bunch of old photo albums stashed in the attic. I've been meaning to go through them and get everything organized. It's coming up on the two-year anniversary of..." He gritted his teeth.

"I understand," Zinnia said. Jesse's father, Viktor, had passed away two years ago. Grief was one of the things Zinnia and Jesse had bonded over, whether Jesse knew it or not.

"Two whole years," Jesse said. "Sometimes I can't believe he's gone, like when I'm in the house. I feel him everywhere there. In the walls. It's comforting."

Zinnia shivered. Whenever she was at Jesse's house, she felt it, too. Except to Zinnia, the presence was the exact opposite of comforting. The Berman house had some seriously bad juju.

"Hey," Jesse said, snapping his fingers. "How about you come over tomorrow night? I should have all the photos cleaned up by then. I'll cook you dinner. A nice dinner."

She raised her eyebrows. "Dinner? You cook?" He'd never cooked for her before, so she had no idea what to expect.

He laughed. "I know, right?" He waved his hands up and down his body. "All these good looks, and he can cook, too."

"You are a man of many surprises, Jesse Berman."

"It's a date," he said, smiling broadly and blasting her with his effortless charm. "Saturday night. Don't be late."

* * *

3:30 PM

The office was quiet. Too quiet. Zinnia removed her in-ear headphones and listened. Nobody was typing or clicking mouse buttons, even though they were all staring at their computer screens.

Carrot looked up and around, caught Zinnia's eye, and guiltily looked back at her screen again. Gavin and Dawna were both focused on their screens, hands on their laps. Margaret was in the same pose.

Carrot suddenly burst out, "Is this Tracy person supposed to be me? Seriously?"

Nobody said anything.

Carrot repeated her question. "Seriously? Is Tracy me? She's got my hair and tattoos."

Zinnia asked her, "What are you talking about?"

"The book," Carrot said, gesturing to her computer screen. "Annette's manuscript. I'm reading it on my computer. That's pretty much all I've been doing since lunch time."

"Same here," said Gavin.

"Me, too," said Margaret.

"Good," said Dawna. "It's about time everybody caught up." She cupped her hand around her mouth and called out, "Jesse?"

Jesse's voice came from his office. "You guessed it, Dawna. I'm on chapter five."

Carrot yelled to Jesse, "Do you think this Tracy character is anything like me? I know she has orange hair, but she's so annoying. Tracy always makes a point of being different from everyone else, like she's a special snowflake."

Nobody said anything.

Carrot said, "I guess she's okay. Tracy has some good qualities. But why is her name Tracy?"

"There's a code," Dawna said with an air of authority. "I already figured out the code the first time I read it, last night. Annette warned me she was going to use all of us as people in her book, and did she ever! She used lots of our personal details, but she moved the letters of everyone's names around. That's why Carrot is Tracy. Same letters."

Gavin cleared his throat. "Tracy is a *palindrome* for Carrot."

Margaret cleared her throat. "I believe the word you're looking for is *anagram*, Gavin. A palindrome is a word or phrase that reads the same backward and forward, like *Emily's sassy lime*."

Gavin stuck his nose in the air. "Sorry I'm not as literary as you, Margaret. Some of us were having *fun* in our twenties."

"I had fun in college," Margaret said indignantly. "I was in an improv troupe. The MacGuffins."

Carrot said, "Tracy is not really an anagram, either, because she added the letter Y and left out a few other letters."

Gavin stuck his tongue out at Margaret. "See? You're wrong, too."

Margaret rolled her eyes.

Carrot leaned forward and studied her screen. Shaking her head, she said, "But Tracy is a high school student. Maybe she's not supposed to be me after all. These high school kids can't be us."

Dawna said, "Think about it, Carrot. Don't you think there are a lot of similarities between what happens around here and what it's like in high school?" She laughed. "Just look around you. We've got all the high school clichés. Gavin and Margaret are always competing to be Teacher's Pet. Jesse is obviously the Class Clown. Karl is the quiet, weird kid who snaps one day and blows up the chemistry lab. And then Zinnia, well, she's the classic wallflower."

Zinnia felt the sting of Dawna's joking insult. Classic wallflower? Was that how the others saw her? Surely there were better high school clichés to describe her, such as whatever you called a conservative, sensible person who actually did her job. Maybe a nerd? Or, better, yet, the smart girl who accidentally gets stuck in the popular clique?

The others were chuckling over Dawna's labels. The only two not laughing were Zinnia and Carrot.

"I never went to high school," Carrot said. "I was homeschooled."

This new tidbit about Carrot's upbringing came as no surprise to anyone.

Gavin snickered. "That explains a lot."

Dawna waved a hand at Gavin and turned to Carrot. "Girl, you didn't miss out on anything. High school was the worst. I was best friends with this girl who was always breaking up with her boyfriend." She rolled her eyes. "The drama! They'd be fighting one minute and making out by the lockers by the next class."

Margaret and Zinnia exchanged a knowing look.

Jesse came out of his office to join the conversation. He eyed Zinnia's desk but didn't come over. He leaned up against his doorway, standing behind Gavin.

"Looks like you're right about where I'm at," Jesse said to Gavin, looking at his screen.

Dawna asked Jesse, "Did you two get to the part where all the kids find out their magic powers?"

Carrot covered her ears with both hands and squealed, "Spoilers!"

Dawna said, "Carrot, keep your ears covered and don't listen for a minute."

Carrot kept her hands over her ears and started humming.

Dawna got to her feet and waved her hands as though beginning a prepared announcement. "Get this, everyone. So, Dawna—I mean Wanda—is a pretty amazing person in the book. She does this thing where she reads Tarot cards and predicts the future. She also does this other cool thing where she picks out winning scratch-off tickets."

Gavin wrinkled his nose and asked, "What are scratch-off tickets?"

Dawna sighed. "You know. Like the ones I buy at the gas station."

"You mean the instant win tickets you always win money on?"

Everyone went quiet and stared at Dawna. She did talk about scratch-off tickets a lot.

Dawna pulled at her collar. She suddenly looked very uncomfortable. Zinnia wondered, was that how Dawna could afford all her designer purses? Did the real-life Dawna share her character's magic ability with scratch-n-win lottery tickets?

"I'm just lucky," Dawna said, her voice high and squeaky. "If you buy enough of those things, you're bound to get lucky sooner or later."

Gavin's eyes narrowed. One at a time, he picked up the personal items on Dawna's desk and named them. "Jade plant. Four-leaf clover. White elephant." He stared up at her as though seeing his on-again-off-again girlfriend in a new light. "These are all symbols of good luck."

Dawna, still standing, put her hands on her hips. "So? Who doesn't like being lucky?"

Gavin rubbed his chin thoughtfully. "I'm starting to wonder if Annette was onto something. Maybe you *do* have some sort of magical ability when it comes to picking winners."

Dawna's eyes widened and she bobbed her head from side to side. "Oh, yeah? If I'm so good at picking winners, then why'd I pick you? Hmm?"

Everyone laughed.

When the frivolity died down, Carrot spoke up. "The magic powers are pretty funny." She dropped her hands away from her ears. "I could still hear you through my hands, but that's okay. I skipped ahead a bit, so I already know about Tracy being a rune mage. That Annette sure had a wild imagination. Tracy works her magic mainly by putting tattoos on people." Carrot put her elbows on her desk and rested her chin on her hands. Her expression was dreamy. "Maybe one day when I finally open a tattoo parlor, I'll tell people I give magical rune tattoos."

"I'd pay for that," Jesse said. "You can give me one of your magical rune tattoos around my bicep."

"Me, too," Gavin said. "Carrot, I want magical rune tattoos on *both* biceps."

"Silly Gavin," Dawna interrupted in a singsong voice. "You're a gnome, and gnomes don't get tattoos, because it affects their ability to teleport."

Gavin choked on the water he'd been drinking.

While he coughed, Dawna explained, "Y'all aren't there yet in the book, but—spoiler alert—Gavin's character is a gnome."

"I am not," Gavin said indignantly, wiping his mouth with his sleeve. "I'm six foot two. I'm not a gnome. Who ever heard of a six-foot gnome?"

"Don't shoot the messenger," Dawna said. "You can blame Annette and her wild imagination. You do know your character is Nivag, right?

"No kidding," Gavin said flatly. "Nivag is Gavin backwards. I figured that out instantly."

Dawna asked, "Did you get to the part where everyone finds out Nivag is a gnome?"

Gavin frowned. "Obviously not." He looked directly at Zinnia, locking eyes with her and glowering.

Zinnia averted her gaze and pretended to be concerned with some loose stationery on her desk.

Jesse said, "Nivag the gnome. I like it." He patted Gavin on the shoulder. "New nickname for you, Gavin?"

Gavin pulled away from Jesse's hand and got to his feet. He pointed at Zinnia and Margaret's shared work space. "Oh, yeah? If I'm a gnome, then what are they? What are Margaret and Zinnia?"

Zinnia tensed, expecting the worst. If Annette had pegged Gavin as a gnome, Carrot as a rune mage, and Dawna as a cartomancer, what were the odds she had guessed—or known—the powers of the two office witches?

Everyone looked at Dawna expectantly.

"They're both witches," Dawna said breezily. "Margaret and Zinnia are witches."

Zinnia had to remind herself to keep breathing. At hearing her secret revealed, she'd nearly turned to stone. Margaret had a more violent reaction. She sent a dozen shin kicks under the desk at Zinnia, rapid-fire.

Zinnia let out a startled pain yip.

Margaret began to laugh in a high, hysterical pitch. Zinnia joined her. Was she laughing too loud? Not loud enough? Would someone change the topic, please?

Everyone stared at Zinnia and Margaret. Dawna looked thrilled. Gavin looked smug. Jesse's facial muscles kept moving, like he didn't know how to feel, let alone react.

Zinnia stifled her fake laughter and quickly asked Dawna, "What about Karl?" If nobody else was going to change the topic, she would. "Dawna, what kind of powers does Karl have?"

Dawna smirked. "I don't want to spoil it for everyone."

Zinnia said, "Feel free to spoil away. I promise I'll still read the book, even if I know some of the twists. With my favorite stories, I love re-reading them, and knowing the twists can actually make everything better."

Dawna bounced her eyebrows excitedly. "Okay. Everyone's gonna love this." She relished the attention for a few seconds. "Karl is a troll named Lark."

Everyone glanced around at each other before slowly nodding. Karl was a troll named Lark. It was perfect.

Jesse circled around Gavin and Dawna's shared work station to peer at Dawna's computer screen. "What's my power in the book? Can you show me?"

"Oh, it's boring," Dawna said with a hand wave. "You might have guessed that already, since your character's name is also Jesse."

Jesse slouched and lolled his head to one side, conveying disappointment. "I guess my secrets weren't juicy enough for Annette to scramble my name."

"Your name is tough," Dawna said apologetically. "She couldn't have done much with J-E-S-S-E."

Jesse grimaced. "How lame are my powers? You can tell me. I can take it." He took a seat on her desk.

"How lame? More like no powers at all." Dawna scratched her chin with her long orange fingernails. "Jesse in the book is a lot like the narrator, because neither of them have any special skills. Maybe it's something Annette was saving up for the sequel." She waved her hand. "Either way, Jesse doesn't do much, except stop some bullying in the high school. He does win a swimming tournament, but that's about it."

Jesse shrugged. "I'm okay with that. And I am a good swimmer, so she got that right."

Dawna was about to say something else, but the ringing of a bell interrupted her. Everyone turned toward the front counter.

Nobody was there.

"That's strange," Margaret said. "I swear I heard the bell ring."

Suddenly, a hand appeared over the top of the front counter. Carrot shrieked. The hand swatted the service bell repeatedly.

The voice of an older gentleman called out, "Who do I have to stab around here to get some service?" Then he cursed all municipal employees in general for good measure.

Everyone rushed up to the counter and looked over the edge to see a familiar customer. It was Randall Wheelchuck, also known around town as Old Man Wheelie. He sat on his trusty mobility scooter, which he had managed to ride in without alerting the staff to his presence.

"This is my least favorite time of year," Wheelchuck ranted. "Every January, I have to come to this godforsaken office to get the permit for my godforsaken Class Three Invalid Carriage, which is an offensive term as far as I'm concerned." He blinked up at them from his seat on the scooter. "Why are you all staring at me? Did I roll through something stinky?" He made a show of checking his wheels and sniffing loudly.

"We didn't hear you come in," Carrot said, wringing her hands.

"Of course not! You were all wagging your chins about some nonsense." He leaned left and right, looking through them. "Where's the only person who knows what's going on around here? The woman. The sexy one with the big eyes and the brown curly hair." He snapped his fingers.

"Annette Scholem. That's her name. What have you done with her?"

CHAPTER 15

ONE YEAR AGO

10:15 AM

On Randall Wheelchuck's previous visit to the Wisteria Permits Department, it had also been Carrot Greyson who'd tried to assist the man. Her desk, which was one of the two smaller ones that weren't shared with another coworker, was closest to the reception counter. Zinnia judged that by the way Carrot jumped up without hesitation, she was the one who helped the majority of the walk-in customers. Zinnia had been working in the office for a few days now, and she was starting to get a feel for how things worked.

Zinnia liked Carrot. The young woman had an unusual appearance, with her many tattoos, and her cute little bug eyes, and her bright orange hair, but she was a dedicated worker who didn't create drama. Zinnia could see the two of them becoming friends over time.

That morning, the orange-haired young woman leaned across the tall counter to speak down to an older gentleman who'd arrived on a mobility scooter.

He muttered something Zinnia couldn't hear.

"This isn't the right department for the permit you want," Carrot said. "I'm so sorry for any misunderstanding."

His voice rose up loud enough for everyone to hear clearly. "You're not sorry, and this is not a misunderstanding."

Carrot said, "Um."

Zinnia felt sorry for the young woman, but Zinnia was so new there, she didn't feel it would be her place to come to Carrot's assistance. Not yet, anyway.

The man demanded, "What the heck happened to your hair? That's the same color as a mango. It's not a color the good Lord intended hair to be."

Zinnia suppressed a smirk. The man had a point.

Carrot said, "Um, sir, my hair is an expression of how I feel. And I'm truly sorry, but we can't issue you the permit for your scooter."

"You could if you wanted to! If you tried harder, I bet you could!" He took a break from yelling to mutter, "Lazy government employees."

"Um..." Carrot glanced over her shoulder at her coworkers, who were all watching the exchange. That was, everyone except for Gavin Gorman, who was pretending to work. Gavin had, from what Zinnia had observed over her first few days, "selective hearing" when it came to anyone needing help at the front counter.

The old man continued ranting. "Just give me my permit so I can get out of this godforsaken building! This place is haunted, did you know that?"

Carrot's voice trembled. "Haunted? City Hall?"

"That's right," he said, with a dash of mischief in his gruff voice. "Haunted by the spirits of municipal employees who didn't do their jobs, and got what they had coming to them!"

Carrot's hands fluttered like birds before she clutched them to her chest. "Sir, is that a threat?"

"Of course not!" He waved both hands in the air. His hands were the only part of him Zinnia could see from her seat at her desk, but she had a good idea of what the man looked like based on his voice and personality.

He yelled, "Just give me my godforsaken permit and I'll be outta your hair *tooty-sweet*. You know what tooty-sweet means, don't you? It's French."

"Oh," Carrot said with interest, as though he wasn't a raving lunatic at all. "I know tutti frutti, but not that one."

But Zinnia did. The man's version of *tout de suite*, a French expression for *immediately*, came out sounding like tooty-sweet. Under more pleasant circumstances, his funny mispronunciation would be charming. Zinnia had enjoyed the way her niece, Zara, had said the word hamburger as a child. *Hangaburger*. She wondered, what was Zara up to these days? The little girl was all grown up now, in her thirties. The last time they'd seen each other had been at the funeral. Poor thing. Raising her child all by herself. It was a shame the Riddle family wasn't closer. Zinnia might have been able to guide Zara in some way, help her avoid the same mistakes she'd made.

As Zinnia's mind wandered, the older gentleman continued to argue with Carrot about everything from the education level of kids her age to the temperature of the reception area and lack of accessibility within the town in general.

Zinnia's ears perked up again when she heard the man demand, "And why's it called City Hall, anyway? Wisteria is a town, not a city. This building should be called Town Hall. Why is it City Hall? Well? Can you answer me that?"

Carrot, flummoxed, turned to her coworkers for help.

Zinnia tilted her head to the side, equally flummoxed. She was new to the office, but not to Wisteria, and yet she didn't know the answer. Why *was* the big municipal building called City Hall? She'd never given it a second thought until now.

Dawna, however, had something to say. The stylish black woman got out of her chair and sauntered over to the reception desk. She leaned over it right next to Carrot. Zinnia noted that Dawna's nails were the same shade of orange as Carrot's hair, and Carrot's nails were black, matching Dawna's hair. Zinnia liked that they matched. She appreciated things that matched in general. It was good to take pleasure in the small synchronicities of life.

Dawna spoke in an exasperated yet civil tone. "Mr. Wheelchuck, we went over all of this last year when you came in. Number one, you need to go get your permit up at the DMV. That's the D-M-V. The Department of Motor

Vehicles. It's on the second floor." The man tried to interrupt, protesting that he knew what DMV stood for, but Dawna cut him off with her voice, growing louder. "Number two, the town's founding families laid out plans for a whopping big city, and they marked a spot on the map for this building as the City Hall site, so when folks built it, that's what it was called. And, more importantly," she put both of her hands around her mouth, like a bullhorn, "nobody 'round here cares what it's called!"

"You're too smart for your britches," the old guy said. He'd been pointing one gnarled finger at Dawna, and now he turned it to jab at Carrot. "And you're not smart enough for any britches. Whoever did that to your hair, I hope you made them pay for their crimes."

Dawna turned away from the man and returned to her desk, hands raised and head shaking. "I can't even," she said. "I. Can't. Even."

Carrot went back to apologizing to the customer and trying to convince him to go to the DMV. "It's only one floor up from here," she said.

"Does it look like I can take the stairs? I don't have any feet, orange-head! A sea monster bit my legs off at the calf. Have you ever seen a sea monster?"

Carrot turned to her coworkers again, her big blue eyes pleading.

Zinnia was new and uncertain, but she was willing to give it a shot. She started to rise from her chair when a hand landed on her shoulder, pressing her down and delivering a static shock of electricity at the same time. She looked up at the friendly face of Annette Scholem, the chatty older woman who'd been training her.

Annette winked at her. "Don't worry about this one, Nina." Annette had been calling Zinnia Nina all day. "I've been here six months longer than you, so I'll jump on this grenade, so to speak."

Annette walked gracefully toward the reception counter, arms outstretched so that her colorful jewel-toned caftan caught the breeze and fluttered. She looked like a beautiful butterfly swooping down to bring peace to all humankind in the midst of a bloody battle.

"Good afternoon," Annette chirped to the man.

"What's good about it?" he quipped back.

Annette tilted her head back and laughed, her curly brown hair shaking in a merry way.

She walked around to the other side of the counter, her colors fluttering. Her head and shoulders were still visible to Zinnia. She laughed once more, tipping both head and shoulders back, and then dropped from sight. She'd thoughtfully taken a seat in one of the reception chairs so she could be eye level with the man.

"Mr. Wheelchuck, my name is Annette Scholem," she said in a professional, friendly tone—not patronizing at all. "I'm fairly new here, but I believe I can help you with your request."

"I just want a permit," he said. He was still gruff, but not as loud.

"So I heard," she said. "Do you want to know a secret?"

He answered hesitantly. "Depends."

"I have a magic button, and it lets me access the permit applications for the DMV."

"Oh," he said, sounding both interested and surprised. "So, you're the smart one around here. Where's this button?"

"It's on my laptop," she said. "Carrot, will you bring me my laptop so I can help this gentleman?"

Carrot was only too happy to oblige. The laptop wasn't Annette's, technically. It was a banged-up old thing anyone could use if they had to work off-site. Carrot grabbed the hefty thing and brought it to Annette without a peep.

Annette and Mr. Wheelchuck continued to speak, but quieter now, so Zinnia couldn't catch all the words. She lost interest and returned to her work. Somehow, in between their chats about social activities, Annette had managed to train Zinnia on enough of the basics so that she might be able to put in a half-day's work.

Zinnia very quickly found the "magic button" to access the DMV permits. It turned out any one of them could have helped the man with his request after all, if they'd tried. Her heart dropped, feeling heavier than usual. She hated it when someone's accusations of laziness or ineptitude turned out to be true.

Dawna's chair squeaked as she rolled over to the work station Zinnia and Margaret shared. She was coming to see Zinnia, since Margaret wasn't at her desk at the moment. She'd been called away for some issue at one of her children's schools.

Dawna had her purse on her lap and was rummaging for something. "Gum?" She offered sugarless gum to Zinnia, who accepted a piece.

"Thanks," Zinnia said. "Sometimes I forget how much I like gum until someone offers me a piece."

"You don't keep gum in that big ol' purse of yours?"

"I like to keep it empty, just in case."

Dawna gave her a confused look. "You mean for packing around your thermos full o' tea?"

"Exactly," Zinnia said. *And sometimes eyeballs of various sizes. Plus powders and ointments and salves. Just the usual witch stuff.* She put the gum in her mouth. "Mmm. Good gum. Thank you." Zinnia hoped she wasn't being too strange. What did people say to each other while sharing gum at an office? She had no idea. Her casual socializing skills were rusty. "Mmm," she said again. "Really good gum."

Dawna chuckled and slapped the half-full pack onto Zinnia's desk. "Here. Keep the rest, New Girl. I've got plenty."

They chewed gum and listened to the pleasant sound of Annette's voice as she soothed the savage beast at reception.

"It's just one of those days," Dawna said. "We get a difficult walk-in about once a week. You'll get used to it." She looked pointedly at Margaret's empty seat. "Too bad your friend Margaret wasn't here. She has a real knack for chasing them off."

I'm sure she does, Zinnia thought but didn't say.

"At least we always have Annette," Dawna said.

"She must have an endless supply of patience," Zinnia said.

"I'll say," Dawna replied. "That woman is a saint. The only way I was going to help that man was with the back side of my hand." She shrugged. "Or the front of my hand. Slaps are pretty effective. It must be the noise it makes. Slap! Smartens 'em right up."

Zinnia giggled. She didn't usually laugh at threats of violence, and she couldn't remember ever slapping anyone, but Dawna's enthusiasm was contagious.

Dawna looked down at her purse and zipped some interior pockets. Zinnia caught a glimpse of a designer label. Unless she was mistaken, the purse was the type that cost more than a good used car. How did someone on a municipal support-staff salary afford a purse like that?

"Hello?" Dawna waved her hand in front of Zinnia's face. The orange nails were startling, coming toward Zinnia's face that way. They looked strong and sharp.

"Sorry," Zinnia said. "I was just in a daze, admiring your purse."

"It's a knockoff," Dawna said quickly. She whipped the purse off her lap and slung it from the back of her chair. She seemed about to roll away but didn't. In a whisper, she asked, "Hey, what do you think of Gavin?"

"He seems nice," Zinnia said politely, which was exactly what any sane person in her position would have said.

"We hook up sometimes," Dawna said. "Annette doesn't approve."

"She doesn't?" Zinnia hadn't taken Annette for the sort of woman who intruded on other people's romantic lives.

"She thinks I should find someone better than Gavin. She offered to go out as my wingwoman sometime. You know what a wingwoman is, right?"

Zinnia smiled patiently. "I may be a few years older than you, but I'm well aware of wingmen and wingwomen."

The main door creaked open. The clip-clop of Margaret's boots announced her return. "I'm ba-a-a-ack," she sang as she returned to her desk. "It turns out two of my least bright children were caught running an illegal gambling ring, betting on hamster races at the school."

Dawna let out a low whistle. "Sounds to me like those two are a couple of smart cookies. When it comes to gambling, it's the bookies who make the money."

"You may be right," Margaret said as she dropped wearily into her seat. "It's a shame they weren't smart enough to not get caught, the little monsters." She leaned to the side and looked at the back of Dawna's chair. "New purse, Dawna?"

"This old thing?" Dawna grabbed the purse and tucked it under her arm as she wheeled her chair away. "Secondhand. Bought it online from one of those auction sites."

Zinnia opened her mouth to ask Dawna why she would buy a knockoff through an auction but stopped herself. Clearly, Dawna was lying about the purse. There was no point in catching her in the lie and embarrassing her. Zinnia would simply file the detail away in her Dawna file.

Within seconds, Dawna's place next to Zinnia's desk was taken by Karl Kormac. His inexpensive suit was already looking more wrinkled than it had been when he'd arrived two hours earlier. Karl leaned across the desk and lifted the lid on a jar of candies that had been sitting there when Zinnia had started working there.

"Don't mind if I do," Karl said to no one in particular, grabbing a handful of sweets. He popped one into his mouth and asked Zinnia, "How's our new hire working out?"

"Great, thank you," Zinnia said. "Annette did a great job showing me how to use the system."

Karl sucked noisily on the candy, clunking it against his teeth. "She is an amazing woman," he said. He glanced over at reception, where Annette was still helping the elderly customer, who was now laughing along with her. Karl said, "That Annette Scholem certainly knows how to soothe the savage beast."

Zinnia said, "That's funny. I was just thinking the exact same thing."

"You must be psychic," Karl said.

Across the desk from Zinnia, Margaret sniggered.

* * *

2:35 PM

(STILL ONE YEAR AGO)

Jesse Berman meandered out of his office and looked around the open area where most of the department employees worked. His office, like Karl's, was separate from the others, due to either his seniority or the complexity of the special buildings permits he worked on. Zinnia hadn't yet learned which.

His eyes, a boyish shade of bright blue, stopped roving when they found the candy jar on Zinnia's desk. He walked toward the candy as though being pulled by a tractor beam. He leaned his tall, muscular frame across the desk and lifted the lid off the jar. Zinnia could look away, but she couldn't help but smell him. The scent of his skin was intoxicating. He was a dozen years younger than her, pulsating with vitality. His dark brown hair was short, but not too short. He had a stubborn curl that made the longer hair on top swirl this way and that. His head was only inches from hers. She could reach up and tousle his hair so easily, if she wanted to. What would it feel like to run her fingers through those thick, dark locks? Her whole body felt warm. Was she having a hot flash? No! It had to be Jesse's presence. Either that or the office's wonky heating system was hot flashing everyone.

Zinnia pretended to be fascinated by something on her computer screen. It was the interdepartmental TPS reports. So interesting! She could be a good actor when she needed to.

"You know, this desk of yours has a certain reputation," Jesse said.

She tore her gaze from the TPS reports, met his eyes, and got lost in their bright blue waters. "My desk?"

"Your desk is the sweet spot."

She felt her cheeks flushing. "Oh?"

"Thanks to your predecessor," he said, smiling. His teeth were straight and white, but not scary blue-white like Gavin's.

"My predecessor was sweet?"

"Sweet enough to keep a jar of sweets." He unwrapped a hard candy, bright yellow, and rolled it between his fingers. Zinnia smelled the lemon flavor wafting off the candy. Her mouth watered.

"Sweet enough to keep a jar of sweets," she repeated.

Jesse continued to smile. "Hey, how many times do you think we can say the word *sweets* in a conversation?" He paused and added flirtatiously, "Sweets?"

Her cheeks no longer felt hot. They had to be on fire. Actually burning.

Across the desk, Margaret groaned, "Get a room."

Jesse straightened up, put one hand on his hip, and said to Margaret in a mocking tone, "Jealous?"

She snorted. "Jesse Berman, the only reputation that desk has is that you and Karl visit it three times a day, and it costs one third of our petty cash fund to keep filling it with candy."

"Everyone eats the candy," Jesse said. "Especially you."

She snorted again. "I never, ever, ever touch that candy." It wasn't true. Zinnia had watched Margaret stuff a handful in her mouth that very morning, right after her kids' school had called about the hamster racing.

Jesse winked at her. "Sure you don't." He gave Zinnia a wink as well. "See you later, keeper of the sweets."

After he'd returned to his office, Margaret fixed Zinnia with a serious look.

"What?" Zinnia rearranged the perfectly square office supplies on her desk. Margaret was probably about to say something bossy. Zinnia had an overwhelming urge to hit Margaret on the head with a pad of Post-It notes. Their relationship was a complicated one, and it would feel good to finally clear the air with a bit of old fashioned witch-on-witch pummeling.

"That's my warning look," Margaret said. "It's also good for confessions. I give the look, and my kids feel guilty about whatever it is they've done and promise not to do it again." Her expression got even more focused and serious.

"But I haven't done anything wrong," Zinnia said.

"Steer clear of Jesse Berman. He's a heart breaker. He and Carrot had a thing for a while."

Carrot? Zinnia glanced over at the young, orange-haired woman, seeing her in a new light.

Margaret said, "He called it a casual, just-friends thing. But Carrot, being Carrot, started to fall in love." Margaret got a far-away look in her eyes. "Ah, young love."

"Are they still involved?"

"Not at all. He broke her heart, and she was a mess. More so than usual. But she's okay now. She's seeing someone else, a guy named Sefu that everyone calls Steve. He's a bit skinny for my taste, but he is polite. And he's a lawyer. As far as I'm concerned, she totally upgraded."

Zinnia turned and studied the orange-haired young woman with the tattoos peeking out from under her shirt. Was that Jesse's type? She was such a meek little thing, like a damsel in constant distress. Zinnia had liked Carrot, but now, in the light of this revelation, she reminded Zinnia of a shivering Chihuahua.

"Now you understand why I gave you the warning look," Margaret said.

Zinnia shrugged. "Carrot is a bit young for him, anyway."

Margaret chortled. "And Jesse is a bit young for you."

"We ought to let him be the judge of that."

Margaret's look of warning turned to one of surprise, and then shifted further, into something like... admiration?

"You go, girl," Margaret said. Admiration it was.

They both got back to work.

An hour later, Annette came over to their work station for some candy and to check on Zinnia.

"Look at you go," Annette said, watching Zinnia type. "You're a fast typist. How many words per minute is that?"

"Oh, about a hundred, give or take," Zinnia said, pretending she didn't know. She regularly clocked one hundred twenty words a minute, but didn't want to brag.

Annette patted her on the shoulder. "I'm glad we hired you, Nina."

Zinnia's typing slowed. Was Nina a common nickname for Zinnia? She didn't think so. A few people had tried calling her Nia, but it hadn't stuck.

"Nina, how do you feel about bowling?" Annette had a hopeful expression.

"I don't have *any* feelings about bowling," Zinnia said. It was true. She had zero feelings about bowling.

"You'll love it," Annette gushed. She looked over at Margaret and said, "What do you think, Margaret? Now that Nina has filled our empty desk, we have enough people to meet league regulations."

"Great," Margaret said flatly. "Also, her name is Zinnia, not Nina."

Annette laughed merrily and apologized to Zinnia for calling her the wrong name. "It's just how my silly ol' brain works," she explained. "The letters of people's names get mixed around. Don't you worry, Nina. I'll get it right eventually." And she did. After a few months.

CHAPTER 16

NOW

FRIDAY, 10:15 AM

It was Friday, at last. The Wisteria Permits Department had almost made it to the weekend without losing another person—not since Karl's departure, anyway. It would be nice for everyone to wake up tomorrow morning and finally have a day away from the place where their coworker had been killed by a wolf.

"Coffee break," Dawna announced at quarter past ten. She stood and looked around at everyone expectantly. "Why's everyone still sitting? I said it's coffee break time. If you wanted to work through coffee break, y'all should have become entrepreneurs."

Carrot slowly got to her feet. "Entrepreneurs? I don't get it."

Dawna sighed. "We get two paid breaks plus lunch. People who work for themselves don't get paid breaks."

"Why wouldn't they give themselves paid breaks?" Carrot frowned. "One day when I open my tattoo studio, I'll give myself paid breaks."

Dawna pulled her head back in surprise. "Your tattoo studio? Girl, that book of Annette's has really gone to your head!"

Carrot gave her a sweet, bashful smile. "I think it has."

"Good for you!" Dawna offered her a high-five. Carrot slapped her hand tentatively.

Dawna asked, "Do you need any start-up money?"

Carrot said, "I asked my brother, Ishmael, for a loan. He's got a pretty good job, I think. He won't tell anyone in the family what it is. He might be doing something illegal."

"That doesn't sound good," Dawna said. "You don't want money that's tainted."

"It doesn't matter, because Ishmael said no. But my uncle, Arden, might help me out."

Dawna said, "Great. Let's get some fresh coffee, and you can tell me all about this generous family member of yours. Is Uncle Arden dating anyone?"

"Just his dog," Carrot said. "Oops. I didn't mean that the way it came out. He's just very close to his dog, Doodles."

"That's sweet. I love a man who's kind to animals. So, Uncle Arden isn't dating anyone human?"

"No," Carrot said, leading the way to the break room. "And he's actually my great-uncle."

Dawna followed, talking about how it was just as easy to love a rich man as a poor one.

Zinnia looked over at Gavin for his reaction to Dawna's hunt for a sugar daddy.

Gavin said, defensively, "We're on a break, okay?"

"Sorry to hear it," Zinnia said, even though she had no feelings about yet another Dawna-Gavin breakup.

Margaret said, "Don't worry. You can get her back. Just think." Margaret pretended to think hard, her chin on her fist. "What would Nivag the Gnome do?"

Gavin frowned. "He'd stomp his foot three times to get away from the two of you witches."

"Do it," Margaret said, still pretending to think hard with her chin on her fist. "Stomp your foot for us, Nivag. Let's see if you're a real gnome."

Gavin gave her a dirty look and walked away.

Jesse emerged from his office, yawning. "Coffee break?"

Margaret waved him toward the break room. "Go ahead. I need a minute to discuss something with Zinnia in private."

Jesse leaned against his door frame. "Something juicy? Office gossip?"

Margaret said, "Just female stuff. About female things."

"Ew." Jesse faked disgust and left for the break room.

Zinnia said to Margaret, "Good one."

"The threat of hearing about female stuff works on males of all ages."

Zinnia grabbed her thermos and opened the lid. She was already out of tea.

Margaret said, "So? You didn't call me last night."

"I was reading Annette's book."

"Me, too. Most of it, anyway." She stifled a yawn. "Did you hear from Fung? What did he say about you-know-who and her pet wolf, and her animal scratch tattoo?"

"He hasn't called me back."

"Figures." Margaret looked in the direction of the break room. The others were laughing about something. Tattoos, maybe. Or the idea of Dawna dating Carrot's great-uncle.

Zinnia shuffled some papers on her desk, accidentally knocking her pen to the floor. She looked at the pen, remembering her experiments with Annette's pen.

She picked it up and said to Margaret, "I should go to the station with Annette's pen. I don't think it's charmed in any way, and I've got no idea why Gavin was after it, but who knows? It might mean something to Fung."

"No!" Margaret exclaimed, her eyes wide with alarm. "Don't do that. They'll put it in an evidence box and we'll never see it again."

"Maybe that's where it belongs."

"Give Annette's writing pen to me." Margaret rubbed her hands together the way she did when she knew there was birthday cake waiting in the break room. "I want it."

"You only want it because Gavin wants it."

"Sure, but so what? At least I'd hold onto it. If Gavin got his grubby little gnome hands on it and figured out the secret, he'd sell it to the highest bidder in a heartbeat. Gnomes aren't sentimental, except about money."

"You're assuming he is a gnome," Zinnia said sagely. "We don't know for sure that he is."

"His uncle is a gnome. Griebel Gorman."

"Yes, but as you know, blood lineage isn't everything. Magic has its own plans."

Margaret was still rubbing her hands together. "It simply cannot be a coincidence that Annette made him a gnome in her book."

She was right. Plus, there was the troublesome detail that Annette had cast Zinnia and Margaret as a pair of witches named Nina and Gretta. Zinnia had read the whole book last night. There was no doubt in her mind about Nina and Gretta. Aside from the fact they were teenagers, they were obviously based on the two real-life witches.

Zinnia asked, "How do you think Annette knew about... Nina and Gretta?"

Margaret raised both hands. "Don't look at me. I didn't tell her nothin'. I barely knew the woman."

"You knew her longer than I did."

"Only by a few months, really. She started working here in August, year before last. I remember the date because she was sitting in here by herself when we all got back from Jesse's father's funeral. Nobody told her we'd be starting late that day." Margaret smiled at the memory. "She didn't know which desk was hers, so she was working on the reception area couch with that old laptop."

"Because she didn't want to offend someone by sitting at their desk?" Zinnia smiled as well. She hadn't heard that story before. "That Annette. She was a special lady."

They sat in silence for a moment, honoring their friend.

Suddenly, an acoustic ceiling tile over Annette's desk came loose and landed on her empty desk with a loud THWAP.

Margaret and Zinnia ran over to see what had happened. The others in the break room had either not heard the crash or hadn't cared to investigate.

A sheaf of papers were drifting down from the rectangular hole in the ceiling, fluttering like white butterflies marked with blue handwriting.

It took only a few seconds for the two witches to determine that it was the first draft of Annette's novel, written in pen.

Margaret clutched some gathered pages to her chest. "We need to read this," she said breathlessly. "Annette wants us to. The way it fell from the ceiling like that. It's got to be a message from the other side."

Zinnia looked up at the ceiling. Several other ceiling tiles were crooked and looked ready to fall at any moment. It could have been a message from the other side, or it could have been physics. Either way, she did want to read the handwritten pages, so she didn't argue with Margaret.

The other witch was already grabbing her purse and coat. "I'm taking it to get scanned somewhere else, like that chain photocopy place. I'll get us both copies, then I'll take the original to the police station." She waved her hand and answered a question Zinnia hadn't asked. "It's not like the pen. We can make copies of this, so it doesn't matter if it sits in an evidence box."

"Relax. I agree with your plan," Zinnia said. "But why don't you scan it here? We have that fancy fax machine that does everything but make toast."

Margaret shook her head. "I'm doing it somewhere they don't know me. I don't trust anyone right now. I barely trust you."

Zinnia's jaw dropped. What had *she* done? Besides pelting Margaret with office supplies and trussing her up like a mummy.

"You took the pen home without even showing it to me," Margaret said, once again answering a question that hadn't been asked—not out loud, anyway.

That's the thing about witches with psychic powers. They're always having conversations with what's been left unsaid. It's rarely appreciated by others, unless they're also witches.

Margaret hustled out the door with the handwritten notes.

* * *

Zinnia walked into the break room without Margaret. Nobody commented on the other woman's absence. Dawna, Gavin, Carrot, and Jesse were still discussing tattoos.

Carrot looked up and asked Zinnia, "What kind of tattoo would you get?" All eyes were on Zinnia.

Zinnia shrugged one shoulder girlishly. "What makes you think I don't have one already?"

Gavin guffawed and lifted his fresh coffee to his lips.

"A feeling," Carrot said, her eyes glazing over. "I feel like I've seen you naked before."

Gavin snorted, shooting two streams of fresh coffee out of his nostrils. Everyone laughed. Gavin grabbed paper towels and started mopping up the mess.

Dawna asked Carrot, "Why would you say something like that about Zinnia?"

Carrot's cheeks flushed. "I don't know. I have a lot of strange dreams."

Jesse took a paper towel from Gavin and dabbed at his sleeve where Gavin had sprayed coffee. Gavin didn't apologize.

Jesse waggled his eyebrows at Carrot. "Do you ever have dreams about me?"

"Yes," she said without hesitation. "Just the other night, I dreamed you were flexing for someone, trying to impress them."

Dawna said, "That sounds more like something Gavin would do. Are you sure it wasn't him?"

Indignantly, Gavin said, "Excuse me? I don't flex."

"It was definitely Jesse," Carrot said wistfully. "I'd know those blue eyes anywhere."

Dawna leaned back in her chair and crossed her arms. "Don't start dreaming your dreams about me, Carrot. I like my privacy."

Carrot self-consciously twirled her orange hair around one finger and looked around the room.

Zinnia wanted to leave the break room, but it was too late for that. She pulled out a chair and joined her coworkers at the table. Gavin kept staring at her. She gave him a squinty look. "Stop trying to picture me naked," she said.

Gavin's cheeks flushed. "I wasn't," he said.

Everyone laughed again. Jesse opened his mouth to say something. By the twinkle in his eyes, Zinnia guessed he was going to say something else about her naked body. Luckily for Zinnia's reputation, he was cut off by Carrot asking the group, "Hey, so what does everyone think about Annette's book? I stayed up late to finish reading it. We all did, right?"

People murmured but nobody spoke up.

"Come on," Carrot said. "We should talk about the book, right? Isn't that why Dawna wanted us all to read it?"

Jesse, never one to give up on a joke easily, said, "Let's get back to your dreams about Zinnia naked."

Another round of laughter.

Zinnia adjusted the collar of her blouse. "That's enough, everyone. I'm still here. At least have the decency to talk about me behind my back."

More chortling.

"Okay. We can talk about the book," Gavin said. "I would say... it wasn't bad."

Carrot said, "It was really good." She quickly added, "For a make-believe novel."

Gavin said, "Carrot, all novels are make-believe."

She frowned at him. "I meant that it's science fiction."

"It's fantasy," Gavin said. "Did you even read it?"

She stuck her tongue out childishly. Gavin returned the gesture."

Jesse said, "It's a shame it won't get published."

Dawna said, "Actually, I was talking to Annette's cousin, and the family might be able to publish it *posturally*."

Gavin corrected her. "You mean *posthumously*."

"That's what I said," Dawna said, eyes flashing.

Nobody corrected her a second time.

"I'll buy a copy," Carrot said. "Ooh! I could buy a whole box and give them as gifts."

Jesse blew over his steaming coffee and said, "It probably won't sell very many copies. I've been asking around, and nobody's heard of AJ Scholem. Not even at the local bookstores."

"I had to special-order the other ones," Dawna said. Everyone looked at her. She explained, "I'm reading all of Annette's older books to see if there are any more clues in there to solve her murder."

Gavin groaned. "Dawna, it was a wild animal attack, not a murder. Will you let it go already? There aren't any clues to be found. This isn't one of those murder mystery party games. It's real life, and the case is closed. Remember how we got that memo yesterday to check the windows? That was the end of it."

Dawna crossed her arms and glared at him. Oh, they were definitely broken up again.

The room was quiet.

Everyone remained subdued until the coffee break was over. People started tidying up their coffee mugs and preparing to get back to work.

Jesse paused, looking at the calendar on the fridge. "Hey, gang," he said with a mild note of alarm. "It's Friday today, right?"

"All day long," Gavin said. He was the kind of guy who always said "all day long" instead of simply answering yes to the day of the week question. He didn't get to say it often, because if Karl was around, he'd jump on it first, but today was Gavin's lucky day.

"We've got bowling league tonight," Jesse said.

Everyone stopped in their tracks and looked at each other. They'd all forgotten. Should they go? Should they carry on in Annette's honor, or cancel out of respect?

Zinnia was eager to get home and start reading the handwritten version of Annette's book, in case it contained the secret of how she'd known or guessed that two of her coworkers were witches. But Zinnia did have the whole weekend to do that, minus Saturday night's dinner at Jesse's. The book could wait. It wasn't going anywhere. In fact, she would cast a steadfast spell on her scanned pages to make sure stray ghosts didn't mess with it.

After a discussion, the group unanimously agreed that since Annette was the one who had initiated the bowling league, they should go. They were short a couple of players, since Annette was dead and Karl was taking some vacation days, but they still had six bowlers. The league would allow them to play. The scores wouldn't count toward their average, but nobody really cared about their average except for Annette.

"Then it's settled," Jesse said. "Tonight, the Incredibowls will knock down some pins. Hey, maybe we'll beat the Wisteria Wizards."

"Not without Karl," Gavin said.

The others murmured in agreement. Say what you wished about Karl Kormac, the man could bowl.

* * *

By the end of the work day, Zinnia was dreading the bowling night. Why had she agreed to go? They all were probably feeling the same way, but wouldn't admit it. Who wants to spend more time with their coworkers after five o'clock on a Friday? Only a person like Annette, which was why she'd organized the team. What a strange and lovely woman she had been.

Margaret dropped a storage stick on Zinnia's desk as she walked by. "Here's a digital copy of that *document* we discussed," she said.

"Where's the original now?"

"At the, uh, customer's workplace."

That meant Detective Fung had it.

Margaret turned off her computer monitor and started packing up for the day. "I tried running the character recognition software so I could convert it into searchable text, but the original handwriting was too messy."

"That's too bad." Zinnia tidied her desk as well. "Smart of you to try." She thought about how long it would take to read the same book again in messy handwriting. Probably the whole weekend. She would only be reading it to figure out how Annette had known their secret powers. She doubted there'd be anything in the original draft that would shed light on what had happened to Annette.

The book itself was just a typical novel for the young adult crowd. It was enjoyable and well written, as far as those things went. There was the standard plucky orphan pitted against the super-nasty villain. Aside from the characters who'd been inspired by Annette's office mates, it didn't feel realistic. The bad guy, a kidnapper with a sadistic streak, was not evil in a believable way. He was just a wee bit too evil. Twirling-his-mustache evil.

Five o'clock arrived. Everyone got ready to leave in absolute silence, which was not typical for a Friday, but then again, this was not a typical Friday.

The group of six walked out together and stood in the hallway while Margaret locked up.

Someone was approaching them. He called out, "Heading out to the staff parking lot?"

It was Xavier Batista, a cocky young man in his early twenties who worked in the building. Zinnia had seen him around, but didn't know him well.

Jesse replied, "Yes, we're just locking up and heading out."

"Good," Xavier said, and joined the group. "Don't you hate the whole month of January, how you get to work in the dark and then leave in the dark? It would be great... if we were all vampires, right?" He shuffled himself into the center of their group of six.

Jesse looked at the newcomer with curiosity. "Xavier, are you trying to merge with our pack? Careful what you wish for, buddy. We're heading straight to the bowling alley from here."

"Uh, no thanks to the bowling," Xavier said. "Unless you *want me* to come along." He looked directly at Carrot, who was about his age. He made goo-goo eyes at her.

Carrot, who'd been chewing her thumbnail, said coolly, "I have a boyfriend, Xavier."

"Same one as before?"

Carrot glanced at Jesse briefly then back at Xavier. "If you mean Sefu, then yes. He's quite dark-skinned. Kind of hard to miss in a town like this."

"I thought his name was Steve," Xavier said. "I guess that's sort of a nickname, huh? What is Sefu? Swahili?"

Jesse cleared his throat. "If you'll excuse us, Mr. Batista, we should be going to Shady Lanes. The latecomers have to buy rounds."

"Sure, sure," Xavier said. "I just thought we could watch each other's backs. That parking lot sure is dark."

Carrot said, "I can look after myself, Xavier."

"Didn't you hear? There was a second attack." Xavier paused. As he observed their looks of confusion, a smile crept onto his lips. "Another wolf attack," he said excitedly. "In broad daylight. At lunch time today."

Dawna made one of her pre-barfing hiccups. "Oh no," she said, pressing her hand to her mouth. "Not again."

Gavin's face got waxy. He asked, "Was it here? At City Hall?"

Xavier, still grinning, said, "No, man. It was at one of the schools. Some kids were playing behind their school, and a wolf come out of the woods and tackled a small boy. Don't worry, though. The kid's shaken up, but he's going to be okay."

A second attack! They all exchanged worried looks.

Jesse said, "Good thing we all stayed in for lunch today, or it might have been one of us."

"Good thing," Gavin said, frowning and looking more waxy.

Dawna hiccupped again.

Carrot became more pale.

Margaret muttered something almost imperceptible under her breath. Zinnia guessed she was rehearsing a spell in case they needed protection in the dark parking lot.

Jesse was the only one who didn't look concerned. He looked right at Carrot and grinned. "You're off the hook as a suspect, Carrot. If I recall correctly, you were with all of us in the office break room at lunch time, nibbling on a bean sprout and hummus sandwich. I can be your witness. You definitely weren't out with your pet wolf Alfie, hunting down another kill."

Carrot frowned. "That's not funny. I might have an alibi, but if people think it was Alfie, they'll grab their guns and start shooting wolves."

Gavin snorted. "Knowing the people in this town, they'll just shoot each other in the butts."

All three men started laughing.

"Good one," Xavier said. "It's funny because it's true."

Encouraged by Xavier, Jesse and Gavin worked together and did a short improvised show right there in the hallway, impersonating two local hicks going out to shoot a wolf and accidentally shooting each other in the butt.

"Ya done shot me, Jeremiah," Gavin said to Jesse, clutching his stomach and fighting laughter.

Jesse clutched his buttocks. "Ya done shot me, too. And I thought *you* were Jeremiah. If you're Jeremiah, what's my name?"

Gavin wheezed. "You're Jebediah, Jebediah." He moved his hands up to clutch his chest. "Ow! Ya done shot me again, Jebediah!"

"That's not funny," Carrot said. "I have twin cousins named Jeremiah and Jebediah. They're nothing like that. They're both vegans."

That only made everyone laugh harder. Dawna was no longer in any danger of being sick. She leaned on Zinnia's shoulder and wiped tears of laughter from her eyes. How she did it without stabbing herself with those long nails, Zinnia didn't know. Margaret was doubled over, hands on her knees. Zinnia felt something warm trying to sneak into her heart. Some unwanted emotion trying to blossom. Meanwhile, Xavier had joined the improv scene as a talking wolf who goaded the hunters about their marksmanship.

Despite the grim news about a wolf attacking a child, the mood had certainly lifted. Perhaps it would be a good night of bowling after all. Perhaps Annette's spirit was watching and smiling.

CHAPTER 17

SHADY LANES BOWLING AND ALES

5:45 PM

Shady Lanes was a twelve-lane classic-style bowling alley that had been owned and run by the same family for three generations. The youngest owner had recently expanded the building to add a microbrewery and pub next door. Rumor had it their most popular beer, Shady Lanes Shady Ale, was the most profitable part of the whole endeavor. The ale sold well nationally, and subsidized the bowling alley, which otherwise might have been shuttered.

A newcomer to Wisteria might have had a hard time distinguishing which parts of the bowling alley were original, and which had been lovingly "restored" to look even more 1950s than the actual 1950s.

The place was noisy, thanks to the rolling balls and crashing pins, but not too noisy, because they didn't blare music on the stereo. The lighting was soft and flattering, which made Shady Lanes a popular location for first dates. That Friday night, ten lanes were taken up by the league regulars and the other two lanes were an assortment of people who'd come for dates and been put into ad hoc teams so they could compete for the night's usual prizes.

The Incredibowls—the team name that unanimously won the office vote—kept one seat empty in honor of Annette. Everyone at Shady Lanes had heard about Annette's death. Some came by to pay their respects while others simply stared while looking sad.

The Incredibowls made it through their first game before any of the other teams. They were short by two players, sure, but everything moved along faster without their usual tomfoolery. It wasn't that they weren't enjoying the game. It was more that they could feel everyone watching and whispering to each other about what may or may not have happened to their coworker.

They took a break for dinner. While the others ordered their burgers and fries, Zinnia excused herself to the washroom. Unfortunately, this gave some of the other league members the opportunity they'd been waiting for, and Zinnia was waylaid in the women's room by an endless chain of women who wanted to hug her and tell her that Annette Scholem had been a special woman.

When Zinnia finally made her escape from the washroom, she paused behind a room divider screen to check her appearance in a compact mirror. Just as she'd suspected, her eyes were looking red at the corners. All the better to encourage more hugs from strangers.

A female voice pierced her thoughts. "Hey, wait up, Jesse."

Jesse Berman—Zinnia would know his voice anywhere —replied, "What's up, Carrot Top?"

Carrot giggled. "A carrot top is green, silly."

He laughed unselfconsciously. "I don't write the jokes, sweetheart, I just deliver them." The two of them stopped on the other side of the room divider screen, mere feet away from Zinnia. She could see Jesse's shoes under the bottom of the screen. She took a step back so he didn't see hers. She could have kept walking and returned to the table with the others, but didn't. Could you blame her? Who wouldn't be tempted to listen in on a private conversation between their boyfriend and his ex-fling?

Carrot said to Jesse, "Sorry if this comes out all weird and everything, but I have to ask you a question."

"Ask away."

"Last week at bowling, I saw you and Annette talking."

"So?"

"Well, you looked upset about something she was saying."

"Are you sure it was me?"

"Jesse, I know what you look like."

"Then are you sure I was upset with Annette? A lot of my balls were ending up in the gutter that night. Plus, I had a few bad splits I couldn't salvage."

"I heard you fighting, okay?" Carrot sounded upset that he wasn't taking her more seriously. "You told her to mind her own business."

"Ohhhh," he said. There was a snap—Jesse snapping his fingers. "Now I remember. She was asking me about my childhood. Like my mother's maiden name, and other things. For a few minutes, I thought she was trying to figure out my banking password or something like that."

"Why do you think she was asking about your mom?"

Jesse chuckled. "I think it's pretty clear now, in hindsight. She was looking for a few more details to flesh out her book."

"Gosh, do you think that was it?"

"Sure, Carrot. Not everything is a big, spooky conspiracy. Most of the time, the simplest explanation is the right one."

"I guess you're right," she said. "So why were you mad at her for asking about your childhood?"

He paused before answering. "I don't like talking about that time in my life."

"It must have been so sad and lonely, being an only child. I can't imagine growing up without any siblings. Except maybe Ishmael, because he's kind of a show-off."

Jesse agreed, "Ishmael Greyson is not my favorite guy."

"You know my brother?"

"Uh... just by reputation."

"You mean from what I've told you about him?"

"Exactly."

Carrot sighed. "Still. You must have been a lonely little kid."

"Not lonely. My father was able to give me a lot of attention."

"But wasn't your dad kind of... you know?"

"Tough?" Jesse took a big breath. "He wasn't easy, that's for sure. But he made me into the man I am today. He made me strong."

There was a pause. Neither of them moved.

Carrot asked, "How are you doing? Are you seeing anyone?"

He chuckled and replied, "I thought you were dating that Steve guy."

"I am," she said quickly. "I just worry about you being lonely there in your dad's house."

"Don't you worry about me," he said. "As a matter of fact, I have been seeing someone. She's a strong, sexy lady who knows what she wants and goes after it."

"Oh, really?"

"Really. I've never known anyone like her. We're keeping it quiet, because, well, it's complicated. But hopefully I can bring her by the office soon."

"Complicated? How? Is she married?"

"Come on," he said in a joking tone. "I'm not a home wrecker. Trust me, she's single and she's... sensational. Far better than a guy like me deserves."

"Sounds like a special girl."

"Oh, she's no girl. She's all woman. In a good way."

"Good for you," Carrot said. Her shoes moved out of Zinnia's view as she backed away. "I guess I should let you go to the men's washroom."

"Either that or stand watch while I make use of this potted palm tree."

"I don't get it."

"Probably for the best," he said, chuckling. "See you back on the lane."

Zinnia picked up her cue to hide the fact she'd been snooping. She returned to the women's washroom, where she was immediately grabbed and hugged by all eight members of the Gutter Dusters. When Carrot entered the washroom, she shot Zinnia a bug-eyed look of apprehension as she snuck into one of the bathroom's stalls unscathed.

* * *

Most of the night's prizes would be going to the Traveling Beer Bellies, though the Wizards of Wisteria weren't far behind. The Wisteria Permit Department's Incredibowls were headed for last place, even behind the notoriously lousy Pin Pushers. It was a good thing the Incredibowls' score wouldn't count toward their average, because tonight's games were sure to be low scoring.

"We need more carbs," Gavin said. "Let's get that energy up, Incredibowls!"

"No more carbs for me," Dawna said. "Unless they're liquid." She smiled and tipped back her beer.

Their lane went quiet—as quiet as a lane can be in a busy bowling alley. Zinnia knew why everyone was subdued. If Annette had been there, she would have volunteered to buy the group pretzels right about now. Was her spirit there, ghosting around them at that very minute? Offering to buy pretzels and not being heard or seen by anyone? Ghosts had difficulties with time and space. It had to be so confusing, being somewhere and also not being there.

Zinnia felt a chill trying to catch her. To get away, she jumped to her feet with so much energy, she slid forward an inch on her soft- soled rental shoes.

"Pretzels," Zinnia announced. "Pretzels are on me!"

Everyone murmured appreciation and agreed to put the game on hold for a break.

Zinnia walked over to the snack counter and ordered a large, group-sized bag of pretzels.

Someone joined her at the counter, standing much closer than a stranger would.

"Nice bowling form," he said. It was Jesse.

"Not my best game tonight, I'm afraid."

"But you look so good bending over," he said. "Handling those big balls."

She shot him a look, giving him the offended expression he seemed to crave whenever he'd had a few drinks.

He chuckled, pleased with himself. Then he leaned over and kissed her on the top of her shoulder.

She kept her gaze straight ahead and took two steps to the side, away from him.

"Hey, don't pull away," Jesse said, his voice low and thick. "You're always trying to get away from me."

"No, I'm not."

"Yes, you are. You're a pull-away-er-er." He chuckled at his mangled joke. "I get it when we're at work, but lighten up. We're not at the office now." He made an exaggerated pouting face, lips pushed out childishly. "Sometimes I think you don't even like me."

"I like you."

He took two steps closer to close the distance and grabbed her hand. "Prove it. Come with me into the arcade. I peeked in and it's deserted. We can make out and then play Donkey Kong. Or forget all about Donkey Kong. I don't have any quarters, if you know what I mean." Shady Lanes had a collection of vintage arcade games, and she did know exactly what he meant. Jesse's eyes fixed on hers as his pupils dilated. "Like that first time you let me kiss you."

"Tempting," she said, and it was. Just like it had been the first time, when their subtle office flirtations had led to physical contact.

He leaned into her, merging his body heat with hers. "I'll make it worth your time." He licked his lips. "Again."

"But we're not done our games." She pulled her hand from his. "People will know something's up if both of us disappear."

His upper body twitched. "So what if they do? Don't you think it's about time we became official? What are we even waiting for?"

Official? *Sure*, Zinnia thought. They could officially be broken up. That would save a lot of hassle.

"Come over to my house tonight," he pleaded. "Sleep in my bed." He nodded his head forward and looked her in the eyes. "Stay with me the *whole* night. Don't get up and leave. I want you to be there when I wake up."

But Zinnia didn't want to spend the whole night. Not tonight. Not ever. Jesse's inherited home wasn't in the worst condition, considering he was a bachelor, but it wasn't welcoming to someone with her sensitivity. She could never shake the feeling that his house disapproved of her. That it actually hated her. How could a house hate a person? Was it prejudiced against witches?

She couldn't tell Jesse his house had bad juju, so she focused on something mundane. "You want me to stay over so you can laugh at me tomorrow morning when I try to make breakfast out of thin air plus the old condiments in your fridge."

"I don't care about breakfast." He turned away from her and waved to get the attention of the snack bar attendant. "Toss me five bags of those pretzels, would you?" The attendant did. Jesse paid and tipped, then turned to Zinnia, grinning like someone who'd just won a major debate. He waved his hand over the five large bags like a magician performing a reveal. "I've got plenty of breakfast right here."

"But it's already so late," she said, feigning a yawn.

"It's barely eight o'clock."

"But it will be later by the time we all get out of here. You know how it goes with the last game of the night."

He ripped open one of the bags of pretzels and frowned at the contents. "Fine," he said, pouting. "I'll eat all these amazing pretzels by myself."

"I'm still coming over tomorrow for that dinner you promised." She pushed some warmth into her voice. "I'll make it up to you then."

He looked up, his blue eyes bright and gleaming. "Okay."

"Forgive me?"

"Yes, but only if you kiss me." He flashed his eyes. "Right now. Do it." He looked over her shoulder and then back at her. "Nobody's looking, I swear."

Begrudgingly, Zinnia kissed him. In public. For anyone to see.

He gave her another victorious grin. He had won. But what was the prize?

As Zinnia returned to the Incredibowls' lane with the first bag of pretzels, she noticed Carrot was staring at her. The orange-haired young woman's eyes were droopy at the edges. Her mouth wouldn't stay closed. She looked like a goldfish who'd been spilled from its bowl.

Zinnia didn't need witch powers to know that Carrot had seen the kiss. She wondered, had that been Jesse's intention? He didn't strike Zinnia as the type to be cruel, to flaunt his new romance in front of a former flame, but then again she didn't know the man that well, did she? She probably should have taken the time to acquaint herself with him outside of the bed. What kind of woman had she become? Not the good kind. Not the kind her family had raised her to be. She was forty-eight, carrying on with a coworker in the careless manner of someone half her age. And it evidently wasn't sitting well with Jesse, either. He wanted more.

She should have been more of a traditional woman toward him, but thanks to the stone surrounding her heart, she couldn't. She had no interest in growing closer to any man, softening herself so that she could merge into his life and add her mass and energy and passion to all that he possessed. Not again.

* * *

The Incredibowls finally finished their final game. The last one always took three times as long as the first, and despite being short a couple of players that Friday night, the gang was as dawdling as ever.

"Time to settle up," Gavin said between yawns. He leaned over Dawna's shoulder to look at the piece of scrap paper she was scribbling on. "Whatcha doing?"

Dawna picked up the paper and showed it to the group. She'd been rearranging the letters for one of the characters' names in Annette's book: Villobek.

"Seriously, you guys don't get it," Dawna said, shaking her head. "I thought once you all read the book, you'd see it like I did."

Her coworkers exchanged confused looks.

"The guy who killed Annette was Villobek." As soon as she uttered the villain's name, the bowling alley grew eerily quiet, as though everyone was now listening.

"You've had too much to drink," Gavin said. "I'll drive you home." He pulled Dawna's jacket from the back of her chair and started putting it on her.

She pushed him away. "Don't you get it?" Her voice was louder, verging on yelling. Now that the balls had stopped rolling and the pins had stopped crashing for the night, Dawna's voice was loud and clear over the soft music. "We need to find Villobek!"

At the second mention of the name, Zinnia felt a distinctive chill run up her spine. She looked across the table to see Margaret rubbing her arms. The two exchanged a knowing look. The bowling alley was quite warm. A chill like that only happened when a ghost was present, or when the name of something truly evil had been invoked.

Jesse stifled a yawn and patted Dawna on the shoulder. "Time to call it a night. Let Gavin drive you home."

Dawna struck her fists on the table. "No. I'm not leaving until all of you wake up and see what's right in front of your eyes."

Carrot continued to look like a goldfish out of water.

Gavin looked annoyed, holding Dawna's jacket.

Margaret leaned over, looking very interested in Dawna's paper with the scribbled letters.

Jesse finished his stifled yawn. "And what's that we're supposed to see, Ms. Jones?"

"Let me field this one," Gavin said to Jesse. He turned to the others and explained to them as a group, "Villobek is the bad guy in the book. He's kinda like Voldemort from Harry Potter, which is where I think Annette got the inspiration."

Carrot said, "We all read her book."

Gavin continued. "Then you know that Villobek is the one who kidnaps the main character's best friend, and..." He trailed off. "Did the book ever say the name of the main character?"

"No," Margaret said. "It's a nameless character. I'm not even sure it was a girl. I assumed it was an artistic decision."

Carrot said, "That was confusing. There were two main characters, but sometimes there was just one. I think Annette needed an editor."

Dawna's eyes had the glazed, unfocused look of inebriation. She banged her fists on the table again. "Villobek!" She got to her feet, cupped her hands around her mouth, and yelled, "Hey, do any of you bowling people know a guy named Villobek?"

Nobody answered. Everyone in Shady Lanes—about fifty people—stared at the woman yelling drunkenly. The stereo system glitched. The song that had been playing softly turned into noise that grew increasingly louder until someone shut it off with a crackle. In the silence that followed, alarms started going off with the pin-setting equipment.

Dawna made an excited whooping sound. "Something's happening!" she exclaimed. "Villobek! Come out, come out, wherever you are!"

Margaret clamped her hand over Dawna's mouth. "We need to get her out of here," she said.

The two guys, Jesse and Gavin, each grabbed one of Dawna's arms and steered her toward the exit.

* * *

Five minutes later, Jesse waved goodbye to Gavin, who was driving Dawna home in her car. Jesse walked over to where Zinnia stood on the walkway between the parking area and the entrance to Shady Lanes.

"Dawna will be fine after she sleeps it off," Jesse said. "I didn't realize how hard she was hitting the drinks."

Zinnia asked, "What do you think about what she said? About the villain in Annette's story?"

Jesse shrugged. "I dunno. The guy seemed like a stock villain to me. I'm not even sure what the guy's motivation was. Why does someone act like a monster?"

"Some people are truly evil," Zinnia said. "Evil in a way that makes them less than human."

Jesse fixed his eyes on her. The light from the entrance caught his irises and made them pale and gray, like the sky in the middle of January.

His voice got low and gruff. "Less than human? I'm not sure what you mean by that."

"Never mind." She took a deep breath of chilly night air and let it clear her mind. "We ought to be running along home, I suppose."

He raised an eyebrow. "If you won't come to my place, should I come over to yours? I could stay all night to protect you from wolves and monsters and things that go bump in the night."

"I can take care of myself. We Riddle women are tougher than we look."

"Oh?" His raised eyebrow climbed higher. "There are more than one of you?"

She waved a hand. "Just a family saying." She made a shoo gesture. "Go on home. I'll see you on Saturday, for dinner at your house."

"You will?" Judging by the wavering in his voice, he'd forgotten about his promise. "Right," he said, more solidly. "Dinner. I'm cooking you something spectacular." He grinned. "A spectacular dinner for a spectacular woman."

Zinnia said nothing. Was he using the word *spectacular* because he knew that she'd overheard his conversation with Carrot? She couldn't tell by his face. Ordinarily she could get a decent sense of when people were being honest with her, but something about Jesse clouded her senses. Something about the way he made her feel when he stayed over, perhaps.

"See you then," he said, and he went to his vehicle.

Zinnia watched his taillights disappear into the night.

Margaret finally emerged from the Shady Lanes building. "There you are," she said. "I was waiting inside to get a word with you in private."

"And I've been waiting outside to do the same."

"So it would appear." Margaret looked around. They were alone. "You felt it, didn't you? When Dawna yelled out that name?" She was careful to not say Villobek.

"I did," Zinnia said. She'd felt it in her spine and then everywhere else. The chill of evil.

"The locating spell could work, if the name holds that much power."

"You read my mind."

"I need to go home first," Margaret said. "Get the little animals into their animal pajamas so they don't stay up all night. Their father is too lenient."

"Shall we meet at the regular place?"

"Yes. I'll be there by nine o'clock," Margaret said.

Zinnia knew that Margaret's nine o'clock would be nine-fifteen, but didn't quibble.

CHAPTER 18

DREAMLAND COFFEE

9:16 PM

Zinnia stood alone in the dimly lit storage room of Dreamland Coffee, surrounded by metal shelves stacked with bags of coffee beans. This was the witches' "usual place" for casting multi-witch spells. The walls were made of cinder blocks, the ceiling was metal, and the floor was gritty concrete. Nobody cared if things got a little messy back here. The storage room was not exactly fit for a scene in a Hollywood movie, but it was sturdy and secure, and their fellow coven member Maisy Nix trusted them to lock up after themselves. Dreamland had two locations in Wisteria, but the coven always met at this one, near the center of town.

Zinnia lifted a bucket of used coffee grounds out of the way so she could put the table under the light. The coffee grounds were still fresh and damp, heavy with moisture. She groaned from the weight of them in the bucket. After setting the bucket down, she looked at the redness on the palm of her hand. Her palm returned to its normal light pink immediately. She caught her breath, and then lifted and set down the bucket a few more times, just for the exercise. It was good to strain her muscles and use her body. She could heal quickly no matter what, but her muscles were bound to get rusty if she didn't use them.

She centered the table under the storage room's only light. The table wobbled. She tipped it with her hands and used magic to turn the adjustable knobs on its feet. The table still wobbled. She adjusted the other knobs. Now the wobble was even worse. She ripped a piece of cardboard off a box containing plastic utensils, and used the cardboard as a wedge under one foot and then another. Good? No. The table still wobbled.

Margaret Mills arrived to find Zinnia on her hands and knees, removing and inserting different-sized wedges of cardboard under the feet of the table.

"Don't bother trying to level that thing," Margaret said.

Zinnia hadn't heard the gray-haired witch come in, and bumped her head on the underside of the table in surprise.

"But I've almost got it balanced," Zinnia said, rubbing her head.

"That table has been cursed one too many times," Margaret said. "It won't hold a flat plane anymore."

"That's ridiculous. It's just a table. It ought to be able to do the one thing a table is meant to do."

"Oh, it functions just fine," Margaret said. She reached into her purse and pulled out a marble. It was a lovely cat's eye marble, yellow with a red eye. "This is just a little keepsake from the funny vasectomy doctor," Margaret explained, and she placed the marble on the table.

The red and yellow marble didn't roll.

No matter which way the table wobbled, or where Margaret set down the marble, it didn't roll.

"This table isn't cursed," Zinnia said. "Clearly, it's charmed."

Margaret shrugged. "Cursed. Charmed. All depends on how you look at it." She gave the marble a loving glance and tucked it back into her purse. "Did you bring the map?"

Zinnia frowned. "I thought you were bringing the map. Oh, Margaret, if I'd known you were going to forget the map, I could have asked..."

Margaret was already placing the aforementioned map on the table, smoothing out the fold lines. She had brought the map after all.

"It was a joke to lighten the mood," Margaret said. "We're about to touch the edges of evil itself. We might be taking our last mortal breaths in here, surrounded by coffee beans and boxes of whatever that is." She pointed at the damaged cardboard box Zinnia had been ripping apart for table wedges.

"Plastic utensils and stir sticks."

Margaret wrinkled her nose. "Stir sticks are so wasteful. I like it better when a place has a jar for clean spoons and a jar for dirty spoons. It's like a test for people, to make sure they're conscious, and not sleepwalking through life, using other people's dirty spoons to stir their coffee."

Zinnia blinked at her friend. "I suppose."

"Anyway, we could be taking our last mortal breaths right here in this concrete bunker, so I figured it might be funny to pretend I didn't bring the map."

"It was sort of funny," Zinnia said.

"You didn't laugh."

"Ha ha."

"I can be a funny person, Zinnia. People used to think I was funny, before I had kids. Did you know I did improv in college?"

Zinnia said nothing. She did know about the improv. Margaret told her about it at least once a month.

They stared at each other a moment, and then both looked down at the map. They were only quibbling because neither one of them wanted to do the spell. Touching the edges of evil seemed even less appealing than going bowling when you weren't in the mood. But the worst thing that could happen at bowling was a pulled groin muscle. If the witches screwed up and let a demon slip through, well, a pulled groin muscle would look pretty delightful by comparison.

Margaret looked down and finished smoothing the fold lines in the large sheet of paper. It was a full color map of the town of Wisteria, with select amenities and attractions highlighted. Businesses paid to have their locations featured, which covered the costs of production, since the maps were available for free at the Wisteria Tourist Info Center. This particular map was two years old. Some of the businesses had changed in the interim, but the old map would still work for their purposes.

They settled in and centered themselves before beginning their two-witch locating spell. It would, in theory anyway, work on the resonance of a name to find its evil power source. When they couldn't find any more reason to stall, they leaned across the table, joined hands, and prepared to chant.

They chanted.

And they chanted some more.

After several minutes of non-stop chanting while weaving Witch Tongue through their words, they took a break to relax their tongues. They continued holding hands so they could pick up where they left off.

Margaret grumbled, "We could have used a third set of hands to prevent flowback."

"Sure, and we ought to be wearing pointed hats to access the higher source, but we're not."

"Just saying it might have been nice." Margaret squirmed in her seat, her sweaty palms slipping around in Zinnia's hands. Their chairs, like the table, were rejects from the front of the coffee shop, and equally wobbly.

Zinnia knew exactly who Margaret wanted to be there. Maisy Nix, the owner of the coffee shop. Her niece, Fatima, was not nearly as useful.

Zinnia said, "She did offer to cancel her plans and help us, but you're the one who insisted we could handle it ourselves."

"Yes, well, is it my fault I can be a stubborn cow sometimes?"

"I'll assume that's a rhetorical question and not answer."

"Zinnia Riddle, you're just as stubborn as—" She cut herself off, but it was too late. She'd uttered Zinnia's name. Her full name.

Zinnia kicked Margaret's shin under the table. "Thanks a lot, *Margaret Mills*."

Margaret kicked her back.

The thing about using a locating spell to find evil through the resonance of its name was that you were not supposed to mention any other names, especially your own. The only thing worse than flowback on a spell like that was payback. As soon as they located the evil, it would see its way straight back to them.

"Cancel," Margaret said, trying to pull her sweaty hands from Zinnia's. "There's too much risk. We should—"

But it was too late to cancel. The magic spell suddenly took effect, and their hands locked together.

The map on the table glowed. Power fluttered through the paper fibers like ripples on a pond. The corner of the map took a tentative crinkle, and then the whole map trembled. It folded and bunched, transforming from two dimensions to three. Paper buildings rose up like architectural models from the flat surface.

Zinnia felt the magic throughout her whole body, and it was not an unpleasant feeling at all. She'd all but forgotten the wonders of casting a dangerous spell. Her heart raced, but not with fear. Anticipation. Oh, how she'd missed practicing powerful magic. And there was darkness inside her as well. It was wrong and dark, that dear, sweet Annette's death had led Zinnia to this place on this night, to this feeling of being so alive.

Across the table, Margaret's face glowed red and green, lit by the soft glow of streetlamps appearing on the map, as well as the streaks of car taillights.

Margaret squeezed Zinnia's hands with a painful grip. The map was fully realized. It was time. If they didn't ask now, the spell would ask for them, and they might not like what it queried.

With hands gripped tightly, the women asked in unison, "Show us the one named Villobek."

The map's miniature streetlights flickered, but nothing more happened.

Zinnia asked on her own, "Show us the one whose name contains the letters V-I-L-L-O-B-E-K."

The map crinkled and pulled in on itself, becoming a fraction smaller than when they had begun.

"Or someone connected to Villobek," Margaret said. "Do you have anything at all for Villobek? Or some form of that name? Some related—"

A bolt of lightning shot down from the space above their heads. The map seemed to catch fire.

"Wow," Margaret said. "That's a very convincing illusion. I swear I can smell paper burning."

Zinnia yanked her hands free, grabbed the bucket of wet coffee grounds from the floor, and dumped it on the map.

Margaret jumped back and brushed the coffee grounds from her clothes. "What did you do that for?"

"The map was burning," Zinnia said. "That wasn't an illusion."

"You could have let me cast a water spell," Margaret said.

"The coffee grounds were sitting right there."

Margaret started pawing through the brown, muddy grounds. "The lightning strike was too bright. I didn't see where it landed."

Zinnia put her hand on Margaret's wrist. "I did," she said softly.

They looked into each other's eyes. Margaret's gray irises had disappeared. The magic had turned her eyes almost pure black. Zinnia was sure her eyes looked equally odd. The only sound was their breathing. Rapid, excited breaths. The air smelled of ozone and smoke and damp coffee grounds.

Margaret licked her lips. Her black eyes flicked left and right wildly. Her hair had more curl. She was having as much fun as Zinnia.

Her voice came out raspy, desperate. "Where?"

"Towhee Marsh," Zinnia said.

The entity known as Villobek was, at that very minute, in Towhee Marsh.

CHAPTER 19

OUTSKIRTS OF WISTERIA

10:10 PM

Margaret Mills drove, leaning forward against her seat belt, her knuckles white from her tight grip on the steering wheel. Margaret's vehicle was a typical family van, littered with the usual family debris, and it did smell exactly as bad as Jesse had implied. Like sour milk and beef jerky.

They drove toward Towhee Marsh, a man-made freshwater wetland near the edge of town. The marsh served as both a wildlife preserve and a park, with a mile-long looping path for walkers. No dogs or bicycles were permitted. The marsh was inhabited by hundreds of species of birds, which made it a popular destination for bird watchers and wildlife photographers. Zinnia's favorite birds were the great blue herons, magnificent creatures with long necks. They patiently stalked the reeds at the water's edge for minnows. Of course she wouldn't see any herons tonight. Maybe a few bats. Or whatever had ripped open the front of Annette Scholem.

Zinnia swallowed the lump of fear in her throat. She rubbed her hands together, practicing the delicate hand movements that would help her control her blue lightning powers, should she need them.

Margaret, who hadn't spoken for several minutes, said, "I sure hope Tansy Wick isn't involved in any of this business." Zinnia guessed Margaret had brought up Tansy Wick because her property wasn't far from the marsh.

Zinnia snorted at the idea of Tansy being involved.

"I'm not being paranoid," Margaret said. "You have to admit a lot of this town's problems trace back to Tansy and her business."

"Margaret, are you suggesting that one of Tansy's larger left-handed snails has escaped the garden and gone on a killing spree?"

"You know what I mean."

"Some of those snails can grow quite big." Zinnia smiled in the dark. Teasing Margaret Mills was nearly as fun as doing dangerous magic.

Margaret made an indignant rhino noise. "The thing is, and I mean no disrespect to our mutual friend, she does hang around some dangerous people."

"That's her business," Zinnia said crisply. She didn't regard Tansy as a friend, exactly. How could one be friends with a hermit who despised people? But she did feel a certain kinship with the older woman. Tansy Wick wasn't wrong to live away from everyone, content with the companionship of her left-handed snails, her magical plants, and her dogs, Jasper and Coco.

"She should be more..." Margaret trailed off.

Zinnia finished the sentence. "More like us? Sitting in the dark underbelly of City Hall, tapping away on our keyboards, earning our meager salary, like good little secret witches?"

"Well, no, but she shouldn't consort with the sort of people she does."

"Oh, but Margaret, those are exactly the sort of people who have the best cuttings and seeds. Nice, well-behaved people don't spend years of their lives breeding stronger strains of black scarabyce."

Margaret said nothing. She knew when she'd been beat. She was only too happy to purchase magical herbs from Tansy Wick without ever asking about their origins. She couldn't justify being judgy about Tansy Wick's supply chain.

They were nearly at the marsh, anyway. No time for jibber-jabber.

Margaret's knuckles were still white as they drove past the lookout point, where teenagers sometimes parked their vehicles to do whatever it was teenagers did those days. A single car was parked there. With steamy windows. No mystery what the teens were doing in that car.

They arrived at the visitor parking, where Margaret angle-parked across two spots. She turned off the van's engine, they double-checked their magical supplies, and then both witches stepped out into the night air.

It was colder than either of them had expected. With the first breeze, the damp from the swamp seemed to seep into their bones.

*　*　*

They explored the bushy area as best they could without calling attention to themselves. The outer ring of the marsh was dry enough to walk on, but as they neared the reeds and water, the earth was only partly frozen, so it got mucky and tried to slurp off their shoes.

Margaret said, "Aw, shoot. My favorite boots are getting ruined."

Zinnia asked, "Why didn't you cast the dry shoes spell like I did?"

"I didn't think of it," Margaret admitted. "Go easy on me. I don't exactly get to do a wide variety of spells lately, so I might be a bit rusty."

"Here. Hold still." Zinnia cast the spell onto Margaret's boots for her.

"Perfect. And did I detect a little—shall we say—*stank* on that spell of yours?"

"Maybe." Zinnia smiled in the dark. She'd cast the dry shoes spell along with an extra clause to warm up Margaret's feet and dry her socks. Maybe Zinnia's magic wasn't so rusty after all. Maybe she could track down this Villobek entity and save the day.

They kept searching, using a variety of magical supplies to illuminate different types of cloaking magic.

After an hour, they'd circled the pond twice and had nothing to show for it but empty glass jars.

"I'm nearly out of eyeballs," Zinnia said.

"And I'm completely out of everything I brought," Margaret said. "So much for that location spell. Maybe the map was too out of date."

"There is one place we haven't looked yet. The steamy car back at the make-out point."

Margaret snickered. "There are some things I'd rather not see, not even with something else's eyeballs."

"Come on. We have to be thorough."

"But it's late, and I'm freezing my buns off."

"Margaret Mills, don't make me play the dead Annette card."

Margaret sighed. "Fine. But when we get to the steamy car, you be the good cop and I'll be the bad cop."

"I wouldn't have it any other way." No one could play the bad cop like Margaret.

They finished circling the pond and returned to the van. Margaret wanted to drive her van to the lookout point, but Zinnia convinced her it would be better to walk. All the better to have stealth on their side.

The distance was further than it had seemed when driving, but no more than half a mile. The car was still parked where they'd seen it.

The witches weren't yet close enough to see if the windows were still steamy when the passenger side door opened with a metallic creak.

A young woman stepped out of the car, her feet scuffing unevenly on the dry road. "You shhhtay there," she told someone inside the vehicle. She sounded more than a little tipsy, her words slurring. "Gimme a minute, okay? Shhtay there while I find a," she paused long enough to hiccup, "swamp bathroom."

Margaret elbowed Zinnia and whispered, "Definitely a couple of criminal masterminds at work. Should we glamour up some disguises and give them a scare? I've been working on a new accent."

A twig snapped nearby in the darkness.

"Shh," Zinnia said, swiveling her head to listen. "Did you hear something?"

"Sorry," Margaret said. "That was me. I shouldn't have ordered the chickpea burger at Shady Lanes. But it's so good with the mango chutney."

"Not that," Zinnia said. She knew the sound of a chickpea burger rumbling around Margaret's stomach, and what she'd heard was something else. "There's something out here with us," she said.

The young woman who'd been stumbling around looking for a "swamp bathroom" let out a terrified scream.

Zinnia turned on her heel and ran toward the scream without hesitation, both hands crackling with blue lightning. Margaret was right behind her.

They rounded the parked car and saw what had made the young woman scream. Both women stopped in their tracks. Margaret whispered a spell to amplify the moonlight in the vicinity.

There was an animal standing on the poor girl's chest.

Zinnia whispered over her shoulder, "Margaret, are you seeing what I'm seeing."

"That's not a wolf."

"No, it's not."

Straddling its captive prey was a giant cat. From end to end, it had to be over seven feet long. As it sniffed the young woman's face, the tip of its tail dusted the toes of her shoes. The only giant cat species native to the area was the mountain lion, also known as the cougar.

Margaret whispered, "Is that a cougar or something else? A jaguar?"

"Let's ask it." Zinnia snapped a branch from a nearby tree and whipped it against the ground. "Hey!"

The big cat turned its head and made eye contact with Zinnia.

She nearly dropped her stick. Oh, the eyes it had. Dark yet sparkling. Dangerous. Like refreshing water teeming with sharks.

Zinnia gripped her stick tightly. Who was scared of a kitty cat? Not this witch. She whipped the branch against the ground and raised her free arm over her head. A smart way of dealing with a cougar was to make yourself appear as large as possible. The conventional wisdom was to look big while backing away slowly. But Zinnia was walking toward the beast, not away. *Riddle women are tougher than they look.*

"Bad kitty." She whacked the ground again. "Go home. Shoo!"

The cat swiveled its ears and flattened them back, fangs bared. It didn't budge.

As she drew nearer, she determined the cat was definitely a cougar, with a tawny coat and lighter patches on the jaws and chin.

The cat let out a growl, gruff and desperate. Unfortunately, Zinnia wasn't gifted with a talent for understanding animals. If only they'd brought their junior coven member Fatima along, the young woman might have been useful for a change! But even without translating the growl, Zinnia sensed the big cat was hiding something. Bluffing, even. But what would a cougar be bluffing about?

The woman pinned beneath the cat let out a whimper. She didn't show any signs of having been bitten or scratched, but the cat had to weigh nearly two hundred pounds, if not more. The beast might not be eating its victim, but it was crushing her.

Margaret stepped up to stand shoulder to shoulder with Zinnia, or at least shoulder to bicep, given her stature. "Time to break out the big guns." Margaret raised her hands, palms together, and prepared. Margaret's lightning was as green as Zinnia's was blue. It flickered between her palms, buzzing audibly.

"Wait," Zinnia said.

The driver's side door of the car swung open. Out jumped a young man with a familiar face. He was Xavier Batista, the City Hall employee they'd seen five hours earlier. He reached into his pocket and whipped out something. The blade of a pocket knife flashed under the enhanced moonlight. It was a very small flash for a very small knife. He would have been better armed with a big stick than the tiny blade, but he brandished it bravely as he advanced on the cougar. Xavier stared straight ahead, unaware of the two witches huddled in the darkness.

Margaret whispered, "Xavier Batista's going to be Cougar Chow if we don't do something."

"Hold your fire," Zinnia said. "Don't you dare shoot that green lightning of yours and blow our cover."

"I'll do it quick, while Xavier's back is to us. He won't know what happened."

Zinnia dropped her stick and clapped her hands over the top of Margaret's, snuffing the green electricity.

"Tandem lighting," Zinnia said. "Tandem."

"Of course," Margaret said. "I can't believe I forgot. See? I told you my magic was rusty."

She stepped behind Zinnia, placed her hands on the taller woman's shoulders, and willed her energy forward.

Zinnia felt the borrowed magic flood her body. So much power! She could set the whole swamp ablaze if she wanted.

Luckily, Zinnia's training kicked in through muscle memory and she reeled in the power. She focused the energy in her hands, making it invisible. Then she pulled back her arm, and released. The movement was not unlike releasing a sixteen-pound bowling ball down a hardwood lane.

Her aim was true. The invisible ball connected with its target. The big cat made an OOF sound. It flew off the girl and tumble rolled. The dust settled, and the cat scrambled up to four paws. The swamp was silent except for the scratch of its claws in the dirt. The cat looked Zinnia directly in the eyes as it slowly backed away.

Just then, Xavier darted toward the cat. He lunged out, brandishing his tiny knife. He slashed the cat clumsily across the top of its head.

The cat howled as it whipped its head. Blood sprayed from its wound, spattering Zinnia's face.

Xavier Batista retreated swiftly, hopping from foot to foot like a boxer. "You like that?" He flashed the blade in the moonlight. "Want another taste?"

The cougar retreated, stepping away. It moved slowly, taking its time to look at each of them. It seemed to be memorizing their faces.

The young woman on the ground rolled to her side and used her hands to push herself upright. She groaned and mentioned that she no longer needed to find the bathroom.

Margaret let out a near-silent whoop. "We got him. Or her. We got it. Bam. Right in the kisser." She did a little of Xavier's boxing footwork herself.

Zinnia blinked the blood from her eyes and wiped her mouth. She licked her lips. The blood was still warm, and it had a taste. A magical taste. This was no ordinary local cougar.

She looked into the dark eyes of the retreating cougar and asked softly, "What are you? Who are you?"

The cat blinked at her slowly, growled again, then turned and disappeared into the darkness.

CHAPTER 20

MIDNIGHT

The secluded lookout point was now a chaotic scene of flashing lights and emergency vehicles. The sound of idling engines covered the wetlands' owl hoots and frog noises with a rumbling blanket of noise.

The female victim was being treated by paramedics for minor scrapes and a bump to the head. There was some confusion over what kind of animal had attacked. She and Xavier had called it a wolf to some people and a cougar to others.

Zinnia left the young woman in capable hands and joined Margaret for some mutual grumbling.

After two hours at Towhee Swamp, both witches were ready to go home. They'd been ready to leave right after the cougar attack, but Xavier Batista had spotted them standing next to the car. He'd called the police on his phone immediately, and then asked that the two women stay to corroborate his statement. Now Zinnia regretted being such a responsible citizen. The weather had been chilly enough at ten o'clock, but it had dipped further below freezing since then, and now rain was falling. Icy-cold January rain, bordering on sleet.

Meanwhile, Xavier Batista was having the time of his life. The young man had found an audience with the first responders. He puffed out his chest and bragged about how he'd shown that "big, bad kitty cat" that he could be just as big and bad. "And that's when I stabbed the beast right in the jugular!" Xavier swung his right arm and small pocketknife to demonstrate.

One of the male first-responders, who was in his early twenties like Xavier, said, "Come on, bro. You don't even know where the jugular is."

"I know where *your* jugular is," Xavier said with adrenaline-fueled bravado. "Step up and I'll show you."

"Oh, yeah?"

"Yeah." Xavier puffed out his chest even further.

"Sure, why not. I could use some practice giving stitches." He started removing his reflective safety jacket.

Xavier's shoes scuffed on the dirt road as he did his boxing footwork again, like he had with the cougar.

"That's enough," said one of the more sensible of the crew. He calmed down his coworker and put an end to the fighting talk.

Margaret and Zinnia watched everything from their seat on the bumper of Xavier's car. They had charmed the bumper to be a source of heat. It was pleasantly warm, but not too hot. They didn't want to drain the car's battery, which was the power source. The witches had to use the battery since they'd drained their magical energy on the invisible lightning ball. Both witches would recharge, but it would take time and high calorie food. Zinnia usually steered clear of junk food, but she would open up her emergency supply as soon as she got home.

Margaret, who was taking the temporary loss of her magic harder than Zinnia, leaned over and grumbled, "I feel like I've been dosed with witchbane."

"Witchbane feels nothing like a power drain. You don't even notice a smaller dose until you try a spell, and a high dose feels like you've been run over by a paving crew."

"Since when are you the resident expert on witchbane?"

"My mentor had interesting methods of teaching lessons."

"I'll say." Margaret rubbed her hands together rapidly. Nothing magical happened. She sighed. "Look at that. Not even a spark."

Zinnia elbowed her. "Cool it. Detective Fung is coming over."

"Oh, pfft. He knows I'm a witch."

"Yes, but he doesn't know that you know that he knows."

"I'm too tired to keep up on who knows what." Margaret hopped off the bumper. "I smell granola bars. Watch my back while I go for a quick recon."

"Sure," Zinnia said. She had very little power remaining for protecting Margaret, but a quest for granola bars was unlikely to prove dangerous.

After Margaret left, Fung took her spot on the bumper. "Wow," he said, twisting to look down at the magically warmed bumper. "Margaret Mills must have a hot butt."

Zinnia said, "I shall pass along your compliment."

He rested his hands on the bumper and looked down again. "It's magic, right?"

"Do you really need to ask?"

He chuckled. "Impressive, whatever it is."

She turned her head and studied his face. The lines around his eyes looked deeper, and his cheeks seemed to be hanging from his face. He'd lost weight recently, but given his current state of near-exhaustion, he looked sick.

"You need to sleep," Zinnia said. "You're only human."

"I hate it when you remind me of that." He reached into his suit jacket, and handed Zinnia a crisp white handkerchief.

"No, thanks," she said.

He put the cloth in her hand. "You've got something on your face," he explained.

She touched her face, contacting something crusty on her upper lip. "It's blood," she said. "I forgot about that."

"Yours?"

"No." She spat on the handkerchief and started wiping her face. Fung tilted his head and gave her a somewhat disgusted look. He didn't know any better. Unladylike though it seemed to spit on a hankie, it was the best solution. Witch saliva was an effective agent for many things, such as breaking down blood or magical compounds. Witch saliva could deodorize a musty room in less than ten minutes. Plus, it was naturally antibacterial.

"There's something funny about this blood," she said, sticking the tip of her tongue against the red spots on the handkerchief.

Fung's face kept contorting with disgust. It was a normal human reaction, so Zinnia didn't hold it against him.

She handed him the soiled hankie. "Thanks."

He reeled back. "That's yours to keep. I have plenty."

Zinnia smiled. She'd missed freaking out Fung during her last year of staying under the radar.

"You might want to take the blood for evidence," she said.

Fung asked, "To test that it was a cougar and not a wolf? That young woman is so shaken up, she doesn't know what attacked her. She was babbling about a wolf, then she said it was a cougar."

"Margaret and I both saw a cougar."

"And you're sure it wasn't a wolf using one of those masking spells?"

"You mean a glamour?" She frowned and looked down at the handkerchief she was folding into a tiny square. "I have been wondering if it might have been a magical disguise. It is possible my eyes deceived me."

Fung turned his head toward Xavier Batista, who was hopping from foot to foot, demonstrating his fighting technique for a trio of bemused ambulance attendants.

Fung turned back to Zinnia. "My money is on the witches. Cougar it is. I believe your eyes over anyone's." He pulled a plastic evidence bag from his pocket and gingerly accepted the folded, stained handkerchief. "Maybe we can test this blood for something at the, er, special lab."

A moment that might have been quiet, if not for the idling engines, passed.

"It might not have been a glamour at all," Zinnia said. "Group hysteria has been well documented over the years. If our young lovers were psychologically primed to see a wolf, then fear could have made them see what they expected."

"But you and Margaret didn't see a wolf."

"We weren't afraid," Zinnia said, which wasn't entirely true.

"Neither was Mr. Batista, according to... Mr. Batista."

Zinnia smirked. "He didn't even cut the cat until it was already retreating."

"What do you think made it retreat? It didn't hurt Liza Gilbert at all."

"Gilbert? Are you telling me that drunk girl is related to the Gilberts?"

"It's a common last name, and I believe she has sobered up." He fixed his gaze on Zinnia and didn't waver. "You were saying? Something made the cougar retreat?"

"Oh, just a little something Margaret and I whipped up."

"Which was what?"

"A *secret* little something, Detective." She gave him an enigmatic smile. It was always better for others to not know the full depth and breadth of a witch's power. It was always better to be underestimated.

"Secret witcher-i-doo." Fung smiled.

Zinnia wrinkled her nose. *Witcher-i-doo* was one of Wick's favorite taunts. Not Tansy Wick, but her brother, Vincent. She wondered for a moment if he might be involved in these cougar incidents. She glanced around. He was probably watching her right now, thanks to all his cameras. The thought made her shiver.

"You're freezing out here," Fung said. "You should go home."

"I will, if you think you can handle—"

Headlights swept across them, interrupting the conversation. A new vehicle was coming up the road toward them. The driver stopped before reaching the lookout point, and began doing a multi-point turn to leave.

Zinnia recognized the vehicle immediately. It would have been hard not to recognize the long, shiny, white 1991 Cadillac Brougham.

"That's Carrot Greyson's car," she said to Fung.

He rubbed his chin. "Your coworker with the suspicious wildlife connection? What are the odds?"

"She might have a logical reason for being here."

"Such as?"

Zinnia had nothing.

Fung jumped up from the heated bumper. "I've been meaning to talk to Ms. Greyson ever since you left me that phone message, and now here she is. Great how things work out, ain't it?"

Zinnia checked the time on her phone. "Detective, you promised you'd have Annette's case closed by Friday. It's now Saturday morning. I'd like my money back."

Fung hung his head in mock shame and pressed his hands together in a prayer position as he backed away. "Give me another day. You won't be sorry. I'm so close, I can feel it."

"You'd better hurry up." Zinnia waved for him to speed up. "Carrot's going to get that giant boat of a car turned around eventually."

* * *

Margaret didn't talk much on the drive home. She was too busy cramming granola bars into her mouth.

Zinnia was also nibbling on one while she reviewed notifications on her phone. Dawna Jones had been drunk-posting up a storm all evening, ever since Gavin had driven her home from Shady Lanes. Dawna had put up a tribute page for Annette Scholem, and she'd added photos from that evening's bowling game in Annette's honor.

Zinnia got an unsettling, disassociated feeling as she reviewed the pictures that had been taken just a few hours earlier. Everything was so flat in a photograph, like a memory but different. The way a flower pressed in a book is not a flower.

Zinnia gasped when she spotted a photo of Carrot goofing around with her bowling ball. One side of Carrot's V-neck shirt gaped open, revealing her full tattoo.

"Cougar," Zinnia said excitedly. "It's a cougar! Margaret! A cougar!"

"Yes, Zinnia. I was right there with you when it happened. Wow. You must really be drained."

"I mean the tattoo," Zinnia said. "Carrot's tattoo with the animal paw. It's not a wolf. It's a cougar, just like the one we saw back there." She leaned over and showed Margaret the picture.

"I see it, I see it," Margaret said. "Get your phone out of my face before I crash this van."

Zinnia settled back into her seat. "I'd better send this to Fung. No, wait. Turn the van around. We have to go back. He could be in danger."

"We're going home."

Zinnia didn't like the sound of that.

"Turn around," Zinnia said.

"No."

Zinnia felt a sharp pain in her gut. Was it a premonition or a side effect of being drained? She had no idea. Her patchy psychic abilities had not come with a user manual. The pain persisted.

"Margaret, I think Fung is in danger. We have to go back." She rubbed her stomach. "Or he will be in danger soon. I don't know. You know how I get these premonitions sometimes. The more distant it is, the less clear it comes through."

Margaret didn't even slow down, let alone prepare to turn the van around. "Detective Fung is currently surrounded by half the cops and firefighters and medics in the town. I think he'll be okay without us."

"I don't know." The feeling in her gut was only growing stronger.

"Plus, it's just Carrot. I mean, come on. Last week, I had to help her open a milk carton." Margaret ripped open another granola bar using her teeth and spat out the wrapper. "Driving and eating without magic is hard," she complained. "There should be a drink we can use, like a Gatorade for witches."

Zinnia sighed. Margaret would not be turning the van around. Whatever it was Fung was about to discover from questioning Carrot, he'd have to deal with it himself.

She looked down at her phone. Coincidentally, the battery was as dead as her magic. One percent power remaining. Zinnia sent a message to Fung, including the photo of Carrot's tattoo. Her phone blinked off. And that was that. She had tried. She wasn't a police officer or a detective. Forwarding the photo was all she could reasonably be expected to do.

"Exactly," Margaret said, conversing with Zinnia's unspoken thoughts without realizing it. "Let the police handle it from here. It's no witch's duty to put herself in danger.

"You're right," Zinnia said, making an effort to be agreeable despite being irked by Margaret's attitude. Zinnia had to let it go. Margaret didn't want to put herself in further danger. And Zinnia might feel the same way if she had four kids who counted on her coming home at night.

Zinnia had been the one to lead the charge toward the screaming and the cougar. Margaret had helped tonight, with the location spell and the trip to the swamp, but she had her limits. And who could blame her for setting reasonable boundaries?

Zinnia had to accept one key fact: she was only willing to take risks because she had absolutely nothing to lose.

CHAPTER 21

SATURDAY, 8:00 AM

Zinnia stood under her shower nozzle and experimentally turned the temperature down. The water turned chilly, yet it didn't bother her. She turned the lever all the way to cold. Icy! Under normal circumstances, she would have been jumping out of the tub, teeth chattering. But this morning there was no shivering. No discomfort, even. Cold was simply a temperature, just another option.

Last night at Towhee Swamp, she'd helped Margaret cast a spell to warm the car bumper for both of them, but now that she thought about it, she hadn't really needed an external heat source. They'd simply used the spell because they were witches, and they could.

The chilly shower water continued to pour down.

Riddle women are tougher than they look. The old family saying was true.

She rotated in the shower and let the icy water run down her other side. No effect. If anything, the cold water was stoking her internal fire.

She rinsed her hair and turned off the water. The air in the bathroom felt warm by comparison. She called for her towel magically, and it floated over obediently. Her magic had recovered from the previous night's tandem lightning spell.

She changed her mind about the towel, snapped her fingers to send it away, and then cast a drying spell on herself instead. Hair and body dried instantly. She lifted one foot to the edge of the tub and checked between her toes. Dry! The spell didn't usually work that well, but this morning it was perfect. The interior of the tub and shower curtain were similarly dry.

Her magic hadn't just recovered; it had increased. She was like a character in a video game who had... what was the term? *Leveled up.*

The new and improved, leveled-up Zinnia Riddle got dressed. She pulled on a cute pair of green corduroy stretch jeans and a flowered silk blouse. Zinnia liked to dress casually on the weekend, so she didn't fasten the top two buttons of her blouse. She closed the doors on her closet, which contained dozens of variations of the same basic outfit.

Her mentor had always stressed the importance of minimizing frivolous decisions, leaving the mind free for more important matters. Choosing a wardrobe and sticking to it was one way of simplifying. So was waking up and going to sleep at the same time each day, or drinking the same tea.

More important than routine, though, was adversity. Too much comfort makes a witch weak. A tree that takes no wind gets fragile and topples in the first storm. Etcetera.

Zinnia had been well served by her mentor, even if it hadn't felt that way at the time. Only now, at forty-eight, she was finally able to fully appreciate the wisdom that had been passed on. Her training had truly saved her bacon the night before. If she hadn't developed good muscle memory thanks to countless drills with fundamental spells, she might have accidentally incinerated all of Towhee Swamp. Or herself. Or poor Margaret.

If Zinnia Riddle were ever in the mentor position herself, she would teach the way her mentor did. With the stupid egg drills and everything.

* * *

Half an hour later, Zinnia found that the dreaded egg drill wasn't so stupid after all. One might almost call it fun. Fun and useful. A witch would be hard pressed to find a better way to practice accuracy than by peeling the shell off a levitating egg. The egg was raw, so the real trick wasn't in removing the shell, but keeping the wobbly liquid egg in its egg form.

The doorbell rang.

Doorbell!

She smiled as the word *doorbell* reverberated in her mind. Zinnia and her older sister, Zirconia, used to yell *doorbell* and fight each other to reach the front door first. They did the same for the ringing telephone, back in the days before voicemail—before answering machines, even.

The doorbell rang again.

Zinnia's egg wobbled. Long drips formed, straining to break free of the magical tether and succumb to gravity. Zinnia managed to hold the half-peeled egg together long enough to get it over the sink. It plopped with a wet crunch.

She ran to the door, excited to see Jesse. They didn't have plans until dinner, but sometimes he surprised her on Saturday mornings by dropping in with fresh croissants. Whenever he did pop in, it was about this time.

Zinnia was surprised to see a woman standing on her porch. The woman was in her late twenties, and she wore a shiny silver jumpsuit that made her look like the flight crew for a spaceship in a cheap sci-fi movie. Golden blonde ringlets framed a round face that was as perfectly symmetrical as it was pretty. She looked up at Zinnia with eyes that shifted between blue and something else—the gray of cast concrete statues. Her natural beauty was enhanced by a light dusting of shimmering makeup, frosty pink. The blonde was neither tall nor short. Some might describe her as petite, which was probably what she wanted. Better to be underestimated. She stood solidly, with her feet apart. A power pose. And, oh boy, did she have powers.

Zinnia took an automatic step back and crossed her wrists, palms forward.

The blonde smirked as she looked down at Zinnia's hands. Her light eyebrows rose in amusement.

"Easy now, Ms. Riddle," she said. "There's no need for either of us girls to mess up our hair and makeup."

Us girls? It was just like a twenty-nine-year-old to refer to a pair of women as *girls*. The label offended Zinnia, and yet, on some level, she also enjoyed being lumped into a category with the young woman on her porch. Such internal conflict. Being called a *girl* at forty-eight was nearly as flattering as it was patronizing.

Zinnia took a second step back and relaxed her arms into a welcoming swing. "Won't you come in, Ms. Wakeful?"

Charlize Wakeful's smirk blossomed into a grin. Zinnia felt the tautness in her muscles relax. It was hard to hate someone so beautiful and happy. But not hard to fear them. Some of the tautness remained.

"Please, take a seat anywhere," Zinnia said as she led Charlize to the living room.

Charlize looked past her. "Isn't that the kitchen over there?" She didn't wait for a response.

Zinnia followed her guest into the kitchen. The young woman's silver jumpsuit looked even more incongruous in that room than it had on the porch. Where exactly would one wear a silver jumpsuit? Besides the set of a music video.

"Kitschy wallpaper," Charlize said. "I like what you've done with the place."

Zinnia walked around the blonde, keeping a safe distance, and grabbed the kettle. "Tea or coffee?"

"Coffee. Unless there's tequila. Do you have tequila?"

It wasn't even nine o'clock in the morning. "I'll make coffee."

Charlize ran her hands over the wallpaper and continued to snoop around the kitchen while Zinnia put the kettle back and pulled out the coffee maker.

"Hah!" Charlize exclaimed.

"Hmm?" Zinnia turned to find the blonde leaning forward, her nose practically touching the stone object Zinnia had left resting on a dusty stack of recipes.

Charlize asked, "What's this supposed to be?"

What did it look like? "A paperweight," Zinnia answered flatly.

"Family heirloom?"

"How'd you guess?"

Charlize chuckled. "Ms. Riddle, that is not a paperweight."

Zinnia replied crisply, "I believe the papers it is currently weighting down would beg to differ. I've had it since—"

Charlize touched the lump with her fingertip. The lights overhead flickered. Zinnia felt all the air in her lungs forcibly leave. A charge of electricity pulsed through the room. Zinnia inhaled, gasping, just as the lumpy paperweight did the same. It had transformed into a mouse. A very confused-looking mouse, who skittered to the edge of the counter and jumped to the floor. It looked left and right, soiled the floor, and ran away.

Zinnia kept her shock to herself. *Poker face, Zinnia. Poker face. Don't let your guard down around a gorgon.* She reached for a paper towel and cleaning spray, and tidied up after the frightened mouse.

Charlize asked, "How long was that," she made air quotes with her fingers, "*paperweight* in your family?"

"A couple of generations, at least."

"Someone in the Riddle family tree must have been acquainted with a Wakeful or two."

"It would seem that way." Zinnia finished tidying the floor and washed her hands thoroughly. She fought the urge to spit on her hands for extra sanitization. Who knew what sort of germs a decades-old mouse carried? It could have fleas with bubonic plague.

Lightly, Zinnia asked, "How have you been?"

"Keepin' busy."

"Has there been any improvement with your sister?"

Charlize didn't answer. Zinnia looked up at her—not directly into the gorgon's eyes, but slightly to the side of her face. Safety first.

Charlize was frowning. "Uh, can you keep a secret?"

"Only the dead keep secrets, and even they aren't perfect."

"Then never mind. You'll find out soon enough." The sunny smile returned. The young gorgon yawned and stretched, snakelike in her movements, before changing the subject. "I'm here about something else, anyway. I'll give you three guesses and the first two don't count."

"You must be working with Detective Fung, investigating the Scholem homicide."

"Ding ding. We've got a winner!"

Zinnia pursed her lips. Annette Scholem had been her friend.

Charlize Wakeful continued, unperturbed. "Have you heard from her lately? By which I mean, have you heard from her ghost?"

"No."

"Aww, come on. I thought you witches were tapped in with the ghost world, what with all your archaic, demonic ways."

Zinnia pursed her lips even flatter. The gorgon was actually calling *her* archaic and demonic. The nerve.

"I'll take that as a no," Charlize said. "How about you do something for me right now? Call her up on the witch phone. I've got a few questions for the lady."

"It doesn't work that way."

"No?" Charlize blinked her powerful blue-gray eyes. "Fung says you saw the dead lady on Tuesday morning, right here in your kitchen." She looked around the room with a theatrical whipping of her blonde hair. As the ringlets swung out, Zinnia caught a glimpse of the hidden magic, a glimpse of the copper snakes that sprung from the gorgon's head. The snakes were both there and not there. Seen and not seen. Like a glamour.

"Well, I don't see any ghostly people," Charlize reported. "Can you tell if she's here right now?"

"No."

The snakes in her hair twitched. "But you saw her. Don't lie to me, witch." The copper snakes flashed their fangs.

Zinnia made her voice soft and non-confrontational. It was the same tone she took with her boss, Karl Kormac, when he was having a mood swing. "Ms. Wakeful, I assure you that I only saw Annette Scholem briefly, thanks to a reveal spell. That particular spell only works if the ghost is fresh, and only for a glimpse. I cannot contact her directly."

"You mean you *won't*. I'm sure you *can*."

Zinnia said nothing. There were indeed ways to make contact with ghosts, but the spells were dangerous and required multiple spellcasters.

A tense silence hung in the air.

When Zinnia spoke, she chose her words carefully. "If it were truly that easy, I would have done so already."

"I bet." Charlize, who'd been staring at the candid photos on the vintage fridge, finished her inspection of the kitchen and grabbed a seat, turning a chair around and straddling it. "Hey, Annette," she said in a falsetto tone, imitating Zinnia in a scenario where she called the ghost on a ghost phone. "Tell me something, girlfriend. Who or what killed you, and how? Oh, really? Okay, okay! Slow down, I can't write that fast."

Zinnia was not amused. "Only a few of the most cursed witches interact with the dead." She licked her lips and added, "Poor things." Her older sister had been one of those cursed witches, and she'd taken extreme measures to free herself. But that was none of this gorgon's business.

"Only a few? I thought all of you witches were cursed."

"Charmed or cursed, it all depends on your perspective."

Charlize waved a hand. "Yeah, yeah. Glass half empty, glass half full. Speaking of which, is that coffee ready?"

Zinnia turned her back on the gorgon. The coffee was ready.

Charlize asked, in the most casual of tones, "So, did you know Annette Scholem was one of you? That she was a witch?"

Zinnia's hand missed the handle of the coffee pot. Her fingertips sizzled as they touched the hot glass. She didn't yank her hand away. It was not that it didn't hurt, but the news was so revelatory, she didn't notice her fingertips scalding.

Annette Scholem was a witch?

Zinnia was glad she had her back to the gorgon because she wouldn't have been able to maintain a poker face.

A witch.

Annette!

But of course Annette was a witch. That explained why she knew everyone's secret powers to write them in her book. It had nothing to do with the pen.

Secrets revealed are trouble unsealed.

Suddenly, so many things made sense.

CHAPTER 22

Charlize said, "I'll take it by the way you're fondling that hot coffee pot that you didn't know Annette Scholem was a witch."

Zinnia recovered from the shock of the news and put on her poker face. She shook her hand to fix her burned fingertips, then grabbed the coffee pot by the handle, along with a mug, and brought both over to the table. Charlize, who'd been straddling a kitchen chair, got up just long enough to turn her chair around and sit like a lady. Zinnia considered breaking out the tequila after all, but the impulse quickly passed.

Zinnia lifted her chin and looked directly into the blonde's eyes as she sat. *Face your fears*, her mentor used to say. It was good advice for anyone.

Zinnia took a good look at the young woman in front of her. She was beautiful and fierce, yes, but she was also partly human. Zinnia scanned down to the woman's hands. And there it was. The flaw. The chink in the armor. Charlize had short, ragged fingernails. She was a nail biter.

Seeing this sign of humanity softened Zinnia's edge. Why was she so dead set against cooperating with the people who worked in the shadows? They were just people. Sort of. Why not try trusting them? Or at least this one.

Zinnia spoke softly. "Honestly, I didn't know Annette was a witch. None of us knew." She poured the gorgon's coffee.

"That does explain a few things," Charlize said. "You're not lying to me, are you?"

"I'm telling you the truth. I shall only tell you the truth today." Zinnia moved her hands in a magical threading-the-needle gesture. "My word is my bond."

"Neat," Charlize said. "The hand gesture is a nice touch."

Zinnia wasn't sure if she was being teased or praised, so she said nothing.

Charlize took a big slurp of the steaming coffee and made a face. "Ow. This coffee is hot. I burned my tongue."

Zinnia reached out her hand, two fingers extended. "Here. Let me fix that burn."

Charlize frowned for a moment before understanding what the witch was offering. She hesitantly stuck out her tongue. Zinnia was surprised to see the woman's tongue looked like a regular, human tongue. She'd been expecting something snakelike. Forked.

Zinnia pinched the round tip between her fingers, sent healing energy forward, and quickly released it. The transaction had taken all of two seconds. A burned tongue doesn't take much to heal with magic.

"Much better," Charlize said. "I can see how it would be handy to have one of you around."

"You're welcome," Zinnia said, even though she hadn't been thanked.

"I owe you one."

Zinnia held her peace. She couldn't imagine anything she'd ever want from a gorgon, but whatever.

Zinnia asked, "How did you find out Annette was a witch? I didn't even know, and I've worked five feet away from her for the last year."

"It was her organs."

Zinnia fought down revulsion and asked, "The ones that were removed by the attacker?"

"The attacker didn't remove or consume anything," Charlize said. "It just looked that way."

"Good," Zinnia said. The crime was still horrific, but the news that nothing had eaten Annette's organs came as a small relief.

"As for how we could tell she was a witch, I'm afraid our autopsy guys weren't too generous with the details. Jerry Lund called in Dr. Bob to help, and that's when they figured it out. That's all I know. Dr. Bob's a brilliant doctor, but he can be secretive."

"Yes. Your people can be secretive." Zinnia glanced down at Charlize's ragged fingernails to summon her courage to ask the next question. "As for the wounds, what manner of creature made them? Was it a shifter? One of yours?"

The snakes hiding within Charlize's ringlets appeared and hissed with displeasure. "Whether it was a wolf or a cougar who attacked Ms. Scholem, he or she wasn't one of ours. All of our agents are accounted for."

"Sure they are." *Like protects like.* Zinnia hadn't expected any different. When Margaret got the full report of this meeting, she wouldn't be surprised either.

"The funny thing is..." Charlize paused, her cold blue eyes sparkling now. She was excited about sharing this next detail. "I don't think Annette knew she was a witch. Did she ever mention to you she was adopted?"

The word bond Zinnia had taken made her answer quickly and honestly, without filtering the response through her thoughts. "No, she never mentioned it, but the narrator in her book was adopted, so I'm not that surprised."

"Isn't that funny? She didn't know she was a witch."

Zinnia stiffened in her chair. She crossed her arms. "It's not funny for a witch to be unaware of her powers. It could lead to someone being seriously injured."

Charlize shrugged. "I thought it was funny."

Zinnia said nothing.

Charlize said, "Stonewalling me, huh?"

"Are you actually working the case, or is this a social call, Ms. Wakeful?"

"What's wrong with a social call? Us girls should be closer."

"And do *us girls* have any suspects?"

"There's Villobek, whoever that is. Good job using your witcher-i-doo to track him or her to the swamp, by the way. Any chance I can get you and the other witch to do another one of those spells?"

"There'd be no point. The evil entity develops an immunity after the first casting."

Charlize wrinkled her nose. "You're pulling my leg."

"I don't make the rules."

"How does it work? The immunity?"

Zinnia felt a twinge of mischief. "Are you asking for the investigation, or are you planning to do something evil?"

Charlize laughed. "Good one. But seriously. How does an evil entity develop immunity to witchcraft?"

"It's not like witchbane, if that's what you're wondering. It's just immunity to specific spells. Like how the flu shot gives people a little bit of the virus so they don't get hit harder later."

"Interesting." Charlize looked thoughtful. "I should be taking notes. We should get you to come in and run some workshops. You can educate us about the wicked and wonderful ways of witches."

Zinnia spoke with honesty. "That will never, ever happen. The less other people know about witches, the better. Especially the 'people' you work with."

Charlize pouted.

"I don't make the rules," Zinnia said again.

Charlize looked down at her coffee. She lifted it to her lips and blew over it carefully before taking a cautious sip. "Perfect," she said.

"You were saying?" Zinnia made a rolling gesture with one hand. "About suspects?"

"There's the obvious one. Carrot Greyson."

"She does seem to be connected."

"Our current theory is that Greyson was remotely operating animals from a trance state. She's got a few other animal tattoos, in addition to the cougar on her chest. If she's controlling animals, it would explain a few things."

"Such as?"

"For example, some of the squirrels in this town are extremely erratic."

"Yes. The squirrels in this town *are* erratic." Zinnia thought of one in particular: Petey the Squirrel. He was a pest who regularly mugged people for their muffins at Wisteria's sidewalk cafes.

"When Carrot was interviewed last night, she told us she'd been dreaming about the attacks. Vivid dreams. On Monday night, she dreamed she was the animal who attacked Annette. When she woke up, the memory was so powerful, it made her violently ill. That's why she called in to work sick on Tuesday. The next night, she—"

Zinnia interrupted. "Why would Carrot do something that made her sick? It's more logical that she was picking up a stray signal, maybe from someone else." Zinnia shook her head. "Carrot is as innocent as they come."

Charlize drank more coffee and continued. "Carrot went to bed early last night, right after she got home from bowling with your office. She dreamed that she was stalking two women in the woods. When she recognized them as her coworkers, Margaret Mills and you, she woke up, jumped in her car and drove to the marsh, which she'd recognized in the dream. She didn't understand what was happening, but she wanted to see for herself if she was crazy." Charlize smirked. "I find that people in this town do that sort of thing a lot."

"That explains why she showed up, but I think you're barking up the wrong tree with her as a suspect. Are you absolutely certain it wasn't one of your shifter pals? For example, your brother-in-law?"

Charlize chewed on one of her ragged fingernails. "He's not my brother-in-law. Chet and Chessa were only engaged before the accident. Not married."

"But he is a wolf. Or at least he's a wolf when he wants to be."

Charlize said, "Since you're being honest with me, I won't deny it. Yes, Chet Moore is a wolf shifter. No, he didn't kill Scholem. He was working late that night on a project, and I can personally assure you he's accounted for."

Zinnia pressed on. "And how about your other brother-in-law, Jordan Taub? He spends his days baking, but how does he spend his nights?"

Charlize chewed a new fingernail. "How interesting. You think Jordan is a shifter. You don't know very much about what goes on in this town, do you?"

Zinnia licked her lips, remembering the taste of the cougar's blood. She didn't know everything, but she was finding out more every day.

Charlize yanked her fingers out of her mouth. She couldn't resist tearing off a piece of ragged fingernail and setting it on the table next to her coffee mug.

Zinnia stared at the torn fingernail and thought of something she'd noticed at the crime scene. "There wasn't any blood on the windowsill of the office. You'd think that a wild wolf or cougar would leave a few drips or smears behind when they climbed back out through the window."

"True," Charlize said. "But there were blood stains on the carpet near the window. Not enough that we needed to replace the carpet, but the cleanup crew did steam it."

"But there was no blood on the windowsill." Zinnia kept staring at the piece of fingernail on the table. "Whoever attacked Annette might not have gone out through the window, which leaves the door. But with the way the chair was wedged up against the door, that seems unlikely. It's almost as though the attacker simply stomped their foot three times and disappeared."

"Like a gnome?"

Zinnia looked up into the gorgon's eyes. It was getting easier each time. "Exactly like a gnome."

Charlize frowned. "I suppose we could look into Gavin Gorman's alibi."

"Unlike Carrot, Gavin actually had motivation to get rid of Annette. She was always telling Dawna that she could do better than him." Not that it had done any good. Even with Annette gone, the two had already broken up yet again.

"You make a good point," Charlize said. "I'm glad I came by to talk to you." She looked past Zinnia, at something that made her smile. "I've learned so much."

Zinnia asked, "Where is Carrot right now, anyway?"

"Don't worry. She's fine. Carrot doesn't know it, but she's got friends in high places."

Zinnia's interest was piqued. "Oh?"

"Her brother, and also her—" Charlize frowned. "Forget I said that." She waved a hand while her semi-visible hair snakes hissed. "Forget I said anything about Carrot's friends in high places." More hissing. "Forget thisssssss."

Zinnia waved her own hand in the opposite direction, countering the spell. "Witches don't forget so easily."

Charlize sighed. Then she slugged back the rest of the coffee and jumped to her feet, her silver jumpsuit rustling as she did.

"Thanks for the coffee," Charlize said. "I should be on my way. I only came here for information, and now I've got it."

"What information? Do you have something else on Gavin?"

Charlize quirked one eyebrow and spoke stiffly. "I'm afraid I can't let the cat out of the bag yet, so to speak."

Zinnia snapped her fingers in a *darn* gesture. "Ms. Wakeful, I would threaten to turn you into a frog right now if I wasn't sure you'd turn me into a statue first."

Charlize grinned. "You're fun when you get loosened up. We should hang out more often." She headed for the door. Zinnia followed.

When they reached the entryway, Charlize paused, looking up at the garden painted on the ceiling. "You should be careful, Ms. Riddle. Stay close to home for a couple of days. Don't invite anyone over."

"Am I under surveillance?"

Charlize kept staring at the ceiling. "I'm not at liberty to discuss that matter."

"I thought we were being honest with each other."

Charlize looked at Zinnia. She unzipped a pocket in her silver jumpsuit and reached for something. "Do you have the switchboard number for the DWM?"

"The DWM?"

Charlize winked. "DWM. It's short for Department of Water," she lowered her voice and finished in a dramatic whisper, "and Magic." She produced a business card and handed it over. The card looked exactly like an ordinary card for the Wisteria Department of Water, except it had the words *emergency line* written in red, along with a phone number.

"Department of Water and Magic," Zinnia said, dumbfounded. That was the cover for the people in the shadows? The Department of Water? It did explain why their office operations weren't housed at City Hall along with the other municipal services.

Charlize hadn't left yet. She was looking at Zinnia closely, and her hair snakes were doing something as well. Sniffing the air.

Zinnia glanced around. "Is something wrong? I have protective wards on the house, but they're not infallible."

"It's something else." Charlize pointed to Zinnia's heart. "Would you like me to help you with that?"

"With what?" Zinnia wasn't being evasive. She truly didn't understand what the blonde gorgon meant.

"Easier to show you than explain," Charlize said. "Plus, I owe you one for fixing the burn on my tongue." She placed her hand on Zinnia's chest, over her heart. The gorgon's hair erupted in snakes. Each snake grew, until it was three feet long, then six feet long, then the small entryway room was nothing but snakes, hissing and writhing.

The breath whooshed out of Zinnia's lungs. Up was down and down was up. Lights flickered. Zinnia felt her skin cracking, her mind melting. It was like what had happened to the paperweight mouse, except now it was happening to her. A hot wet feeling burst through Zinnia's chest, as though she was a volcano erupting.

This is how I die?

Zinnia was more than a little surprised. She'd always expected to get a psychic preview of her demise, even if it only preceded the event by two to five minutes.

CHAPTER 23

12:30 PM

Zinnia Riddle hadn't died. It just felt that way.

She lay on the cool tiles of her bathroom floor, curled in the fetal position. The only sound was the soothing drip-drop of a tap.

Drip-drop. Drip-drop.

She had been there a while. An hour, maybe? She should have said no to Charlize. She shouldn't have accepted the gorgon's "help."

Drip-drop.

But the gorgon had placed her cursed hands on Zinnia's chest, and now...

Zinnia squeezed her eyes shut. In the darkness, she kept seeing the body. *No.* She saw Annette. No. The body. *Annette's body.*

In her mind's eye, the body stirred and became Annette again. She hadn't died. Not yet. She was reaching out, bloody arm trembling, reaching for Zinnia. Her big, brown eyes pleaded for help. Annette's voice came out raspy. "Help me. I don't understand what's happening. What's wrong with me?" But those weren't Annette's words; they had been Zinnia's words, long ago. From yet another time she'd been trying to forget.

Zinnia opened her eyes and stared at the edge of two planes, where the wall met the floor. She turned her head and pressed her forehead on the cool tiles. She had to get up. She had to keep moving, stop closing her eyes and seeing the body. *Annette.* The body. *Annette's body.*

The pain in Zinnia's chest was unbearable. She let out a low, continuous moan that didn't help at all except to make her feel even more pathetic.

She propped herself up using her hands, then collapsed on her other side. Ah, the tile was so cool on her hot cheek. And there was so much new information to digest.

The shadowy people in town were more organized than she'd ever imagined. They were operating in plain sight, under the Department of Water. And those people—the DWM—were working on Annette's case, which was back to being considered a homicide, not the animal attack the public believed it to be.

Zinnia placed her cool fingertips against her hot eyelids. In less than a week, her whole world had changed. She didn't even know the people she worked with.

Carrot Greyson had mage powers, whether she knew it or not. She also had a brother who was working for the DWM. That had to be Ishmael Greyson, since he was the only sibling of Carrot's who lived in Wisteria. Zinnia hadn't thought much of the young man. What powers did he have, she wondered. And was the other friend Carrot had in high places her boyfriend, Steve? He was a lawyer, according to Carrot. But was he, really?

And then there was Annette. She'd been like Zinnia, like Margaret. A witch. Three of them had worked side by side for a year and not even known they were a triad. How could Zinnia have been so blind?

Zinnia stopped rubbing her eyes. She'd been pressing too hard, making herself see patches of unreal light behind her eyelids. She was harming herself.

Just like she'd been harming herself by drinking that tea every day.

She moved her hands down to her chest. Her heart continued to beat despite the pain.

Charlize had used her powers to peel away months and months of potion. Now Zinnia's heart was bare, with no magical stone around it. No protection. She could feel all of her feelings, and they were agony.

Aiden.

Now that her heart was raw and open, she thought of the sweet child. Aiden. How he'd been so hopeful, and how she'd let him down. The pain knocked the wind out of her lungs. How could she breathe when Aiden did not?

Zinnia Riddle hadn't died, but it sure felt like it.

* * *

There was something purple at the edge of her vision.

Zinnia blinked to refocus her eyes. Purple? A little spark of curiosity pushed through the curtain of pain.

What was that purple thing? Annette's pen? How had it gotten into the bathroom? She blinked again. It wasn't the pen. It was an old purple toothbrush that had fallen behind the laundry basket. Just a toothbrush.

But now she was thinking about the pen, and the more she thought about the pen, the less she thought about Carrot Greyson, or Annette's body, or all the times Zinnia had let people down.

The pen?

She unrolled from her ball, stretched, and got to her feet.

The pen!

The pen was the answer. As long as she stayed on mission, stayed focused on something concrete, the pain in her raw, meaty heart stayed in the background.

She went to her bedroom and retrieved the box containing Annette's pen. She stared at the simple plastic thing. It was no less ordinary than the fallen toothbrush. And yet, this was what Gavin had been searching for on Annette's body.

But why? Gnomes were naturally drawn to objects of value, but the pen was worthless. Zinnia had already checked it for enchantments. It didn't have never-ending ink, tidy handwriting, or even spell check.

She stared at the room's pretty wallpaper and searched her mental database for other explanations.

Movement in the room pulled her from her thoughts. Something was moving. Something right in front of her. It was... her own hand. Zinnia's hand was gripping the pen and moving. Writing. Guided by Annette's simple plastic pen. She was writing, but she didn't have any paper, so she was writing on the leg of her green pants. The pen was too eager to bother waiting for paper. Why now? Why not when she'd tried to figure out the pen the first time?

She used her other hand to catch herself by the wrist and lift her scribbling hand. The pen resisted, but not very much. Just a little tug.

Zinnia smoothed out the fabric ripples on her slacks and examined the markings. Were the scribbles a spell? Runes? Secret messages from the dead?

She squinted, and the lines became letters and then words. Words she could read. Zinnia stopped breathing. She had written on her pants leg the title of the memoir she and Margaret used to privately joke about her writing: *The Life and Times of Zinnia Riddle, A Not-too-Witchy Witch.*

Below the title was an unfinished sentence. *Once upon a ti—.* If she hadn't stopped the pen, it would have kept on writing. Writing... her story?

Zinnia remembered to breathe.

The magic imbued in Annette's pen was very powerful indeed. She could have gathered some of her printer paper, settled at a flat writing surface, and had a complete tell-all memoir written in a matter of days. How... wonderful? Her battered heart throbbed. It was not wonderful. More like terrifying! All her secrets, exposed on paper.

She carefully removed the pen from her hand. She didn't dare set it down, so she held it in her non-dominant hand. The pen felt surprisingly heavy all of a sudden. She dropped her hand to her leg, and the pen immediately began writing. Zinnia gasped and lifted her hand again, but not before it completed the sentence: *Once upon a time there was a girl named Zinnia.*

Annette's book had also started with the phrase "Once upon a time." Was the pen charmed to begin all stories that way? It was not the most original of openings, but you could only ask so much of a pen.

Zinnia used her magic to twirl the pen through the air while she pondered what to do next. After a moment, she leaned forward and caught it between her teeth. She kept it there and waited. The pen did not attempt to use her head as a writing appendage. Not yet, anyway.

Still holding the pen between her teeth, she went to her concealed cupboard and withdrew a single magical book. She cast a basic page-finding spell, and the pages riffled open to the chapter she needed.

The page read: *Animata Energy. A witch may, at times, unknowingly enchant or encurse the objects that she comes into contact with regularly. This phenomenon of Animata Transference is more likely to occur when the witch has not been keeping up her magical practice. In extreme cases, the objects may become dangerous, but the phenomenon is largely benign. However, as with all enchantments or encursements, there is the potential for great danger should the objects fall into the wrong hands.*

Zinnia read on with the pen gripped safely between her teeth.

When she finished the chapter, she understood. The pen had become enchanted—or encursed—due to Annette's frequent use of it. The only reason Zinnia's or Margaret's pens didn't take on Animata Transference was because they knew they were witches and dispersed their magical energy regularly. Even during Zinnia's period of trying to "go straight," she still used her magic weekly at minimum.

Zinnia looked down at the pen, still held between her teeth. Once the Animata from Annette had been transferred, the pen had developed the ability to tell the writer's most heartfelt story.

Zinnia touched her chest. Now she understood why her tests with the pen on Wednesday morning had yielded no results. While her heart had been magically cursed with its stone coating, the pen couldn't have worked in her hands. Even with its powerful Animata magic, it was still just a pen. It couldn't reach her heart through its protective coating.

She turned her head and carefully dropped the pen on her bed next to her. It still appeared to be nothing more than a simple plastic pen. And to think she hadn't realized what she had, until now.

Could Charlize have known? Was that why the gorgon had been so eager to "help" Zinnia's heart break free of its granite box?

Her mind reeled. Were Zinnia's choices even her own, or had she been directed to this point in time by design? Was she simply a pawn in a game controlled by powerful players?

Zinnia's paranoid mind churned with conspiracy theories that were so convoluted, they would make Margaret's rants seem tame by comparison.

The redheaded witch sat on her bed with the pen next to her for several minutes while she gathered her thoughts.

When her head finally cleared, it was crystal clear. She jumped up. She knew what she had to do. It was time to put some pressure on Gavin Gorman. First, she would change into a fresh pair of slacks, and then she would go press on the gnome. She would press until one of them broke.

CHAPTER 24

THE CANDY FACTORY APARTMENTS

1:25 PM

Zinnia stood near the front door of the Candy Factory Apartments, cupping her hand over her eyes to block the sunshine as she tried to read the digital intercom screen. She couldn't complain about the nice weather that was rare for January, but the sunshine did make reading the screen difficult. For the third time, she scrolled through the Candy Factory's tenant listing looking for Gavin's apartment number. She'd probably resort to jinxing the front door open, but not yet. It was best to avoid using magic when regular means would suffice.

The pain in her chest had dulled since she'd gotten herself off the bathroom floor, only to be replaced by a heavy ache that was in some ways worse because it fluctuated. Sadness would come in waves, making her eyes blur. She missed Annette Scholem. She missed the life she'd tried to have. Her eyes blurred. Zinnia didn't know what grief was good for, but it sure wasn't for helping her see names on the intercom's digital scroll.

She had just found Gavin's apartment number when movement on the other side of the building's glass door caught her eye. A gentleman with pink hair was standing by the communal mailboxes, sorting a handful of mail. When he saw Zinnia looking at him, he came to the door to let her in.

"Good afternoon to you, Zinnia Riddle!" He gave her a pearly smile that was nearly as bright as Gavin's. "We're not supposed to let random people into the building, but I'll vouch for you personally."

Zinnia forced a light laugh. "Thanks for that, Fred."

"Frank," he said, correcting her. "Frank Wonder."

She touched her fingers to her forehead. "I knew that. Sorry, Frank. I haven't been feeling like myself today."

"Oh?" His voice and body language were playful, his skinny form undulating, noodle-like. "Who *have you* been feeling like?"

"That's a good question. I shall get back to you on that when I see you at..." She trailed off, confused by her own words. The ache of her grief pulsed with each heartbeat.

The older man cocked his head. With his bright pink hair, Frank Wonder reminded Zinnia of a tropical bird. Not everyone could pull off the flamingo-pink hair look, but Frank did so with wondrous panache. It was the perfect hairdo for his career. He worked as a children's librarian, and all the kids adored his fun style.

He finished Zinnia's sentence for her. "When you see me at the next fundraiser?"

"Yes," she said, although she'd been thinking of something completely different. She'd had the strangest premonition she would be seeing Frank soon, at a dinner party. Perhaps this was a side effect of the gorgon pulsing Zinnia's heart back to life. Or she was truly going crazy. Either way, there was no time to dwell on it now. She had to apply some pressure to a certain gnome.

Frank Wonder wished her a pleasant day and went back to his mail sorting.

Zinnia headed for the stairwell and took the stairs two at a time. The old building was chock-a-block with ghosts and foul energy. Most of the bad juju pooled in the stairwells and common areas. The individual apartments had been treated by the magical equivalent of an exterminator, for the protection of residents. Most ghosts were harmless, but they could be provoked by the living. The Candy Factory was not Zinnia's favorite building, yet the owners always found long-term tenants with ease. It was particularly popular with divorced or single men who valued the building's top-of-the-line fitness room.

Zinnia banged on Gavin's door until it opened.

By the look of his shirtless, sweaty torso, Gavin Gorman had recently made use of the gym facilities. The apartment behind him was tidy and quiet; Dawna didn't appear to be there.

"Zinnia Riddle," he said with grim politeness. "To what do I owe the pleasure of seeing your frowning face and flowery attire on a Saturday afternoon?"

"I'm here about the pen," she said. The time for subtlety had long passed. "Annette's pen. The one you were groping her lifeless body for."

He didn't even blink. He'd been expecting this conversation.

Zinnia tapped her toe. "We ought not conduct our business in the hallway."

He smirked. "We *ought not*? You're a funny bunny, Zinnia." He blocked the doorway to his apartment with his body. "What's the magic password?"

She raised her eyebrows. Was he serious?

"You should be able to guess the password," he said. "Or are you not much of a witch?"

Not much of a witch? His words reverberated down the open hallway for anyone to hear. Zinnia bit back her fury. It was unforgivable for a person with supernatural powers to reveal another person's gifts in a public forum. Not to mention the height of rudeness.

Tersely, she replied, "If you're a gnome, then I suppose that makes me equally special." Louder, she said, "That is, if you, Gavin Gorman, truly are a gnome."

The skin on his bare chest contracted visibly, goose bumps forming across his pectorals. His nipples might have hardened, but Zinnia avoided seeing them do so. She had the good manners to not stare at a man's nipples, unlike Gavin, who didn't have the good manners to pull on a shirt before answering the door.

Finally, Gavin stepped back and waved her into the apartment.

Zinnia felt a sense of relief as she stepped into his ghost-free personal space and away from the haunted hallway.

"Make yourself at home," Gavin said. "Don't mind me. I just worked out, and if I don't power up with my smoothie right away, I'll crash." He walked over to the open kitchen area and picked up smoothie preparations where he'd apparently left off. He didn't say anything about the pen. He was stalling for time, mentally preparing a cover story. Zinnia decided to let him try.

Gavin used a pair of shiny scissors to snip greenery from a row of plants he had growing in pots on the windowsill.

Zinnia looked around the apartment. Her gaze was drawn by a framed painting of a woman. A nude woman. She had red hair and creamy pale skin. Every inch of her was naked.

"Nice painting," Zinnia said.

"Local artist," Gavin said. He narrowed his eyes. "Any chance you've done a little figure modeling? I can't see much of her face, and I always thought my girl bore a resemblance to you."

Zinnia gave him a thin smile. "I am *not* your girl."

"If you say so." He finished snipping greenery from the plants on the windowsill.

Zinnia joined Gavin in the kitchen area, walking over to the window to inspect the plants. Herbs were one of Zinnia's specialties, so she recognized the plants instantly. All except for the basil were magical species.

She pinched off a leaf and rolled it between her fingers. Potent magic released in a puff of colored crystals. An idea began forming in Zinnia's mind, and as it did, the weight in her chest grew lighter. *Yes.* Staying on track was the answer. Moving forward. She would keep moving. She would find Annette's killer, avenge her death, and then the pain would go away. Not all deaths could be avenged, but this one would. Annette Scholem would have justice.

Zinnia turned to face her spray-tanned, bare-chested coworker. "Gavin, are you sure you know what you're doing with these herbs? Some of the combinations can have strong side effects."

He snorted and continued sprinkling the herbs into his blender. "Don't worry about me. Wick gave me very clear instructions."

"Which Wick was that? Only one of them can be trusted, and even then I'd be cautious."

"You worry about your smoothies, and I'll worry about mine." He shot her a knowing look. "Or should I say... *your tea.*"

"Fair enough." She washed the crushed herb from her hands. "Speaking of the Wicks, are you aware that their family operated a poison factory within these walls for twenty years?"

An expression of shock registered on Gavin's face before he regained composure. "This building was a candy factory," he said indignantly. "There are a bunch of old-timey photos of the factory in operation, down in the lobby."

"Yes, at some point it was a candy factory," Zinnia agreed. "But it's a good, sturdy building. A fortress, really. These old stone walls have housed a great many operations over the years. Candy factory. Poison factory. Prison for the criminally insane. At one point it was even—"

"Nope!" He cut her off with a waving hand, brandishing the flashing scissors. "That's more than enough. I still have to live here, thank you." He set down the scissors and hit a button to fire up the blender. Over the noise, he yelled, "What do you want from me, anyway?"

She waited until the blender was finished and said, "Answers. Why were you after Annette's pen?"

His cheeks slackened and his eyes widened. "Do you have it with you? Give me the pen and I'll tell you everything."

"Tit for tat? Is that any way to treat a coworker? I thought we were a team. We're the Incredibowls. What happened to cooperation?"

"You don't understand gnomes at all, do you?"

She looked down at his socked foot. "I know that if you stamp your foot three times, you'll go away."

"That's just an urban legend," he said.

Zinnia knew he was lying, but let it go.

He poured his green smoothie into a glass and started gulping it down. When he was done drinking, he wiped his mouth with the back of his hand and glanced around the apartment as though looking for an excuse to end their visit.

"Listen, Zinnia, it's not personal. I like you. And Margaret, too. I like everyone at the office. Even Karl."

"How about Annette? You liked her, but you killed her because she wouldn't give you her pen."

Gavin held his fist to his solar plexus and stifled a burp. "Of course not. How could you even say that? How could you think that about me?"

"Are you protecting someone else? Maybe your girlfriend?"

He blinked three times. "Dawna didn't do anything. She doesn't even know she's a cartomancer. The crazy girl thinks she's just really lucky at picking scratch-off tickets."

"What about Carrot?"

"What about her?"

"There was another attack last night, at Towhee Swamp. Carrot showed up. According to her statement, she went to bed early and started having vivid dreams about stalking people. So she jumped out of bed, got into her car, and drove to the swamp, but she was too late. The attack had already happened. I witnessed the whole thing."

Gavin stifled another burp. "Did anyone get hurt?"

"No."

He made a *phew* noise. "Life in Wisteria is stranger than fiction."

"You must know something," Zinnia said. "You must have some ideas about Carrot's powers. You've worked with her a lot longer than I have. Why was she receiving visions from a cougar?"

"A cougar? Don't you mean a wolf?"

"I'm not sure there ever was a wolf," she said. "Just a cougar." She explained what had happened at the swamp the night before, leaving out the fact Margaret had been present.

When she had finished catching him up, Gavin shrugged. "Magic stuff is weird. I don't know what you want from me." He put his glass in the sink, grabbed a too-small gray T-shirt off a chair, and pulled it on. He started cleaning the kitchen, carefully avoiding eye contact the whole time.

"Tell me what you're hiding," she said, weaving a bluffing spell between the spoken words with Witch Tongue. The charm wouldn't work on the gnome, but she had a different plan. She let her tongue hit her teeth sloppily, so that the gnome would hear something of the spell. "Tell me what you're not saying."

He licked his lips. "I heard what you did just now, with your witcher-i-doo. Don't bother trying to hocus pocus me, Zinnia. Gnomes can't be charmed by your witch spells. You're not getting anything out of me."

He'd heard the spell, exactly as she'd intended. He had fallen for her bluff. She suppressed her smile, though she felt it ripple through her body.

"I suppose you're too clever for me," she said with resignation. "But your kind is still susceptible to certain potions." She set her purse on the counter with a dramatic thunk.

"So what?" He looked at the purse on the counter and frowned. "I'm not an idiot. I'm not going to drink anything you give me."

"No need," she said lightly, allowing her internal smile to curve her mouth. "You already fed it to yourself. You made a smoothie with three magical herbs, but you didn't add the fourth. I suppose you made that choice because the fourth one has wilted and doesn't look so appealing. If you'd like to revive it, try putting the pot in your bathroom for a few days. The steam from your shower will do wonders. You can make a new smoothie by tomorrow, but

I'm afraid that by then," she paused and gave him a concerned look, "it may be too late."

"Too late for what?"

She knew very well what the four herbs were used for. She had helped Tansy perfect the combination. The woman could have made herself rich selling the herbs online to men who wanted to be more impressive in the bedroom. Gavin, vain as he was, was an ideal customer.

Zinnia held up one hand and made a drooping gesture.

Gavin understood. He swallowed hard and frowned at the plants on the windowsill. He cursed under his breath. "I shouldn't have trusted Wick. I shouldn't have messed around with those herbs. My kind is much better with mechanical devices."

"But you can't use mechanical devices for..." She stopped herself. "Actually, I'd rather not know what you gnomes do."

His cheeks reddened. "Never mind about gnome stuff. Should I chew down some of that other plant right now? Will that help?"

"No."

His cheeks got even more red. "Thanks," he spat out. "Thanks a lot. You had to come in here and distract me, didn't you?"

Zinnia reached into her purse and pulled out a glass baby jar full of orange mush.

Gavin stopped making sputtering sounds and stared at the jar with a hopeful look.

"Don't worry your pretty face," Zinnia said. "I happen to have something with me that will reverse what you just poisoned yourself with. As a matter of fact, if you ration yourself, there's more than enough here for you to keep Dawna happy for a long time."

He lunged for the jar, as she knew he would. She used magic to levitate it out of reach.

The grief in her chest was gone now, replaced by something not unlike happiness. It felt good to practice magic openly in front of a new person. She and Gavin were not the best of friends, but they could be open with each other now.

"Aw, come on, Zinnia," Gavin whined. "What happened to teamwork? Cooperation? We're the Incredibowls."

"The pen," she said. "Who wanted it?"

"Me," he said. "I've, uh, always wanted to write my life story."

Zinnia coughed and fixed him with her gaze.

"Fine," he said with a sigh. "I was going to sell it to the highest bidder through my uncle. Are you happy now?" He jumped for the floating jar, but it was up too high.

"Tell me how you knew about Annette's powers. Do you have some sort of detection device? Even Annette didn't know she was a witch."

He kept his gaze on the floating jar while he crossed his arms. "Have you ever heard of gnome intuition?"

"I've heard your type has powers of perception when it comes to acquiring items of value. I didn't realize it was supernatural." She'd thought it was simple greed, but didn't use this word with Gavin.

"Yeah, well, we do have intuition, and let me tell you, it's both a strength and a weakness. Why do you think I can't stay away from Dawna?"

"Are you telling me you aren't in love with Dawna?"

"I'm telling you it's *why* I'm in love with her."

Zinnia frowned. "I didn't want to know that. Poor Dawna. You're only after her for her cartomancy magic."

He took a raspy, irritated breath and moved his hands to his hips. "Dawna's powers are just part of the whole Dawna package. I thought you witches were more pragmatic about love. Especially at your age. If it's okay to love a person for their looks or their mind, why not for their powers?"

"It's *not* okay to love a person for their looks."

Gavin raised an eyebrow. "Oh, really? And I suppose you're carrying on with Jesse Berman because he's an appropriate mate for you?"

Zinnia had nothing to say about that.

Gavin jumped for the jar again. "Can I have this now? I told you everything I know about the pen."

"Let me get this straight. You sensed the pen had value, and you immediately guessed that Annette was a witch?"

"Not immediately, but I started watching her more closely. It's easy enough to find support for an idea once you have a theory."

"That's true."

"Didn't you or Margaret sense something was different about Annette? There were plenty of signs."

"Like what?" Zinnia had seen lots of odd things around the office, but they were always the result of one of Margaret's spells. Or so she'd assumed.

"Just little things," Gavin said. "For example, her mood would affect the thermostat in the office. Whenever Karl went over to her desk, the whole room got chilly. But she did like Jesse, so if he came out of his office, that would warm the place back up again. Their two offices were like hot and cold taps on a water faucet."

Zinnia considered the office's heating and cooling issues over the last year. Gavin was right. The proof was in the past four days. The temperature had been absolutely consistent since Tuesday. Annette's emotions must have been causing the fluctuations. And the poor woman hadn't even known she was a witch.

Zinnia snapped her fingers and let the jar drop into Gavin's hands. "Take one teaspoon now, and then a quarter teaspoon as needed. It will give you what you need to make Dawna a very happy lady." She pursed her lips. "So you can maintain your access to her," Zinnia coughed, "items of value."

"Thanks, I guess." Gavin looked at Zinnia's purse with new interest. "Do you carry this sort of thing with you regularly?"

Yes and no. The male stamina compound was something she'd been making for Margaret to give her husband. Earlier that morning, Zinnia had slipped it into her purse planning to bribe Gavin, but he didn't need to know that. She would continue to bluff the non-magical way.

Snippily, she said, "My romantic life is none of your business." For Zinnia, pretending to be offended wasn't difficult.

"What else have you got in that big ol' purse of yours?" He held the jar tightly to his chest while trying to peer in through the top of the purse. "Is this how you got Jesse interested in an old lady such as yourself?"

"I beg your pardon?" She didn't have to pretend to be offended.

He raised his free hand. "Easy now. Don't shoot. I think it's cool you two are hooking up. Older women are hot, in their own way. Lots of young guys are into cougars."

Zinnia grabbed her purse, turned on her heel, and headed for the door.

"Wait, Zinnia. Don't go mad! I don't have a lot of friends."

"I'm not surprised." She kept walking.

"Wait! I just thought of something else, something people don't know about. It's a secret."

She paused at the door. "I don't have time for games, Gavin. Either tell me or don't."

"It's about that other wolf attack," he said. "The one that never happened."

She turned slowly to face him.

"The attack that happened on Friday afternoon?" She felt her curiosity surge and her rage settle. This business of feeling all her emotions unfiltered by the spell on her heart would take some time to get used to. Feeling everything—every little thing—was like being in a room full of stereos with the volume cranked up to eleven.

Gavin practically sparkled with excitement. "The attack that *didn't* happen."

"What do you mean? Did it not happen, or did it not happen the way they reported because it was a cougar, not a wolf?"

"There was no wolf, no cougar. I heard about it in the gym this morning, from the divorced guy who lives down the hallway, who heard it from his kid who was there. It was just a bunch of dumb kids. They pushed some other kid down into a dry creek bed. He got banged up, and they all agreed to blame it on a wolf."

"There was no attack, wolf or cougar, on Friday afternoon?"

"Just regular dumb kid bullies. Not wild animals. You could chalk it up to," he grinned, "the boy who cried wolf."

He waited expectantly for Zinnia to laugh at his bad joke. She did not.

Instead, she asked, "Have any of the other people from the office been here, to your apartment?"

He frowned. "Why?"

"Just answer the question."

He rubbed his chin and said, "There was a poker night, not that long ago."

"My invitation must have gotten lost in the mail," she said.

"Sorry," he said. "But it was just a guys' night thing. You know how it is. We let Xavier Batista tag along."

"I understand. Was that the only time?"

Gavin scratched his chin again. "I think so. I haven't entertained much since I moved into this place. Dawna doesn't like being here."

"No, I would imagine she wouldn't."

They stared at each other.

Ten seconds later, Zinnia was running at full tilt down the stairwell. She took the steps two at a time once again, but not because she was scared of the building's bad juju. She was on a mission.

Friday's attack wasn't real.

That meant...

She knew exactly what it meant, even if she didn't dare think it clearly. The pieces snapped together. Annette's magical pen. Her murder. The book she was writing. Questions about people's past. All the secrets revealed. All the magical powers her coworkers had. The dating and breakups. Everything was coming together now.

CHAPTER 25

Zinnia ran out of The Candy Factory and jumped in her car. She checked that she still had the digital storage stick containing the scanned version of Annette Scholem's handwritten draft. Thankfully, it was in her purse where she'd put it the day before. If she hadn't gone straight to bowling after work, and then traipsing around Towhee Swamp, she would have started reading it already.

She started her car's engine but didn't pull out of the parking lot yet. She was forgetting something, but couldn't put her finger on it. If only there was a spell that worked on the mind the way a page finding spell worked on a book. If only she could query her brain directly. *Dear brain, what am I forgetting? Oh, thanks for asking, Zinnia! You're forgetting... uh, I don't know.*

She shook her head and started driving. The brain did respond to queries, it just took a while. The result would come eventually, and once you'd forgotten about your need and moved on. Like when you ask for a glass of water in a busy restaurant.

The traffic light ahead was yellow. No. Red now. Zinnia slammed on the brakes. Her mentor's voice echoed in her head. *One thing at a time, Zinnia. What do you know to be true?*

What did she know to be true? For starters, she had to pay attention to what she was doing. Just like spellwork, driving a vehicle came with rules and parameters that existed for everyone's safety, including the operator.

She took a calming breath, deep into her lungs, and blew it out between her lips.

Two pedestrians began crossing the street in front of her. One of them immediately drew her eye. Charlize Wakeful. Zinnia leaned back in the driver's seat and tried to blend in. Just a few hours earlier, Charlize had warned Zinnia to stay home, and here she was, out of the house, getting a gnome riled up, bartering potions for information, and nearly running red lights.

The blonde looked her way and then past her. The young woman clutched her bulging stomach protectively with one hand while she used the other to grab the arm of the man walking at her side.

Zinnia relaxed enough to get a better look at the blonde, who was not Charlize after all. The woman was a gorgon, all right, but not the one who'd unfrozen Zinnia's heart. Charlize was one of triplets, and since Chessa was in a coma at the moment, that left only Chloe. Chloe and her husband, Jordan Taub, owned the Gingerbread House of Baking. They appeared to be enjoying the unseasonably pleasant weather by going for a Saturday afternoon stroll. Zinnia's focus narrowed in on Chloe's stomach. Either the blonde gorgon had been sampling too many of the bakery's excellent donuts or the woman was pregnant. Maybe six months along, judging by the size of the bump.

Suddenly, Zinnia's imagination turned down a dark corridor. Six months along with *what*? She pictured Chloe sweating on a hospital bed, giving birth to a flood of snakes. Or some other, even more terrifying monster. Chloe was, after all, a member of the Wakeful family.

Chloe's head suddenly whipped around, and she was staring through the windshield at Zinnia. Her cold blue eyes locked on the witch's.

There was a loud cracking sound. A small rock chip that had been in the windshield since the day Zinnia had acquired her car was no longer just a rock chip. A web of cracks radiated from the divot.

Zinnia maintained eye contact with the gorgon. She smiled and waved.

Chloe frowned and zipped her jacket, hiding her baby bump. She clutched her husband's arm possessively, and continued crossing the street.

Zinnia was so focused on Chloe and the crack in her windshield that she barely registered seeing the person crossing the street in the opposite direction. It was a grown woman dressed up as the little girl character, Dorothy, from *The Wizard of Oz*. The woman was Dorothy Tibbits, one of the town's more colorful real estate agents. Dorothy Tibbits' gimmick was that she regularly appeared around town wearing a blue pinafore and sparkling red shoes, and carrying her house sales materials in a picnic basket. Today she was parading around as usual, walking a brindle Cairn terrier she borrowed for such occasions.

Zinnia paid very little attention to Dorothy Tibbits. The witch was still staring at the cracks on her windshield. Did insurance cover "glare by gorgon?" Probably not.

Someone honked.

It was the car behind her. The light had turned green.

Zinnia pressed the gas pedal. At the same moment, the busy waitress inside Zinnia's mind finally served up what she'd been forgetting: Zinnia's printer at home was nearly out of paper. She'd made two copies of Annette's final, typed manuscript, which had used up most of the sheaf of paper she'd borrowed from her neighbor. If Zinnia was to have any chance of using spells to find what she needed in the original version of the book, she needed paper, and she needed it to be bound, just like a regular book.

Zinnia thanked the waitress inside her mind for mentioning the paper issue now, while she was still in the car.

She drove to the little shop that offered photocopies and other digital and paper services.

The place was busy. Saturday afternoon appeared to be prime time for people to get their menus laminated and their garage sale fliers printed.

Zinnia took her place in the long line. The single employee working the counter was currently helping a woman in yoga clothes, and there were three more people between Yoga Lady and Zinnia. Not a single one of them looked like the kind of person who had a simple five-minute request. The man closest to Zinnia was carrying a large plastic container full of dusty floppy disks that had to be three decades old. There were hundreds of floppy disks.

Zinnia didn't need psychic powers to predict that she would be stuck in line for an hour, minimum, before she got her printed and bound book.

She turned to leave, resigning herself to reading the pages on her computer screen, but stopped herself.

You're a witch, Zinnia! Her internal voice was cheerful yet insistent, like a personal trainer. *You're not going to let a long line of regular humans stand in your way, are you?*

She frowned at her internal coach. The task that had brought her into the shop was certainly an important one. She was trying to determine who or what had murdered her dear friend and coworker. And yet, nobody visited a photocopy shop unless they had a need that felt urgent or important to them: Lost Dog posters, wedding invitations, memorial cards for funeral services. Did Zinnia have any right to distract the people in front of her from their own tasks?

No, she had no right. But she already had her hand inside her purse. She was already reaching for something. A shimmering silver powder.

She took a pinch of the powder, silently begged for forgiveness from whomever it was keeping score on a witch's rights and wrongs, and dropped the powder down the back collar of the man standing in front of her.

By the look of the man's changing posture, the magic took effect immediately. He wavered and wobbled, then dropped the box of disks. It fell with a loud clunk and subsequent clatter that made the other customers turn and stare.

Once the other customers were facing the counter again, Zinnia placed her hand on top of the man's shoulder. "Are you okay?"

He gave her a dumbfounded look. "I feel great," he said. "Why do I feel great?"

"It must be the weather," she said sweetly. "We're so lucky to get a little sunshine in the middle of January."

He looked even more dumbfounded. "But I feel so light and free."

Zinnia continued smiling. Of course he did. The shimmering silver powder she'd dropped down the back of his neck was for body buoyancy. She could have cast the same spell with Witch Tongue, but the powder was much safer, because it was less likely to interact with any pre-existing spells and kill the recipient. Body buoyancy powder could be used in an emergency for making an injured or unconscious person light as a feather so they could be easily transported elsewhere for medical attention. When a conscious person was dosed with the powder, they experienced profound euphoria. The magic didn't just lighten their physical weight; it also took away all the thoughts and worries that weighed them down. The man most likely was feeling better than he'd felt since early childhood.

Zinnia was actually a tiny bit jealous of the man. She would love to be free of her worries, but the powder wasn't affecting her in the same way. A witch's fingertips were naturally impervious to most powders and potions, and for good reason: pulling on a big pair of rubber gloves was a surefire way for a witch to draw attention to her spellcasting.

Zinnia said sagely, "Sounds like you should enjoy this great mood with a walk outside in the sun."

"Wonderful idea! I believe I shall do just that." He leaned over to retrieve his box of disks.

Zinnia grabbed the box before he could. The man didn't have much more mass to him than a ghost. The body buoyancy magic had real, physical effects. The man couldn't carry the box of dusty disks because he didn't have the weight to counterbalance its heft.

"I'll take care of this for you," she said. "Come back in half an hour, after your nice walk. Your disks will be waiting."

He tipped back his head and laughed, then he sneered at the box. "Who cares about those old disks? I've been living in the past for too long, hanging on to things I shouldn't." He shook his head. "Listen, lady. If I'm not back in half an hour, tell the staff to throw everything in the dumpster."

"Are you sure?"

"Lady, I'm more sure than ever that I don't need to archive a bunch of thirty-year-old disks!"

He winked at Zinnia, rolled back his nearly weightless shoulders, and headed for the door. Zinnia used telekinesis to nudge the door open so that he wouldn't struggle with its weight. And then the unburdened man was off, marching down the sidewalk, heading in the direction of Wisteria's pleasant seawall promenade.

Zinnia silently wished him well. The effects of the body buoyancy powder would wear off gradually. He would be completely back up to his regular mass again before sundown, but it was possible the psychological effects would linger. Perhaps she had done the man a favor by ruining his plans. So, had she cursed him or charmed him? It all depended on how you looked at it.

The next two obstacles in Zinnia's way were removed just as easily.

She felt a little bad thinking of people as *obstacles*, but she did have a crime to solve. She was trying to keep the town safe. The end would justify the means. If Margaret Mills had been there, that was exactly what she would have said.

* * *

Back at home, Zinnia dropped the freshly bound copy of Annette's Scholem's handwritten pages on her kitchen table in front of her. A page-finding spell would help her find the specific spots she was looking for, but she wasn't ready to cast the first spell just yet.

She picked up her phone and called Detective Ethan Fung. He didn't answer the call, so she tried again, this time sending a modified compulsion spell over the line, using her pepper grinder as a magic wand to do so.

Fung answered, sounding sleepy. "What?"

She didn't apologize for waking him or ask if now was a good time. She charged ahead like Margaret Mills would have, telling Fung about the gorgon's visit and then Zinnia's subsequent visit to the gnome, as well as what she'd learned.

Fung broke in to ask, "Gavin Gorman is a gnome? But he's so tall."

"Roll with it," Zinnia snapped. "That's not the key point here." She went on to tell him exactly what the key point was. She'd rather have told him everything in person, but she couldn't wait. She finished explaining her theory and paused for a response, tapping her fingers on her table impatiently.

Fung was very quiet, and then finally his sleepy voice came over the line. "Last night, before I got called to the swamp, I was reading Annette's handwritten copy of the book. She did have certain details that she omitted in her final version."

"Such as?" Zinnia would find out for herself in a few minutes, but it wouldn't hurt to get a summary from a live person.

"Zinnia, I don't have infinite time and resources. I'm just one man. I only checked a small sample. I don't have a definitive index, if that's what you're asking."

"Never mind. I'll be checking it myself right now."

"Great! You can be my research assistant."

Zinnia snorted. "That'll be the day."

"Seriously. I could put you on the payroll."

"There's no time to talk about such nonsense." She patted the bound copy in front of her. It was still vaguely warm from the print shop. "I have to start reading."

"Good luck. For what it's worth, you may be right about the narrator being a trick, a gimmick. I didn't study much literature in school, but I've picked up on a few things over the years."

"You know I'm right."

He chuckled. "Maybe I'll stop by later and see what you've found. You can make me some tea. The good stuff."

"Don't bother. I've got plans for dinner." She said the next word with focused weight. "Elsewhere."

Fung was slow to respond, then said, "You should stay home. By yourself."

"You sound just like your snake-haired buddy."

"Zinnia, stay home. I'm serious. Lock your doors and do what you need to do to stay safe."

"I've got a better plan. How about you meet me later, just... not at my house?"

He groaned. He didn't like the sound of her plan. "Let me think about it," he said.

"Whatever," she snapped. "I can take care of myself."

"Zinnia, why do you have to be so stubborn?"

"I'm self-reliant. It's a totally different thing." And with that, she ended the call. She didn't have time to argue about her character strengths or weaknesses. She had to review Annette's original notes—the first draft, that had been written truly from her heart, thanks to the charmed pen.

Secrets revealed are trouble unsealed.

CHAPTER 26

JESSE BERMAN'S RESIDENCE

6:50 PM

Zinnia Riddle parked on the street in front of Jesse Berman's house, turned off the car engine, and sat quietly. She was early. Being early to dinner was even more rude than being late. Worse than being early, she was also sweaty. *Nerves*. And for good reason. She was about to do something that, if her theory was correct, could be very dangerous.

She cast a drying spell on her armpits. It didn't work. Sometimes the body resists a witch's magic. This evening her body wanted her to feel every sign and side effect of her fear. Sometimes the body knew better than the witch.

She checked her phone for messages, even though she knew there wouldn't be any. Where was Detective Fung? Was she actually going to do this without him? No backup?

She pulled out the business card Charlize Wakeful had given her, with the emergency number for the Department of Water and Magic. She punched in the number before she lost her nerve. The voice that answered was male.

"Chet Moore speaking," he said.

"Who?" She'd heard him, but needed to buy time to recover from the shock of hearing from a known wolf shifter.

He repeated his name and asked, "What is the nature of your emergency?"

"I, uh... I don't know. It's more of a hunch."

"A hunch?"

"Never mind," she said hurriedly. "I shouldn't be bothering you. I just wanted to check this phone number."

"It works."

"By which you mean I've reached the DWM?"

Chet Moore made a displeased sound. "You have reached the Department of Water, ma'am. Do you have a water-related emergency?"

Just my sweaty armpits. "No. I suppose I don't."

"Then thank you for keeping this emergency line clear."

The line clicked and he was gone.

The phone buzzed in her hand. There was an incoming message.

Detective Fung: *All systems are go. I will meet you there at 7:20pm.*

She stared at the screen. Normally when she read a text message, she heard the sender's voice in her head. This time she didn't. The message had no dimension, no depth. She shook her head. *Nerves.*

She checked her appearance in the rearview mirror. Her eyes were tinged with red, but, all things considered, she looked okay. Good, even. There was a bright glint in her hazel eyes, and fresh color in her cheeks. More bounce in her long red hair.

She checked all the supplies in her purse, then applied some fresh lipstick. As she inspected her mouth in the mirror, she thought of her older sister, Zirconia. This lipstick was Zirconia's favorite shade. Zirconia had been raised with the same manners as Zinnia, yet she had a bad habit of using cutlery as a mirror at the dinner table. In Zinnia's mind's eye, she saw her sister checking her lipstick on a butter knife. It wasn't a memory, exactly, but something else. A premonition? In the vision, Zirconia's red hair had turned as black as night. All at once, the vision was gone. Only grief remained. Zinnia's sister was gone. Everyone was gone. Grief and fear mixed together in a paralyzing concoction. She felt for a moment like she was being swallowed by a creature with a mouth as large as her body. Swallowed and digested.

Tap tap.

Someone was tapping at the car window.

The sun had set hours ago, so the person's face was in shadows.

"Are you going to sit out here all night?" It was Jesse Berman. Even muffled through the car window, Zinnia would know his voice anywhere.

She waved apologetically.

He said, "I thought I heard your car, but then you didn't come in. What are you doing out here in the dark? Don't tell me you've started meditating."

She smiled and pushed open the door a crack. The automatic car interior light illuminated his face. His blue eyes looked pale in the yellow light, like the bleached-out fliers hanging in the windows of a convenience store.

"I was just thinking," she said.

"Come inside and have some wine. It makes thinking more enjoyable."

She laughed lightly as she stepped out of the car. "Yes. I suppose that might even be the true purpose of wine."

Jesse didn't wait for her to close the car door before he kissed her. On the cheek. He'd seemed to be going for her lips and then changed his mind at the last minute.

"The wine is a Valpolicella Classico," he said. "That's your favorite, right?"

"Oh, I don't have a favorite, but that particular blend is nice."

"Isn't it the first wine you got drunk on? Back when you were just a kid, and you had a crush on your big sister's boyfriend?"

She pointed a finger at him in the dark. "I shouldn't have told you that story." She'd meant her tone to be light and teasing, but it came out angry. Jesse didn't pick up on her irritation.

He asked, "What was that guy's name? It was something odd. Ricky? Ricky Rocker?"

"Rhys Quarry."

"I knew it had something to do with rocks."

She sighed. "Are we going to stand out here on the sidewalk discussing the most embarrassing moments from my childhood, or are you going to invite me in?"

"Touchy, touchy," he said, grinning. "You do need that glass of wine."

"I'm looking forward to it."

"Right this way, ma'am." He offered her his elbow, like a gentleman. She took it, and they walked up the overgrown pathway to the front door. The house had been Jesse's childhood home. The old bungalow was showing its age and neglect, from the cracks in the concrete pathway to the moss on the roof. Jesse had moved back in recently, after his father had passed away but before Zinnia had begun a relationship with him. She hadn't known Jesse to live in any other place, yet the house had always felt wrong for him—or wrong to Zinnia, anyway. The floorboards always creaked when they shouldn't have creaked, and were quiet when they should have creaked. The walls felt as haunted as the stairwells at the Candy Factory. Why was that, anyway? Jesse's father, Viktor Oliver Berman, had passed away peacefully in the town's hospital after battling a common type of cancer. If a ghost haunted the Berman residence, it seemed unlikely it was Viktor. Whatever or whomever it was lingering in the residence, it made Zinnia prefer entertaining Jesse at her house. She rarely had dinner here, let alone slept over. One time, she'd accompanied Jesse to the washer and dryer in the basement, and the dark underground space had given her the heebie-jeebies. For a witch to get the heebie-jeebies meant the house had some wicked bad juju.

She began to cast a protection spell as she stepped through the threshold of the home, as was her habit.

Jesse's arm stiffened under her grasp. "What?"

She abruptly aborted the spell. "I didn't say anything."

"Oh. I thought I heard you mutter something."

She studied his face in the bright light of the entryway. Could he have detected her spell? He might have. She was nervous, after all.

* * *

Zinnia leaned casually on the kitchen counter, sipping a glass of wine while Jesse cooked dinner.

She munched on the crackers and soft cheese that he'd set out for her. The herbed cheese wasn't her favorite—too much dill—but she was hungry. Charlize had interrupted her breakfast that morning, and then there had been the whole thing where Zinnia thought she was dying. Understandably, she'd lost her appetite for a while. It was coming back now with a vengeance.

She checked the time. 7:10 pm. Another ten minutes until Fung showed up. Another ten minutes to act normal. She glanced around the room. Jesse's kitchen was as dusty and neglected as her own. What a matched pair they were.

Her gaze came to rest on a cardboard shipping box sitting on a side table. Either the box had a magical glow, or its faint shimmer was a trick of the light.

"What's in the box?" she asked conversationally.

Jesse tossed more chopped vegetables into a pot before answering. "That's Annette."

"Her personal stuff from her desk?"

He kept his back to her as he stirred the stew on the stove. "No. I mean literally. *That is Annette*. She doesn't have any next of kin in town, so her cousin asked me to pick up the ashes from the cremation place. I'm supposed to hang onto her until one of the family members can drive up."

Zinnia didn't want to say anything. She wanted to let that fact pass without comment, but she had to act normal. She had to say what she would normally say in a situation like this.

"Poor Annette!" she exclaimed. "You just dumped her on a side table along with a pile of unopened mail. Poor thing!" She made a tsk-tsk sound.

"It's only temporary," he said. "Don't you worry about good ol' Annette. If one of her cousins doesn't turn up, I'll put her to good use. There's a scraggly rose bush in the back yard that could use some fertilizer."

Zinnia gasped in mock horror. "You're terrible." She laughed and took another sip of wine.

What she didn't say was that cremated ashes wouldn't do the rose bush any good. Human ashes were extremely high in salt, and didn't contain manganese, carbon, or zinc. The imbalance could actually hinder plant growth. The high calcium content could reduce the plant's supply of nitrogen. She didn't say any of these things because it wasn't normal for a permits department clerk to know so much about growing plants. That was the realm of the Kitchen Bewitched.

Instead, she got up from her stool, grabbed the box containing Annette's ashes, and set it on the other stool next to hers.

"That's better," she said, patting the box.

Jesse turned and gave her a curious look. "Shall we pour a glass of wine for Annette, too?"

"I don't think that's necessary, but you can top up mine."

Jesse grabbed the bottle and refilled Zinnia's glass.

"Don't forget yours," she said, pointing to Jesse's glass, which he'd barely touched.

He held still and looked into her eyes. Zinnia's breath caught in her throat. He was so handsome, so virile. And his eyes were so pure, and blue, and penetrating. She felt the floor giving way beneath her, and the sensation of falling backward, tumbling down the rabbit hole. Jesse's eyes had always had such a powerful effect on her. Now that her heart was unguarded, the sensation of being seen by him was almost unbearable.

Keeping his eyes locked on hers, he downed his dark red wine in three gulps and refilled the glass. He held up the wine glass—it was heavy, cut crystal, one of his father's—and clinked it against Zinnia's.

"To Annette Scholem," he said.

"Our dear friend and coworker," she added.

"Leader of the Incredibowls."

"And future bestselling author."

Jesse's nostrils flared. He opened his mouth as if to say something but tossed back the wine instead. "We'll see about that," he said, licking his lips.

Zinnia said nothing. She pulled her phone from her purse and checked it again.

Jesse said, "Expecting a call from someone?"

"Just my boyfriend," she said, teasing him the way she normally would.

The pot bubbled over and hissed on the stove element. Jesse turned away and tended the dinner.

Zinnia tried to check the time on the digital clock of the microwave to see if it was different from the one on her phone but found her vision was blurry. She hadn't consumed that much wine, had she?

With an eye on Jesse's back, she cast another reveal spell on the wine she was drinking. She'd cast it on the first glass and found the contents to be safe and true, but now she worried she'd missed something. Her head was fuzzy and her tongue felt thick. If her tongue got any thicker, she'd be unable to speak in Witch Tongue.

The wine revealed no encursement or poison, magical or otherwise.

Zinnia rubbed her temples and checked her phone again. The screen blurred. She rubbed her eyes. Still blurry.

She jumped off the stool and headed for the door.

Jesse moved, blocking the exit with his body. "Zinnia? Are you feeling okay?"

"I'm fine. I just need some fresh air."

"With your phone?"

"Yes. I also need to make a call, and I wouldn't want to be rude."

"Make your call here from the kitchen. I don't mind."

She kept her gaze down, not meeting his eyes. "But I would mind." She took a step to the side, dodging him, but he moved and blocked her way.

"What's wrong?" There was a cruel, taunting tone to his voice. "Do you think it was the wine?"

"Why? Did you put something in the wine?"

"Of course not."

She shoved him, but her arms were weak, and he was so big. He barely swayed. He laughed, sounding more cruel by the second.

"I didn't put anything in your wine, Zinnia," he said.

"You didn't?" Now she looked up at him. His blue eyes were bright and wide. Not fearful. Excited.

"I put it in the cheese, which you put on the crackers." He grinned. "You served it to yourself."

"What did you put in the cheese? All I tasted was dill."

"The dill was to cover something that you and your people don't like. A little something called *witchbane*."

Witchbane! That explained the blurred vision, the weakness. The thickness of her tongue. How could she have been so cavalier? How had she walked right into his house, even when she knew that he knew she had powers? He had felt the lightning blast at the swamp. And of course his kind knew of witches. Had she really expected him to keep bluffing, not letting on that he knew what she was? Had she believed his personal feelings toward her were some kind of protection? Yes, she had. And now she was going to pay the price.

She tried to pool lightning in her hands. Nothing came. Just as she'd expected as soon as he'd uttered the terrible word. *Witchbane*. The filthy weed.

Her thoughts scrambled for a solution. At least Fung would be coming soon. Fung would be more prepared. He wouldn't make the mistake of believing that sharing a bed with someone meant anything at all. What could she do now? She could play dumb, stalling for time.

"Witchbane?" She blinked up at Jesse. "You're being so strange tonight. Now get out of my way so I can get some fresh air outside."

"Make me."

Through gritted teeth, she said, "Step aside. Now. I'm not joking."

He laughed, mocking her. "You redheads are so cute when you're angry. It's a shame you're a witch. Why'd you have to go and be a witch, Zinnia? We could have had a great time together."

Together? Her vision was narrowing, shrinking to a circle of light. Her magic was gone, but the herb hadn't stopped there. The dose must have been very strong. Why did she have to eat all those crackers? She was about to lose consciousness. The witchbane, powerful as it was at that dose, might even kill her.

She backed toward the stove and prep area, grabbed a sharp knife from the counter, and lunged forward, slashing at the man who threatened her.

Jesse hadn't been expecting a physical attack. Blood sprayed from his forearm before he'd even moved a muscle.

Zinnia stepped back and licked the tip of the blade. Jesse's blood was spicy. It matched the blood she tasted from the cougar. Her hunch had been correct. Jesse Berman was a shifter. He was the cougar she'd seen at Towhee Swamp. And she'd only figured it out thanks to Carrot Greyson's visions. Carrot had dreamed about seeing Zinnia nude. Who else had been seeing Zinnia that way except Jesse? The nude painting at Gavin's apartment had jarred the facts into place in her mind. Carrot must have formed a bond, a psychic link, with Jesse during their brief romance. And he didn't even know his ex had been watching his every move in her dreams. He should have been more careful about who he took to bed. And he shouldn't have messed around with Zinnia Riddle.

"Step aside," she said, brandishing the knife.

Jesse slowly wrapped a tea towel around his cut forearm. "You barely scratched me," he said. "I'll give you one point for catching me by surprise, but I assure you, witch, it will not happen again."

She kept waving the knife. "Step aside now, or you'll be sorry."

"What are you going to do? I'm bigger and stronger. You can't zap me. You're all out of witch juice."

She dropped the knife, grabbed the pot of bubbling stew from the stove, and flung it at him. He screamed as the boiling mass struck him. He buckled, flailing both hands at the boiling stew on his clothes as he crumpled to the floor.

The only way out of the kitchen was through Jesse or over him. As soon as he hit the ground, she started running.

She was jumping over him when she felt a strong hand clamp on her ankle. *So close.*

He yanked her feet out from under her violently. She used her arms to protect her head from hitting the stone floor. Distantly, she noted a shooting pain in her wrist and elbow.

Jesse snarled, "Not so fast, witch."

"I'm Zinnia," she said, panting. "Jesse, it's still me. I'm just Zinnia. I'm not your enemy."

But he wasn't listening. He dragged her to the center of the kitchen and straddled her, locking her arms down with his knees. He leaned forward, his face inches above hers. His face was contorted with rage. Half of it was red, burned by the stew. He would heal by magic and bear no scars, but it had to hurt like hell. And over his face there was something else. Another layer. His father. What was this magic? Was Jesse possessed?

Annette had been wrong about Jesse. Zinnia had read through the original handwritten draft earlier that day, after leaving Gavin's place and before coming to Jesse's. Annette had originally cast Jesse as a selkie named Sej. Sej was a creature who could shift at will into the form of a seal. Sej had been sired by an evil man, but then he turned away from his evil father, away from the dark side of magic. Sej had been good. Pure of heart. But the magic pen only wrote from Annette's rose-tinted version of the truth. She'd been wrong about Jesse Berman. He was nothing like Sej. Even the love of his mother couldn't save his soul. In her dying moments, Annette must have realized how wrong she'd been.

Pain ripped through Zinnia, pinning her to the present.

Jesse's upper lip twisted up in a catlike snarl. "You tasted my blood last night in the swamp," he said. "I was hurt, and you didn't even try to help me. You just licked my blood from your lips."

"But I didn't know it was you," she said, her voice pleading. "It was Xavier who cut you on the top of your head. Xavier Batista. From City Hall."

"You liked it," Jesse snarled. "You're a demon spawn. Since you like the taste of my blood so much, here. Get your fill." He ripped off the blood-stained tea towel and shoved his forearm into her mouth.

She did the only thing she could. She bit him with all her strength.

He laughed. "That barely tickles."

He was right. Her bite was weak. The witchbane was draining away even her human strength. It was only the flood of fight-or-flight adrenaline coursing through her veins, keeping her conscious. And that wouldn't last forever.

She bit him again anyway.

"Isn't that cute," he teased. "You've been defanged. You're like a kitten with no teeth."

He pulled his arm from her mouth and looked down at her. His expression softened to something like pity.

She said nothing.

"Ah, peace and quiet," he said. "I don't know why shifters hate witches so much. A witch isn't a problem if you feed her enough witchbane." He leaned forward again, sticking his face in hers. "You're not much of a threat, are you?"

She spat a mouthful of his own blood back in his face.

He recoiled.

She said, "What about you? You're not much of a man, Jesse. You turn into a cougar and you attack innocent women. You're a coward. You're a filthy, nasty creature who slinks around at night."

"I wasn't going to hurt that stupid girl. Xavier's girlfriend, whoever she was."

"Then what were you doing at the swamp?"

He made his eyes wide and innocent. "Getting some fresh air. Stretching all four legs."

"I don't believe you."

"Such a suspicious little witch you are."

The ceiling above Jesse's leering face blurred. Her vision was closing off again, the white ceiling becoming blue. Zinnia closed her eyes, just to rest them for a moment. She thought of the blue painting that hung in Detective Fung's office behind his head. Sea. And sailboats. Were there sailboats in the painting? It didn't matter. With the right tactics, sailboats could sail against the wind. She stopped struggling under Jesse's grip and took another direction. She opened her eyes and faced her fears.

Softly, she said, "Jesse, I'm sure you didn't plan to kill Annette. I know how sweet and good you are. It was probably an accident, right?"

He seemed surprised. "It was an accident," he said agreeably. "I only wanted to talk to her."

"About what?"

"About her past. My father used to tell me about a woman named Annette. She was a friend of my mother's."

"Annette knew your parents?"

"Yes, but she wasn't a very good friend. That's why my dad warned me about her. Annette tried to take me away from my father after my mother died."

"She did? I had no idea."

"My father always told me to be on the lookout. I forgot about it until last week, when Annette asked me about things that happened when I was a little kid."

That was what Carrot had overheard him talking to Annette about. "So, you went to the office on Monday night just to talk to her?"

"That's right. I only wanted to talk. But then..." His blue eyes took on a malevolent gleam. "She said terrible things."

"Like what?"

"Lies," he seethed through gritted teeth. "Villobek is supposed to be my father. She rearranged the letters of his name."

"Viktor Oliver Berman is Villobek."

"No, he isn't," Jesse growled.

"Villobek kidnapped his wife when she tried to get away from him. He made her bear his son, and then he left her for dead."

"My father didn't do that. He would never. He was a man of honor."

"But Annette..." She chose her words carefully, delicately sidestepping the truth. "Annette knew your parents. Like the narrator in her book."

"Maybe she knew them, maybe she didn't. Annette was a storyteller. A liar. My father was a good man. He's the one who raised me by himself after my mother ran off."

"Your mother ran off? But you always tell people she died."

He seized her shoulders and shook her against the floor, slamming her skull hard enough to make her see stars.

"Don't put words in my mouth! You're trying to trick me, witch!"

"No, no. Jesse, I'm just trying to get everything straight in my head."

"This is a trick. I don't feel right." His face flickered, becoming another face. That of his father, Viktor. He said, "You're doing something to me right now. My father always said, if a witch can talk, she's a threat. I should have given you something stronger."

"Calm down and take a deep breath. We can get through this together."

"Don't pretend you care about me, witch. You don't love me. You never loved me. I gave you my heart and you threw it away. You threw me away."

"What are you talking about? Of course I care about you. Jesse, I—"

Her words were choked off. He had his hands around her throat.

Jesse grinned. "Your boyfriend's not coming for you, by the way."

Fung? He wasn't coming?

Jesse smiled with more cruelty than seemed possible for a human—but then, he wasn't exactly human. He was two people, possessed by his father's spirit. And he was part demon, like all shifters. His kind looked down on witches for being part demon, yet they were all cut from the same cloth.

Jesse said, "I'm afraid the detective is a bit tied up at the moment. He didn't send you that last text message, Zinnia. I did."

The world turned red.

Zinnia fought him with all her remaining human strength, but the high dose of witchbane took away her consciousness before the strangling could.

CHAPTER 27

Zinnia Riddle had never liked Jesse's basement. Not when she helped him fold laundry and got the heebie-jeebies, and certainly not now, when she found herself a prisoner there, bound and aching on the cold cement floor. The basement was chilly, damp, and nearly pitch black. A couple of green and orange lights on the washer and dryer were the only source of light.

With a hopeful heart, she flexed her swollen tongue and cast a spell for light. It didn't work. Her mouth tasted sour. She tried again. Sourness. And again. No light. If anything, the darkness around her seemed to grow darker with the failure.

Her magic was still snuffed out, thanks to the witchbane. Her throat ached as though it was on fire. She could still feel Jesse's hands around her neck, choking her. She could still see the raw hatred in his eyes. Or was that his father Viktor's hatred? Her head throbbed. Did it matter? Jesse could have resisted his father's influence, if he wanted to. If the old man's ghost had been attached to the son after his death, it had been there for two years. Viktor had little power over Jesse, unless Jesse gave it up willingly.

Zinnia allowed herself to feel every ache and pain in her body as punishment. How could she have walked into this house with only a few supplies in her purse? Jesse knew she was a witch, even if he didn't know that she knew he knew. He had been aware of her magical status for nearly twenty-four hours. He had prepared. *Of course* he had prepared. Jesse was a be-prepared sort of guy. He'd gotten witchbane from some unethical dealer, and then he had, to use his own hateful words, *defanged* her.

She tasted her regrets, rank and acidic in her mouth. And then she tasted something new. White-hot rage, pure and clean. Anger was growing inside her, fiery and ancient and demonic. Yes, she was demon spawn. And Jesse would pay for his crimes against his fellow demon-spawned family member.

Careful, she told herself. *One moment at a time. Keep your wits about you.* A mad witch is no good to anyone, especially herself.

She let her mortal senses expand. She couldn't see much, but there was something to hear. Someone was breathing right behind her. Jesse? Was he waiting for her to regain consciousness? And then what?

She lay still in the dark with only her human senses. She pulled her rage into a compact ball, just below her solar plexus. *One moment at a time.* Her internal warnings took on the voice of her mentor. *Zinnia, what do you know to be true?*

What did she know to be true?

For starters, her tongue was still badly swollen from the witchbane. Next, she wasn't dead. What else? Nobody besides Ethan Fung knew she was in Jesse Berman's basement because few people knew they were dating. Well, Margaret Mills knew. That was one good thing. But Margaret wouldn't notice Zinnia's absence until Monday morning at work, and that was at least thirty-six hours in the future. Zinnia's mouth turned even more sour.

What did she know to be true? Here was the big one. Her lover was a murderer. And a monster. Zinnia Riddle, who'd always tried to be a good witch, had shared a bed with evil. And now, if she survived this basement, she would forever be tainted by it. She shouldn't have been so careless. This predicament, this being tied up, helpless and defanged, in a basement, was what she'd brought upon herself. She knew it was no time for a pity party, but what the heck. Bring on the parade, with all its floats and streamers, and the marching band booming out the chorus of YOU DID THIS TO YOURSELF.

Meanwhile, the breathing behind her continued, louder than her own.

On some level, she knew exactly who the other person was, but she delayed rolling over. She didn't want to confirm even more of her worst fears. She closed her eyes and allowed the marching band of the pity parade to stomp all over her.

The person behind her coughed between labored breaths.

Zinnia finally put the parade on pause and wriggled from her side onto her back. The ties around her wrists chafed, especially on the wrist that had been injured in the kitchen. It might have been a sprain or a break. Her body was working hard to repair the bones, but it would take time. Riddle women were tougher than they looked, but they couldn't mend broken bones instantly.

In addition to having her wrists tied with something hard and plastic, she'd been bound with duct tape from shoulder to toes. She probably resembled a lumpy gray bookwyrm. Something flashed in her mind's eye: herself, making bookwyrm dough in her kitchen. She had made the compound a few times over the years, so the flash might have been a memory, but she hoped it was a premonition. If she was still getting future flashes, it meant she might survive this basement.

The other person coughed again. This cough sounded wet. Not a good cough.

Zinnia wriggled toward to her other side. Her arm twisted unnaturally under the thick layers of tape. Her wrist screamed in pain, the healing bonds breaking again before they could solidify. She caught another flash, this time of a woman with Zinnia's face snapping her forearm. A compound fracture. Bloody as hell. *Oh, good.* She might survive this basement only to get herself broken again.

Zinnia came to a stop on her side, staring into the darkness. Slowly, a face formed in the dim light. He was further away than she'd expected. His breathing was even more labored than she'd imagined.

"Fung," she said.

He didn't open his eyes. The last vestiges of her pity party abruptly flung away. All she cared about was him. Forget herself and her regrets. Her friend was in trouble.

Detective Ethan Fung's face was shiny in the dark. His sweaty nose had a spot of orange and a spot of green from the laundry station's lights.

"Ethan," she said.

His eyes flashed open, unfocused. "Zinnia?"

"It's me."

"Please be real," he chanted. "Please be real. Please be real."

"Look at me, Ethan. I'm right here."

"I can't see anything. Zinnia? Are you really here?"

"Unfortunately, yes."

He cleared his throat. "I'm sorry if this makes me a jerk, but I'm really glad you're here."

"We are quite the pair of jerks, then, because I'm glad you're here." She looked over his dimly lit body, which was as bound as hers. "Though it would be better if you weren't tied up."

"Please tell me you're not tied up, too."

"Good news: I'm not tied up. Technically, I'm taped up. With duct tape."

Fung chuckled until he wheezed and then coughed. "Don't make me laugh. Do some magic and get us out of here."

Ah, if only. She quickly tried the spell she had recently used on Margaret to make her packing tape cocoon lose its stickiness. The spell didn't work. Oh, the pain of knowing the perfect spell for a sticky situation and being unable to use it.

"I can't," she said glumly. "I can't do any magic right now."

"Why not? Did he dose you with witchbane or something?"

Zinnia said nothing.

Fung cursed in the darkness. "Why does witchbane even exist? Why can't you witches get rid of every last bit in existence?"

Zinnia snorted. "Why doesn't Superman get rid of all the kryptonite? Or at least keep it away from the supervillains?"

"Because it comes from another planet," he said, as though the reason was obvious to anyone with eyes.

They were quiet for a moment, then Zinnia said, "I'm glad you're here, because you'll have to hold me back. As soon as I get myself un-mummified, I'm going to kill someone."

Fung wheezed wetly. "This is where I'm supposed to tell you not to kill anyone because it would be wrong." He coughed. "Or at least make sure I'm not looking when you do it."

"How did he get you?"

"This person we're talking about, is it Jesse Berman?"

"Yes. We're in his basement. Don't you remember? Did you get hit on the head?"

"No and yes. I mean, yes and yes. The last thing I remember is leaning over a gravestone at the cemetery. I went there to check the name of Jesse's father. I guess someone got the jump on me."

"Did he drug you, too?"

"Judging by the throbbing on the back of my head, he went caveman and hit me with a rock. Or a stick. Or maybe a whole tree."

"You were alone? No backup?"

"You know I work alone. And I didn't think I'd need backup to check a gravestone in the middle of the day."

"I should have anticipated you'd go there. Jesse visits his father's grave on Saturday afternoons. Why didn't I warn you?"

"You did enough by calling me today. You did more than enough. I'm the one who got sloppy. It's my fault we're both down here."

She didn't argue with him, which she supposed was cruel, but she was feeling bitter.

After a moment, he asked, "How did you know it was him?"

"A few things started adding up. When Margaret and I cast that location spell—the one that led us to the swamp last night—the spell didn't work until we asked for anyone connected to Villobek. In spellwork, *connected* can also mean *related*. That's why the map showed us Villobek's son."

"How did the map know that Villobek was another name for Viktor Oliver?"

"Magic has a mind of its own."

"Like artificial intelligence?"

"Sure, except the exact opposite of artificial. It also has a weird sense of humor." They lay still in the darkness for a moment. The floor above them squeaked. "Jesse and I were dating."

"Tell me something I don't know."

"That's how I knew he was the cougar. On Friday morning, Carrot told the whole office she thought she'd seen me naked. She also said she saw Jesse flexing for someone. Those must have been visions she was having, through Jesse's eyes. When she saw him, he was looking in a mirror."

"Yeah, Zinnia. I know. You told me most of that when you phoned me today. It's too bad you didn't figure it out a bit sooner, like last night."

"But I couldn't have known until after the attack in the swamp."

Fung asked with a hopeful tone, "Does anyone else know you're here? Gavin? Margaret?"

Zinnia regretted not calling Margaret. She hadn't called the other witch because Margaret would have tried to talk her out of doing something stupid. Something that could get her injured and tied up in a dank basement.

"No," Zinnia said. "Nobody knows I'm here. Except..."

Fung waited expectantly, unmoving in the darkness.

"I did call the Department of Water and Magic when I got here."

Fung pursed his lips. "I don't know of any such department."

"Sure, you don't." She winked, even though he wouldn't see it. "Unfortunately, I don't think they'll be coming to our rescue. I told them it was just a test call to make sure the number worked."

"Did you talk to Wakeful? She's been working the case with me."

"No. It was some guy. Chet Moore. Her sister's fiancé. The wolf shifter."

"Ugh," Fung groaned. "That guy won't care about a cop and a witch in trouble." He wriggled pointlessly on the concrete. "It's a crying shame I lost those five pounds for my New Year's resolution. It made me too easy to kidnap."

Suddenly, light flooded the basement as the door at the top of the stairs opened.

Zinnia craned her neck to look, hopeful to see Charlize, or Chet Moore, or one of the other shadow people.

But it was Jesse.

He kicked something down the stairs. It was the cardboard box containing Annette's ashes.

"There you go, Annette," he said. "Join your friends."

And then he slammed the door shut.

The box took its time thumping down the stairs before landing a few feet from Zinnia's head.

Fung said, "Please tell me that's a box full of scissors. I think I've got one pinkie free."

"No scissors," she said. "It's Annette Scholem's ashes."

Fung muttered something Zinnia couldn't understand.

She said, "Pardon me?"

"I was just saying that two's company and three's a crowd."

Zinnia groaned. "We need to get you to the hospital. That bump on the head has made your sense of humor even worse."

"The bump on my head isn't nearly as bad as the compound fracture on my leg. It busted when your boyfriend threw me down here like a sack of potatoes. But the good news is, I probably have another hour left before I bleed to death. You can tell me the story about when you found out you were a witch."

"Stop trying to make me laugh. It's not helping the situation."

"I'm not joking." He coughed and wriggled backward. The tiny amount of light in the basement revealed a pool of blood where he'd been lying. His movement also afforded Zinnia a glimpse of something white. His bone. Sticking out through the tape.

CHAPTER 28

Zinnia screamed. She screamed until she was hoarse, and then she kept going. It was partly to summon her captor and partly because what she was doing to her hand hurt so bad.

Eventually, the door creaked open again. Jesse's familiar shape formed a shadow. He said nothing. He just stood there.

"Please. You've got to help Ethan," she said. The hoarseness from screaming had made her voice extra scratchy. All the better for pleading.

"Why? He doesn't care for the accommodations? This is the best I could offer on short notice."

"He's bleeding out from a broken leg. You broke it when you threw him down here. It's a compound fracture."

Jesse didn't respond.

With her scratchy voice, she pleaded, "We need to get him to a hospital right away. We need to do something."

"What's this *we* nonsense? You and I are not a *we*, Zinnia."

"You, then. Do you really want another person's blood on your hands? That's not the Jesse I know."

Jesse sighed. "Don't freak out. As soon as I'm on my way out of this hellhole of a town, I'll call someone to come check the basement."

"There's no time for that. He's already lost consciousness."

The shadowy form shrugged. "Then he's as good as dead. There's not much the hospital could do for him anyway." Jesse took a step back but didn't close the door. "Them's the breaks. He knew what he signed up for when he became a cop." He didn't move from the doorway.

Zinnia decided to try another tactic. "Are you really that insecure, Jesse? Are you that jealous of my friendship with Ethan? If I didn't know any better, I'd think I was talking to Gavin right now."

Jesse snorted. "That greedy goblin? Yeah, right."

Gavin was a greedy gnome, not a goblin, but Zinnia didn't correct Jesse.

"You're just like Gavin," Zinnia said. "You should know, back when I started at the department, I liked both of you equally. Did I ever tell you that? You were just the first one who happened to make a move."

"Don't say that. I'm twice the man Gavin is. Anyone can see that."

Not from where I'm lying on your basement floor. "Gavin wouldn't leave someone to die," she said.

"Oh, well," Jesse said tiredly. "I guess the little goblin has a few good qualities." He started to close the door.

"Wait!" It was time for the real ploy. "Don't you want to meet your mother?"

He paused. "You're trying to trick me, witch."

"Jesse, your mother didn't die when you were little, but you already suspected that, didn't you?"

He didn't argue.

"She left your father, and she hid from him," Zinnia said. She knew the details, thanks to the handwritten version of Annette's book. "She hid away until she knew he was dead. Until she knew that the big bad man who'd held her captive, Viktor Oliver Berman, was dead."

Still Jesse said nothing.

She continued. "Don't you get it? Your mother was trying to make contact with you, through Annette."

"What? That's crazy."

"Think about it. Annette was asking you those questions about your childhood, not for her book, but because she wanted to be sure you were the right person."

"She was?"

"Doesn't it all match up? You read the same book I did." *But not both versions.* "I know where your mother is."

Jesse took one step down the stairs. "How do you know where my mother is?"

"We witches have our ways."

"But how could you know? I never even told you her name."

"Doesn't matter. She changed her name. To hide from your father."

He growled. "You're lying. I know it's a trick."

"It's not a trick. I can tell you everything, Jesse. I swear."

"Do it. Swear." He took another step down. "Swear by your word, witch."

"My word is my bond," she said solemnly. The word bond would take effect even without her magic functioning. "I shall give you your mother's name, but you have to swear you'll call the paramedics for Ethan."

"Tell me first."

"You have to swear."

His growl turned to a groan, and then he spat out the words. "My word is my bond. If you give me my mother, I'll see that your boyfriend gets help right away. But I can't guarantee he's going to make it." Jesse took three more steps down the stairs. "Now tell me."

"I need my purse. There are supplies in it. I don't know your mother's name, but I didn't lie. I can get it for you, right now."

"Liar! How can you do any spells if you've got no powers?"

"The potions will work, because the magic is in them already."

He growled again. He didn't quite believe her, but he wanted to. He wanted to have his mother's identity.

He disappeared and returned a few minutes later. He flicked on a light. It was blinding, and it illuminated Ethan Fung, lying unconscious in his blood. Zinnia only looked at Fung long enough to determine that he was still alive. If only she could get him some of the supplies from her purse. She would certainly try, but she wouldn't have long.

Jesse stayed at the top of the stairs, and then he melted. He shifted into another shape. A cougar.

The cougar picked up Zinnia's purse in its powerful jaws and crept silently down the stairs on padded paws.

Each step the cat took sent a shiver of emotion down Zinnia's spine. Fear mixed with rage. She'd trusted the man inside that cat, once upon a time. She'd cared about him. True, she had never loved him, and maybe she'd even used him, but she sure didn't deserve this.

The cougar padded up to her face. The big cat didn't seem so menacing, now that he was down in the damp, cold basement with her.

"Impressive," she said. She knew a compliment was what he wanted to hear. Jesse was that kind of guy. He craved attention, which was why he was always making jokes, and why he'd been attracted to her. Few men can resist the admiration of a witch in her prime years.

She went on, gushing. "Even with the cut on your arm and the burn on your face, you were able to shift form."

He dropped the purse with a thud and shifted back to human form. "You barely scratched me," he said.

She dropped her gaze to her purse. If only she had magic, she'd smash him in the face with everything she had. She'd show him how she could scratch. Jesse Berman wouldn't shift again when she was done with him.

"Thanks for getting my supplies," she said sweetly. "I suppose you'll be acting as my hands? Unless you'd prefer to untie me?"

"I don't think so, dear," he said in a singsong voice. "But I have brought you some more of that herb you don't like."

He pulled from his pocket a handful of crushed witchbane. It had no scent, yet it made Zinnia's nostrils burn.

"No," she said, pulling her head back as much as she could. "No more. Too much will kill me."

He shoved it into her mouth anyway. "Be a good girl," he said. "Chew it up. Now say ahh."

She wanted to spit it in his face. *Bide your time, Zinnia. Ball up that rage and use its power as your own. Be a good girl.* She chewed, said ahh, and showed him her mouth was clear.

"Now tell me how we find my mother."

"First, unzip my purse and take out the three vials with the corks."

"I'm not an idiot," he said as he dug out the vials. "I'm not going to drink anything you have me mix up, so don't waste my time."

"I won't poison you. I promise. My word is my bond. I shall not poison you."

That reassured him enough to get started.

For the next fifteen minutes, Zinnia walked her cougar shifter ex-boyfriend through the complicated procedure of creating what she called Tracing Ink.

When it was ready, he said, "Now what? Do I need paper?"

"We need something connected to your mother."

"I'm connected. I'm her son. What more can you want?"

"Something else. Do you have anything of hers? A lock of hair? A favorite article of clothing?"

He stared down at her with a murderous haze in his pale blue eyes. "You know I don't. I have nothing of my mother's. I never have. My father threw everything away. Is this part of your trick?" He started getting to his feet. "Never trust a witch."

"Wait," she said. "We can use Annette."

They both looked over at the cardboard box lying near Fung's head.

"Her ashes," Zinnia explained. "Gather a handful. That will work."

"I'm not touching Annette Scholem's cremated remains. No way."

"Then untie me, you big chicken," she teased. "I'm not afraid of a few ashes."

He stared at her, his expression no less furious than when they'd started the potion.

Finally, he grabbed the box. He ripped off the packing tape, lifted out the urn, and opened the lid. The cremated ashes were packed in a vacuum-sealed plastic bag. It was a thick bag, designed to not spill easily. Jesse picked at the seams ineffectively. Zinnia noted that he hadn't learned all the shifter tricks that others like him knew. If he had been taught by a better man than his father, he would have known how to turn his nails into cougar claws without fully shifting form.

"Those vacuum-sealed bags can be tricky," Zinnia said.

He growled.

"There's a small knife in my purse," she said. "It's on my keychain."

He pointed a finger at her. "This had better not be a trick."

"There is no trick to having a small knife on my keychain, I assure you." She met his gaze with grace, with her chin raised—or so she hoped. It was hard to have dignity while trussed up on a cold cement floor. "My word is my bond."

He used her tiny knife to open the bag of ashes.

"Now what?" He looked down with disgust at the gray chunks and flakes.

"Pick up a handful and toss it into the air so it spreads evenly on the floor, then sprinkle the Tracing Ink over it to spell out your mother's name."

He did as she directed. The dark drops puddled on the ashes randomly. Nothing magical happened.

He kicked at the dusty, inky mess in frustration. "I knew it! You're just wasting my time, as usual."

"I forgot one thing. Oops. Sorry about that. Of course it didn't work, not without the key ingredient."

He glared at her. "What did you leave out?"

"The ashes need to be awakened. They need a bit of life force."

"Blood?"

"No," she said carefully. "Good thinking, but blood would sour the ink. Hmm." She looked around the basement. "It's too bad we're not at my house. I have everything there."

Jesse snorted. "We're not going to your house. Forget it." He started to get up.

"Wait," she said. "I have the perfect thing, and I have it with me at all times. We can awaken the ashes with a few drops of my saliva."

He glared at her.

"Don't stop now," she said, craning her neck to look pointedly at Fung. "We're almost there. Come on, Jesse. I'm keeping up my end of the bargain."

"Okay. What do I have to do?"

"Gather another handful of ashes and bring it over here."

Slowly, glaring at her the whole time, he did so. He held a handful of Annette's ashes under her face.

"Spit," he said. "Do it now or I'm out of here."

She paused, as though stalling for time, even though she didn't need any more time. She was ready.

Zinnia said, "As soon as I give you your mother's name, you're going to call an ambulance, right?"

"Yes. Just do it already."

She opened her mouth and flicked her tongue over her lips. "My mouth is so numb from the witchbane," she said. "I can't tell if there's any saliva coming out of my mouth. Can you look? We don't want too much. Just a few drops."

He leaned in over his hands, his gaze on her mouth. "Go ahead."

She felt a bead of saliva fall from her mouth to the ashes. Oops. She hadn't meant to do that. He started to pull his hands away, but she said, "Wait. We need three drops."

He growled and held the ashes steady.

She took in a deep breath, and then, instead of spitting, she blew as hard as she could. She blew with all the hate and grief and fury in her body. The ashes flew up into his face and eyes.

Jesse howled and stumbled backward, tripping over his own feet as he retreated. He landed heavily on his butt, groaning from the impact. From his seat on the cement floor, he dug at the gritty ashes that had filled his eyes.

"You witch!" he howled. "You'll pay for this!"

"You're the one who wanted to meet your mother." She powered up her voice for the big one. The whopper. The secret revealed. "Jesse, your mother is in your eyes. She's on your filthy basement floor. She's all over you. Your mother's death is on you. Her ash is in your face. Her blood is on your hands."

Zinnia wriggled and pushed down the top half of her gray cocoon. She was nude from the waist up, except for her bra. Her long-sleeved floral blouse was still sticking to the tape. She brought her hands around to her front, both of them free of their bonds. Blood sprayed from one hand, the most mangled one, but she paid it no attention.

Jesse groaned and continued rubbing his face. He didn't know that Zinnia had her arms free. She couldn't move very far with her lower body taped up, but she could move enough.

He moaned, "Annette was my mother's best friend. What are you talking about?"

"Annette was your *mother*. She was her own best friend, and her own worst enemy. That was the gimmick in her book. The main character was pretending to be two people, so she could get some distance, because the truth was so awful."

"But why?"

"Because your father was a monster, and she was worried you were one, too." Zinnia grabbed the urn containing the remainder of Annette's ashes, raised it high over her head, and struck Jesse on the skull.

A mighty crack reverberated through the damp basement. Ashes flew everywhere.

Zinnia toppled over from the exertion. She had poor balance with her lower body bound this way. But she managed to hold onto the metal urn. She got to her feet again, and raised her weapon once more.

The bare light bulb illuminating the basement flickered. The air compressed around Zinnia, becoming viscous. All around her, the basement crackled with juju. Heaps of juju, good and bad. The viscous air thinned again, and a breeze stirred up from out of nowhere.

Zinnia lifted the metal urn high over her head. She was ready to strike. The death blow. Fung wasn't watching. Her arms trembled but did not move. Something was stopping her. Not weakness.

The opposite of weakness.

There was a force suddenly coursing through her. Power. Like when Margaret had stood behind her and they'd shared powers for the tandem lightning spell.

Was her magic back? Witchbane didn't disappear that quickly, and yet, she felt no pain whatsoever. Only strength.

If she brought the urn down again, she would keep going until she'd killed her captor. And she wanted to. But the rational part of her mind, the part that was not boiling with white-hot rage, was asking a question. Where was this magic coming from?

The breeze that could only be magical ruffled her hair and evaporated the sweat on her face.

Something strange was happening to the ashes on the floor around her. The breeze was swirling them. The ashes were rising up, taking form, just like the darkness that had taken form inside Zinnia's kitchen.

The breeze kept swirling, until the ashes formed a body. The body stood between Jesse and Zinnia.

It was Annette. Standing there. Made of ash. Facing Zinnia.

The form was silent as she leaned forward and patted Zinnia on the shoulder. Zinnia felt nothing but power and peace. The form gently took the urn from Zinnia's mangled, bleeding hands, and placed it on the ground. Zinnia dropped her arms to her sides. She kneeled. She brought her bleeding hands together in a prayer position.

Ash-Annette smiled at her. She was Annette, and she was also someone else.

The holy name sounded in Zinnia's mind. *Mahra.* The spirit of Mahra was with them in that dank basement.

Zinnia felt the peace radiating from her raw, unprotected heart. Spreading to the rest of her like pure white light. She was broken, and yet, she was whole.

And then the woman of ash turned toward Jesse. He was also down on his knees, reeling from the blow to the head but still conscious, rubbing his eyes and squinting up at her.

All at once, the dust pulled away from his eyes and merged with Annette's form. He stopped rubbing his eyes and dropped his hands to his sides.

Jesse stared up at her, blinking, eyes watering. "Annette?"

She did not speak. She patted his head.

He began to smile. He beamed up at her. "I'm so sorry," he said. "I didn't know it was you. You're my mother?"

She nodded and kept patting his head.

"I love you." His eyes darkened. "But you shouldn't have said those lies about my father."

She pulled her hand away.

"My father never left me," Jesse said. "He never abandoned me. But you did."

She slowly shook her head. Zinnia couldn't see the ash woman's face, but she knew the body language. Jesse didn't understand, and he never would.

His face, which had been gentle for a moment, contorted back to rage. "I'm glad you're dead," he said, spitting the words with venom. "You would have only insulted my father's memory with that stupid book of yours."

She kept shaking her head, but moving faster now. Ashes broke free from her form and swirled around them. The air in the basement ceased being damp and chilly. The heat was rising. The concrete space was rapidly becoming a boiler room.

Jesse snarled, backed up, and shifted once more into a cougar. The big cat growled at Annette, teeth flashing brightly under the single light fixture.

Ash-Annette stood her ground. Zinnia couldn't see the woman's face, but she saw the ashy fists ball up at her sides.

The big cat pounced, passing through her middle.

The ashes flew out, swirled, and reconfigured. Ash-Annette was still there, but her form was less stable. The temperature in the basement rose a few more degrees.

The cat jumped at her again.

The ghost woman's center washed out once more. Her form was slower to reform this time.

The cat swished its tail, preparing to leap again.

Ash-Annette made a gesture that Zinnia had seen in martial arts movies. It was the come-get-some gesture.

Cougar-Jesse jumped, but before his paws and snarling jaw could connect with the ashes, Annette flew up all at once and spread across the ceiling. She still looked vaguely human up there—a face in the midst of a flattened puddle of ash.

The cat paced below, growling at the ceiling.

And then, all at once, the ashes came down. They snaked down in the shape of a tornado, narrowing as it reached the cat.

Jesse-cougar opened his jaws to growl, and the tornado snaked in through his mouth. The ashes funneled in until they were all gone, every last gritty speck, consumed by the cat.

Zinnia whispered, "Jesse. Don't—"

Her warning was late. Far too late.

The big cat's tawny coat turned gray. Then black. Then red, like hot coals. There was a rumbling sound, like that of a volcano about to explode.

Zinnia wormed her way over to Fung and covered his face with her own.

The cat exploded, blown up from within.

Red ashes fell down around Zinnia, hissing as they touched the exposed skin of her bare back.

A minute passed. All was quiet except the hissing and popping ashes.

Zinnia slowly pulled her head up and looked around.

Jesse was gone. Steaming chunks of burning flesh and ash surrounded the two captives.

Jesse was dead, and the ashes were spread across the basement floor, and yet, Annette was still there.

Annette Scholem stood at Zinnia's feet. No longer ash. No longer corporeal, but visible. She wore her green dress. The one that brought out the bright flecks in her big, brown eyes. Her chest and neck were intact. She was radiant. She was the embodiment of one of the original Four Eves. Mahra. Mother and destroyer.

Annette mouthed something that looked like *thank you.*

Zinnia was dumbfounded, but she managed to ask, "For what?"

Annette only smiled. She leaned down, placed her hands on Zinnia's bound feet, and then disappeared in a flash of bright light.

Some of her light remained, and worked its way up over Zinnia's body. The thick, sticky layers of duct tape that bound her lower body fell away like tissue paper. She was free. She was shirtless, wearing only her bra, but she was free.

Zinnia looked around on the dirty floor for something. Her thumb. The one she'd ripped off so she could free herself from the handcuffs. She found the thumb, grabbed an empty jar from her purse supplies, and tossed it in.

Then she picked up the vial of Tracing Ink. Half the liquid remained. It actually wasn't ink at all, let alone the tracing kind, since such a thing didn't exist, as far as she knew. She'd promised Jesse she wouldn't poison him, but she hadn't promised not to lie.

She ran to Ethan, crouched at his head, and carefully dripped a few drops of the dark liquid into Ethan Fung's slack mouth. He was still breathing. The dark drops disappeared when they touched his tongue. The potion would keep his heart beating, but not forever.

Zinnia grabbed her cell phone and immediately dropped it. She'd forgotten about the missing thumb. Thumbs come in handy for holding things like phones. She switched the phone to her other hand, and redialed the emergency number for the DWM.

Chet Moore answered again.

Zinnia said, "Unless you want me to blow all your secrets out in the open, you'd better get your best medical crew to my location in two minutes. Can you do that?"

There was the sound of typing on a keyboard. "Will three minutes be okay?"

"It'll do," Zinnia said. "It'll have to."

"They're on their way."

"Do they have black scarabyce blood in their supplies?"

"What's that?"

"Never mind. I have something I can use."

Zinnia ended the call and took a seat under the basement's single light fixture. She dug through her purse, found a salve she hoped would do the trick, and reaffixed her thumb. She'd lost a lot of blood. There was so much of it on the floor. Hers. Ethan's. Jesse's.

She wiggled her reattached thumb. The angle wasn't quite right, so she yanked it off and tried again.

She paused to check on Ethan. Still breathing. She considered dusting him with her remaining body buoyancy powder so she could carry him upstairs, but decided against moving him. If medical assistance didn't arrive within three minutes, she would carry him to her car and start driving. But she did have some faith in Chet Moore's promise.

Now, for the next order of business. She looked at her thumb. It wasn't quite right. She adjusted it once again. Straight? No. But thumbs weren't straight anyway. The repair was good enough.

She retrieved her blouse from the pile of unsticky duct tape and dressed herself.

Then she went upstairs to open the door for whomever —or whatever—the DWM was sending.

Zinnia walked out the front door and sat on the step. The night air was cold, but she barely felt it. She glanced over her shoulder at the house. It didn't feel menacing anymore. Whatever bad juju had infested the walls, it had been vanquished, along with...

Zinnia stopped her thoughts. Now was not the time to think about Jesse Berman.

She peered down the street. Unlike pots of water on the stove, which don't boil any faster or slower when watched, watching for a bus or other vehicle does make it come sooner, if a witch is doing the watching.

There was no sign yet of the DWM emergency crew.

Zinnia looked down at her thumb. It was rapidly healing.

She cast a spell to make the moonlight in the vicinity brighter. It worked. A little too well. She dimmed the moonlight back to regular levels.

Then she took a seat on the front step and waited, looking up and down the street periodically to help the crew arrive sooner.

She picked absently at a ridge of white glue that had remained stubbornly stuck to the cuff of her blouse. Annette had cast the spell for unsticking the duct tape almost perfectly, nearly as well as Zinnia had cast the same spell a few days earlier.

Annette hadn't known she was a witch in life, but she'd been a quick study in death. She must have been haunting around the office the day Margaret and Zinnia had battled in the supply closet. That must have been how she'd learned that spell. After her death, Annette must have seen everything they did, heard everything they said. Of course she'd stuck around the office. The people there were her family. One of them was her son. That was why Annette had always organized the group to spend time together outside of the office. She wanted to be near her son. She wanted to be near...

Zinnia's back tickled. She reached under her blouse and pulled out a smoldering chunk that had embedded near the edge of her shoulder blade. She studied the smoking chunk, which was about the same size as Margaret's lucky marble. Had Annette arranged through her cousin to have Jesse pick up her ashes so they would be here, at the house, when Zinnia needed them? *No.* Zinnia shook her head at her thoughts. Annette's spirit couldn't have known. Could she?

Zinnia was still thinking about how little she knew about ghosts when the unmarked vans pulled up and the crew rushed out.

CHAPTER 29

SIX DAYS LATER

Zinnia Riddle woke up, climbed out of bed, and cast the first spell of the day. Her bed made itself with no sass or fuss, not even from the pillow.

Next, she retrieved a feather duster from her linen closet. Overnight in her dreams, she had finally remembered the spell for dusting. She twirled the duster up into the air, pink feathers fanning out, and set it in motion with quick hand gestures. Off it flew, flapping like a tiny, pink flamingo, magically dusting the tops of doors and window frames.

She took an ice-cold shower, reveling in the refreshing water. She shut off the water, and then didn't touch the decorative towels she'd hung on the towel rack. She dried herself by magic—her third spell of the day, cast with perfect syntax, but who was counting?—then went to her closet to look over her wardrobe. Several newly purchased blouses hung at the ready in Zinnia's closet, along with a new floral skirt. She'd considered buying some plain blouses to wear with the patterned skirt, but decided against it. Life can get dark sometimes. We all need more of the bright flowers that come after the rain.

* * *

Zinnia was approaching the hospital's front doors when she saw a familiar, friendly face. Another woman her age was holding open the door for her, and the woman had the chin-raised posture of someone anticipating a pleasant exchange. Ah, life in a small town.

Zinnia quickened her pace so as not to keep the woman waiting. Her name was Kathy Carmichael. Kathy had a compact build, medium-brown skin, and medium-brown hair that coiled in ringlets. She was dressed in conservative, earth-toned clothing, and wore an old-fashioned pair of wire-rimmed glasses on the bridge of her narrow, sharply pointed nose. Zinnia had known Kathy for many years, but she had not yet determined if Kathy had any magical abilities. Kathy dropped plenty of hints from time to time, but the two had never come into the sort of calamitous situation that forced a supernatural woman to reveal her true self.

"Good afternoon, Kathy!" Zinnia said brightly. "How are things at the library?"

"Wonderful, thank you, Zinnia. Frank mentioned he saw you recently."

"Frank?" Zinnia's mind fired a blank. She thought of the name Fred and promptly went blank again. How was it she could name any herb in existence, yet certain people's names and faces wouldn't connect in her mind?

Meanwhile, someone else was approaching the entrance of the hospital. The two women instinctively moved away from the doorway. They both stepped inside, even though Kathy had been on her way out. They carried their conversation over to an unpopulated waiting area.

"You know Frank. Our children's librarian," Kathy explained. "An older gentleman with bright pink hair. You can't miss him." Kathy winked a golden-brown eye behind her round glasses. It was a slow-motion wink, very controlled, which made Zinnia feel for a moment like she was making small talk with an owl.

"Yes, of course," Zinnia said, recovering graciously. "Frank Wonder. One of my coworkers also lives at the Candy Factory, so I happened to see Frank there last week." Had it only been last week? It felt like a hundred years ago.

"The Candy Factory." Kathy shuddered and rubbed her arms through her puffy winter jacket. "That old building gives me the creeps. Did you know it used to be a prison for the criminally insane?"

Zinnia replied, "A polite society has to hide the crazy ones somewhere."

"Grandma Kay always warned us kids to steer clear, because of all the ghosts." Kathy tilted her head and snapped her fingers. "That reminds me. I believe you work with my cousin, Karl Kormac."

Zinnia was stunned. Kathy and Karl had zero family resemblance. She said, "Yes, I do work with Karl. He's an interesting man."

"Interesting? I suppose that's one way to put it." Kathy winked again.

"And you two are related? Cousins, you said?" Zinnia's mind spun new threads. Annette Scholem had cast Karl in her book as Lark, a grumpy troll. As far as Zinnia knew, trolls weren't real, but there were other creatures who had troll-like attributes. Was Karl one of those creatures? Was his cousin, Kathy Carmichael?

Kathy removed her glasses and rubbed the bridge of her narrow nose. "Karl and I share a set of grandparents, Ken and Kay. Here's a funny thing: every one of us kids was given a K name. Isn't that odd?" She chuckled. "Whooo does such a thing?" She drew out the word *whooo* like an owl hooting.

Zinnia kept a straight face. "That doesn't seem odd to me, but then again, we have a lot of Z names in my family."

"Is that right?" Kathy pulled a tiny spray bottle from her purse and began cleaning her glasses thoroughly. "I'm so glad I ran into you today. The library is thinking about hiring someone with a name similar to yours. She's not from around here, but now you've got me wondering if the two of you might be related."

"What's her name?"

"Zara Riddle."

Zinnia took a step backward as a flash flood of premonitions nearly knocked her over like a bowling pin. Powerful magic was afoot. She tried to focus on one of the visions to catch details, but the imagery cut off as quickly as it had come on.

Kathy took a step forward, closing the space between them. "Is something wrong, Zinnia?"

"Not at all." Zinnia forced a calm smile. "Zara Riddle is my niece. I didn't realize she was applying to work at our local library." More questions bubbled up. Was Zara already living in Wisteria? How had Zinnia not noticed something like that? She'd been so blind to Jesse's true nature. Was she blind to everything that mattered? Was it something that happened with age?

"Your niece will have to move here if she takes the position, of course," Kathy said.

That answered one question, at least. Zinnia nodded sagely. "Moving here would be wonderful for her, and her family."

"Family?" Kathy blinked one golden-brown eye and then the other. "Oh, you mean her daughter."

"And me. Since I'm her family."

Kathy laughed. "Of course! Silly me. Well, I guess that's that. We simply *have to* hire her now, so you two can be reunited. I'll throw out all the other resumes."

Zinnia couldn't tell if the other woman was joking or not.

"Oh, no," Zinnia said. "Don't hire her simply on my account. That wouldn't be right."

"It would be more right than wrong." Kathy hooted happily as she returned her round glasses to her face. She grabbed Zinnia's forearm. "If she's half as fun as you, Zinnia, I'm sure she'll be a hoot!"

A hoot? Zinnia played it cool, even though the news, in addition to Kathy's powerful grip on her arm, was surprising. "You could do worse than hiring one of us."

"One of you?" Kathy raised both eyebrows expectantly.

"Yes. One of us Riddle women. You should know, we Riddle women are tougher than we look." Zinnia gently pulled her arm away from the town's head librarian and massaged her reattached thumb.

Kathy looked down at Zinnia's hand, frowned, then glanced over at the door. "Well, I suppose I should let you go see whomever it is you're here to see."

Zinnia said nothing, even though she sensed Kathy was waiting for an explanation about her business at the hospital. It was no secret that Zinnia was friends with Ethan Fung, yet she didn't want to share that she was there to visit him. Zinnia didn't divulge personal details easily, and for good reason. Even the smallest slip-up could get a witch in trouble. That's why two witches who might be best friends in their coven could pass each other on the street without so much as a glance. Witches do well to avoid each other except when necessary. Margaret and Zinnia had been practically courting disaster by working together.

Kathy scrunched her eyes and did a little hop. "Zinnia, would you mind writing a personal recommendation letter for your niece? Just for my file. I won't tell her about our conversation."

"A personal recommendation? Of course," Zinnia said. Never mind that she barely knew her niece. The last time she'd seen the young woman was at Zara's mother's funeral, five years ago. But it didn't matter that they were practically strangers. Zara was a Riddle, and so Zinnia would vouch for her. She would do anything for her family.

Kathy said goodbye, reached into her yarn-filled purse for her car keys, and continued on her way outside.

Once Zinnia was alone, she allowed herself to collapse into one of the waiting area's chairs. Sitting down after big news always felt good. The witchbane she'd been fed on Saturday was no longer affecting her magic, but she hadn't quite recovered from the changes in her life. There was still the pain in her heart to contend with. Since Charlize had unfrozen her heart, she hadn't touched the special tea. She was dealing with her emotions. Taking them and feeling them all, good and bad. She would need time to find her balance. How long did she have until her niece arrived in town? She should have asked Kathy.

Zara's daughter would be turning sixteen shortly. Little Zoey. Rhys, the girl's grandfather, called the girl Zozo. Was their Zozo about to become a witch? Zoey's mother, Zara, wasn't a witch herself—not as far as Zinnia knew.

What strange things did magic have planned for the three of them?

Zinnia moved on from massaging her thumb to wringing both hands. There was so much to do. She had to talk to Margaret about everything, and warn the others in her coven. Then again, maybe it wasn't any of Maisy or Fatima's business.

She had to finish the wallpaper in the guest room so it would be perfect, in case her niece—*her niece!*—wanted to stay over while she looked for a suitable home. Perhaps the girls could move right in with Zinnia? Wouldn't that be something!

Zinnia suddenly clutched her hands together at her chest in girlish glee. Her family was coming to Wisteria!

* * *

Once Zinnia had recovered from the news given to her by the town's head librarian, she took the hospital's antiseptic-smelling elevator upstairs to visit her dear friend, Ethan Fung. He'd been released from wherever the DWM had him, released from whatever they'd been *doing to him*, and was now recovering in a regular, non-magical hospital room.

She walked into the private room to find the detective sitting up in bed. He had a slipper on one foot and a giant cast covering the other leg, from his foot to his upper thigh. She hadn't seen him since that night in the basement, and was glad to see his face had regained its normal tan coloring, though his cheeks were gaunt. He'd lost weight since the ordeal. And his typically short black hair had grown out just enough to look messy.

But, even in hospital-issued pajamas, he was a beautiful sight for Zinnia's eyes.

By the time the medical crew from the DWM had arrived and taken over, she'd worried he was too far gone. There'd been so much blood on the concrete floor. The amiable man in charge of the crew, a doctor who called himself Dr. Bob, had promised to fix up Fung as good as new. No, that wasn't quite what he'd said. Dr. Bob had promised to make Fung "better than new." Zinnia hadn't liked the way the doctor had made the promise, but now here Fung was. Alive. She couldn't complain.

Fung didn't hear Zinnia enter the room. He was busy flicking through channels on his tiny television.

"Catching up on your soap operas?" Zinnia asked. "I understand they're easier to follow if you stay on the channel more than five seconds."

Fung gave her a wry smile and waved the remote control in his hand. "I'm trying to find the station that's playing old episodes of *Wicked Wives*. I heard it playing in someone else's room. Do you know which channel I'd find that on?"

Zinnia blinked rapidly. "Why would I watch a show about housewife witches?"

Fung snorted.

Zinnia took a seat in one of the visitor's chairs. Her mind was still buzzing from her conversation with Kathy, but she kept the big news to herself. Fung had enough to worry about.

She asked politely, "How's the leg?"

"Itchy under the cast, but I think they put me back together the right way around."

Zinnia eyed the angle of his toes compared to his body. "It's a better job than I might have done." She rubbed her thumb self-consciously. Fung didn't know about her thumb, or the drastic measures she'd taken. Perhaps it was for the best. He'd endured enough horror.

Fung turned off the television and pulled himself upright on the bed. "I should be getting out of this place in a couple days. I'm only here now because they were worried about my blood tests. They detected high levels of strange chemical compounds they couldn't identify."

"Oh, really?" Zinnia feigned surprise.

"You wouldn't know anything about that, would you?"

The compounds were probably the potion she gave him that night for his pain, but then again, it might have been the work of Dr. Bob.

She answered, "No, I wouldn't know anything about strange chemical compounds, but it does sound very interesting." On that note, she pulled her trusty tea thermos from her purse and set it on his side table. "You'll want to sip this between meals."

He narrowed his eyes at her. "More of your trickery? I know what chamomile tea smells like."

"No chamomile in there today," she said. "Just the good stuff."

"Thanks. I think." He opened the thermos and sniffed the tea. "That smells nice, actually."

She smiled. She knew he would say that.

He rolled his blanket up and then smoothed it down. The room was quiet. Someone in the hallway pushed a cart with two squeaky wheels off into the distance. An elevator dinged. The scent of disinfectant tickled Zinnia's sensitive nostrils.

Fung asked, "And how are you doing, Zinnia?"

"Great," she said. "Never been better."

"No, I mean, how are *you* doing? How are you feeling?"

She shrugged. "I'm feeling however it is you think I ought to be feeling."

"That's not much of an answer. Jesse was your boyfriend, and now he's dead."

"These things happen."

"He poisoned you. He choked you. He left us both to die."

"He only left you to die. He left me to watch you die."

Fung's eye twitched. "I stand corrected."

"These things happen," she repeated.

Fung closed his eyes and rubbed them. "Zinnia, you're going to have to start letting people in some day."

"I will if you will."

He stretched out his arms. "Me? I'm an open book!"

She raised her hand and wiggled her thumb. "Look at this thumb. You'd never guess it was completely detached last Saturday night."

Fung's jaw dropped open. "It was?" He looked horrified. She instantly regretted her decision to tell him about her method of escape, but, on the other hand—pardon the pun—she had successfully changed the topic of conversation.

They talked about her thumb for a while, and she shared with Fung how she'd been able to slip out of the handcuffs and then out of the duct tape thanks to her loose-fitting, long-sleeved blouse.

After a while, the conversation died down peacefully, like a campfire. They were two old friends enjoying the flickering embers of what remained.

Fung said, "I'm going to be out of commission for a while. Maybe I'll take a vacation with all those days I have stockpiled. The department will be bringing in someone new as my replacement."

"They could never replace you."

"I'll say. It'll be some poor schlub who doesn't know anything about magic."

"It's so cruel to do that to someone. Why do they do that?"

"They do that because only the people who've recently had their minds blown become the most creative problem solvers. Whoever they hire, that man or woman will become an incredible detective, assuming they survive the trial by fire."

Zinnia nodded slowly. "Whatever doesn't kill you makes you stronger."

Fung gestured at his cast. "Stronger, but with a limp."

Zinnia's mind went back to the idea of Fung being replaced. She asked, "How many of these vacation days do you have saved up, anyway?"

He answered immediately. "A year's worth." He'd been anticipating her question. "Some people would call that a sabbatical."

"Where will you go?"

"What makes you think I'd go somewhere?"

"We both know you're not going to putter around the house while some other detective takes care of your town. For one thing, your mother wouldn't allow it."

"She's probably lining up blind dates for me at this very minute. And I'll be on crutches, so I can't get away as easily."

Zinnia giggled. She had a mental image of Fung on crutches, being chased by his dear mother and a dozen eligible women.

"Which is all the more reason why I need to leave town," he said. "Any ideas?"

"Venice," she said without hesitation.

He did a double take. "You sound sure about that."

"You should go to Venice," she said.

"Maybe I will."

A nurse came in to check on the patient. Zinnia excused herself and quietly left to give them some privacy.

If she had known how long it would be until she saw her friend again, she might have stayed. But she didn't know, and so she made her way out of the hospital and then home.

CHAPTER 30

7:30 PM

Zinnia got home that Saturday evening to find Charlize Wakeful sitting on her porch. The pretty gorgon wasn't in a silver sci-fi jumpsuit this time, but she was wearing shiny silver pants. She'd paired them with pink sneakers and a puffy white ski jacket. The day had been warm for late January, so even though the sun had set an hour ago, her jacket was unzipped, revealing a T-shirt with gray and white stripes.

Zinnia's thumb throbbed. She switched her bag of takeout dinner to her other hand. She maintained steady, confident eye contact with the blonde as she approached the porch.

Charlize was nibbling on a fingernail and reading on her phone.

Zinnia should have said hello, but what came out was, "You knew." Her voice was raspy. Angry. Nearly as hoarse as it had been one week ago, when she'd been screaming in the basement of the Berman house. "You knew," she repeated. "You knew about everything."

Charlize looked up from her phone. "Me?" She blinked her light eyelashes innocently. "I suppose I had my own theories, but I didn't know for sure."

"Do you expect me to believe that you, of all people, didn't know what Jesse was?"

She blinked again. "That sort of information is kept under tight wraps. Top level eyes only." Another evasion.

Zinnia tried another direction. "What does Special Buildings do?" That was the permits division that had been run solely by Jesse Berman.

Charlize replied airily, "Just what the name says. Issue permits for special buildings."

"Such as?"

"Such as the facility you insisted we rush your friend Ethan Fung to. The facility you were so happy existed, when you needed it."

Zinnia jerked her head, tossing her hair over her shoulder. She wasn't going to let herself be distracted. She pressed on. "So that means Jesse knew all about everything going on in this town."

Charlize smirked. "Not everything, Ms. Riddle. Nobody knows everything."

"But he was working for your people the whole time."

"Just on the building projects." Charlize looked down at the ground briefly. "The other incident had nothing to do with the DWM."

The *other incident.* She meant Annette's murder. If Charlize had stopped by to make friends, she was doing a lousy job of it.

"You knew," Zinnia said.

"We didn't know about what he did to your friend," Charlize said. "We didn't put it together until after the cougar attack in the swamp."

"But you do know how his kind feels about my kind." Zinnia stepped closer. Charlize was still sitting on the step, so Zinnia towered over her. Zinnia was feeling a storm inside again, like what she'd felt when Annette's spirit had manifested in the basement. She spat out her words. "You knew what Jesse was, and how he felt about my kind, and you didn't even try to warn me."

Charlize leaned back before snaking her way up to stand. She was on the porch, so now she had the higher ground and towered over Zinnia. "That's not true," Charlize said coolly. "I did warn you. I came here in person, on my own time, and I warned you."

Zinnia took two steps up to the porch so they were about the same height. She looked the gorgon in the eyes with no fear whatsoever.

Through gritted teeth, Zinnia said, "You told me to stay home and not invite anyone over."

"That's exactly what I said. Good memory. And if that's not a warning, I don't know what is. You would have been perfectly safe if you'd done what I told you to."

Zinnia curled her free hand into a ball. Her power was spotty, but she had blue fire. She felt it ignite.

Zinnia said, "This is precisely why your kind can't be trusted."

"Ouch." Charlize backed up, leaned down, and picked up the cardboard box she'd been sitting next to. It was the same width as the one that had contained Annette's ashes, but twice as tall.

"Here," the gorgon said. "I brought you a peace offering."

Zinnia didn't move. "I'm not interested in your bribes, your panaceas."

"It's not a *panaceas*, whatever that is." Charlize wrinkled her nose in what might have been a cute gesture, if Zinnia were not so angry.

Time to cut to the chase. "Get off my porch."

"Take my gift. You mussssst take my gift." As she pushed the box toward Zinnia, Charlize's copper hair snakes appeared between her golden-blonde waves of hair. They showed their magical fangs and hissed as she spoke, entwining their hypnotic hiss with her regular voice, the way Witch Tongue did with spellwork. "I insissssssst."

Zinnia took the cardboard box without looking at it. The box weighed about five pounds. "Listen, Ms. Wakeful. If you want peace, you've got it. I'll stay out of your business, and you stay out of mine." She continued to stare into the gorgon's eyes. "We can have peace."

"Aren't you curious about what's in the box?"

"No." Zinnia's lie sounded hollow, even to her. Who could resist a mystery box? Nobody. Not even Zinnia. She glanced down briefly. There were no markings on the box. "I might open it later, after I've checked it for traps."

"Traps?"

"Spying devices, or things that might weaken a person such as myself."

"Like witchbane."

"Yes." Zinnia felt a light shudder. Even hearing the name of the herb brought back unpleasant feelings. Her thumb itched.

Charlize said, in a teasing tone, "Or other, more abstract things that weaken us girls. Such as love." Charlize raised her eyebrows twice in a playful expression. "Or lust." Her snakes twisted sensuously.

Zinnia held her ground and said nothing. She could only deny the truth so many times before it exhausted her.

"Interesting," Charlize said, squinting. "Your heart is no longer stone, and yet it is still so guarded." She leaned in and sniffed, with both her human nose and her snake tongues flicking scent particles into their vomeronasal systems—assuming the mythical snakes shared their physiology with real ones.

Charlize studied the witch and asked, "You are alive, aren't you? Not some creature of the grave?"

"Don't be ridiculous," Zinnia said. "The spell on my heart was metaphorical stone. Not gravel and rocks, like the kind you make."

"I can make all kinds of stone. That's what I do. And I can unmake it whenever I want." The snake-haired woman sniffed Zinnia again. "What kind of spell has made you like this?"

Zinnia tapped her foot and glanced around. They weren't exactly alone. People were out walking their dogs, strolling up and down the sidewalk, illuminated by the bright streetlights. Zinnia's street was smack-dab in the middle of a peaceful yet bustling neighborhood, which was just how she liked it, because she never felt alone there. It wasn't the right place for an open-air talk about magic and spells.

"That's a discussion for another time," Zinnia said.

"Why not now? I've got the time. And by the look of that sad little Thai takeout meal for one, so do you."

Zinnia looked down, past the box she was holding, at the bag in her hand. A sad little takeout meal for one? Not true. There was actually enough food in the bag for several people. The owners of Kin Khao were fond of Zinnia and always made her portions generous.

"Let's talk," Charlize said. "Our people should be working together."

"Your people should leave my people alone."

"What are the odds of that happening?"

"Slim," Zinnia said, agreeing with the gorgon for the first time that night. As she gave in by an inch, she felt her chilly walls melting. Charlize was just another gifted person, not that different from a witch, trying to make her way in the world without accidentally destroying those who crossed her path. In a way, Zinnia felt pity for her. Charlize had the powers of a goddess, but she was still so young. She didn't have the wisdom to handle her gifts. Was that the real reason she was on Zinnia's porch? Was she seeking a mentor?

"Our families' paths are entwined," Charlize said. "We can resist our fates, or we can accept and adapt. You and I both know what nature does to those who resist."

A sweet, spicy smell wafted up from Zinnia's Thai food. The longer she stood outside, the colder her dinner got. She didn't want to re-heat the food. She kept no microwave—confounded, cursed appliances!—in her house, and the oven always took so long.

Why not invite the gorgon to join her? Charlize had guessed correctly that Zinnia did have time. Also, if Margaret Mills found out Zinnia had declined a friendly dinner with a gorgon, she'd pitch a fit. Margaret was always hungry for gossip about other supernatural people. Gorgons never showed up on Margaret's porch. Come Monday morning, Margaret would berate Zinnia for passing up on juicy details to share with the coven.

Zinnia held the mysterious cardboard box and takeout food with one arm, opened her front door, and waved Charlize in. "You might as well come inside."

"I thought you'd never ask." Charlize reached down behind her and picked up a slender paper bag—the type that holds liquor bottles. "I brought my own supply of tequila this time. A little birdie told me this one's your favorite."

Zinnia snorted. She didn't have a favorite tequila. Not unless...

Charlize lifted the bottle to reveal the label. Hot diggity! It was Zinnia's favorite after all. How had Charlize known? It would have to remain a mystery. Zinnia was not going to give the gorgon the satisfaction of being asked how she knew.

"I have salt, but I don't have any limes," Zinnia said.

"Fine by me."

"I do have something much better than limes."

"How much better?"

Zinnia shrugged nonchalantly. Hidden inside a compartment of her fridge was a bottle of preserved fruits that enhanced the positive effects of tequila while minimizing the negative. Charlize would see for herself.

They entered the kitchen together.

Zinnia flicked on the light, thinking about how glad she was that the dusting was up to date. She was surprised to see something moving. A mouse sat atop the table, chewing on a piece of crust Zinnia had neglected to clean up that morning. Drat. Her charmed feather duster could only do so much. It didn't wash dishes or catch vermin. Zinnia reached for the broom to chase the mouse toward the front door. Charlize stopped her with a raised hand.

"Allow me," the gorgon said.

Zinnia held still with the broom in hand, watching. Ordinarily, she would never let someone see her holding a broom for more than a few seconds. It was too easy to attract a comment along the lines of, "Hey, you look just like a witch with that broom in your hand!" But Charlize and Zinnia already knew each other's secrets, so there was no point in hiding.

Charlize inched toward the mouse. Her hair snakes flared out, not quite filling the kitchen the way they had filled the entryway last weekend, but close.

The mouse froze in place, whiskers twitching, more curious than fearful. Zinnia understood exactly how the poor mouse felt. Charlize leaned over and made a twirling gesture with her finger. The mouse obediently twirled, wrapping its tail around itself. Then Charlize touched the mouse with the tip of her finger. It became stone.

Charlize picked up the mouse, which was now a paperweight, and returned it to the stack of recipes. She brushed off her hands.

"Time for tequila," she said.

Truer words had never been spoken.

Zinnia cleaned the small kitchen table, sanitizing it to remove all traces of mouse, and set out the plates and Thai food. She gathered the small, slender glasses she used for tequila, and prepared the fruit slices.

"Elegant," Charlize said, lifting one of the long-stemmed, narrow glasses. "Most people use a shot glass."

Zinnia smiled. "Well, most people prefer to swig it straight from the bottle, but we're not like most people, are we?"

"I'll drink to that." Charlize raised her glass and clinked it against Zinnia's.

They began dishing out the fragrant Thai food.

After a few minutes, Zinnia decided to ask Charlize about something that had been niggling at her. "Jesse's last name was Berman," she said.

"Yes. And?"

Zinnia frowned. "It's just that *Berman* sounds a lot like *Bear Man*. Don't you find that odd?"

Charlize seasoned her food with extra chili pepper flakes. "Not really."

"So, it's just a coincidence that a cougar man is named Berman?"

"My mother didn't raise me to believe in coincidences."

"Neither did mine," Zinnia said. "So, what does it mean?"

"I'm not really at liberty to discuss such things."

"Not even with me?" Zinnia batted her eyelashes. "Your friend?"

Charlize cracked a smile. "Okay, but you didn't hear it from me. The thing about shifters is it's all one genetic line. Everything from cougars to wolves and eagles. A wolf shifter father can have a son who turns into pretty much anything."

"Oh." Zinnia had always suspected something like that, but she hadn't known for certain.

"And they can even change," Charlize said. "Some shifters go through a sort of midlife crisis and change forms completely."

"Fascinating."

Charlize looked down at her food. "But nobody talks about it. When it happens, you're supposed to carry on as though they've always been that way."

"What about Jesse's father, Viktor? Was he a cougar?"

Charlize's forehead wrinkled. "From what I've read, he was a shifter of some kind, as well as a very bad man. He really did kidnap Jesse's mother, except it was worse than it was in the book Annette wrote. She was even younger, and she wasn't his wife. He'd been a stranger."

Zinnia's skin crawled. "That's..." She was at a loss for words, imagining what happened to Annette as a child. It was almost too much to bear. Her heart ached.

Charlize topped up the glasses of tequila. "He's gone now. And his son."

"Did your people know about Jesse? About his nature?"

"Jesse never did anything wrong, until he killed Annette. The thing is, we can't judge people by their parents."

"Not even when they're as evil as Viktor Oliver Berman?"

Charlize looked into Zinnia's eyes. "Jesse's mother was Annette. He was half evil, and half good. Can any of us say any different of ourselves?"

Zinnia snorted. "I'm not half evil."

Charlize tilted her head to the side, still holding Zinnia with her gaze. "What were you about to do when Annette animated those ashes in the basement?"

She'd been about to cave in Jesse's skull with an urn. "Nothing," Zinnia said, swallowing hard. "Escaping. I'd been trying to get away."

Charlize didn't blink. "Escaping. Yes. That is exactly what's in the report. But sometimes certain details are left out of reports. Is there anything you'd like to add?"

Zinnia shook her head.

"That's what I thought," Charlize said.

Zinnia tore her gaze away from the gorgon's. She cleared her throat. "On a lighter note, I've been offered a promotion at work."

"Good for you," Charlize said cheerfully. "I'm glad we have something to celebrate."

They both raised their glasses, clinked, and drank tequila.

CHAPTER 31

WISTERIA PERMITS DEPARTMENT

2:35 PM

THE LAST MONDAY IN MARCH

Zinnia Riddle sat in her private office, completing the paperwork for a new special building permit. She had recently been promoted, and was now the head—as well as the entire body—of the Wisteria Permits Department Division of Special Buildings. She even had new business cards with the long-winded title to prove it. Not that she had anyone to give the cards to. Since taking over Jesse Berman's old office and job, she'd been keeping a low profile.

She submitted the permit paperwork and stretched her arms over her head. She rotated her chair so she could gaze at the painting on her wall. It was a seascape, Ethan Fung's painting. He'd given it to Zinnia in February, before he left on his sabbatical. By now, Fung's cheery ocher walls had all been painted white. The police department didn't usually redecorate for a new detective, but Fung had felt bad about the holes in the wall left behind by the fastenings of his bookshelf, so he'd paid for a painting crew out of his own pocket.

By now, the end of March, there would be a new man sitting in Fung's chair. He was some poor schlub from out of town, who didn't know about magic. His name was Theodore Bentley. Zinnia hadn't met the man, but she knew she wanted nothing to do with him. From now on, the town's law enforcement agencies could solve their own crimes. She had permits to keep herself busy.

Zinnia slowly rotated her chair away from the painting. Her gaze landed on the printer's proof copy of Annette Scholem's novel. It would be released by Annette's small publisher later that year, under the name AJ Scholem, the same as her other books. The editor predicted it would sell very few copies, since it was a spin-off about a side character, but had agreed to publish it anyway to honor Annette's final wishes.

Zinnia closed her eyes and rubbed them. In her mind's eye, she saw the ash version of Annette. Vengeful and loving at the same time. Facing her son and her killer, then becoming a killer herself. It was a perfect circle; Annette brought him into this world, and she took him out. She had embodied the spirit of one of the original women, one of the four Eves. *Mahra. Mother and destroyer.*

It had been ten weeks since Annette Scholem's death. Almost three months. The office had stabilized to a new range of normal. The chemical carpet smell was gone. They even had some new hires. There was Xavier Batista, the self-anointed hero of Towhee Swamp, who'd taken over Annette's position. And Liza Gilbert, the young woman who'd survived being attacked by Jesse in cougar form. She had taken over Zinnia's job and desk, much to Margaret's annoyance.

Karl Kormac was back from his leave of absence. The others thought he was back to the usual Karl Kormac, alternately blustery and pouty, but Zinnia noticed he wasn't the same. For one thing, he had stopped announcing the number of days he had left until retirement. She wondered if he'd changed his plans about retiring, or if he feared he wouldn't live that long and didn't want to tempt fate. She hadn't asked. Karl would talk about it when he felt ready. Whatever he was, troll or otherwise, the man had his private issues. He had falsely confessed to killing a coworker, after all. A smart witch gives a guy like that some space.

Zinnia leaned over to peer through her office doorway at her old desk. Nobody had touched the candy jar in months. Not Karl, who claimed to be off sweets. And not Margaret, who felt the candy had been cursed by Jesse Berman's spirit. Nobody else wanted them, so they were starting to melt together into a lump.

Zinnia planned to eventually take the hardened lump to the cemetery and drop it on Jesse's grave. *Closure*, the psychology people called it. One last goodbye. The cougar shifter had been laid to rest next to his father—if you could call it "laid to rest." After Annette's ghost blew him apart from the inside, there hadn't been much to lay to rest. The DWM had cleaned the basement and scooped up the organic materials—ash and bone and flesh—and given it a controlled cremation. First time 'round for Jesse, second time 'round for Annette. Ashes to ashes, dust to dust. Mother and child reunion.

The official story in town was that Jesse had learned Annette was his mother and killed her in a fit of rage when she told him the truth about his father. He'd made her death appear to be an animal attack to cover his trail. Then he'd kidnapped a police officer, confessed, and shot himself. Case closed.

Nothing to see here, folks. Just a regular, everyday murder-suicide. Case closed!

Zinnia rolled her chair over to see what Margaret Mills was up to. By the look of her face, slightly frowning, Margaret was doing data entry, minding her own business and being a productive employee. In fact, the whole office looked and sounded productive. Zinnia could hear Carrot Greyson talking to a customer who'd walked in with some questions. Carrot was saying how she loved working at City Hall, but one day she planned to be a full-time tattoo artist.

Underneath that chatter, there was a quiet exchange going on between deskmates Gavin and Dawna. She was telling him to stop making puppy-dog eyes at her because they were not getting back together again. Not ever. Zinnia rolled her eyes. Dawna was as drawn to Gavin as he was to her. A gnome and a cartomancer. What could possibly go wrong? If they could stop bickering over petty things, they could become a real power couple.

The phone on Zinnia's desk rang. It was her direct line.

She answered, "WPD, Special Buildings Division. Zinnia Riddle speaking."

"Zinnia, it's Kathy. Kathy Carmichael. From the library."

"Oh, hello, Kathy. I've been meaning to follow up—"

"She's here now," Kathy said abruptly. "The woman named Zara Riddle. She's been telling people she doesn't have any family here in Wisteria, but she looks exactly like you. It has to be your niece, right? I mean, what are the odds?"

"I don't know. Riddle isn't that uncommon a last name. It might not be my niece, but it sure sounds like her."

"Which begs the question, why doesn't she know about you living here?"

"Things with our family are... complicated."

"Oops. I think she's heading toward the staff lounge now, so I might have to hang up." Kathy snickered. "I've been giving her a hard time."

"You have?"

"She cleaned out the fridge." More snickering.

"That doesn't sound too bad to me."

"Gotta go."

And she was gone.

Zinnia hung up the phone and looked at it. Zara was in town, working at the library, not far from City Hall. Zinnia could leave work early and catch her there before the library closed.

Or not. It was only Zara's first day at her new job. Better to give her some time to settle in.

The phone rang again.

Zinnia answered, "WPD, Special Buildings Division. Zinnia Riddle speaking."

An old man's gravelly voice came over the line. "You've been holding out on me, Ms. Riddle."

"I have? May I ask who's calling?"

"It's me. Griebel." It was Griebel Gorman, Gavin's uncle. Griebel was a gnome who actually looked like a gnome ought to look, according to storybooks, anyway.

"Hello, Griebel. What's this about me holding out on you?"

"There's another lovely redhead in town who looks just like you. I made a fool of myself on Saturday because I didn't have my glasses on."

Zinnia leaned back in her chair. "Oh, Griebel. I'm sure it won't be the last time you make a fool of yourself."

"She's related to you," he said, more statement than question.

"Easy now. She's way too young for you, mister."

He cracked up for a bit, then asked, "How do you like your new lamp?"

Zinnia put two and two together. When Charlize had come to apologize to Zinnia in January, she'd brought a bottle of Zinnia's favorite bottle of tequila in addition to the world's ugliest lamp. That was what had been inside the box. The two women had laughed themselves senseless over the lamp, particularly when they had reached the end of the tequila.

Zinnia asked the gnome, "Did that horrible thing come from your repair shop? The person who gave it to me wouldn't say where it came from, just that it was very old and very valuable."

"True, true. The lamp is both of those things. Plus it really brings a room together."

Zinnia snorted. "It's a shame that being old and valuable doesn't make up for a lack of aesthetic beauty."

Griebel made a tut-tut sound. "I'll have you know it's a stunning piece of ancient craftsmanship."

"The only craftsmanship was yours, when you unloaded it on someone to give to me. Why did you suggest that particular piece? Was it the flowers? Just because I'm fond of floral patterns doesn't mean I'm bonkers for anything with a flower slapped onto it."

"You don't like it?"

"Why? Can I exchange it for something else?"

"No refunds or exchanges. Final sale."

Zinnia sighed. It had been worth asking.

Griebel said, "The only reason you don't see the lamp's beauty is because you are not its intended owner."

"Good." She glanced over at the darkest corner of her office. "Do you think I should bring it into work? Or maybe a dark alley between my house and City Hall?"

"You must not do that," he said emphatically. "Keep the lamp inside your home. When the time is right, it will tell you who its next caretaker should be."

Zinnia paused to consider this. Griebel was a wily, squirmy guy, but he didn't lie. Not to her, anyway.

She asked, "Is it cursed?"

"Would I pass along a cursed item?" He quickly added, "To you?"

"So, it's enchanted? Charmed?"

"Cursed, charmed, who can say? Only the writers of history. If it's not for you, give it to the one for whom it is for."

Zinnia was quiet for a moment. How curious it was that the gnome had chosen to phone her just seconds after someone else had called about her niece. Curious, indeed.

The old man on the phone cleared his throat. "How is my young nephew doing?"

"You could ask him yourself. I can transfer you to his desk."

"No need," the elder gnome said hurriedly. "He doesn't like it when I check up on him. Such a defensive young man. So touchy."

Zinnia couldn't argue with that, even though she and Gavin Gorman had been getting along better than ever lately. She'd started supplying him with a compound that he valued greatly. He'd been sweet as honey.

"I should let you get back to your busy job," Griebel said. "Don't be a stranger. Bring your lookalikes along, and come see me sometime at my shop."

Zinnia agreed and said goodbye.

She sat quietly in her chair, thinking about her two phone calls. Both had been surprising. Her short-range psychic previews seemed to be limited to her cell phone. She and Margaret had tried to figure out why Zinnia's gift didn't work with her direct line at the office, but they'd found no charms or enchantments. It stood to reason that City Hall had some dampeners in place, and whatever the mechanism was, it was too sophisticated for the witches to detect. If Zinnia really wanted to know, she could always contact Vincent Wick. He did owe her a favor. But it would be better to save that for a time she genuinely needed him.

She looked around her private office, wondering if anyone would mind if she put up some wallpaper—paid for personally, of course. Decorating made her happy. Even just thinking about decorating improved her mood by several degrees.

She found herself smiling. Life for Zinnia Riddle had been pleasant over the past ten weeks. She enjoyed her new job, since special buildings were much more interesting than regular buildings. The position had first been offered to her coworkers, who all had more seniority than Zinnia, but none of them had wanted it. Probably because the pay was the same while the role came with more responsibility. Zinnia, unlike the others, had been thrilled to accept more responsibility. She'd immediately thrown herself into her work. Working hard gave her a purpose, a wind with which to sail her boat.

But soon the winds would be changing direction. New family members often came, much like her new job, with more responsibility. Zinnia didn't know how she felt about that, but she found herself frowning.

A fresh pot of her tea, the regular, non-magical kind, would help.

She got up and walked out to the main office area. There was a loud crack as the heel of her shoe broke. She looked down, stunned. The heel had simply snapped, like a diseased tree in a snow storm. As if by magic.

Margaret Mills was looking at her with mild interest. Zinnia instinctively gave Margaret a dirty look. Was this payback for that time Zinnia had whipped the other witch's shoes off? Witches weren't supposed to keep score. And they didn't cast sneaky spells on each other.

Margaret commented, "A snapped heel is bad luck, Zinnia. You should go to a shoe store straight after work. You need to purchase a new pair before sundown, or you'll get showered with bad luck."

Zinnia was not amused. "I have to replace my shoes before sundown? I've never heard of that particular superstition. Did you just make it up?"

"Everyone knows that about a snapped heel. Right?" Margaret looked for support from her new deskmate, Liza Gilbert. Liza, however, had headphones in her ears. The young woman hadn't heard anything.

Margaret frowned and shook her head at the oblivious Liza. She got up from her chair and came over to where Zinnia stood, albeit lopsided thanks to one broken heel.

"Yup. It's broken," Margaret said.

"Thank you for your expert opinion."

"Since we're chatting, I've gotta say I don't like this new office setup." She rolled her eyes in Liza's direction. "That one is no fun at all. I miss sharing a desk with you."

"Well, I *don't* miss getting kicked in the shins."

"I hardly ever kicked you in the shins." Margaret put her hands on her hips and leaned her torso forward, ready to charge like a rhinoceros. "Wait. Is that why you took the special buildings promotion? To get away from me?"

"Of course not, Margaret. You're one of my most treasured friends."

Margaret snorted. "You must not have a lot of friends."

Zinnia shifted her balance and steadied herself with one arm around Margaret's shoulders. Then she looked the woman in the eyes and said, "Oh, Margaret. Who needs friends when I have you?"

* * *

Zinnia lifted her face skyward and enjoyed the spring sunshine as she walked past the old stone buildings and churches lining the streets between City Hall and the shops of Wisteria. A shadow passed, darkening the sidewalk. She caught a glimpse of an enormous bird, too big to be anything but supernatural. She kept her pace and looked straight ahead. Best to ignore these things and stick to your own business!

Just to be safe, though, she quickly darted into a store and waited for the giant bird to move on. The store sold vintage teacups, among other things. Zinnia took some time to browse the selection and pick out a few pieces for her house. One could never have too many pretty teacups.

After the dishes had been wrapped up, Zinnia crossed the street and headed for Open Toad Shoes. She had cast a steadfast spell on her broken heel, but it wouldn't last on the long walk home. What odd luck that today, the day she left her car at home and walked to work, would be the day her shoe broke? Magic clearly had something in mind for her. What had Charlize said? *We can resist our fates, or we can accept and adapt. Fate punishes those who resist.*

Fate or magic had something in mind, so Zinnia would play along with Margaret's superstition. She would buy new shoes today. Not much of a sacrifice, really.

She opened the door to Open Toad Shoes and said hello to the owner, Thomas Rose. He gave her a surprised look, his mouth dropping open below his large, white mustache. Zinnia barely noticed his reaction. Her eye was drawn by a curious selection of saddle shoes. Who would wear such a theatrical thing? She bent over to examine them.

The shopkeeper went back to helping another customer, a redheaded woman. After some friendly chatter, the woman selected a pair of boots. Zinnia glanced over her shoulder at the footwear. *Good choice*, she thought. They were very nice boots.

Thomas Rose said to the first customer, in a voice loud enough for Zinnia to hear clearly, "I hope you don't mind me asking, but how closely are you two gorgeous redheads related?"

Two redheads? Related? Zinnia turned around to find herself staring at a nearly identical copy of herself. The effect was like looking in a mirror.

Zara Riddle! Zinnia's niece. There was no doubt. The pair had the exact same coloring, from red hair to hazel eyes, and the same oval-shaped faces. Zara was younger by sixteen years, but other than that, they were remarkably similar. No wonder the shopkeeper had done a double take when Zinnia had walked in.

Thomas said, "You must be sisters."

"I don't have a sister," the younger one said, breaking eye contact and looking down at Zinnia's clothes, a floral blouse and flower-dotted skirt. Zinnia was glad she had worn her nicest outfit that day. Best to make a good impression right from the start. Zara had been in Wisteria since at least Saturday, so Zinnia had already lost two days. Her breath caught in her throat. She shouldn't have been feeling so much emotion, but she was.

Zinnia was at a loss for words. Where was the conversation? She rewound it in her head. Zara had mentioned she didn't have a sister. Right.

Zinnia replied with a playful, "Such a shame you don't have a sister." The words spilled out before she could consider them. Zinnia's spine stiffened. She'd simply been trying to keep up the conversation, but she'd inadvertently lied to her niece. What a way to start a relationship. Zara *did* have a sister. She had a sister and she probably didn't know.

Zara looked her aunt in the eyes. "But I do have a few stray relatives," she said with a knowing look. "Weird ones."

Zinnia suppressed a smirk and played along. "Is that so?"

The conversation continued playfully. They exchanged names, just to be absolutely certain, and Zara confirmed that she had bumped into one of Zinnia's friends—not that Zinnia considered Griebel Gorman a friend. Zara's hazel eyes twinkled when she described Griebel's appearance. Did she know he was a gnome? Did Zara know about magic after all? Her mother, Zirconia, had sworn her daughter didn't know, and that Zirconia had "protected" her, and yet here Zara was, in Wisteria. A town brimming with magical creatures.

Zara gave her aunt a pleasant smile. "Well, this is quite the coincidence," she said knowingly. There was that twinkle again. She *had to know* about magic having a mind of its own. How could she not?

Zinnia tested her by replying, "Don't tell me your mother raised you to believe in coincidences."

Zara leaned back and gave her aunt a surprised look, her hazel eyes wide and her brow furrowed. Thoughts were definitely churning inside that sharp mind. What could Zara be thinking? Was she eager to get to know her aunt? Or had she been poisoned against her by Zirconia? Zinnia's older sister had been dead for five years—nearly six—and yet her controlling ways still extended out into the world from her grave. That bitter ex-witch.

Zinnia looked away quickly, ashamed she'd been having negative thoughts about her sister. That "bitter ex-witch" had been Zara's mother. This meeting today had to be difficult for Zara. Seeing someone who resembled Zirconia so closely had to be unsettling.

Thomas Rose, who had always been such a sweet, simple man, clapped his hands like a schoolboy being presented with a birthday cake full of sparklers. "How wonderful," he exclaimed. "A surprise family reunion happening right here in my shoe store. I knew something was afoot, so to speak, when I noticed you were foot twins."

Zara's face wrinkled up. She sneezed three times, and then her face relaxed. The scent of peppermint hung in the air.

Zinnia detected a change in the room tone. Something had been altered. Magic was afoot, but what kind?

"Zinnia, darling," Zara said in an otherworldly tone. "You simply *must* come for dinner at my house. We shall have rack of lamb, and you can meet my daughter. How about seven o'clock? We'll have cocktails at seven and dinner by eight, like *civilized* people. How does Friday work for you, *darling*?"

Zinnia was so shocked, she could have been knocked off the shoe store bench with a feather. Her niece seemed to be possessed by someone or something. Zinnia turned away slowly and began taking off her shoes. It had to be a muscle memory from being inside the shoe store, because she didn't know what she was doing.

Keeping her composure as best she could, Zinnia said, "Friday works for me."

Just then, Thomas returned with a pair of boots for Zinnia to try on.

Zinnia forced herself to continue the polite conversation. Whatever force was at work on Zara, Zinnia couldn't let on that she knew. Her niece did have powers, and she'd been saddled with the most dangerous one of all. She was Spirit Cursed. Or, to be more politically correct, Spirit Charmed. The poor thing.

Zinnia asked, "When did you move to Wisteria? Myself, I adore living here, but most of the country has never heard of the place."

Sounding more like herself and less like something otherworldly, Zara said, "What makes you think I'm not here on holidays?"

Careful, Zinnia. Zinnia couldn't let on that she'd talked to Kathy Carmichael about the librarian job. Zara struck Zinnia as the type of independent woman who wouldn't appreciate having her fate be meddled with by others.

Zinnia covered coolly, logically. "You invited me to dinner at *your* house, which I presume is here in Wisteria."

"Oh, yes. *My house.* How I've always loved the sound of that phrase. My house. Mine. I'm going to be working that phrase into every conversation I have for the next year."

Zinnia felt herself relax. Her niece was charming. A bit daffy and talkative, but in a pleasant way. "You're so much like your mother," Zinnia said. "She did love having things that were all her own." Zinnia leaned over to tie her laces and hide the tears that welled in her eyes. "I miss her so much."

The younger redhead didn't say anything.

A moment of silence passed, and then Zara was writing her address on a slip of paper.

The address was on Beacon Street. It was the exact address of Winona Vander Zalm's house. If the Red Witch House was Zara's house now, that meant... Winnie was no longer of this world. Zinnia kept her shock to herself. But how shocked should she have been? Winona Vander Zalm had been old. Older than most people would imagine. The only surprising part about the news was that Zinnia hadn't heard it before now.

The two women talked for a moment about the house and its previous owner. Zinnia finally found the courage to ask her niece, "How did she die?"

Zara shrugged, seemingly unconcerned. "Peacefully, in her sleep. Or so I heard. It all happened long before I arrived on the scene. I only got here on Saturday."

"The day before your daughter's sixteenth birthday."

Zara's red eyebrows rose. "For a lady I haven't seen in years, you sure keep close tabs on me." There was suspicion in her voice.

Zinnia panicked and lied. "I have an excellent memory for dates." She did not. She'd forgotten her own birthday in January. But what else could she say?

Zara edged toward the store's exit, looking uneasy. Her eyes narrowed. "Did you follow me in here?"

Had she? Zinnia couldn't say for sure. She'd followed something. A feeling. A superstition.

"Of course not," Zinnia said, trying to sound casual and fun. "Don't be a ding-dong." She immediately regretted calling her niece a ding-dong. She hadn't used the term in years—no, decades. It was the insult she and her sister used to trade, because all the other bad words had been banned in their house.

Thomas Rose clicked away at his computer and announced the total for Zara's new boots.

Zinnia waved her hand and said, "Put my niece's boots on my tab, please." She turned to Zara and tried to set things as right as she could. "I know it doesn't make up for missing out on so much of your life so far, but I hope you'll accept this small gift from me. It's the least I can do, considering your kind invitation to dinner."

Zara looked confused, but just for a moment. "Uh, sure, but you might change your mind after you taste my cooking on Friday."

Zinnia sensed it was time to do something. What did people do in a situation like this? Hug? She should hug her niece. She started extending her arms then pulled back. She ended up awkwardly grabbing her niece's arm and making an alarming sound as she nearly lost her balance.

To cover, she said, "Zara, darling, I'm sure whatever you whip up, it will be intriguing!"

Too much, Zinnia! She tried to pull back and be more normal, but another alarming sound came out of her mouth. It sounded to Zinnia an awful lot like a cackle. A witch's cackle. *Oh, floopy doop.* This was not going well at all.

CHAPTER 32

ONE WEEK LATER

Margaret Mills couldn't hear enough about Zinnia's recently-reunited family members.

"That Zoey *does* sound sharp," Margaret said. "I don't know about Zara, though. She sounds like a loose cannon."

"Takes one to know one," Zinnia said.

Margaret barreled on. "There's no way you can bring Zara into the," she lowered her voice, even though they were talking within the relative privacy of Zinnia's new office, "book club." She winked three times.

"Margaret, it's not much of a secret code if you say *book club* and then wink three times."

"But you know what I mean. You can't bring your niece into our secret book club." Two more winks. "Not until she's been prepared. Maisy would eat her alive."

Zinnia chuckled. Margaret was right. Their fellow witch, Maisy Nix, didn't mean to be brutal, but she did have a special knack for making novice witches cry. Maisy was the one who'd developed the spell that felt to its victim like a vicious animal bite on the buttocks.

Margaret's expression turned serious. "It's bad enough poor Zara is Spirit Cursed. You can't bring her into the group unprepared."

"Spirit *Charmed*," Zinnia corrected. "And I don't know for certain yet. I certainly haven't told her my theory, anyway. When I get a chance, I'll have her consult one of my books. For the moment, I'm letting her enjoy the experience. She's absolutely delighted about having powers. Can you imagine that?"

Margaret tilted her head thoughtfully. "Learning you're a witch turns your whole world sideways, but it is kind of a blast."

"Whether she's Spirit Charmed or not, when you do meet her, please promise you won't say anything negative about that specialty."

Margaret frowned and leaned back in her chair. "But isn't that the same specialty the girl's mother had? Isn't that why she poisoned herself?"

Zinnia crossed her arms and frowned. "Yet another detail you need to keep to yourself."

"But does Zara even know about her father? Or her—"

They were interrupted by a knock at the door.

Zinnia called out, "Come in!" She was glad they were getting interrupted. She and Margaret had been talking about Zinnia's niece and great-niece for the last half hour, and Zinnia was starting to feel guilty about taking so much personal time when she was supposed to be working.

The door opened. One of the department's new hires, Liza Gilbert, stood in the doorway. Liza had her blonde hair up in a sporty ponytail. Next to the twenty-one-year-old was a much older woman who bore a strong family resemblance. She was shorter than Liza by two inches, and her hair was as snowy white as Liza's was blonde, but both had the same large, honey-brown, wide set eyes.

Liza looked from Zinnia to Margaret and back again. "Are you two having another one of your secret parties in here? Who do I have to kill to get an invite?" She cracked one of her usual smiles.

Liza wasn't the hardest worker, and she frequently got in trouble with Karl for filing her reports late, but she was an energetic, outgoing young woman. It was hard not to like Liza Gilbert, unless you were her desk mate, Margaret Mills. Margaret was not a fan.

"We aren't having a party," Margaret replied without a shred of humor in her voice. "We don't get paid to have parties, Liza." Margaret got up from the visitor's chair and said to Zinnia with formality, "Thank you for clearing up that important WPD business for me."

Margaret squeezed past Liza and the older woman, and returned to her desk.

Liza said in a loud whisper to Zinnia, "I can see why you took the promotion to get your own desk. Margaret's kind of a stickler for the rules."

"When it suits her," Zinnia said. She rose from her chair, walked over to the doorway, and extended her hand toward the visitor. "Hello." She watched for a spark of familiarity in the older Gilbert woman's eyes, and when it didn't come, she said, "I'm Zinnia Riddle."

The woman smiled sweetly and pressed her hand into Zinnia's. Her handshake was weak, like shaking an empty glove.

"Queenie," the woman replied. She gave her head a little shake. "It's actually Beth Gilbert, but I never liked the name Beth, so everyone calls me Queenie." She withdrew her hand from Zinnia's and patted Liza on the shoulder. "Even my granddaughter calls me Queenie."

"It's true," Liza said. She beamed at her grandmother before turning to Zinnia. "Queenie's treating me to lunch. She's a bit early, and I have to finish something that Margaret's waiting for. Do you think anyone would mind if I set Queenie loose in the direction of the cafeteria?"

"I'm sure that would be fine," Zinnia said. The City Hall cafeteria wasn't open to the public, but thanks to their limited menu, it had never been an issue.

"There you go," Liza said to the white-haired woman. "Don't wander off and get yourself lost."

Queenie, still smiling sweetly, said to her granddaughter, "I told you, Liza, I know my way around here better than most people. I was here when they built the building. I know all its secrets." She waved goodbye to Zinnia. "Lovely meeting you."

"Same to you," Zinnia said politely. Zinnia had met Queenie Gilbert before, on a number of occasions over the years, but hadn't mentioned it. She didn't want to embarrass the older woman, plus it didn't matter. Zinnia's coworker, Gavin, wouldn't have let that type of fact go unmentioned, but Zinnia didn't share Gavin's compulsion for correcting others.

Zinnia got back to work on her computer.

Her mind wandered, and soon she was thinking about her niece's situation, and all the secrets between them. Zinnia hadn't yet confessed to Zara about the reference letter she'd given to Kathy Carmichael at the library. Now Zinnia had a funny feeling in the pit of her stomach that she should have said something straight away.

For the past week, Zinnia had been playing dumb about so many things that she couldn't remember what she had or hadn't told her niece. It was very difficult to be a witch and know about other people's secret abilities and not be able to share everything she knew with the town's newest witch, but she had her rules. People with supernatural powers don't "out" each other.

Margaret knew almost everything Zinnia did, but that was different. Margaret had helped herself to most of Zinnia's secrets, thanks to her psychic abilities, limited though they were: Margaret could only pick up on Zinnia's thoughts when she wasn't trying.

Zinnia stared at the wall behind her computer monitor. She wondered how her niece was getting along with her coworkers at the library.

Thirty minutes passed. Zinnia had made zero progress on her computer work. It was past time for lunch, and the space outside her office door was quieter now. Everyone had gone to the cafeteria or the break room for lunch. Everyone except...

There was a clomping sound as Margaret returned to Zinnia's office. Margaret had the non-magical ability to clomp her shoes on carpet.

Without any lead-in, Margaret paused in Zinnia's doorway and asked, "What's their deal, anyway?"

Zinnia rotated her chair and threw her hands in the air. "You'll have to give me a hint, Margaret. I'm not sitting here all day trying to read your mind just in case you want to come in and ask me questions."

Margaret's gray eyes widened. "You can read my mind?"

"No. That's your thing. Remember?"

Margaret waved one hand dismissively. "Oh, that? It's about as useful as a pogo stick in quicksand. I don't even know when I'm doing it."

Zinnia rubbed her temples and thought, very clearly, *Margaret, you want to buy me lunch.*

"Of course I'll buy you lunch," Margaret said, completely oblivious to the fact she'd just read Zinnia's mind perfectly. "It's my turn, isn't it?"

* * *

They got to the cafeteria, ordered their food, and took a seat at their usual table.

That was when Margaret asked Zinnia, once again, "What's their deal, anyway?"

This time, however, Margaret was looking directly at the two Gilbert women when she asked, so Zinnia did understand to whom her witch coworker was referring.

Zinnia glanced over at Liza and her grandmother, Queenie. The two were laughing and enjoying green salads. They looked like a stock photo that might be used in an advertisement to sell salads to women of any age.

So, what was their deal? Were the Gilberts descendants of supernatural creatures? The majority of the people working in the Wisteria Permits Department had special abilities, so why not Liza Gilbert?

After a moment of thought, Zinnia said to Margaret, "Your guess is as good as mine. But I do suspect they have a few secrets in that family tree. Queenie was good friends with Winona Vander Zalm, and Winona always hinted that her friends had some very interesting stories to tell."

Margaret nodded and ate a fistful of crinkle-cut french fries without taking her eyes off Liza Gilbert and her grandmother. Margaret smacked her mouth noisily, affording Zinnia a full view of Margaret's half-chewed food.

"They eat funny," Margaret said of the Gilberts, who were still enjoying their green salads.

"If by *funny*, you mean they chew their food with their mouths closed, and refrain from talking while they do so, then I suppose the Gilberts do *eat funny*."

Margaret continued talking around her half-chewed crinkle-cut french fries. "We really don't know much about people outside our little circle, do we? I bet the older one has probably forgotten more magic than we'll ever know."

"Don't say that. We're both still learning."

Margaret tore her gaze off the Gilberts and met Zinnia's eyes. "Are we? Are we really? What have you learned lately?"

Zinnia was pleasantly surprised to find that she had an answer. "I'm learning more about spirits, thanks to my niece."

"But you aren't interested in ghosts. You hate them even more than you hate microwaves."

Zinnia wrinkled her nose. "Cursed things."

"Exactly. You aren't actually learning anything new that you want to learn."

Zinnia shrugged. "I'm learning a lot about special buildings permits."

"But don't you crave more? Don't you wonder what else is out there?"

Zinnia blinked at her coworker. "Are you having a mid-life crisis? You're only forty-two. It's too soon. I haven't even had mine yet, and I'm six years older than you."

Margaret let out a good-natured snort. "Good one. You could actually be funny if you tried, Zinnia." She stared into Zinnia's eyes as she grabbed another french fry and lifted it to her lips. "You know, I was really funny once, before I had kids. I did improv in college. Our troupe was called the MacGuffins. Did I ever tell you ab—"

Margaret stopped talking abruptly when Zinnia grabbed her by the wrist.

Speaking calmly, so as not to cause alarm, Zinnia said, "Don't act erratically, Margaret, but that's not a french fry in your hand."

Margaret slowly rolled her eyes down. When she saw what she'd nearly put in her mouth, her face went through a dozen emotions before settling on quiet horror.

"Easy now," Zinnia said.

Margaret held absolutely still, like a gorgon's statue.

Zinnia had her purse at her side. She reached in for an empty jar and calmly held it under Margaret's fingers. "Okay. Nice and easy. Drop it in here."

Through clenched teeth, Margaret asked, "Is that what I think it is?"

"I've never seen one that size, but I do believe it is a brainweevil."

Margaret dropped the long insect, which was the size and coloring of a stubby, overcooked crinkle-cut french fry, into the jar.

Zinnia quickly twisted on the lid. She didn't need to poke any breathing holes in the container. Brainweevils could live without oxygen for several hours.

Margaret asked, "Is that lid on tight?"

"Yes."

Margaret kept staring straight ahead into Zinnia's eyes. "Are there any more on my plate?"

"No. You ate them all."

Margaret made a retching sound.

Zinnia hurriedly said, "You ate all the fries. I'm sure that was the only one that wasn't a fry. They typically travel alone until they find a suitable victim, then they send out their pheromone flares to attract the others to feed on..." She didn't say the word brains because she didn't have to. Every person with supernatural powers knew about the dangers of brainweevils.

Margaret cursed under her breath, then asked, "What if it had crawled in my ear?"

Despite the seriousness of the situation, Zinnia smirked. "They only eat brains, Margaret. It would have starved to death."

Margaret reached for her glass of water and gulped it down.

Zinnia asked, "Did you do something, Margaret? Did you conjure that thing?"

Margaret looked aghast. "That's not funny."

"Well, you were talking about wanting to know more about book-club related things."

"It's against the rules."

"You do plenty of things that are against the rules."

"Even so, I would never want to see or touch, much less eat, something like that." Her face scrunched as she stared at the wriggling thing inside the jar.

"If you say so."

Zinnia took another look at the creature in the jar before tucking it away in her purse. She hadn't yet looked around the cafeteria to see if anyone was looking their way. Looking around to see if you were being watched was a sure way to get unwanted attention. It was best to assume most people were oblivious to the comings and goings of others.

This time, however, two people were looking at the witches. The Gilberts. Liza and Queenie.

Zinnia waved at them, smiled, and then picked up her fork and resumed eating her meal. After finding a rare, brain-eating insect on her cafeteria table, eating a chicken pot pie was the last thing Zinnia wanted to do, but she had to avoid arousing suspicion.

Margaret picked up on Zinnia's cue—or she found her appetite again—and moved on to her cheeseburger.

They ate in somber silence. Despite Zinnia's joke about the brainweevil starving inside Margaret's head, the situation was alarming. The first protective ward any witch cast on her residence was to keep brainweevils out, and this was in spite of their rumored extinction. Last week, Zinnia had arranged for Vincent Wick to put the appropriate protective wards on Zara and Zoey's house. It had seemed like an overreaction at the time, but after this afternoon's harrowing encounter, Zinnia was glad she had done so.

As Margaret finished her cheeseburger, she asked, "Do you think the Gilberts saw everything?"

"So what if they did? They're a good twenty-five feet away. Perhaps they saw me put a single one of your french fries into a specimen jar. What of it? If Liza asks, I'll tell her I liked the color and I'm thinking of painting the wainscoting in one of my rooms that exact shade."

Margaret wiped her face with a napkin while Zinnia finished every bite of her chicken pot pie.

They left the cafeteria and went outside for a walk. Margaret cast the rolling sound bubble so they could be sure of privacy.

As they walked, Margaret kept looking down at Zinnia's purse with a grim expression, as though she expected a nest of brainweevils to suddenly pour out of the zippered opening.

"Stop staring," Zinnia said. "The jar lid is screwed on tight."

"What are you going to do with that thing?"

Zinnia patted her purse protectively. "As much as I'd love to dry and crush this little guy to use in some experimental potions, the right thing to do is report it to the authorities."

"Fung's replacement?"

Zinnia snorted. "No, not Detective Bentley. I haven't met him yet, but I'm sure he doesn't have a clue about what he's gotten himself into." She shook her head. "No. I'll contact the DWM and tell them to deal with it. That's what they get paid for."

"Good. Someone has to sweep the whole building in case there are more."

"I'll pass that along, but I'm sure this won't be their first rodeo," Zinnia said.

Margaret shuddered and rubbed her arms. "Where do you think it came from? I thought brainweevils were completely extinct, except for a few in captivity."

"They're supposed to be."

A van pulled up alongside them and continued to roll at walking speed. The passenger-side window rolled down, and Charlize Wakeful leaned out of the window.

The gorgon said hello and asked, "Have either of you seen or heard or felt anything unusual?" Her voice was muffled by the sound barrier spell around the two witches, but her words were easily heard.

Margaret broke the sound bubble spell and replied, "Why? What sort of unusual thing do you think we saw?"

"There was a flicker," Charlize said. "A power surge. We detected it emanating from this area about thirty-five minutes ago."

Margaret asked, "What kind of power surge?"

Zinnia elbowed Margaret and walked up to the van. In a hushed tone, she relayed what had happened in the cafeteria and then handed over the jar containing the captured brainweevil.

Charlize let out a low whistle as she looked through the jar. "That's a brainweevil, all right. It must have slid through during the surge."

Zinnia asked, "Slid through from where?"

The man in the driver's seat said, "Ma'am, that's none of your concern."

Zinnia stepped back from the van, hands raised. "Very well, then. You're right. It's not my concern at all. It's yours." She leaned forward briefly, as though bowing, and said, "Thank you for your service."

The van was already driving away.

Margaret said, "You could have bartered for a little more information. You had something they needed."

"Why?" Zinnia brushed imaginary dust off her hands. "So we could get drawn into some sort of dangerous mystery involving power surges and horrible creatures that slide through from the other side? No, thank you. Between my new job, plus being a mentor to a young witch, I'm busy enough. I'm sure the DWM has things under control."

"If you say so," Margaret said. "If you say so."

The witches returned to City Hall.

A month passed, and they'd nearly forgotten about the brainweevils when another one showed up.

For a full list of books in this
series and other titles by
Angela Pepper, visit

www.angelapepper.com